ERI'DORIAN KNIGHTS
&
THE ORACLE OF VALEMÌR

Written By; Anthony Ochoa

To my lovely wife and family
who supported me throughout this journey.
I wouldn't be here without you.
To my daughter, thank you for
giving me courage.
To my favorite Teacher Mrs. Phillips,
Who said I could be a writer,
thank you for believing in me
all those years ago.

Contents

INDEX

Dru'Ny – DROO – NAI

Soferian – SO -FEER – REE – AN

Umoya – OO -MOI – UH

Valemìr – Vaa -Leh – Meer

Kinừ - Kai – Nu

Eri'Dorian – Eh – Ri – Door – Ree - an

Eri'Dor – Eh- Ri - Door

Dereli – Dair – Ruh – Lie

Manu – Mah - Nu

PROLOGUE

Ama stared at the blank page in her old journal. She tapped the end of her pen rapidly on the stone desk, making a repeating rhythm. Even though she was in her normal workspace she couldn't help but feel restless. All day she felt as if someone had been watching her, the mere thought of it felt ridiculous, but the nagging feeling hadn't gone away.

The overhead light in the corner of the room flickered repeatedly; breaking her concentration. She brushed the long locks of her dark brown hair back with her free hand and then fiddled with her glasses to make sure they were on correctly. After she wasted more time, fixing the sleeve of her white tunic she flipped the grip on her pen and began to write.

I can't help but feel nervous as I write this. I feel like I've done something wrong…

The history of the Oracle is well known and thought of as nothing more than conjecture of old mythology passed down from teacher to student until it is ingrained in their mind.

My studies have been extensive, I've spent the better half of the decade searching, finding and deciphering old transcripts to unlock the mystery of the Oracle. All of my studies have taught me one thing—that the last Oracle may not in fact have been the last Oracle. She was just the last one seen…

She stopped writing glancing up at the door again. The incessant flickering of the light wasn't anything new. No matter how many times she brought it up to be fixed, she was met with the usual runaround. Staring at the flickering light, she knew there was nothing different about it than yesterday, but the pit of her stomach told her to be careful. Instinctively, she pulled her journal inwards, covering it with her arm. With an unnecessary quick scan of the room she continued.

…I think the Oracle is alive… somewhere, I think the Oracle has returned and we just don't

know it yet. I think the return of the Oracle will change the world…

I just hope that if I am right, the Oracle is okay and will be safe until we need them…. God knows that we do...

Ama took another deep breath before closing the small leather-bound journal and with another glance around the room she placed it in the backside of a drawer behind a hidden divider. She closed the drawer locking it with a key attached to a chain necklace that she promptly placed around her neck.

She shuffled around her desk trying to find the old historical books of the Order and the Oracle. When she found them she stacked them on top of each other. Impulsively she touched the key around her neck to make sure it was still there. She began to walk around her workspace, stopping to stare at the flickering light. With a sharp inhale and slow exhale she tried to calm her jittering nerves, but no matter what she did, she couldn't ignore the nagging feeling that she was being watched.

CHAPTER 1

A New Beginning

Gwynne Hartley laid flat on her back staring at the white ceiling of her small room. Her clothes stuck to her sweaty body as she tried to catch her breath.

"Get up," Isobella commanded between short and precise breaths. Her self-defense training that her mother insisted she partake was longer than normal.

She could remember when it was just for self-defense and the movements were easy to master. As she grew older, the training never stopped, and the movements and techniques became more and more complex forcing their training time to last longer and longer until it took nearly the entire morning. In fact, she wouldn't even consider it self-defense anymore but instead; a full-on assault class.

Gwynne willed herself up to see her mother standing with her arms raised. It made her feel a little better to see that her mother was sweating too. They had matching light blonde hair that were both pulled back into tight ponytails. They were similar in size, though her mother was in much better shape. Her mother wore tight black leggings and a short tank-top that showed her midriff.

"You ready?" Isobella asked, no longer breathing heavily. Gwynne hesitated, knowing that the moment she nodded, her mother would attack. With a shake of her hands, she nodded.

Just as she predicted, Isobella crossed the small room they were in. Gwynne backpedaled to try and give herself some distance, but she took too long. Gwynne parried the first jab, and ducked the wide haymaker that followed after. She kicked out, hitting her mother in the stomach, knocking her back, and charged.

She launched a flurry of attacks at her mother. With every punch, kick, or knee, she felt a surge of confidence encouraging her to move faster.

Normally, by now her mother would have parried or countered, leaving Gwynne on the ground and feeling foolish for ever thinking she had a chance. Today it felt like, for the first time, she was actually winning the fight.

Gwynne ducked under a wild swing and struck her mother in the abdomen, causing her to stumble backwards. She followed up with a straight kick forward that hit her mother in the chest, knocking her backwards. Isobella managed to recover with a one-handed cartwheel and was back on her feet. Gwynne let out a frustrated grunt. The rule was whoever hit the ground first lost.

She pressed the attack, doing her best to keep her breathing under control instead of gassing herself out. Today was the day she was determined, to beat her mother, just once. In desperation, Isobella grabbed Gwynne and they began to grapple. Gwynne dropped to one knee and pivoted off her knee so that she was behind her mother. She gripped her abdomen, lifting her off the ground in an attempt to slam her.

Isobella moved her leg back so that she could hook onto Gwynne's, preventing the slam. Gwynne let go, pushing her mother forward. When Isobella didn't fall, Gwynne slammed her right elbow in between her shoulder blades. Isobella let out a shout of pain as she stumbled forward, trying to catch her balance.

~~~~

Isobella spun around and with a wide kick, caught Gwynne on the side of the face. She took a deep breath trying to control her frustration, the last shot into her back was enough to piss her off. Though, she couldn't help but be a little proud. Their training sessions were getting longer and longer simply because Gwynne was getting harder and harder to beat. Isobella just couldn't tell if it was because *she* was getting worse or if Gwynne was just getting better. Either way, today was not the day she was going to lose. She had given Gwynne enough chances to finish the fight. Isobella would never lose on purpose, but to build confidence, she would take a few hits and kicks.
~~~~

The kick to Gwynne's face definitely reminded her who was the better fighter, if only for a moment. Gwynne was already charging again, but her attacks were less precise as she tired. Isobella ducked the first swing and absorbed the second in her chest. She grabbed Gwynne's arm, torquing it so that Gwynne yelped and stumbled. Isobella stepped into Gwynne and with a sudden jerk, lifted and flipped Gwynne over her shoulder. Gwynne crashed into the floor gasping for air as she attempted to sit up.

"We're done," Isobella said, doing her best to catch her breath.

"I almost beat you," Gwynne said as a smile crawled across her face.

"You did well, but you need to control yourself. You were tiring out at the end, which is why you are on the ground *now*."

"I still don't know why we have to do this every day." Gwynne grunted as she finally sat up.

"Because you never know when you're going to need to defend yourself," Isobella replied, throwing a towel to Gwynne.

"From who? We live in Olessa, you know, the place where *nothing* happens." Gwynne sighed. "Besides, all I ever do is sit in my room and read. So, unless one of my books comes to life and tries to kill me. I think I'm okay." She laughed as she wiped the sweat off her face.

"You'd be surprised how quickly things can change," Isobella said quietly sitting down on the ground next to her daughter. "Besides, there actually *is* something happening tomorrow."

"What?" Gwynne asked furrowing her brow.

"The fall festival," she paused if only to steady herself. "Do you want to go?"

"A-are you serious?!" Gwynne asked excitedly, jumping up as if she had all the energy in the world.

"Yes, as long as you calm down," Isobella replied stifling a laugh. "I have to go into town anyway, figured we could spend the day out of our rooms."

"I would love to!" Gwynne said cheerfully.

"All right, well, we're done and don't worry about school for the rest of the day. Just get your chores done. I'm going to shower."

~~~~

Gwynne wasted no time going to her room. Her room was bare. Only the necessities— a bed, closet full of old worn out clothes, a mirror and a small dresser with a makeshift bookcase that she fashioned with the head of the bed and an old wooden drawer she had found a few years ago on the side of the road. Normally she would read one of her books again, but today she was too preoccupied.

Gwynne couldn't keep her mind still as it raced about the thought of going to Olessa. The town itself wasn't worth getting overly excited about, it was that Gwynne rarely got to go into town. She was typically forced to stay at home and within the confines of the small apartment they shared. With nothing to do except read the books she'd already read.
~~~~

She would often hear the other kids playing outside while she read. Every now and then she would take a break from reading and just watch and have pretend conversations that would never happen. She always wanted to have a friend she could talk to her, and though she considered her mother to be her best friend. She wouldn't mind talking to someone else for a change.

More than that, now was her chance to prove that she was mature, or at least mature enough to be able to go to the town center. If anything, she could at least enjoy the day away from her dwelling in the apartment.

~~~~

Isobella let out a small sigh when she thought about Gwynne's eager reply. She wiped the steam and stared at the mirror. She let down her dirty blonde hair that dropped down and covered her pale blue eyes. Isobella was petite with an athletic build with strong legs and a toned upper body. She was 44 years old and though everyone always told her she
~~~~

never looked her age, she hated the compliment. She *wanted* to look different. She dressed herself and moved to her bedroom. There wasn't anything in there but a white dresser, an old body mirror and a small bed that lay in the center of the room.

In the bottom drawer of the dresser she pulled out a small cloth bag. Moving quickly, she packed the bag with a few items. Water, food packets, and flares, she knew Olessa was within walking distance, but she was always over-prepared. She could see down the hall, Gwynne's door was still shut, and she could just barely hear Gwynne humming likes always, when she read. She lifted the bottom drawer out of the dresser and on the underside was a small leather bag taped in place.

Opening the bag, a coin fell into her hand. The golden coin had a faded symbol that could no longer be recognized engraved in the center. She placed it into the front pocket of the bag, placing the strap of the bag over her shoulder.

She paused to make sure Gwynne was still in her room before she stepped over to a mirror placed in the center of the back wall. She lifted and twisted a small box that appeared to prop the mirror up. When opened, it revealed two daggers. She pulled each from their sheaths revealing that the blades were made of black metal, the hilts were worn down light brown wood. After a brief inspection, she placed them back into their sheaths and returned them to the box. Tomorrow she would be carrying them which always made her nervous. She never wanted to carry them, let alone use them.

She carried the bag to the main living area, placing it down on one of the two chairs, draping her gray coat over the bag. She wondered if going to the town center was a good idea or not. She knew she couldn't keep Gwynne trapped inside here forever, but the thought of going sent a chill down her spine.

"You okay, mom?" Gwynne asked as she entered the room. Isobella forced a smile and nodded her head. "Worried about tomorrow?" Gwynne asked her happy expression fading.

"No." Isobella lied, making her smile seem less forced.

"It's okay if you are." Gwynne said moving closer. "I know last time we went to the festival I didn't exactly do the best job of keeping out of trouble."

"You were eight." Isobella countered. "I shouldn't have been so hard on you." Guilt rose in her chest and created a lump in her throat.

"Well, that was a long time ago." Gwynne said with a laugh. "I'm excited to go, and I promise I'll follow all the rules and paths, and if anything happens, I won't just run away."

"Thank you, sweetheart." Isobella said. "No go shower, you stink."

CHAPTER 2

Return

The next morning came faster than Isobella wanted. It was hard for her to fall asleep, her mind had been filled with all the things that could go wrong. She made sure to be up long before Gwynne, even then she rushed to get ready.

She strapped her daggers just below the small of her back on a thick leather belt that held up her black pants. She brushed her white shirt over the daggers and then placed on her grey coat.

She turned to see Gwynne waiting eagerly, her hair tied back in a tight ponytail showing her youthful face. She was already dressed in a long dark gray tunic with a leather belt wrapped around the waist over black leggings that tucked into her worn down black leather boots.

"Ready!" She proclaimed.

"All right, you know the rules," Isobella said quietly.

"Yes, stay with you, don't talk to anyone," Gwynne muttered her smile fading. "Can we just go, please?" she asked as she passed, rushing towards the door.

"Your jacket," Isobella called out. Gwynne changed her trajectory and grabbed the small brown coat before returning to her intended path.

~~~~

Once they were outside, Gwynne ensured that they kept a brisk pace towards the city center. They had very specific paths her mother insisted they take. Once they chose the specific path of the day they were never allowed to deviate from that path. The paths were never the easiest or the quickest way to their destination, but it was easier to follow the rules than it was to question them. She rushed as fast as she could to make up the time.

Gwynne couldn't hide her excitement about being able to go into town especially with the festival going on. There would be food and sweet treats, and people with their families. She knew her mother was protective, perhaps too protective. Whenever she asked it
~~~~

was usually met with silence and a comment similar to "I'll tell you when you're ready." It seemed that Gwynne was never going to be ready, so she stopped asking.

The day to day routine of school, training, and sleeping was all Gwynne had, so anything that disrupted that routine was exciting. The only entertainment she had outside of her normal duties was reading. She would read whatever books her mother would find and bring back, but her mother hadn't brought a new book in months. Her favorite book was a book that told stories about old mythologies, but after reading it over 10 times. Gwynne was ready for something new.

Olessa was a small industrial town where the majority of the poor stayed. Her mother was always so overly cautious of the people around them that Gwynne rarely went outside or interacted with anyone. Despite being such a small-town Gwynne loved going to the town center. It wasn't anything great, but it was the beginning of the Fall Festival. She hadn't been allowed to go near the city market during a festival since the last time they went when she was 8 years old. Her running around getting lost in a maze created by the local steel company was definitely to blame.

She was stuck in the maze for almost two hours until her mother finally found her. Though, it wasn't necessarily a happy reunion. She was scared, and her mother seemed both angry and relieved at the same time. It was the anger that won in the end.

As they approached, she could see the colors of the city center and the fall festival. Olessa fell under The Dorrennian Empire which was known for its bright red and gold colors and immense wealth. But, here, normally everything was dingy and gray — the buildings, the roads, even the policemen that patrolled on foot or on the back of hover-bikes wore gray uniforms. Olessa wasn't meant for the rich and powerful. Here was where the poor and the workers lived and died. The vibrant video-trons and the massive holograms that danced around in the sky or street vendors selling whatever merchandise that was there. Just beyond the center she saw the old watch tower of the Temple of Valemìr, a safe haven for the Eri'Dorian knights. Gwynne never understood why there was a temple there. She had never seen any Eri'Dorian knights and Olessa certainly didn't seem like a place where a knight would ever visit.

The sight of the town center was always jarring to Gwynne. She always expected the town center to be as run down as the apartments they stayed in. As they came closer, she could hear people talking and bouncy pop music blaring over the loudspeakers scattered throughout the area. Announcements for the transit system on the north side of the town blared over the music, allowing everyone preparing to leave to gather their belongings and head to destinations she'd never heard of. To Gwynne, the city center was a reminder that they weren't alone in the world. That there was something beyond their little town and the outskirts they lived in.

~~~~

To Isobella, the city center was a tremendous hazard with danger lurking around every corner. She had become paranoid over the years, and rarely spoke to anyone
~~~~

unless it was absolutely necessary. Even then, she only gave them what information they needed, nothing more and nothing less.

She could see Gwynne was entranced by the small city lights. She couldn't blame her. Living in Olessa wasn't glamorous, but it was safe, and that was all that mattered to her.

Isobella scanned the area as they walked through the first block of the center. She saw the police guards who paid them no attention, the drug addicts eyeing them both before changing their focus to whatever was in their hands, and even the escorts waving and winking at anyone who passed them.

She locked eyes with the man in a dark corner staring at Gwynne, and he quickly averted his gaze. None of them were threats, not *real* threats at least. Still, she noticed and watched.

After controlled breaths and constantly telling herself that everything was okay, she eventually felt calm enough to relax a bit. She was still alert to every little thing that was near them, but she would try to temper her reactions, at least for today. They were surrounded by everyone dressed in warm decorative clothes. The smell of sweet baked apples and the spiced cakes battled for supremacy, stealing the noses of everyone around.

Gwynne had rushed ahead towards a large crowd circling a small stage. There were signs for a magic show followed by some singer who Isobella assumed was quite popular though she didn't know anything about them.

She finally caught up to Gwynne, who was standing up on her toes to try and see the show over the crowd. Isobella scanned the area again and then looked back to where she needed to go—a small boutique and next to it a food store where she could get ingredients for a special Fall Solstice meal.

"Gwynne, honey," Isobella called out. She watched as Gwynne turned and started sulking back towards her. Isobella knew what she was about to say was going to be a surprise, to both of them.

"I'm going to see Tylex and then the food store." She saw Gwynne's eyes light up. "You can stay and watch the show."

"Are you sure?!" Gwynne asked. When Isobella nodded, Gwynne threw her arms around Isobella knocking her off balance.

"Listen," Isobella interjected as she gently pulled away and looked for a place for her to sit. She pulled Gwynne by the arm muscling her way through the crowd to a spot near the aisle and towards the back. "Stay here," Isobella commanded. "If anything happens—"

"I know, I know," Gwynne replied, rolling her eyes. Isobella shot her a stern look. Gwynne changed her tone and added a smile. "I will do what you have always told me to do. Get out and find my way home using the correct routes." Her words were overly rehearsed. Isobella regarded her for a moment as a sudden rush of panic overtook her for a moment. She smiled, doing her best to ignore it.

She kissed Gwynne on the forehead, who pushed her away wiping the kiss off and looking around making sure no one noticed.

"I'll be careful. I promise," Gwynne said with a hint of a whine.

"Okay," Isobella replied, not truly trusting the statement. She looked up and saw an old woman speaking to the crowd before her attention moved to the large person standing to the side of the stage. Her stare lingered for a moment before looking back down at Gwynne, who was no longer paying attention to her. Isobella bit her bottom lip, nodding her head and walked away.

~~~~

Gwynne could barely sit still in her seat. She found herself looking at all the people instead of the actual show. The families and the other kids her age were what caught her attention.

The parents were focused on the show and seemed happy to be there. The younger children shared in her excitement but didn't seem to know what was actually happening. The other kids her age were more mixed. Some
~~~~

seemed completely bored while others intrigued. She averted any eye contact when they looked over at her. Despite all of the fake conversations in her mind, she had no idea what she would actually say if someone spoke to her. There was a collective gasp as a dragon made of orange fire flew through the sky before turning into a puff of smoke and a burst of glitter, causing an eruption of cheering and laughter.

Gwynne continued watching the crowd. Their reactions were more interesting to her than what they were reacting to. Being so isolated all the time, she couldn't help but watch their reactions. To see them smile and laugh almost made her forget she didn't know any of them. She would spend a few moments watching a particular person or family and then move to the next.

When she got bored of watching the audience, she began to look around them. There were policemen in their gray uniforms and with electric batons holstered to their belts. They stood in a pattern, one officer every 10 rows, and most of the 15 officers seemed to be enjoying the show rather than standing guard. She hated that she noticed them and hated even more knowing that her mother would be pleased with her observation

But it wasn't the officers that held her attention. It was the one figure standing at the edge of the stage. She recognized the symbol on his black cloth surcoat; it was the symbol of the Eri'Dorian Knights of Valemìr, an ancient order that lived in a realm far away called *Eri'Dor.* The symbol on their chest was 3 circles, the right and left circle each had a triangle, the left facing up with a line through its bottom left corner and the right; pointing down with the line through its upper right corner. The center circle had another circle inside that had three breaks evenly spread out.

She had never seen an Eri'Dorian Knight before, at least not in person. She only assumed that this one was a Sentinel. They were the large protectors that often enforced the magical laws passed down from the Kingdoms. It was something she'd learned from reading about them during her school curriculum last year. She had grown curious about how the Eri'Dorian Order worked and how they lived. Whenever she brought the Order up to her mother, she was met with the usual dismissal and again, Gwynne found it easier to just let it go instead of pushing the issue.

This Sentinel stood at the edge of the stage on the far left. Gwynne couldn't tell if it was a man or a woman due to the surcoat and the heavy armor they wore. They were large, with wide shoulders and a broad upper body. They wore black armor made of sculpted metal that covered their entire body, though she noticed it had small breaks at the joints.

The faceless helm was what unnerved her the most. She couldn't tell where they were looking and the way they were positioned it looked as if they were staring right at her. She kept glancing over at them, but the Sentinel never moved. They seemed more like a statue than a living person.

Eventually, she grew bored of watching the unmoving statue of a knight and the people around her, and turned her attention to the woman on the stage who was chanting some kind of language she didn't understand while shooting balls of light into the air.

~~~~

Isobella tried her best to ignore the panic that set in when she left Gwynne. She had more important matters to take care of and she had to be cautious of her own surroundings. Noticing the Sentinel at the show made her even more nervous than usual.

She moved through the crowd looking straight forward not bothering to look at anyone directly, especially the men. She was used to their advances working at the steel mill as she was one of the very few women that worked there or was even in the city itself. Most of the men here were young and single, doing their best to move up in an industry that was never going to make them rich, but would give them a home.

She approached the small boutique of old trinkets and furniture. Nothing with too much technology, simple to use which Isobella enjoyed. It was easier to maintain, and she didn't have to worry about anyone trying to spy on her through electronic means.
~~~~

"Bella?" A voice called out. The man to whom the boutique belonged, stepped out into the middle aisle. He was an older man with bright white wispy hair. Tall with a frail body in a beige apron over a dark gray jumpsuit. He shuffled forward wiping his hands with an old rag as a smile formed over his wrinkled face.

"That *is* you!" he said with a hearty laugh.

"Hi, Tylex," she answered. "How have you been?"

"I've been well," he said as he embraced her. "But I assume you are not here just to talk to me." He moved back towards his seat at the back of the store.

"You know you mean more to me than just information." She threw the golden coin to him which he caught and promptly threw back.

"You've been coming here for nearly 15 years and for those 15 years, have I ever taken that damn coin from you?" He chuckled. "No one is coming for you, Bella. They think you're dead."

"Can never be too sure these days," she muttered, placing the coin back into her coat pocket. She began looking through a box of old metal trinkets. Most of it was decorations, or old mechanical devices that she had no use for. Tylex was a friend who, throughout her time in Olessa, had helped her every step of the way with no desire of payment.

She at first assumed he would want something from her eventually, but it never came, and she often felt guilty for that assumption.

"I let Gwynne go off on her own today," she said with a shaky voice breaking the silence.

"Did you?" he asked, turning towards his desk. "And, how are you handling that?"

"Not well."

"You gotta let her grow up," he said with a chuckle.

"I know." She shook her head. "I never used to be this paranoid. I used to never care."

"Children have a habit of doing that to you," he replied without looking back.

"Yeah, well, I didn't expect it to be this bad," she said with a stifled laugh.

"Have you told her who you are?"

"Not yet," she replied sharply. "I don't… I don't know how to," she added in a softer tone.

"She should know the dangers of who she is and who *you* are."

"I will when the time is right." She couldn't tell if she was trying to convince him or herself. "So, nothing?" she asked, trying to change the subject.

"What? Oh, no. There are a few knights here and there but, none of them are looking for you. Dorrenna is in a conflict with Ardonia of the South, but that is neither here nor there except they may increase their need for steel."

"Great." Isobella let out a sigh. "Exactly what I need, more work."

"You know you don't have to work there, right?"

"They give me a place to sleep and feed me. I can't ask for much more than that."

"Yes, you can," Tylex said, turning back to face her. "You're holding yourself here because of fear."

"You're damn right. If I'm ever discovered. I'll be executed, Tylex. Then what? What happens to Gwynne?" She took a deep breath and softened her tone again. "I'm sorry."

"She's growing up fast," Tylex noted.

"Yes, she is…" she answered. "She's going to start rebelling against me and go do what she wants to do anyway. So, I'm just trying to steer into the turn and hope for the best."

"You're doing a fine job." He continued working on an old mechanical fan, and Isobella sat on the small stool beside him to watch. She wasn't ready to go into the food store. Even if it meant sitting watching him work, which never bothered him, at least she wasn't alone.

~~~~

The performer had climbed down from the stage and was calling for volunteers to join
~~~~

her as she walked the aisles. She spoke in a very melodic way, her words running together as she sauntered up the main aisle. She commented on those who waved their hands frantically.

Her laughs and giggles echoed through the loudspeakers spread throughout the audience as she danced and twirled around even kissing one of the police officers on the cheek as she made her way up. Gwynne watched her approach and panic began to set in when the woman's eyes locked onto her.

"You," she said pointing her long finger directly at Gwynne. She laughed when Gwynne glanced around hoping that the woman was pointing at someone else. "Yes, you."

"Uh…" Gwynne's heart began to race as the panic set in. She could feel a lump in her throat as beads of sweat began to form on her brow. She wanted to get up and run, but her legs didn't want to work. She wasn't sure what to do.

Her mother had said not to move from that spot. Then a fit of anger filled her. Why?

Why did she have to always stay put and out of the spotlight? Why couldn't she talk to the other kids? Why was she always being forced to be alone?

"Okay," she said quietly trying to gain some courage from her waning anger. It took a moment longer than the woman wanted to wait. She grabbed Gwynne by the arm helping her stand, and Gwynne finally managed to will her legs to work.

The woman hooked her arm into Gwynne's to escort her down the aisle. The people waved and cheered at the beckoning of the performer. Gwynne was surprised by how short the magician was. From a distance she seemed taller and much younger. Her make-up was cracking, and her heavy eyeshadow was smeared. She smelled of a mixture of a strong flowery perfume and ash. She yanked Gwynne when she started to fall behind causing her to stumble which made the crowd laugh. Gwynne could feel her cheeks reddening as regret began to swell in her chest.

When they were on the stage, Gwynne looked around and for once everyone was looking at her. It was the first time she felt like anyone noticed her. It was an exhilarating feeling being in front of everyone and while the regret disappeared, she still wasn't quite sure if she liked it, but she was stuck there now so it didn't matter.

The woman spun around her once they reached center stage, stopping to address the crowd.

"In the old days, magic ruled the world!" she said, making a first with her hands. "As time has passed, we have forgotten the magic that lives *inside* all of us. Today, I want to show you that we can access that magic and become greater than we ever dreamed!"

Gwynne wasn't so sure. Clearly magic was real as the Eri'Dorian knights used it. She had even read about witches, wizards and other races such as the Soferians, but magic was forbidden in their realm with the exception of Eri'Dorians and certain other people.

The magician spun around, stopping abruptly in front of Gwynne. She grabbed her hands firmly and lifted them up. Gwynne jumped at how cold the woman's hands were.

"Place your hands together like you're making a bowl," she instructed sweetly. "I'm going to help you unleash the fire that is within you!"

Her brown eyes locked with Gwynne's as she discreetly placed a small drop of liquid and a piece of green paper in her hands. The woman put her finger over her lips and winked.

Gwynne couldn't help feeling a little disheartened to know the woman could not use magic and instead was using tricks and potions to create the effect. She knew it was a long shot that the woman had any actual magical ability, but she'd been hopeful with the Sentinel there.

The woman spun around so fast that the skirt of her dress flared outward. She let out a small squeal of excitement.

"Now, just believe!" she sang out. "Just believe and you will release the fire from within!"

As the woman began singing to the crowd, Gwynne *did* feel something, but it wasn't in her hands like she expected. She looked over at the woman, but she was too busy flailing her arms as if she were summoning the fire from Gwynne's hands which only frustrated her more.

The eerie feeling started in her chest and then moved to her stomach, it burned at first, then was suddenly soothing. She imagined it was electricity pulsing through her, spreading outward and through her arms until it finally reached her hands.

The fire in her hand burst into the air in a blue flare. The crowd gasped and cheered as the flame danced in her hands. The woman seemed slightly taken aback by the burst of flames, but quickly replaced her expression of surprise with a wide smile, glancing back at Gwynne every few seconds.

"You see!" The woman shouted. "If you believe in yourself you can make magic happen!" She twirled around as music blared overhead. The crowd applauded; all of them staring at Gwynne.

"Now, we should contain our inner fire, or the handsome Sentinel over there might get a little nervous!" she said with a high-pitched laugh that prompted the audience to laugh with her.

Gwynne stared at the Sentinel who had still made no movement; further cementing the idea that they were in fact a statue. The performer twirled around and again placed a small drop of a potion into Gwynne's hands. She pursed her lips placing her finger over them and gave another wink.

"Now, take a deep breath and call the power back in!" The woman spoke in a slow methodical pace and the audience quieted, hanging on her every word. Gwynne shrugged and inhaled deeply as she was told to call back in her power.

The flame was dying in her hands, she could even feel the electric feeling in her hands recede down her arms before it surged forward. The flame burst higher into the air now burning white. There was another collective gasp from the crowd and then more cheering. Gwynne looked to the woman who stared at the fire with scrutiny and then doubt. She rushed over to Gwynne.

"What are you doing?" she hissed, making sure to cover her mouthpiece.

"What are *you* doing?" Gwynne asked indignantly. She was doing her best to stay calm as fire danced in her hands. The woman scoffed adding more of the liquid into Gwynne's palms. She then twirled away making sure to smile to the crowd.

"She's feisty one, eh?" she asked the audience with a giggle. "One more time, shall we?" she raised her hands and then gave Gwynne a slight nod coupled with a glare. The woman began to chant, and beckoned the crowd to join in.

As they chanted, Gwynne could again feel the power receding. Again, it surged forward and this time it was far more powerful. The flame skyrocketed into the air and the feeling she had was engulfing her. She looked over at the woman who was cowering near the edge of the stage. She could hear the crowds cheering turn to confused shouting.

She frantically tried patting out her hands, but she couldn't smother the flames. Looking over she saw the Sentinel statue was now approaching her.

"Stop whatever you're doing!" one of the officers shouted.

"I'm not doing anything!" Gwynne screamed trying to speak without her voice breaking. "Help me!" she cried at the magician who had jumped off the stage to hide behind a police officer.

Yelling from her left drew her attention. She saw a group of police officers and they began to circle around her. They were all shouting over each other, their commands muddling together. Some wanted her to stay where she was while others wanted her to get on the ground. Some told her she was only making it worse for herself while others just asked her to be calm.

She kept trying to look for someone to actually *see* her and realize she was scared. That's when she saw the Sentinel walking through the wall of officers. Their approach was slow with one armed raised.

"I need you to calm down," the deep voice said through the helm. Before she had time to react, she saw an officer move towards her. "Wait!" she could hear the Sentinel shouting, which made the officer stop.

The Sentinel took the momentary distraction and closed the distance between them. He grabbed her arm by the wrist, making her jump in surprise.

She didn't think, just reacted and screamed out in fear trying to pull away, and the power she had felt before, released. An explosion of energy sent the officers and the Sentinel flying backward, crashing into the stage. Gwynne tried desperately to stop doing whatever it was that she was doing, but quickly realized that she was no longer in control. She could only watch as her hands created havoc.

~~~~

Isobella wasn't overly interested in what Tylex was doing. She knew that her shopping wouldn't take very long, but she didn't want to cut Gwynne's time at the festival short.
~~~~

She hugged Tylex from behind and he paused from working to pat her head. As she turned to leave, the sounds of screaming began to drown out all the music from the festival. She turned back to Tylex who was already making his way towards her, but Isobella ran through the door.

Her heart stopped when she saw her own daughter standing over a Sentinel, blazing white fire covering her arms. The Sentinel stood back up and charged her but was thrown into the audience by a gust of wind. Gwynne raised one hand as vines rose from the ground to wrap around the Sentinel's limbs. He let out a shout of frustration as he struggled to stand up.

The sky grew dark over him, and Gwynne summoned a lightning bolt from the newly formed black cloud. The impact was deafening. What was left was scorched Earth and the Sentinel—dead.

Isobella shook her head to snap out of the shock induced trance she was in. She threw her jacket back at Tylex and raced towards Gwynne, who had turned her attention to the police officers. They were now cowering with their weapons raised. Gwynne effortlessly waved her hand and a gust of wind sent them flying off the stage.

Isobella struggled to push through the crowd of people as they all began running in hysteria, scrambling over the railings that lined the walkway. When she was finally close enough, she was cut off by another Sentinel.

The Sentinel had their *Umoya* in their hand. It had been years since Isobella had seen the weapon of the Eri'Dorian Knight. It gave the user the ability to conjure any handheld weapon. Each was an extension of themselves, different and unique to the user.

Sentinels were known for using heavy weapons, such as hammers or maces made of metal or stone. The Sentinel took a moment to grab a small handle that was attached to the back of his armor. His armor seemed to almost liquify as some of the metal moved to his hand forming a square shaped shield.

There was no hesitation as Isobella threw herself at the Sentinel. She knew in a full-on fight she was not prepared for it. This particular Sentinel was quite large. She deduced that he was a Dru'Ny—a large giant-like race that was known for their strength and durability. She was small and agile and that was going to be her best tool against him.

She leapt over a railing landing on a second railing and ran across it keeping her balance. She glanced over to see Gwynne had turned her attention towards the second Sentinel as well.

Isobella launched herself forward grabbing the daggers from behind her back. She landed on the back of the Sentinel wrapping one arm around their neck and stabbing them in the back with the other.

The blade of the dagger cut into the armor which surprised the Sentinel and prompted him to rear backwards with a shout. He began thrashing around when he couldn't pull her off.

Sentinel armor was notorious for being impervious to most metals, however her daggers were made of Eri'Dorian Steel — enchanted to be nearly indestructible and uncharacteristically lightweight. The blades never dulled or rusted making them incredibly rare and high in value.

The Sentinel finally managed to throw her to the side. She rolled through the momentum and landed safely on her feet in front of Gwynne. Gwynne glared at them as she raised her hand.

"Gwynne!" Isobella screamed. Gwynne's face distorted and suddenly her emotionless face was full of fear.

"Mom!" she screamed. "I can't—" her voice cut out as she began rising into the air and another burst of white light erupted from her body.

Pillars of light shot into the sky from the ancient Valemìr Temple in the city. Isobella stared up at her daughter and then spun around looking at the pillars of light as far as the eye could see.

Gwynne fell to the ground crying. She staggered to her feet, reaching out to Isobella.

"Go, now!" Isobella yelled. "Go!" she yelled again as the Sentinel charged them. The Sentinel lifted their Umoya that formed into a metal mace and swung down in a diagonal arc.

Isobella sidestepped the swing and dropped to one knee pivoting around him to cut at the back of his knees. The first blade was a glancing shot, but the second cut drew blood.

They stumbled forward and swung their mace backwards wildly to get distance. The metal mace morphed into a long spear that they whipped around to face her. Their left hand lifting his shield defensively.

"Great." Isobella muttered as she raised her daggers. She had to make the first move. She could tell the Sentinel was young and inexperienced in their movements.

Sentinels were trained to be defensive and they were never going to break that mold. Isobella looked and realized Gwynne was gone and so were the police officers. Glancing over she saw that people were watching from a safe distance. The pillars of light distorted the sunlight making everything brighter.

Isobella charged forward. The Sentinel shouted as he lunged with the spear, just as she expected. She was already ducking by the time he was starting his thrust. She pivoted, to try and get behind him, but he simply mirrored her movement raising his shield. He swung the spear outwards forcing her to duck underneath. She wasn't prepared for his counter, slamming his shield into her side.

The power of the hit made her crumple to the ground. Pain shot through her right side as she rolled to her left side to get back up. She was near the walkway with a metal railing. To her left was a young man who jumped back to try and get away, but Isobella grabbed him. She didn't want to hurt the boy, or even the Sentinel, but it was them or her daughter, an easy choice.

Pushing him she realized the Sentinel felt the same way about the boy and swatted him away with the base of his shield. The distraction gave Isobella another chance to attack. She had to get close — his shield was heavy, and his spear was too long. She knew being up close was her best bet at beating him.

She made her first attempt. He tried to backpedal, but she was too fast in closing the gap. Her agility allowed her to get between his spear and shield, throwing one of her daggers. It sunk into his abdomen. Shouts rang through his helm as he staggered backwards. With a desperate swing of his spear he attempted to create distance. Isobella was already on the move and his swings hit nothing but air.

She jumped onto his back, but he shrugged her off stabbing his spear downward. She moved just in time as the blade pierced the ground. She kicked the inside of his thigh causing his leg to buckle, dropping to one knee. She then kicked him in the side of his face knocking him backwards.

He managed to stay on his knee but lost his grip. The metal clanged against the ground and the spear disappeared into the air.

He reared back swinging his closed fist at her. She scrambled to her feet and then lunged forward. She stabbed him again. This time he dropped his shield and grabbed her hand. With his other hand he gripped her throat and lifted her into the air.

Isobella struggled to wrest herself free of his grasp, but even with his wounds he was far too strong. She could see that the armor was beginning to regenerate, forcing the first dagger out of his abdomen and onto the ground.

Isobella wrapped her outside leg over his arm and with her inside leg began to kick him in the face. He lowered his arm allowing her to get one foot on the ground. She pulled his thumb, breaking his grip from her throat and lifted herself onto his arm still holding his hand. She was straddled on his arm just above the elbow and she forcefully pushed down with her left leg trying to break his shoulder.

To her dismay, he simply stood up lifting her back off the ground. She swung her other leg back to hit him in the face again, then lifted herself over his head and dropped back down on his other shoulder with her legs dangling behind him. She wrapped her arm around his neck and tried to rear backwards torquing his neck.

The Sentinel began to flail around, trying to pull her off. She held on with everything she had squeezing as hard as she could to cut off his air supply. He slowly dropped to one knee still struggling to throw her off. He managed to grab one of her arms and used a lightning shock that sent pain shooting down her arm and into her chest. With a loud scream, she dropped to the ground behind him. He spun around swinging his arm wildly and a powerful gust of wind sent her scraping across the ground until she crashed against the stage.

He stood back up shaking his head and then his arms. He rushed her, punching as hard as he could. Isobella ducked in the last moment. The impact of his punch shattered the stage wall behind her. He ripped his hand from the wall and backhanded her back onto the ground.

The blow caused her vision to blur. He slammed his knee into her chest, pinning her down. He swung again but hit the ground as she avoided the blow on instinct.

Gasping for air, she managed to pull herself from beneath him and grab his arm as he swung down again. He pulled back up, lifting her off the ground. She pressed her knee against his throat and grabbed the back of his head pulling as hard as he could. He pushed against her, trying to avoid the chokehold. She wrapped her other leg around his head, trapping him, and squeezed.

He roared in anger and desperation as he stood up, slamming her back against the wall. She held on until he lifted her up to slam her a second time. She let go and jumped over his head landing on the ground. She rolled through the tumble, grabbing the dagger that had fallen to the ground from his armor and threw it as he turned. The blade cut through his helm, knocking him back into the stage.

The Sentinel grunted in pain as he attempted to pull the knife from his face. Isobella was upon him too quickly. She ripped the dagger away and kneed him one final time in the face knocking his head back against the stage. He crumpled forward unconscious.

She stood over him gasping for air, and before she could catch her breath, she grabbed her other dagger, sheathing them both, and ran. The people had stayed out of the way and watched everything transpire. The crowd was so thick that she could hear the police shouting but couldn't see them.

As she ran, the Umoya of the fallen Eri'Dorian caught her attention. She made a split-second decision and grabbed the weapon. She had a designated path that Gwynne should have gone down. That was her next goal—to find her daughter.

~~~~

Gwynne ran as fast as her legs would allow. The fire that had once engulfed her arms was gone, at least for the moment, but she didn't have time to think about that. She wasn't alone. A single police officer managed to keep track of her and was catching up. She could hear him shouting for her to stop.

She just kept moving despite her legs and lungs burning for her to stop. She rounded the fifth corner and then darted down the first alley. She saw the familiar red brick walls of two identical buildings. She had gone down this path so many times in random drills her mother conducted. She was confident she could do it blind folded.

The officer was relentless and gaining on her as she began to slow down. Finally, he tackled her to the ground. She rolled to her
~~~~

stomach and pushed up to run away again just as she felt the searing pain of the stun-baton hitting the back of her thigh.

She collapsed to the ground holding her leg. It began to spasm every time she tried to stand, forcing her to fall.

"You almost killed me!" he shouted as he began to beat her with the baton. Each time the baton connected, it sent a jolt of electricity through her body. The officer didn't let up despite her pleas. The pain was excruciating. She eventually gave up, curling into herself, no longer trying to get away.

Gwynne laid there accepting the pain until it began to fade. She could still feel him hitting her. The heat from earlier returned only this time it was greater. It enveloped her chest before it released.

The officer yelled as he flew backwards crashing into the wall. He scrambled to his feet, still gripping his baton. Gwynne sat up. She could see everything happening, but again it was as if she was there to just watch. When she stood up the pain was gone. In fact, she felt amazing. She felt powerful. She felt angry.

~~~~

Isobella rounded a corner and sprinted as hard as she could when she heard desperate cries for help. When she came upon them, she stopped. Her eyes widened in amazement and then horror.

She watched Gwynne – who was *glowing* – march towards an officer cowering as he tried to crawl away. Her eyes glowed bright white and her face was contorted with anger. She lifted her hand and Isobella shouted for Gwynne to stop, but it was too late.

White flames erupted from her hand and engulfed the man. He screamed for only a moment before his charred body collapsed to the ground.

When Gwynne stopped, she looked to Isobella. They held eye contact. Isobella couldn't decide if she was more afraid or worried.

Her breathing was very controlled and her gaze blank. Suddenly her eyes returned to normal and the golden glow disappeared. Gwynne staggered forward, collapsing to the ground.
~~~~

Isobella ran to her daughter, dropping to her knees at her side. She tried waking her, but Gwynne was unresponsive. She grunted as she lifted Gwynne off the ground, throwing her over her shoulder and running the rest of the way home.

~~~~

At the city center the police had managed to push their way through to the scene of the fight. As they set their own perimeter, a lone rider on a black hover-bike arrived. The engine hummed as she came to a slow stop.

The rider was dressed similarly to the Sentinel, though her surcoat was white with the symbol of Valemìr embroidered in teal. Instead of flat black armor, hers was shined silver with teal accents on the shoulders and obliques. Clasped to her shoulders was a heavy velvet teal colored cape that draped over her shoulders and dangled behind her, hanging just above the ground.

She was armed with a dagger strapped to the back of her right shoulder. Its polished white handle adorned with silver markings.
~~~~

The hilt of her Umoya fastened on her left hip was shined silver with a white leather wrap and a lioness head as the pommel.

Her helm was much different than the Sentinels. The helm itself was completely silver, and resembled the head of a roaring lioness, its eyes a pale shade of violet. She lifted the face of the helm showing her fair skinned face and eyes that matched those of the lioness.

She lifted the helm off her head revealing her long thick vibrant red hair that was pulled back into a single braid that fell down her back. She placed the helm on the front of the bike as she marched forward ignoring the officers who moved to intercept her. The pillars of light from the temple were beginning to fade.

As she continued forward, her eyes locked on the Sentinel who was leaning against the stage. She could see the second Sentinel lying flat on his back. She knelt in front of the Sentinel resting against the stage. She grabbed the sides of his helm, gently lifting it off of his head. His blue eyes looked at her with a blank stare.

"Sentinel, what happened?" she asked calmly. When he didn't answer she placed her hand on the side of his face. She waved her hand through the air creating small droplets of water. She placed her hand with the water on the wound, closing her eyes to concentrate. His eyes darted up at her and he swatted her hand away.

"Girl…" he mumbled. "Too powerful…" He let out a slight cough.

"Who did this to you?" She asked leaning in as his voice grew softer.

"Oracle," he whispered. As he spoke the words, Arilynn looked up at the pillar of lights then back down at the Sentinel. He was still looking at her, but there was no life behind his gaze. She looked back up to the pillars of light.

"The Oracle has returned…"

CHAPTER 3

Lioness

Arilynn stood at the cross section of the city center of Olessa. The perimeter was set, and the witnesses were giving their accounts to the police officers. Every so often, she would glance over to the Sentinel who lay dead against the wall. She didn't know who he was or anything about him, but he was a knight of Valemìr, and for all intents and purposes, he was a family member to her.

She stood with her arms crossed, waiting for the police to get their information. Typically, Eri'Dorian Knights did not handle simple disturbances between people. They only interfered when magic or paranormal activity was involved. This was magical but more importantly a knight had been killed.

Blinking lights illuminated on her forearm. She looked around to see if anyone would disturb her before pressing the button to accept the incoming. Lifting her arm as a small holographic screen emerged from her gauntlet to display the face of an onyx colored man with dark orange eyes. He was a handsome man with a strong jawline with long white hair that was pulled back into a high ponytail.

"How bad is it?" His voice was low, and he spoke in a slow deliberate manner.

"Bad," Arilynn replied, glancing to the fallen Sentinel. "Two dead."

"Damn. Do you know who they are?"

"No, I had one of the Clovi tell me their names: Terrence Pulliver and Jordan Gallin," she answered. "That isn't the most important part."

"What is?"

"The Oracle."

"I saw the light from the temples same as you, Lynn, but this is the issue at hand."

"No, Lorrennius, before he died, he said, 'Oracle'." She waited for him to reply, but when it was obvious he wasn't going to, she continued. "Sir, the people here are saying that the girl went crazy during a magic show. She was here."

"We don't know that," Lorrennius replied.

"We do," she countered. "From what I can gather, she summoned a bolt of lightning from the sky. It killed Lord Gallin."

"You can summon lightning from the sky, Arilynn."

"It took me years to master that and this was a young girl," she argued. There was a moment of silence as Lorrennius mulled over this information. "I think he may have been the first one to see her."

"The Oracle was just born. There is no way this girl can be the Oracle," he commented. "Do you know where she is?"

"No," Arilynn snapped. "I'm in Olessa and their finest aren't exactly known for being anything but incompetent. Their surveillance system is outdated and most of it doesn't work. What little does actually work was pointed in the wrong direction."

"What are you doing in Olessa anyway?" he asked. "I thought you were on your way back from your visit with the

Soferian Queen?" When she made no reply, he let out a sigh. "Of course, Jaxon."

"I *am* married to him."

"Very well, find her." with that, the transmission ended, and she let out a sigh of relief. She couldn't help but always feel nervous around Lorrennius. Not because he was the highest-ranking knight in the entire Eri'Dorian Order, the Commandant of the Order, but because he was once her teacher and mentor.

He taught her to fight and how to use her power. He was relentless in her training and studying. Whenever he was around, she felt the need to be perfect. Even as a youth, when she was considered a prodigy, she felt the pressure to live up to *his* expectations, which were far higher than anyone else's. All of this was intensified by the fact that they were both Soferians.

Soferians were known as the "First Race" or the "Immortal ones". Soferians weren't the first race and they certainly weren't immortal, but they did live far longer than humans or Dru'Ny. The oldest Soferian to have ever lived had been well over fourteen hundred years old.

Their culture was one of perfection. Anything less than your absolute best was considered an insult and if someone failed simply because they weren't good enough. It was considered incredibly shameful. Arilynn was only forty-five, barely a child to most Soferians, and yet, she was a grown woman in the eyes of the Order. She worked hard and it paid off with a great reputation. She was the one they sent in first. It just so happened that today she was already near this small town.

Olessa wouldn't have been her first choice of places to visit her husband, but it was out of the way and no one of importance would ever bother them here. At least, that's how Jaxon explained it to her. Not that it mattered as he never showed.

She refocused herself and placed her thoughts to where they needed to be. Ignoring Lorrennius' disdain for her husband and her need to be perfect all of the time. The dead Sentinel kept grabbing her attention, but it wasn't until she heard the heavy footsteps of the Police Chief approaching did she finally turn away.

He was a heavyset man in a gray uniform that was a few sizes too small. As he waddled towards her, the fat under his neck moved. His pale face was reddened from the exertion and beads of sweat began to form on his forehead. She glared at him letting out a sigh of annoyance when he finally made it to her.

"Anything?" she asked impatiently.

"Found the body of one of my officers, completely burned to death," he answered in a huff. "But there was another person here. A woman, she killed your friend over there."

"Where is she? What did she look like?"

"A blonde woman, short and very fast is all the people said. They were pretty scared."

"Clearly," Arilynn replied dismissively. "Which way did they go?"

"I'll show you where the body was found. From there they have no idea."

"Any surveillance?"

"No."

"Of course." Arilynn commented clenching her jaw. "All right, let's go."

~~~~

Isobella moved so quickly returning home that when she finally stopped, her body felt like it was shutting down. The fight with the Sentinel had taken a lot out of her. Then having to carry Gwynne the rest of the way. The constant running up and down stairs and across rooftops drained her even more.

Gwynne was still unconscious and was now laying on her bed where Isobella had left her. She made sure she was breathing before rushing through the house to gather all the things they would need. She still wasn't sure what happened but was positive that it wasn't something good. Gwynne wasn't supposed to have magical power. She had taken precautions to make sure it could never happen.

Yet, she saw her own daughter use the very power she was never supposed to have. She saw her own daughter kill a man with no remorse and then stare at her as if she didn't know who she was.
~~~~

She stopped and crumpled to the floor hugging her knees as she tried to catch her breath. As she sat, tears began streaming down her face and she couldn't stop herself despite her desperate attempts to do so.

How could I have been so stupid? She thought to herself. She should have never let Gwynne go out on her own. Now she would have to leave everything behind and run - again.

"Mom?" the sound of Gwynne's voice woke Isobella out of her breakdown. Jumping to her feet she did her best to wipe the tears off her face. When Gwynne entered, she threw her arms around her, squeezing her as tightly as she could.

"What happened? What's going on?" Gwynne asked, confused.

"We have to go," Isobella replied, pulling back to look at her daughter's eyes. "Pack what you can carry and do it quickly."

"Why?" she asked. "Mom. What's going on?"

"I'll explain everything. Just grab your things, okay?" Isobella said, trying to control the strain in her voice.

"Go," she said again with more force. Gwynne hesitated before she ran to her room.

It didn't take long for Isobella to get ready. She had prepared for running many times and had always hoped the day would never come. The prepared bag was strapped over her shoulder as she grabbed another coat and a small bag that clanged with more of the golden coins.

When she went back to Gwynne's room, she found her sitting at her desk looking at her books. Isobella stood at the doorway, a lump forming in her throat as guilt washed over her. How could she be doing this to her daughter, how could she have not warned her about everything?

"We don't have time for that," she said. Her throat was dry, and the words caused physical pain to say. Gwynne made no reply, just nodded her head and placed the book in her hand in a small bag she had hanging over her shoulder.

Isobella opened their front door to a group of men who were making their way down the hall. She ushered Gwynne out pushing her in the opposite direction of where the men were going. As the door closed, she did her best to make it as quietly as she could hoping to not draw any attention. One of them still looked back.

"Anna?" he said with a cheery tone. "I didn't know you lived over here." he walked over to her. She recognized him— his name was Gerald, though she had never cared to learn his last name.

"Yup," she said curtly. "Well, I have to go. Have a good day." She forced a smile and tried to walk away.

"Well, wait. If you're not busy tomorrow maybe…we"

"No. I have to go." She turned.

"Hey!" he whined pulling her back around. "That's rude."

"I have to go," she repeated pulling his hand off her shoulder.

"Well, if you're busy tomorrow…"

"Gerald, stop," she said firmly. "No, that is your answer. We've been through this." She turned and again he placed his hand on her shoulder. This time, she twisted his wrist so that he fell forward and kneed him in the groin and when he doubled over, kneed him in the nose. She pushed him so that he fell on his backside holding his bloody nose.

"Anyone else want to ask me out on a date?" she asked, looking to the other men. They all took a step backwards shaking their heads. She turned back and rushed Gwynne down the stairs and outside.

They quickened the pace to just below sprinting. Gwynne was gasping for air just trying to keep up. They rounded a corner to an old abandoned shed. Isobella stepped towards the wall and reached behind a piece of metal that looked to be fixed onto the stone. Behind that hid a small compartment. Inside there were a set of keys. She thumbed through them and when she found the one she was looking for promptly opened the shed. Gwynne let out a gasp when she saw the vehicle sitting inside.

It wasn't much to look at. Just an older model *Volant.* Like most vehicles it had four wheels and six thrusters underneath that would propel it up into the air and act as a flying vessel.

"Get in," Isobella commanded, ignoring Gwynne's stammering.

~~~~

Arilynn stared down at the burned body —there wasn't much left of him— and took a few steps back as she surveyed the area around them. A small alley with three different ways to go and no sign of which way they went. She let out a frustrated huff walking further down the alley looking down the three avenues they could have gone.

She glanced down at the communicator on her forearm. Again, there was nothing, no light indicating an incoming message. She stared at it a moment longer before refocusing on the task at hand. All three avenues of escape led to main streets which would lead to the rest of the small, dingy town. Glancing up to look at the gray clouds she saw the fire escape.
~~~~

She walked over to the building and looked up at the rusted ladder. It was out of reach for her; standing at 6 feet, which meant that it was out of reach for the fugitive who had been described as short and petite.

She scanned the ground and the wall in front of her until something caught her eye. One of the bricks was off kilter just enough that if she weren't such a perfectionist, she would have missed it. At first, she tried pulling at the brick but when it didn't budge, she pressed it. There was a cranking sound and then the ladder descended.

"Huh. Captain, come here," she called out. The fat man hurried his way over to her huffing and puffing as he did.

"Yes, ma'am?"

"She went up the ladder," she commented. "The reason you don't have her on any of your surveillance is because she knows how to avoid them."

"Well, someone said they saw her go into a store back at the center," he croaked.

"Have your men canvas the area. I will go to the store and find out what I can."

~~~~

It didn't take Arilynn long to find the store as it wasn't far from the cross section where everything had transpired. The store was mostly filled with old mechanical parts that were strewn around with no sense of organization. There was one man sitting at a table near the back tinkering.

"Excuse me," she said loudly to get his attention. He slowly turned around, lifting the protective glasses from his face. He stood up abruptly and quickly removed them as well as his gloves. An expression of recognition appeared and disappeared from his face so quickly that she second guessed if it had actually happened. He hobbled towards her with his head lowered.

"Hello there," he said with a warm smile and an extended hand. She accepted the handshake and looked around the room.

"Lot of commotion out there today," he said with a chuckle as he took a step back. "How can I help you, knight?"
~~~~

"My name is Arilynn Harwell, I am a Warden for the Eri'Dorian Order of Valemìr. The reason I am here is because two Sentinels were killed today. There are people who say that the woman who did that came out of this store," Arilynn said walking around the store making sure to notice every detail.

"I'm sorry to hear that…uh, my name is Tylex."

"We all are, Tylex," Arilynn replied. "So, did you happen to have a blonde woman in here? Short, athletic… fast?" She shook her head at the description. "No one seems to know what she actually looks like. They were too busy watching everything else." She grabbed a small spiral made of metal, clearly a puzzle made of old parts, and fiddled with it while she waited for him to answer.

"Well, there was a lot of excitement today in a town that is often quite dull. I may know the girl you're talking about. But I'm not sure if I can help you."

"What's her name?" Arilynn asked, placing the now solved puzzle down. She continued moving through the store.

"Anna" he replied.

"Her last name?"

"I don't know her that well."

"Did she buy anything?"

"No, she just comes in here and looks around and talks to me."

"Doesn't seem like a very good business model to just have people come in and talk."

"Well, most of my business comes from the steel workers and repairs." Tylex walked over towards his desk. "I get by well enough."

"What can you tell me about her?"

"Nothing really, she just comes by once and awhile looks around and leaves."

"She just shows up and leaves?" she was staring at him intently.

"Yes," he replied with no hesitation. He sat down on his seat looking up at her. She studied him for a moment before turning towards the exit.

As she began to leave, she looked around one more time and saw a dark gray coat draped over one of the tables. She looked back at him and then approached the table.

"Is this for sale?"

"Uh, no that- uh, belongs to me." he replied. He kept fidgeting. At first it was his hands on his lap, his two thumbs constantly bumping into each other, then he started bouncing his right knee up and down.

"Seems kind of small for you, Tylex" she replied, lifting the coat off the table to examine it. At the bottom of a side pocket was a golden coin. Lifting the coin up so that he could see the familiar, faded symbol of Valemìr. His already pale face seemed now ghostly white.

"Tell me Tylex, what was her name again?" she took a step towards him. He let out a heavy sigh shaking his head. "You're a defector, aren't you?"

"Yes, Lioness," he replied, lowering his head. She raised an eyebrow at the mention of lioness.

"You're a Clovi."

"Was," he corrected. "I left the Order because I was tired of being treated like a slave." she scoffed at the remark. He was looking up at her now, his hands shaking. "Are you going to kill me now?"

"I'm supposed to. You broke your oath and betrayed the order."

"I just wanted to be something."

"A store clerk?" she asked, gesturing towards the store.

"It's not much, but it's honest work."

"I'm not going to kill you, Tylex. You're an old man now and you are unarmed," she said matter-of-factly. As she approached, he looked down at his hands again.

"It may be hard to believe that a knight such as myself doesn't enjoy killing everyone." She bent down so that she was at eye level with him. She gently raised his head by his chin, so that they were looking at each other. "Tylex, who is she?"

"I already told you everything," he replied firmly. She let out a sigh of disappointment standing up.

"Tylex, you're lying to me."

"I won't tell you anymore than I already have," he said turning towards his desk. "You'll just have to kill me."

"I already told you that I wasn't going to do that." Arilynn replied. "However, killing you isn't the only way to punish you."

"If you take me back, I'll just escape," he answered dismissively as he worked on a small motor.

"I wouldn't take you back, you wouldn't be worth much. However, I can only imagine you and this woman aren't the only defectors around here." He tensed at the mention of other defectors. "I wonder how many old faces will turn up when I tell the Council that I found you. It'll only be a matter of time until they send Rangers and Scholars to find and look through everything, I imagine some irregularities will come up."

"You would uproot all of them for an old oath?" he asked angrily.

"No," she replied calmly. "I will however do whatever is necessary to find the Oracle."

"The…the Oracle…?" his eyes were wide as he tried to make sense of what she said.

"Tell me who the woman is, or I will bring the full might of the Eri'Dorian Order down on you and everyone in this small little town."

He looked up at her. His breathing was uneven, his face flushing red. His knee was bouncing up and down as he frantically tapped his fingertips on the desk. It was only a few seconds before tears began to well in his eyes.

"Okay," he stammered in a whisper. "Just don't hurt the girl, she's innocent," he added, shaking his head. "She's a good girl."

Arilynn stepped out of the store and briskly walked towards her hover-bike. As she climbed on a hand touched her shoulder, causing her to jump.

"Hey, it's me," the man said, raising his hands. He had short greying reddish-brown hair matching his neatly trimmed goatee. He wore the same armor she did, differing only in its flat gray finish. His surcoat was made of black leather with the Valemìr symbol embroidered in dark grey.

He was slightly taller than she was with wider shoulders. Behind him was a young girl, she was around fifteen years of age with long black hair that lay on her shoulders. Her armor matched the man's. Instead of black leather she was dressed in a gray surcoat instead. She had light tan skin with dark-brown eyes. The young girl immediately bowed her head when she saw Arilynn.

"Markus," she said breathlessly. "What are you doing here?"

"We were sent here once it was stated the Oracle had returned." he replied nodding his head to the girl with him.

"That makes sense." Arilynn replied as she leaned back on her hover-bike.

"You all right?" he asked, his pale blue eyes staring at her intently. He crossed his arms over his chest lifting one of his hands to stroke his beard. Markus had strong features; a strong jaw with a ridged nose. He had a scar across the bottom half of his right cheek that stretched back and veered down his neck.

"No," she replied, shaking her head. "Not really."

"Did you know them?" he asked in reference to the Sentinels.

"No, did you?"

"I knew of them. Being on the council, you meet everyone at least once." he paused looking at the young one still sitting against the stage. "He was a good lad, young, a little foolish." he looked back and studied Arilynn. "What is it?

"Isobella Hartley."

"What about her?"

"She's alive."

CHAPTER 4

Seeker

Nya jumped awake, sitting straight up as she gasped for air pulling the blankets to cover her bare chest. She took haggard breaths as her eyes began to acclimate to the darkness of the room. Movement to her left made her jump again until she realized it was Konan who sat up groggily wiping his eyes.

"What is it?" he asked.

"The Oracle," she replied as she threw her legs over the edge of the bed to slide off. She grabbed the robe on the dresser quickly, wrapping it around herself. She turned the lights on with no warning, prompting Konan to curse loudly as he buried his face into his pillow.

"The what?" he asked, throwing the pillow off his face.

"The Oracle," she repeated. "The Oracle is back..." she added, still trying to catch her breath.

"How do you even know that?" Konan asked, rubbing his eyes.

"I'm a seeker, Konan. I'm meant to find the Oracle and bring them to the Temple of Valemìr."

"You're not a Knight of Valemìr anymore," he groaned. "You're a Scorpion now."

"I know that," she replied as she rummaged through a small closet of clothes. "But you don't understand. As a Seeker I'm drawn to them."

"We should go to the boss."

"I don't have time."

"Then make time," he snapped. The sound of his voice made her look over at him. "If you take off without permission, he'll think you turned and will hunt you down."

"How? I'm the best hunter." She turned back to the closet. "I'm your organization's assassin."

"Don't you mean ours?"

"Stop, I'm not running. I need to find the Oracle." Before Konan could reply, there was a loud pounding on the door.

"Does no one sleep around here?" Konan muttered half to himself as he crawled out of the bed to open the door.

On the other side were three men dressed in black and red clothing. They were each wearing different types of clothes, a hoodie, a leather jacket and the one in the middle was in a suit, but all were red and black, the colors of the Red Scorpions. They were a branch of the world's largest and most dangerous gang: The Three Tailed Scorpions.

"The boss wants to see you," the middle one said. He was the smallest of the three with dark brown skin and a shaved head. Konan let out a small sigh and nodded his head.

"The Ice Queen, too," he added before Konan could close the door. Konan glanced back at Nya who was getting dressed. He turned back to the three men nodding his head again and shut the door.

"Well, I guess you don't have to wait," he said as he went to the side to put on a shirt.

Konan had a lean body with substantial muscle definition. His skin was light brown and he had a buzzed haircut. He had light green eyes and a handsome face. His face was clean shaven which made him look far younger than his nearly 40 years. On his right forearm there was a brand of a three tailed scorpion seared into his skin.

"We need to hurry," Nya said, impatiently waiting at the door.

She was now dressed; wearing a black leather jerkin that doubled as light armor. Over her shoulders she wore modest leather pauldrons that buckled into the jerkin. The skirt she wore was armored with black metallic tassels over black leggings that tucked into her boots. Her light brown hair was pulled back into a tight braid. On each of her hips were two dagger hilts that had missing blades clasped to her belt.

She grabbed a bright red cloak and draped over her shoulders lifting the hood over her head. She paused before putting on the glove for her right hand to hide the distorted and scarred skin that plagued most of her right side.

"I'm not worried about it," Konan replied, breaking her concentration. He was dressed in all black. He wore a thick leather studded vest over a thin metallic shirt that was meant to absorb most energy blasts. His arms remained mostly bare except for a bracer on each forearm. Both were black, and each had a red scorpion with three tails embedded in the center. Strapped to his right side were two long-curved daggers attached by a chain that was coiled onto his belt.

"Let's go." Konan commanded.

~~~~

"Are you *sure* it's her?" the voice came from someone she couldn't see. The hologram only showed Lorrennius in his seat within the council chamber.

"Yes," Arilynn said as sternly but as respectfully as she could manage. It was the fourth time she'd been asked. "He told me everything after I promised not to bring the full might of the Eri'Dorian Order here to find other defectors. He was resistant, but I think he understands the gravity of the situation. We have Clara here now with Lord Troyan. She will help us locate the Oracle."
~~~~

"And bring Isobella Hartley to justice!" she recognized the shouting of Andaar Maxwell, Lord Ranger.

"Yes, Lord Maxwell," Arilynn replied.

"This is troubling news," Lorrennius said in his low voice. "I thought you killed her when they attempted to sack our city."

"I thought so too. But clearly she survived."

"Find the Oracle first. If you are able to apprehend her so be it. If not, and you have the opportunity, eliminate her. She is a threat and she could be working with Lionicles Harwell."

"Lio hasn't been seen in over fifteen years," Markus interjected. "It's unlikely he's involved."

"There hasn't been an Oracle in nearly 1,000 years. Anything is possible, Markus," Lorrennius replied harshly. "Find her." The hologram cut out and she was left standing there with Markus and Clara.

"Easy enough," Markus said with a chuckle. "Only have to find the most powerful beings to ever exist who just happens to be running with one the greatest rangers the order has ever known." he smiled and hummed as Arilynn turned to speak to Clara.

"Are you ready?" Arilynn asked Clara who was staring off into the distance. She snapped back to reality and looked over at Arilynn and nodded. "Can you sense her?"

"I think so. I'm not really sure," she admitted. "I can't seem to focus on anything but *your* power."

"Mine?" Arilynn asked, surprised.

"Yes, you stand out more than Lord Markus does. I wouldn't be able to sense the Oracle unless I was near something they were near."

"Fair enough. We will go to where I believe they ascended."

"Of course, and I must say it is an honor to finally meet you, Lady Lynn," Clara said with a bow of her head.

"No need to be honored, child. I just need you to help me find her."

"I will do the best I can," Clara promised.

The short walk back to the cross section was a silent one. Clara made sure to keep in step with Arilynn as they made their way to where everything had started.

For only being the next day the area had been cleaned up and the people moved on with their lives. The town center was relatively empty with most of the town's citizens being at their workplaces.

If Arilynn hadn't seen it herself, she would have never guessed anything had happened here. She stood to the side as Clara made her way to the middle of the cross section, hand outstretched in front of her and eyes closed. She wrinkled her brow in concentration and after a moment her eyes opened wide.

"I sense her," she said with a smile.

"Are you sure?" Arilynn asked, walking up to her.

"Yes," she said confidently. "Her power is…*amazing*, I've never felt anything like it."

"Did you sense anyone else?" Arilynn asked.

"Anyone else?" She looked back to Arilynn raising an eyebrow. "No. Was I supposed to?"

"What about the Sentinel that was here?"

"No," she replied quietly. "Once they die their presence disappears as if they never existed."

"Who all do you sense right now?"

"Just you, Markus and, the Oracle of course." Arilynn furrowed her brow, as looked around trying to understand what the girl had just told her "Are you okay?" she asked awkwardly.

"You do seem distracted," Markus noted as he approached.

"I'm fine," Arilynn replied flatly.

"Clara, go search and see if you can find anything the officers may have missed." Clara glanced at Arilynn and then Markus who tilted his head towards the main stage. Clara took the hint and hurried away.

Arilynn turned to face him, arms folded across her chest. "What, Markus?"

"What's wrong?"

"Where should I start?" Arilynn asked, gesturing around her.

"Where is Jaxon?"

"What?" the question caught her off guard.

"Have you heard from him?"

"No, but that isn't—"

"When is the last time you heard from him?"

Cutting her off only frustrated her more. "A week ago," she replied, looking away.

"Is he the reason you were here?"

"Yes." She paused before looking back at him. "We were supposed to meet here two days ago. He never showed and I've tried contacting him. He hasn't answered."

Markus shrugged. You know how he is."

"I *do* know how he is," she snapped. "I married him, didn't I?"

"Then what's the problem?" Markus asked.

She took a deep breath. "He never goes that long without contacting me." This was not something she wanted to talk about. She didn't enjoy being seen as weak or sentimental — Lorrennius had made sure to force that out of her.

"I'm sure he is fine," Markus said, placing his hand on her shoulder to comfort her.

"That doesn't make me feel any better, Markus."

"Fair enough," he said, removing his hand to stroke his beard thoughtfully. "I'm not sure what to tell you."

"I'm not asking you to do or tell me anything."

"Then you need to focus," Markus said firmly. "If Isobella is alive. She'll be dangerous. We cannot afford to be distracted. Your husband is fine and when this is over, we can find him together."

"Yeah, well if I see him first, he's dead." Markus tilted his head, directing a quizzical expression at her.

"It's not that he hasn't answered. It's about Bella, isn't it?"

"He lied, Markus," she answered with a flash of anger. He nodded his head in understanding, and Arilynn let out a sigh, clenching her jaw.

"That was fifteen years ago," Markus commented.

"That just means he's been lying for fifteen years," Arilynn argued.

"We don't know why he lied, but I'm sure he had his reasons."

"It doesn't matter why. He lied." he retorted. "You can't always defend him."

He opened his mouth to continue, but Arilynn raised her hand to cut him off. "Let's just go."

"Very well," Markus said, waving his hand to call Clara back.

"Thank you, Markus," Arilynn said quietly as Clara approached.

"Are we ready to go?" Markus asked.

"Yes," Arilynn replied. "Do you think you can find her, Clara?"

"It should be easier for me to find her. But it's not like I can just follow her scent like a dog."

"I know," Arilynn replied, "but we have an idea of where she went."

"Then let's go find her," Clara said with a confident smile.

~~~~

"The Oracle. Has returned," Nya announced standing in the center of the suite, Konan stood just behind her to the right. Though, she wished he were standing next to her so that she wouldn't be the only one they were looking at.

"I'm well aware of it," an older man said sitting down. Seticus was wearing a black suit with a bright red scorpion embroidered on the right lapel. His hair was neatly cut with white streaks on each side. "That's why you're here," he said leaning forward.

They were in a large suite filled with other members. The four others who sat beside the older man wore similar black suits, but none of them had the scorpion emblem.

They ranged in ages and races. The largest was a Dru'Ny woman with dark russet brown skin and jet-black hair that was pulled back behind her broad shoulders in a braid.

A Soferian man sat directly next to the elder man. He was dressed in a black gown and had the elegant and pompous presence
~~~~

that most Soferian's showed. He sat with his hands clasped over his crossed legs.

"What do the Red Scorpions want with the Oracle?" Nya asked incredulously.

"I figured you of all people would know the value of the Oracle. The world will go to war to get that child to be theirs." He stood up using a red cane with a large red ruby on top. "I know enough about your ancient order and what they do. The only thing more powerful than money, is magic," he said pacing back and forth. "And magic, powerful enough, can make a lot of money," he added with a grin.

"You want me to bring the child to you?" she asked skeptically.

"Yes," he said adamantly. "And be quick about it."

Konan grabbed her hand signaling not to respond further. She let out a sigh, nodding her head. The man stopped and stared at her for a moment before speaking again.

"Everyone out," the elder man said. "Now!" he shouted when no one moved as quickly as he wanted. They all began hurrying and when Nya went to leave, he raised his hand. "Not you."

Nya glanced to Konan who shook his head as he left the room letting the door close behind him. Nya watched the man as he hobbled over to the couch sitting back down.

"Do you hate us that much?" he asked, breaking the silence, looking up at her. He outstretched his hand motioning for her to sit across from him.

Nya sat and looked closely at his wrinkled face. His short hair looked grayer up-close, blending into the white on the sides. She had never noticed the green in his eyes as he stared at her.

"No."

"Come on, Nya," he said with a smirk. "I know you can lie better than that."

"What do you want me to say, Seticus?"

"Thank you," he replied indignantly. "We helped you, nursed you back to health when you were knocking on death's door." He leaned forward using the cane to prop himself up. "You owe us a great deal of gratitude."

"I have been paying for that for almost fifteen years," Nya snapped. "I'm your greatest assassin and you know it. I find everything you look for and I kill anyone that threatens you. I've built a reputation and made you and your men feared. They call me the damn ice queen!"

"But…?"

"I don't want to anymore," Nya said, exhausted. His eyes narrowed as she lowered her head to look at her hands. She couldn't remember how or where Konan had found her all those years ago. What she did remember was falling and then laying on the ground, broken staring up at the sky.

Konan was the first person she saw when she woke up. He fed her, bathed her, clothed her. When she was finally capable, she was initiated and joined the organization. Her affinity to magic made her a great asset, and she wanted to make Konan proud. Fifteen years later, she was tired and no longer cared if she made him or anyone proud.

"Do you understand what that mark on your arm, the one you keep covered up, means?" he asked, tapping her left forearm.

"Yes."

"It is an eternal bond," he whispered. "You are not *you*. You are a Red Scorpion just as I am. We *serve* each other."

"Who do you serve?" Nya asked, looking up at him matching his gaze. His first reaction was anger then he laughed and leaned back, his smile remaining on his face.

"I'll tell you what. If you bring the girl to me, I'll grant you permission to leave." Nya gave him a suspicious look. "But you should know what that means. No protection, no help, no Konan." His smile grew when he spoke his name. "You sure that is what you want?"

Nya hesitated only briefly before she nodded her head and outstretched her hand. Seticus grabbed her hand and they shook on it. A chill went down her spine as she stared into his eyes.

"Bring her to me," he said, his smile gone. "Then you get what you want."

~~~~

Seticus waited a moment before he pulled himself up using his cane. He slowly hobbled back to the large fireplace embedded in the wall and carefully lowered himself down to his knees. He lifted the ruby gem off the cane, using his index finger and thumb to take a small pinch of black dust from the small compartment which he threw into the flames. The orange fire erupted into a black fireball that nearly burned his face before it settled into black flickering flames.

"We've started," he began quietly. "The Oracle should be with us soon." He waited for a moment for a reply. The flame suddenly turned back to its normal color with a gust of wind.

~~~~

Nya lifted her bag into her vehicle, fitting it snugly between the seat and the back of the bike. She knelt while inspecting the tires and each of the four thrusters.

"You need to get a new bike," Konan said from over her shoulder. The bike was worn down and covered in scratches. Most of the parts had been replaced with unmatching parts she'd find.

"This bike has never failed me."

"Whatever," he muttered.

"Not everyone needs something to be brand new," Nya said, nodding towards him." His expression hardened which made her tense up.

"Where are we going?" he asked, quietly.

"Olessa. That's where they are saying she was sighted."

"What do we know?"

"That the Eri'Dorian Order will have already been there, which means we're already behind." She stood up and climbed on to her bike, which hummed to life as she hit the ignition.

She brushed her brown hair behind her ears, looking over at Konan who sat on his bike. Konan smirked at her when he realized she was looking at him. "Y'sure you don't want a new bike?" he asked with a laugh. "What is it?" he asked when she didn't reply.

"Nothing. Just not looking forward to the ride." He nodded his head understandingly. She stared out towards the horizon. They were so high up she could see far across the city and the outskirts. She revved the engine trying to wake herself from her daydream. She then hit the throttle and flew off the edge of the building, free falling before the thrusters roared to life and propelled her forward.

She wasn't sure she could give the Oracle up. Seekers were bound to their Oracle. It wasn't just an oath, it was a…*need* to protect them.

Nya left the order over fifteen years ago and she still couldn't shake the nagging feeling of performing her duty to the Oracle. From the moment she was discovered as a Seeker, it was ingrained to find and protect the Oracle. Now that the Oracle was actually here, she realized they didn't have to ingrain anything.

Now it wasn't so black and white. She led the revolt against the Order with her friends and followed someone she thought she loved to battle and nearly died in the process.

She couldn't help but feel that she *had* died, and that Konan somehow brought her back. He was the only reason she became a Red Scorpion.

She had fallen in love with Konan during the time he cared for her, and the money and power that came with him was intoxicating.

Her loyalty had always been to Konan and never truly to the organization itself. Now, she was being pulled to something far greater than all of them. The deal she had just struck entered her mind. No matter her decisions; was betraying someone; either herself, the Oracle, or Konan.

CHAPTER 5

The Silver Knight

The light of the full moon fought to break through the dark wall of clouds that loomed overhead. The little light that managed to make it through glistened faintly on the scattered puddles of rainwater outside of the abandoned factory building. Its failing lighting system only illuminated parts of the factory, leaving the entire east side of the building in total darkness where Jaxon Harwell knelt, his gauntlet covered hand pressed against the soft ground. He wore a dark gray leather surcoat with the faded symbol of Valemìr across the chest.

His dark blue eyes darted back and forth as he surveyed the building. Jaxon was half human and half Dru'Ny which gave him his dark russet brown skin and made his eyes seem to glow in the dark. His night vision wasn't as great as a full blooded Dru'Ny, but it at least gave him an advantage over most.

He watched and listened closely, hoping to hear his target make any noise, but a rustling behind him caused him to peek back over his shoulder. Emerging from the shadows behind him were two golden yellow eyes that glowed similar to his. Only they belonged to a much larger creature. The animal skulked forward, her silky black fur gleaming in the spots of moonlight that managed to break through the treetops. Her large paws touched the ground so softly they never made a sound. She let out a soft purr as she settled next to him leaning her body into his.

"Enough, Sani," he hissed. Sani was a Kinừ; a very large cat or lioness, depending on who you spoke to. When she stood on all four of her paws, she was a few inches below eye level to Jaxon's 6'8 height.

She let out a chirp in response. Another attribute he inherited from his Dru'Ny lineage was his ability to *speak* to animals. He couldn't have a full-on conversation and the animal wouldn't reply in words but would in feeling. Over time he could communicate with the animal well enough to understand them as if they *were* having a conversation.

She pressed against him again and this time he patted her on the side. Sani was heavily muscled weighing well over six-hundred pounds, so every time she bumped into him, it almost knocked him over Letting out another chirp, she yawned showing two elongated canine teeth that stuck out on both sides of her mouth just enough to show them.

Sani was more than a pet to Jaxon, she was a friend. She understood him, and he understood her. They were both outcasts to their own kind – powerful and often feared. She purred again, and he gently hushed her.

"You're going to give us away," he warned. She let out a snort in reply resting her head on her paws. Strapped to her was a saddle and a communicator. He didn't often use her as transportation. It was rare for him to even have her around, which explained her overly affectionate behavior. However, tonight he needed her.

Tracking a pack of wolves was dangerous on its own. Tracking a single wolf was safer, but much harder to do. That was where she came in. Kinừ have incredible sense of sight and smell. With her help he never lost his target, only fell behind.

He stood up showing his full size. He had the broad shoulders and the strong build of a Dru'Ny. He was large for a human male, but quite small for a Dru'Ny who would often reach the height between eight to ten feet.

Around his waist over the leather surcoat was a black leather belt that held his Umoya. His Umoya was a sleek and simple design. Made up of shined silver with a black leather wrap around the lower half. The pommel was unique in that it resembled a flanged mace. The top of the pommel spread outward with six thick sharp-edged partitions.

As he went to step forward, the communicator on Sani's back illuminated and began flashing. He pressed a small button to ignore the incoming message and went to leave. The communicator illuminated again. Only this time the alert came on his right forearm. He ignored it a second time. He knew

Arilynn would be angry at him for ignoring her, but he also knew she would understand.

Tracking the animal was hard enough, and he had gone through spots where his communications didn't work. Now, he was finally in a place that he could contact her, but it would jeopardize his mission.

Jaxon let out a sigh as he turned the communicator off, preventing it from illuminating again. Sani shook her small mane letting out a chirp.

"You're right. I'm definitely going to pay for that," Jaxon muttered as he turned his attention back to the factory.

"Stay here, I may need you to cut him off if he runs." Sani made no reply as she laid her head back down on her crossed paws and closed her eyes.

Jaxon looked down at the easiest path to the factory. He could walk the distance rather easily, but it gave him no vantage point and had the potential of exposing him. The only other way would be to go up and over.

He knelt with his hands at his side, furrowing his brow as he concentrated. Pockets of wind began to swirl underneath each palm. The grass swayed violently as the gusts of wind began to gather speed. He couldn't see where he wanted to go yet but launched himself anyway.

The two twisters of wind shot him into the air. He scanned the roof of the factory as he began to descend, adding more wind to carry him forward until he was over the roof. With another gust of wind, he propelled himself further and with the momentum he was able to roll through and land safely on his feet.

The wind dissipated, and he moved on the roof quickly. He was rather agile for his size and moved in almost complete silence, something he had learned from his wife, who insisted that he was always so loud.

He made his way across the roof, where glass skylights framed with metal bars revealed the empty factory floor, reassuring him that the building was abandoned.

The machines below were covered in dust or debris. The floors pooled with grime and water that leaked from the ceiling he was standing on, creating a sour smell of mildew and rust.

He continued moving, but still couldn't see any movement at the ground level. He found a ladder and jumped down the hatch. With a quick gust of wind he landed gently on the concrete floor.

Once inside he could hear the growling of what he could only hope was a man. Wolves were unpredictable, especially a young one. They had no control of their transformations.

He was delighted to hear the voice speak, though it was too quick and frantic for Jaxon to understand what he was saying. He planned each step carefully as he moved forward. He could still hear the muttering that was occasionally interrupted with random fits of coughing and growling.

Jaxon inched closer to the location of the voice. Streaks of dried blood were spread out across the floor as he stepped over a piece of an arm that had begun to rot. The smell was enough that it caused Jaxon to cover his mouth so he wouldn't cough. He pressed himself against a metal wall with scratches and blood down the side.

The factory itself was an old paint and powder coating company. Two very large conveyor belts hung in the ceiling with a maze of staircases and balconies that scattered throughout the main factory floor.

The bottom floor was segmented by metal partitions, separating into four sections. He navigated the small maze moving towards the muttering man. When he found himself close enough to his target he stopped. He stood against the metal partition, listening.

"I…can't…can't….kill…..why….no…ye s…I …killed….why…" The voice was shaky and would break into a high pitch as he spoke.

Jaxon stood still for a moment longer before the muttering abruptly stopped. He could hear haggard breathing and then there was silence.

"I….I know you're there....come out!" the man shouted. Jaxon hesitated, waiting to see if he was speaking to someone else. "I….uh….am very dangerous!" he shouted unsure. "Come out!" his voice dropped low and a low growl followed.

Jaxon shook his head, angry with himself for being so easily caught, as he stepped out of hiding. He was surprised to find the source of the voice was a small frail man lying on the ground in front of a gutted body.

The body was so ravaged and rotted that Jaxon couldn't see anything that could be identified. The smell wafted into the air, mixing with the mildew and rust creating an awful smell that Jaxon was doing his best to ignore.

"Shit…" the man said, falling backwards against one of the partitions. He had short sandy colored hair and a patchy beard that covered parts of his face. He was shirtless with a pair of tattered pants that were being held up by an overly tightened leather belt. His complexion was pale white with red splotches covering his body and dark circles under his eyes.

"It's you..." he said shaking his head back and forth and muttering. "You...killer...no....not...you...."

"What's your name?" Jaxon asked unsure what the young man was doing.

"Doesn't matter," he replied sharply and clearly. "I'm dead regardless." He looked up at Jaxon with bloodshot eyes and a smile crawled across his face and then fear set in again. "I...I knew you'd come."

"Did you?" Jaxon asked, his left hand resting on the pommel of his Umoya.

"They said you'd come. They said..."

"They?" Jaxon repeated.

"Yes, they said you'd come," he muttered. "They said...said you would come for me."

"Of course, I came." Jaxon replied. "You've broken the covenant between your kind and the Order."

"I do not belong to a pack!" he shouted angrily. The sudden outburst made Jaxon jump back a step, his grip tightening on his Umoya.

"You are still required to adhere to the laws."

"Doesn't matter." he coughed. "Doesn't matter."

"It *does* matter," Jaxon corrected. "You killed innocent people, violating the laws," Jaxon said as he stepped forward.

"Doesn't matter."

"Under the authority of the Eri'Dorian Order of Valemìr; I sentence you to die." Jaxon unclipped his Umoya. The hilt crackled as a blade made of lightning formed; As Jaxon moved forward, strays from the blue energy would break away from the blade, zapping anything they touched. "There are two ways this can go," he stated, pointing the tip of his blade at the young man. "You can surrender, and the death is painless, or you can fight it and die tired."

"I'm not dying today," he muttered. "No…no…no…no," he repeated, shaking his head. "NO!" he finally screamed, jumping to his feet. He charged Jaxon, who sidestepped the attack, slashing at him. The edge of his blade cut deep into his back, the energy of the blade left a deep gash that splintered outward, causing him to stumble forward, crashing into the ground. He pushed himself back up as he shouted in pain.

He turned facing Jaxon, his eyes wide and darting around frantically. He charged again. This time Jaxon pushed his hand out, catching the man by the throat and shoving his sword through his abdomen until the blade protruded through his back. Jaxon plunged the blade all the way until the base of the hilt was against the man's stomach.

He screamed so loudly that Jaxon flinched wishing he could cover his ears. The scream turned from an anguished roar to a high-pitched howl. Jaxon took a step back to see that the young man had grown over 3 feet in height and was now towering over Jaxon. His frail body was replaced with hard muscle covered in sand colored fur. His face elongating into a snout with yellow eyes and shaggy fur on top of his head with pointed ears. The beast lowered his head baring its yellow fangs.

"Damn," Jaxon muttered as he stabbed again. The wolf yelped and a wild backhand sent Jaxon sprawling to the ground, ripping the blade from the wolf's stomach. He hit the ground with such velocity that he rolled a few times before he could stop himself.

Jaxon staggered to his feet, his torso throbbing from the impact of the strike. He had no time to recover as the wolf launched itself towards him again.

Jaxon used a gust of wind to propel himself out of harm's way. The wolf was too quick and corrected its course and swung outward catching Jaxon on the back with one of his jagged clawed hands. The impact of the blow and the gust of wind propelled him further than he intended, slamming into one of the metal partitions.

He pushed himself away from the partition trying to shake off the impact. His armor had done its job protecting him from the claws. The wolf tore at him again, Jaxon stumbled backwards narrowly missing the claws coming towards his face this time.

The wolf cut through the metal with such ease that the partition collapsed, and the wolf became entangled in it, giving Jaxon a moment to reposition himself. The wolf snapped its jaw, growling as it tore itself free and dropped down on all fours to stalk towards Jaxon.

Jaxon took a deep breath raising his sword up with both hands. The wolf rushed forward. This time Jaxon met him and went low, avoiding the swipe. He cut into the wolf's side and rolled to the right propelling himself to his feet. The wolf yelped but didn't slow his attack and continued after him.

Jaxon maneuvered and dodged, but each time the wolf attacked, it was just a little closer to hitting him. The first few attacks were already taking its toll on his body.

Finally, one of the strikes caught Jaxon, swatting the Umoya out of his hands. The wolf wrapped his extended fingers around Jaxon's throat, lifting him off the ground. The ravaging beast opened his jaws to bite. Jaxon reacted quickly by shoving his fist down the wolf's throat trying to force him to let go.

He began to bite down, forcing Jaxon to pull his hand out. Throwing Jaxon to the ground, the wolf placed his right paw on to Jaxon's chest and moved to bite at his throat.

Jaxon grabbed a small dagger behind the small of his back and stabbed into the wolf's forearm, prompting a yelp in surprise. He pulled the dagger out and stabbed at the wolf's face. The wolf panicked, jumping away, Jaxon quickly jumped to his feet. The wolf swung another backhand that Jaxon managed to duck under. He caught his balance and punched the wolf with everything he had.

The impact of the punch staggered the wolf. Dru'Ny were known for their physical strength, and it was something Jaxon was able to call upon in special moments like this. The wolf shook its head giving Jaxon enough time to knock down the monster with a blast of fire from his hand into the it's chest.

Jaxon ran over, grabbing his Umoya, and continued towards the wolf who was beginning to stand back up. The weapon ignited with another flash of lightning, this time creating a hammer made of blazing fire.

Jaxon swung the hammer with as much strength as he could muster, hitting the wolf in the abdomen, the fur singing upon impact. He could both hear and feel the bones shatter as the wolf let out a cry of anguish. It limped backwards snapping its jaws the way a trapped animal would.

The wolf, still hunched over, began to retreat swiping wildly to keep Jaxon at bay. He was a young wolf which made him purely instinctual. No strategy, just raw power and speed. This made the wolf dangerous as it would unleash itself with every attack, but also made him susceptible to traps or patterns.

Jaxon stepped forward swinging the hammer down and leaving himself open to an attack. The wolf avoided the blow, but as expected couldn't resist the chance to attack at the opening. It swung down its claws spread out to cut through him.

Jaxon shifted and swung up his Umoya, the fire-hammer turning into a single edged scimitar made of black metal. The blade cut just below the wrist of the wolf's arm lopping the hand clean off.

There was a loud howl that was so piercing to Jaxon's ears that he staggered to the ground covering them. The wolf's survival instincts finally took over and he began to flee. Jaxon put his fingers just inside his lips and whistled as loudly as he could, trying to catch his breath and regain his hearing.

He heard the wolf growling and could hear its footsteps receding until he heard the distinct roar of Sani. Jaxon rushed forward as he could hear the two animals fighting. Sani was an experienced fighter, but the wolf was stronger even with his wound. One bite and Sani would be in a lot of trouble.

Jaxon came upon the two of them entangled. Sani's jaws were biting down on the back of the wolf's neck while her front paws held him close, she was continuously kicking with her powerful hindlegs, her claws tearing away the fur and ripping into its flesh.

"Back!" Jaxon shouted as he rushed towards them, Sani obeyed letting go, and scampering away.

The wolf scrambled to get to its feet, but it was too wounded and stumbled forward until he was no longer a beast but the frail man he was before.

The man used his one good arm to crawl forward while his handless arm dangled at his side. The stump was already healed, a benefit of the curse he was under. He pulled himself to a small broken wooden bench, throwing himself to the side so that he could roll over and face Jaxon.

Sani growled as she paced behind Jaxon who stood over the beaten man. His Umoya blade disappeared but he kept the hilt in his hand.

"What the hell is that thing?" the man asked, looking at Sani who growled at the question.

"She's a Kinừ." Jaxon answered.

"Well, she's an awfully good fighter," he said with a chuckle leaning his head back looking up at the sky. "You…you…you have one hell of a right hook," he added with another laugh that turned into a coughing fit that ended with him spitting up blood. He rested his head on the back of a bench looking up at the sky again.

Jaxon knelt in front of him staring directly at him. The man lowered his head down and looked at Jaxon, his smile gone.

"I... never wanted this, you know?" he said, his voice cracking as he continued. "I just, uh wanted a normal life...with my wife..." He shifted trying to sit up higher against the bench. "I...I was just working on my farm and out of nowhere it came at me. Tried to run but there was no way I could get away. He bit me harder than your beast there." He looked down where his missing hand should have been.

"I knew what it meant. What would happen. Tried to find anyone to help but everyone sent me away telling me to kill myself." He looked back up at Jaxon. "When I finally worked up the nerve, it was too late."

"Why didn't you find a pack?"

"I tried," he said as he spit blood more on the ground. "Novak wouldn't accept me."

"There are other packs besides Novak's," Jaxon said. To his surprise the man laughed again shaking his head. "What?"

"You...you knights don't know anything," he said with a pained laugh as he looked back up towards the sky. He stared at the moon that was beginning its descent.

"What do you mean?" Jaxon asked leaning forward.

"Novak….he….he's taken over the other packs." He answered groggily. "He wouldn't take me. Said I…I was a mistake." He looked back to Jaxon and then shook his head. "It's probably better that way. I don't think I would have fit into his little army."

"Army?" Jaxon asked.

"I…It doesn't matter," he answered with a shrug. "You gonna kill me or what?" he asked with a bloodied smile. Jaxon made no reply standing up. "You take last words or requests?" When Jaxon didn't answer he spoke anyway.

"My wife lives in a small farming town called. Aldirton… She works at the bank there, the only one. Her name is Ariel. If you could just tell her that…I…I'm sorry. That I never wanted to hurt her…" He leaned forward with his head hanging. "I never meant to hurt her."

The man scrunched his eyes and face waiting for Jaxon to cut him down. When nothing happened, he opened his eyes looking up at him.

"You had your final change, right?" Jaxon said, clipping his Umoya on his belt.

"Uh....I...I think so, today."

"What's your name, boy?" Jaxon asked.

"Ethan," he replied, his eyes darting around. "I...I thought you were going to kill me?"

"I'm supposed to," Jaxon replied, looking upward at the sun that was beginning to crest over the distant mountains. He turned so that he was facing Ethan who was now clutching his arm. "It'll never grow back."

"I didn't think it would matter," Ethan said looking down at the stump where his hand once was.

"You realize that you killed innocent people, right?"

"Yes...I...I didn't mean to!" Ethan proclaimed in a sob. "I tried to get as far away from people as I could. I would just wake up and their bodies would be on the ground and I would be covered in blood..." His voice broke as he began sobbing and stammering over his words like he had been doing when Jaxon came upon him.

"You are condemned by the Eri'Dorian Order."

"I know..."

"No pack will accept you."

"Yea...?" Ethan answered confused by what was happening. "Are you trying to make me feel better or worse?"

"I don't care about your feelings, Ethan," Jaxon admonished. "You killed innocent people and should be punished for it." He looked down, his blue eyes glaring down at Ethan. "I would say that you have been."

"Are....are you letting me go?"

"You had your final change. That means you won't change involuntarily except for the full moons." He knelt back down. "Those nights you will need to find a way to barricade or chain yourself down and have your wife be far away from you."

"Wait...what?"

"You need to go home. Tell your wife, Ariel, what you told me," Jaxon said in a whisper. "You tell her everything you've done since you left her. You drop to your knees and beg for forgiveness. If she accepts you, you can learn to live with this curse."

"If she doesn't?" Ethan asked leaning forward.

"Then you learn to live without her."

"I don't know if I can."

"Then you'll have to try harder at killing yourself." His response caught Ethan off-guard.

"Why are you letting me go?"

"Because, I kill monsters and terrible people every day," Jaxon replied. "You're cursed to be a terrible monster, but that does not mean *you* are one."

"Thank you…thank you!" Ethan said lunging forward wrapping his arms around Jaxon. His sudden movement startled Sani, she let out a loud roar jumping forward. Jaxon lifted his hand and she stopped abruptly growling as she began pacing back and forth. "S-sorry," Ethan said sheepishly.

"One more thing," Jaxon said, pushing Ethan away. "If you hurt one more person, accident or not, I will find you and I will not hesitate to kill you. Do you understand?" As

Jaxon asked, he placed his hand on Ethan's shoulder.

Ethan nodded his head and then let out a scream as Jaxon seared his handprint onto his shoulder and torso.

"You've been marked, no other wolf will ever trust you. So, I suggest you don't try joining another pack."

"I didn't know the Eri'Dorian's did this."

"They don't," Jaxon replied. "Now go before I change my mind and let my cat devour you."

"How can I ever thank you?" Ethan said as he stood up.

"Be a good person," Jaxon replied. "Go." Jaxon said with a nod of his head. Ethan obeyed, holding his arm as he ran off disappearing into the woods.

Jaxon let out a long sigh, looking where Ethan had disappeared. After a moment he decided it was time to go. As he walked through the old factory, Sani sauntered behind him letting out random chirps and growls as she passed the body parts scattered on the floor.

"Don't," Jaxon warned as Sani went to take one of the parts. She let out a growl and ran ahead of him.

"You think I should have killed him?" Jaxon asked aloud. Sani let out another grunt and stopped.

"Yea, well what do you know? You're a cat," Jaxon replied with a smirk. Sani let out another growl flicking her tail into the air.

Once they were outside the factory, he checked to make sure she had no injuries. When he was done, he placed his hand on a small medallion on the back of her harness. It was a magical stone that acted as a Shift-gate, allowing him and other Eri'Dorian knights used to travel great distances in a short amount of time.

It didn't hurt the traveler but was certainly disorienting and could be potentially dangerous if there were too many people travelling and not enough power to use the medallion.

She let out a purr as the medallion began to glow and with a flash of light, she was gone. Leaving him alone with his thoughts.

Ethan's mention of an army made him nervous. The last time the packs joined forces under one alpha, there had been a massive war and it nearly tore the realms apart.

He glanced down at his wrist communicator. He knew that Arilynn wouldn't be happy about him not meeting her, let alone not answering. But he also knew that this was potentially a far worse situation that needed his attention.

He lifted his arm and began the transmission to her. She answered almost immediately. He couldn't help but smile when he saw her. Even with her scowl, she was the most beautiful woman he had ever seen.

"Where the hell have you been!?" she asked in such a sharp tone that made the smile fall from his face.

"Tracking a young wolf," Jaxon replied dryly. "It took me longer than I expected and I couldn't reach out—"

"At all?" Arilynn snapped, cutting him off. "I have been worried sick about you."

Jaxon replied with a rush of guilt. "I…I should have reached out."

"It doesn't matter right now," Arilynn replied with a frustrated sigh. "Do you have any idea what is going on?"

"No," he admitted.

"The Oracle has returned," She replied flatly. "I'm here with Markus and Clara right now investigating."

"I miss a few days and the whole world changes," Jaxon replied with a half-smile.

"Now is not the time, Jaxon," Arilynn snapped. "You need to meet me here. Are you done with the wolf?"

"Yes, he's gone." Jaxon replied carefully. She narrowed her eyes regarding him for a moment before speaking again.

"Then get over here," she demanded.

"I won't be able to make it, love."

"Why?" she asked, annoyed.

"The man mentioned that Novak is creating an army."

"Army?" she asked, her tone changing from annoyance to curiosity.

"Yes, I'm going to find Novak and see what I can find out."

"I don't think that's a good idea."

"Why's that?"

"Well, considering Novak absolutely despises you, going there to find out anything is likely to start the war you're trying to prevent. You aren't known for your soft touch and negotiation skills."

"Thanks, Ari," Jaxon replied. "Perhaps you can go there, and I can look for the Oracle."

"Well, you may have a better idea of where she is at considering she was seen with Isobella Hartley."

There was a long pause where they stared at each other. Jaxon let out a long sigh while Arilynn seemed to be holding her breath.

"I'm sorry, Ari," he said breaking the silence. "I—"

Cutting him off. "We don't have time to discuss this right now and I'm hardly in the right mind to do so."

"You will have plenty of time to kill me later."

"I'm not interested in hurting you Jaxon. I have to go. Good luck with Novak, and if you have any idea on where Isobella may go. I would appreciate any help."

She cut the transmission before he could reply. He shook his head, dropping his arm to his side. Jaxon let out a small groan at the thought of where he needed to go next. He would have to deal with Arilynn afterward. Novak's den was not somewhere he wanted to find himself distracted.

He now had to travel and find one of the most notorious wolves in all the realms. He would have to go to *his* domain and question him – *accuse* him. Jaxon couldn't help but think that Arilynn had been right. That he certainly wasn't the man for the job, but it didn't matter anymore. He had no other choice but to go.

CHAPTER 6

Haven

Isobella drove relentlessly through the night, only stopping for fuel as needed. Though Isobella didn't want to spend any money unnecessarily, she caught herself relenting out of guilt, allowing Gwynne to buy something sweet or a small booklet about the local wildlife.

The guilt of pulling her daughter away from everything she had known only grew worse the longer they traveled. Every now and then she would glance down at Gwynne who was either sleeping or reading. She wasn't sure what she was expecting Gwynne to do to make her feel better, maybe a smile or a laugh. Anything would be better than the silence they were enduring together.

Despite *wanting* to break the silence, Isobella cut all conversations short. When Gwynne attempted to ask about what was happening, she dismissed her. She wasn't ready for that conversation yet. She just needed to get Gwynne to safety, and she couldn't think straight until that was accomplished. Unfortunately, it meant that the ride had been quiet except for the constant hum of the engine and the occasional chewing from Gwynne.

They continued down a stretch of road and hadn't seen another vehicle either on land or in the air for hours, but Isobella knew they were close to where they needed to be. It had been years since her last visit, but she could never forget how to get there.

They were in the beginnings of the Askia Desert. It was bare land with jagged cliffs that the road carved into. Though it was still morning, the sun bore down on them and she could already see the heat rising off of the old run-down road ahead. No one wanted to be stuck in the Askia Desert without a way out. It was the perfect place for someone to hide if they could figure out how to overcome the adverse climate.

The road began to curve away from the edge of a cliff, but Isobella stayed the course. The vehicle slowly began to accelerate to the point that Gwynne looked up from her booklet.

"What are you doing?!" she shouted trying to grab the wheel. Isobella swatted her hand away.

"Trust me," she said sternly. Gwynne scrunched her eyes shut and began screaming, pushing herself against the seat.

Isobella floored the pedal causing the engine to roar as they tore across the sand. When they approached the cliff, she lifted a small lever and the thrusters sprang to life. The sudden jolt was enough to make anyone dizzy. Isobella held her breath just as they careened off the edge, Gwynne screaming the entire way down.

Isobella pressed the lever back down shutting off the thrusters as they fell towards the cliff on the other side of the small valley.

She held the wheel so tightly her knuckles were bone white, her eyes concentrating on what was in front of them. She slowly reached over to the console in the center of the dash. She pressed a button that opened a small trap door to present a dusty screen. Isobella quickly typed four digits into the screen while keeping her eyes facing forward. It lit up and retreated into its hiding place.

The rock wall in front of them began to open, splitting into two doors as a metallic platform extended outward, kicking up clouds of dust and sand. Isobella kept her foot floored to the ground, the engines roaring. She flipped the lever again, the thrusters boosting them upward into the air until they reached the platform. Isobella shut the thrusters down, letting off the accelerator as they came to a slow stop. Gwynne was still breathing heavily as she waited in the vehicle for a moment.

They were in the middle of an old worn road that was cut off by a large metal barrier. The light from outside started to disappear as the doors behind them closed. There was a brief moment where the tunnel was completely dark until a row of yellow lights down the center of the ceiling flickered to life.

To their left was a platform where two men were standing at the edge. The first of the two men was a large black man with a potbelly that stuck out over his waistband. He was shirtless and wore brown cloth pants over old dusty work boots. He had heavily muscled arms and a broad barrel chest. His head was shaved bald and a neatly trimmed thin beard lined his jaw.

Behind him was a younger man in much better shape. He wasn't as large but had a lean muscular build. He had long braids that were pulled back with a tie. He wore a loose-fitting sleeveless shirt and pants similar to the larger man. He held a silver tipped spear in one hand while a wooden baton was attached to his right hip.

She exited the vehicle and stared up at the man who narrowed his gaze in return. He regarded her for a moment longer before climbing down the stairs that led to the road.

"Bella," he said with a warm smile. "How long has it been?"

"Too long, Tryxus. Too long." Before she could say anything else, he wrapped his massive arms around her, lifting her off the ground in a tight bear hug. His laugh was so loud it echoed throughout the tunnel.

"Come here boy!" he shouted over his shoulder. "You remember Tyron?"

"Wow," Isobella said in surprise. "The last time I saw him he was barely talking."

"They grow fast." As Tyron approached, Gwynne was now out of the vehicle. She stood on the other side of the vehicle looking at the two of them and then her mother.

"As much as I want to believe this is a social visit. I have a feeling that it's not," he said, looking over at Gwynne.

"We need to talk." Isobella replied flatly. "I need your help." She added.

"Well, this compound is always open to you," Tryxus said loudly, ensuring that Gwynne heard him.

Tryxus led them up the platform and through double doors that opened only after Tryxus placed his hand on a small data-pad. It illuminated and an audible tone rang out his name. Isobella glanced back at Gwynne who was following slowly.

~~~~
~~~~

"My name is Tyron." He was much taller up close than she realized. He slowed his pace to match hers.

"Gwynne," she replied quietly.

"It's a real honor to meet your mother," he said with a sheepish smile that he tried to hide.

"Why?" Gwynne asked, confused by his excitement. He looked at her with a furrowed brow and then laughed shaking his head. "I'm serious, what is so great about my mom and do you know why are we here? *Where* is here?"

"You really don't know do you?" Tyron asked, his smile fading. He shrugged his shoulders as they continued following their parents.

"If I knew, I wouldn't have asked," Gwynne replied, glancing back at the vehicle.

"Yea, I guess so," Tyron replied with another shrug.

"Sorry," Gwynne said quickly. "It's just been a really bad couple days. How do you know my mother?"

"I don't." He replied. "My dad does, and he told me all the stories about her and what she used to do."

"What did she used to do?" Gwynne asked looking over at her mother who was dwarfed by Tryxus walking next to her.

Tyron hesitated. "I don't know what I'm allowed to say, but I would just ask her."

"You really don't know my mother then," Gwynne muttered, crossing her arms.

The tunnel after the double doors was well lit and very clean which shocked Gwynne considering how dusty the tunnel where they left the vehicle was.

Once they passed another set of doors, they were in a large compound that, if she didn't know better, was just a regular building that wasn't built into the side of a cliff.

The room was lit by bright lights scattered throughout the ceiling. The floor was made of carved marble; Gwynne traced her fingers along the smooth sand colored stone walls as they walked. There had to have been at least fifty people — some of them cleaning while others were sitting down to eat at the evenly spaced tables — who all stopped what they were doing and looked over at the new visitors.

"What was it?" a woman shouted. Gwynne looked over to see a heavyset woman with short hair wearing a beige apron.

"Just friends arriving," Tryxus replied with a smile. "No need to worry." The woman stared at them for a moment before going back to serving food, Gwynne's stomach suddenly ached and growled when she smelled the food.

Gwynne continued to look around and saw that everyone was still staring at them. They all immediately dropped their gaze when they noticed her looking back at them. She instinctively wrapped her arms around herself, slumping her shoulders. Lowering her gaze in hopes that people would just forget she was there.

"If you're hungry," Tryxus said motioning to the food. Gwynne looked to her mom for permission. Isobella nodded and Gwynne rushed over to the food, doing her best to ignore everyone's stares.

~~~~

"What's going on?" Tryxus asked as he put on a thin white buttoned shirt.

"I think she's the Oracle," Isobella answered, watching Gwynne get food while Tyron followed behind her.

"What?!" Tryxus shouted. "You brought her here?!" he hissed looking around.

"I didn't know where else to go," Isobella replied frantically.

"Why do you think she's the Oracle?" Tryxus asked, softening his tone.

"It's the only thing that makes sense." She was still watching Gwynne, not paying attention to Tryxus who was glaring down at her. "I need time, Tryxus."

"You can't stay here," he said defiantly.

"What?"

"You know the Order will come after her. It won't take long for their Seeker to find her let alone anyone else who is hunting for her."

"I don't know what to do," Isobella pleaded looking up at him now. "I can't take
~~~~

her to Eri'Dor, they'll kill me at the gates, and God knows what they'll do to her."

"So, you bring her here and risk everyone?" Tryxus scoffed, throwing his hands up in the air.

"We're on the same side, aren't we?"

"That was a long time ago, Bella," he grumbled. "We were at war."

"We still are."

"No," he growled. "We lost the war when Lio disappeared."

"So, that's it? I'm on my own?"

"What do you want from me?" He stepped closer, trying to keep his voice down. "I have responsibilities, most of these people are fugitives or running from the Order themselves. If the Order arrives here looking for her, they'll kill everyone in sight."

"She's my daughter, Tryxus."

"What about *my* son? What about my *wife*?" he argued. "I can't help you. I'm sorry."

"What happened to: I am always welcome?" she asked angrily.

"You can eat what you want and rest. But you will need to leave by nightfall." With that he turned away leaving her standing alone. She went to speak, but knew it was no use. Tryxus was stubborn; when he was done with a conversation, it meant it was over.

She could see that everyone was looking up at her and Tryxus. When they realized she was looking at them, they all quickly averted their eyes.

Isobella walked over and sat next to Gwynne who was shoveling food so quickly down her throat that Isobella was sure she was going to choke.

"Grab everything you want, we're leaving."

"What?" Gwynne asked with a full mouth. She swallowed and cleared her throat before speaking again. "I thought we were staying here?"

"Change of plan," Isobella replied dismissively. "Grab your food. We need to go."

"Ma'am," Tyron interrupted as he placed a black bag on the table. "I brought this for you. It has first-aid supplies, ropes, some dried food packets and water. It's not a lot, but it'll help," he said with a polite smile.

"Thank you, Tyron," Isobella said standing up handing him the bag back, "But we can't take that. I appreciate it though."

"I insist," He stated, pushing it back.

"What about your father?"

"What is he going to do? Ground me?" I already can't leave the compound." he added with a laugh. "Besides, I already talked to him, you saved his life, I know that because he always told me the stories about you and Lio. Take it, please. It's my honor to help you."

"The honor is mine, Tyron. Thank you." She couldn't help but see him as a young child despite the fact that he towered over her in height. He would be nearly nineteen years of age by now, the thought of which only made her feel old and sad. The poor boy had never seen anything outside of the compound, just like Gwynne, who up until recently had never seen anything more than Olessa.

"When will you leave?" he asked looking down at Gwynne.

"Tomorrow," Tryxus said as he approached. "You can rest here tonight. I wish I could help you more, but…" Tryxus' gazed dropped to the ground and then straightened. Isobella knew that was the best she was going to get from him.

"I'm sorry that I brought this to you." Isobella replied regretfully.

"Don't be. I just can't risk everyone here more than I already have."

"I'll get your rooms ready," Tyron said eagerly. "Gwynne, would you like to join me?"

Gwynne looked up with her mouth still full. Her face flushed red with embarrassment, when Isobella gave the okay, Gwynne stood up and followed Tyron.

"We need to talk about this, Bella."

"What is there talk about?" she asked as they both sat down. She was tired; more tired than she was letting on. Dealing with Tryxus' stubbornness was not something she wanted to do.

"Well for starters, where will you go?" She stared at him for a moment. Tryxus had always been a large man, but now he was even bigger than she remembered. He was out of shape, but she was sure he still had all his strength.

"I don't know. I don't know what to do." She dropped her face into her hands shaking her head.

He leaned forward so he could whisper. "How do you know she's the Oracle?"

"The lights of Valemìr, they appeared when she brought down lightning and killed a Sentinel..."

"She killed a Sentinel?" he asked, looking over towards where Gwynne and Tyron had walked off to. "Well, you definitely can't take her to Eri'Dor."

"I know," Isobella replied. "But they're the only ones who are equipped to handle her. She will need to ascend. I can't do that, and neither can you."

"There are other places where she can ascend," Tryxus answered.

"They're all protected by the Eri'Dorian Order," she reminded him.

"Not all of them."

"You can't be serious," she said shaking her head, but when he didn't reply, she looked back at him. "I can't take her to Dereli."

"Why not?" he asked.

"Because, Dereli is a wasteland. There is a reason no one goes there, Tryxus."

"There is an entire civilization there," Tryxus argued. "Lio is there."

"I don't care where he is," Isobella said with a scoff.

"He can help you."

"You may hold out for his triumphant return, but I will not. I can't."

Tryxus made no reply as he leaned back stretching his arms outward before resting them on the table.

"I was going to find Jaxon," she said breaking the brief silence.

"Jaxon?" He raised his voice so loudly that everyone stopped. "Why would you go looking for that son of a bitch?"

"Because, he can help me," Isobella snapped.

"Why would he help you? You're a defector just like me. He'll kill you like he has hundreds of others." Tryxus slammed his hand on the table, causing it to shake. "He killed our friends, or have you forgotten!?"

"I haven't forgotten anything!" She argued. She took a deep breath, no longer concerned with the stares. "Because, he's helped me before."

"Bella, that was a long time ago, you told me yourself that he said if he ever saw you again, he'd kill you." He was still clenching his fists as he inhaled deeply, letting out and an exaggerated sigh.

"He's the only chance I have," she replied. "I have to find him."

Tryxus let out another long heavy sigh shaking his head. "Well, get some rest here and eat." Tryxus said standing up not wanting to continue the argument. "May as well have a full belly and full night of rest before you go get yourself killed."

CHAPTER 7

Wolf's Den

Jaxon drove his vehicle forward slowly, trying to avoid bringing any extra attention to himself despite how much the old-style Phoenix stood out. He was deep in Novak's territory now, and his followers were everywhere, watching carefully as he drove by.

Jaxon's *Phoenix* was a modified all-terrain vehicle; it could travel by air, land and temporarily in water. It was low and wide-bodied, designed for power and agility. His was painted black with tinted windows. It had six wheels, two in the front and four in the back. It had an old-fashioned engine that he had pushed to its absolute limits and thrusters he had stolen from other thieves.

The high council would have never approved of the stealing, which was the main reason he never told them. Arilynn had given him an earful at first but eventually relented and never brought it up again.

The roads were wet from the sporadic drizzle; the night was still young as the sunset colors painted the wall of clouds that loomed in the distance.

Coming to a slow stop, he parked looking out the windshield as men and women walked by him. Some paid no attention while others were so focused on him, he was sure they could see through the tinted double-paned windows.

As he stepped out of his vehicle, his eyes met with some others who either looked away immediately or stared intently first. A woman smiled, turning to her friends who all giggled as they approached the building he was going to — a tower that overlooked that city of Angoria. A large city within the Dorrennian Kingdom that was well known for its nightlife.

Jaxon hesitated before walking in. He lifted the hood of his surcoat to protect him from the sudden downpour that erupted with a faint crack of thunder. He knew that he stood out with his armor, but he knew that in most cases, him standing out would eventually help him.

He made his way inside the building — the guards posted outside too busy flirting with the women to notice. Moving quickly through the lobby, he stepped through an open elevator door with a group of people.

He pushed his way to the back of the elevator; the other occupants that drunkenly stumbled in were too busy flirting and groping one another to realize he was standing there. He waited patiently as they dwindled in number until only a few of them remained when they reached the second to the top floor, level fifty-two.

The metallic doors opened to an entire level that had been turned into a loud dance club. The music was mostly drowned out by the bass that seemingly shook the entire building. The small trio of girls that remained rushed through the doors, noisily making their way to the dance floor garnering everyone's attention.

Jaxon followed, darting to the left and cutting through the crowded club, ignoring the random bumps and the few women who pulled at him. He spotted the bar and made his way towards it. Flashes of light illuminated everything for brief moments. There were a few cages that hung from the ceiling where both men and women danced to the music.

He scanned the area and could see security spread out looking around the large room for anything out of the ordinary. They lined the walls with a few placed in specific areas enhancing their ability to watch everything.

He brushed past another small group and finally made it to the bar. He pulled out one of the seats, sitting down and leaning against the black wooden bar. It was polished so well that it reflected the flashing lights on the ceiling.

"What do you want?!" a voice yelled. Jaxon looked over his shoulder to see that it belonged to a young man with a shaved head and two hooped earrings. He was shirtless, showing his small, skeletal build. His agitated expression told Jaxon he wasn't willing to wait for him to decide.

When Jaxon shifted, showing the symbol of Valemìr on his chest, the bartender glanced over at the guards and then looked over at Jaxon again, eyeing him carefully.

"The strongest thing you got," Jaxon replied. The young man hesitated and then nodded his head. After a moment he returned with a small shot glass with a dark brown liquid. Jaxon grabbed the drink and with a single gulp, ingested it. He placed the glass back on the bar, shaking his head from the potency. The young man waited impatiently with his hand out.

"Novak will pay for it," Jaxon replied. When he spoke the name, the young man hesitated. Then he quickly grabbed the glass, walking away.

He knew mentioning Novak's name coupled with him wearing Eri'Dorian armor would get a reaction.

It didn't take long until he was approached by a well dressed young man in a dark gray suit with a blood red button-down shirt. His dark brown hair was cut short and neatly groomed. Despite the dimness of the room, he wore black sunglasses.

He stood in front of Jaxon with an arrogant smile as he tilted his head, waiting for Jaxon to acknowledge him. "Who are you?" he asked, pushing on Jaxon's shoulder. "You askin' for trouble, knight?" He pushed him again.

"No." Jaxon looked up at him, removing the hood. The man's smile disappeared from his face.

"W-w-what do you want?"

"I'm here to meet with Novak," Jaxon replied, looking away. He could see other men in suits walking around frantically. Some of them spoke into their wrists, or to each other but all of them were watching.

"Well, you're talking to me," the young man said with as much confidence as he could muster.

"You're not in charge. Tell Novak that he has a *friend* waiting for him."

"You don't get to tell me what to do."

"Just tell Novak that I'm here."

"You got balls, I'll give you that," he said with a nervous smile, as the others watching began to move in. "But I don't think you understand the situation."

The guard grabbed Jaxon by the shoulder and attempted to lift him off the seat. Jaxon grabbed the young man's wrist torquing it to the side.

The guard let out a whimper and crumpled to his knees as Jaxon applied more pressure standing up from the seat. The young man attempted to push back. Jaxon simply applied pressure causing him to scream out and stay on the ground.

"Let him go!" a loud voice shouted. The commotion was beginning to gather the attention of the patrons. Jaxon looked over to see a heavy-set, dark-skinned man stomping towards him. He had golden brown eyes and was wearing a black suit with a white button up. His hair was neatly groomed similar to the young man who was still kneeling on the ground.

He moved forward grabbing Jaxon by the shoulder pushing him back. Jaxon let go of the man's wrist taking a step back. The large man helped the guard to his feet and stepped in front of him. He stared at Jaxon for a moment and let out a loud sigh shaking his head.

"Get out of here, kid," he said, still shaking his head.

"What? No! Don't you know who he is?!" the young guard exclaimed, rubbing his wrist

"I know who he is," The man answered as he lifted his wrist to his mouth. "Back off." The command prompted the rest to retreat back to their corners. The large man led Jaxon away from all the music and crowds of people who were beginning to circle around them to a small maroon room with black leather furniture. The man pointed at the two women and then gestured for them to leave, which they promptly did, making sure to stay as far away as possible. Jaxon sat down looking up with a half-smile.

"How have you been, Tobias?" Jaxon crossed his arms as he sat back on the chair.

"I was doing pretty well until now," he answered, motioning to the women who had just left. "Why are you here?" he asked with a heavy sigh.

"I need to see Novak."

"I can't do that. He was pretty clear, no visitors."

"I'm sure he wouldn't mind an old friend."

"I don't think he considers you a friend, Jaxon," Tobias replied.

"It's important."

"I don't care, and I can bet Novak doesn't either."

"I'm not in the mood to argue with you. I'll give you a choice, because I consider you a friend," Jaxon said as he rose to his feet. "You can either take me up to see Novak, or I leave."

"Leave," Tobias said with a smirk and a clap of his hands. "Easy choice."

"You didn't let me finish," Jaxon said with a smile. "I leave and go back to Eri'Dor and see the council and tell them about the rumor I heard that Novak was building an army." Tobias' smirk disappeared and glanced around nervously. "I return with the full weight of the Eri'Dorian Order and crush this establishment and all those associated. We'll hunt the packs down and when we find Novak, I'll be sure to mention it was *you* who betrayed him." Tobias gulped and then shook his head in disbelief. "Your choice, *friend*."

"Dammit, you'd do that to me?" Tobias whined. "That's not friendly at all!"

"I don't want to, Tobias." Jaxon answered. "But I will."

"You're gonna get me killed," Tobias muttered. "Follow me."

Tobias led Jaxon through another small room, this time ignoring the occupants as they opened another door to a long hallway, bright lights on the ceiling. At the end of the hall was another elevator with two men in suits positioned on either side.

"What's this?" one of them asked, stepping forward. He glowered at Jaxon and then back to Tobias who just shook his head. "Novak isn't going to be happy."

"Yea, I know," Tobias muttered as he walked past. The other guard pressed the button and the doors opened. Jaxon stepped inside with Tobias.

"You know, I could just change and kill you in here," Tobias said, glancing over at Jaxon.

"If you think you have what it takes, go ahead," Jaxon replied without looking over at him. Tobias let out another long sigh looking up at the top of the elevator muttering to himself, something about he was dead no matter what he did. The elevator let out a loud bi*ng* as the doors slid open.

The top floor was virtually empty except for a small part in the center of the room. There were five men sitting in the only light of the room, with one standing facing away from them. The furniture consisted of two four seated couches facing each other with a large dark wood table in between them. With two black leather chairs on both ends of the table. The table was littered with half full wine glasses and plates of half eaten raw meat and cheese.

As Jaxon approached, the man standing stopped speaking and turned towards him, prompting the others to do the same. There was a collective gasp between them when they saw him. In the span of a few seconds, twenty guards quickly amassed around the six men. None of them were armed; they didn't need to be. They were all wolves and could change in an instant.

Jaxon took another step towards them. He ignored the guards as he stopped short of the circle they had created. Lifting his head so that he could see over the guards, he waved. "Don't mind me, I'll wait," Jaxon said, placing his hands behind his back. He swayed back and forth with a polite smile on his face. He wanted to keep moving so that he was ready just in case they decided to attack. He felt the guard closest to him was about to strike, but he began nervously glancing around to the others as Jaxon realized they were waiting for their orders.

Something else he noticed was that the guards were all dressed in a type of armor he had never seen. It protected their torso and neck, and it had slats so that it would stretch when they made their change. This realization made Jaxon rethink his arrogant approach. Jaxon refocused his attention back on the men entrenched in the circle of guards. The only one he was interested in was Novak. He wasn't the largest in the room, but he carried himself so well that he had the largest presence. He was the one standing, he never stopped glaring at Jaxon as he refastened the buttons to his suit.

He was at least a head shorter than Jaxon with a medium build that was covered in a black pin-striped suit with a black button down. He had dark-tan skin with long thick silky black hair that he let lay down naturally.

Novak took a long deep breath before speaking in a rough language that the other five men understood. The language wolves used to communicate, Luguia, was a hard language to learn and sometimes even sounded like a dog snarling. He was the only who spoke, making the conversation short.

"You shouldn't speak a language your guests don't understand," Jaxon quipped. "It's quite rude."

"Leave us," Novak snapped. The five men stood up and begrudgingly left. All of them staring at Jaxon as he smiled back at them. As they walked out, he recognized them as the Alphas of the other five major packs.

The guards followed them out until it was only Jaxon, Novak and Tobias, who rushed over with his head lowered. Despite being much larger than Novak, it was clear that Novak was in command. Tobias never lifted his head when they spoke and when they were done, he hurried out of the room.

"You have a lot of—"

"Balls?" Jaxon interrupted. "So, I've heard."

"I was going to say nerve," Novak hissed.

"Well, that is much more mature than your friend down there," Jaxon said, sauntering into the light. He peered down at the table to see if there was anything that would give him an idea of what they had been discussing, unfortunately all he saw was more food. The sight of the raw meat made him think of Ethan.

"Do you want a drink?" Novak asked as he poured himself another glass of red wine.

"Not a fan of wine." Jaxon replied.

"We have beer." Novak replied as he returned the bottle of wine to the table. "For less evolved taste," he added with a sneer.

"Oh, I don't like beer either. More of a hard liquor kind of guy."

"What do you want?" Novak asked with a sharp tone.

"Anything but wine," Jaxon replied with a smirk.

"Why are you here?" Novak asked, forcing a softer tone as he stepped toward him.

"What do you mean?" Jaxon asked, acting surprised. "Can't old friends stop by and catch up?" He knew he had to be careful. Novak was known for his temper. A bad temper with the power of a werewolf was a very strong advantage. It was also a simple tactic to fluster him. Novak was more than capable of changing and even killing him, but Novak was smarter than that and would never jeopardize him or his pack. Killing or even attempting, would bring the Eri'Dorian Order at his doorstep.

Novak took a deep breath and then downed his glass of wine. He poured himself another glass and smiled.

"You're right. How are you, Jaxon?" He asked with a forced smile.

"I'm okay, a little tired," Jaxon replied with feigned yawn. "Oh, hey!" Jaxon said excitedly. "I met a friend of yours, nice enough guy. Hell of a temper, though."

"Is my friend still alive?" Novak asked as he tightened his grip on the wine glass.

"Oh, no. I killed him," Jaxon said pointedly. "Didn't put up much of a fight, but he tried." The sound of glass breaking caught Jacksons attention. Novak stood with the broken glass in his hand as blood and wine dripped onto the rug.

"Do you need a towel?" Jaxon asked, feigning concern.

"Did you come here just to irritate me and tell me you killed a friend of mine?" Novak asked, smiling through gritted teeth.

"Well, I would use the word *friend* loosely. He was more like a stray." Novak's expression darkened. “I don't actually know his name,” Jaxon lied.

“You kill people without knowing their names?” Novak asked as he grabbed a towel to wipe the blood off his hand.

“Don't you?” Jaxon asked incredulously. “Anyway, he had a lot to say about you.”

“You mean Ethan,” Novak said with a growl throwing the towel on the ground. “He wasn't mine.”

“Hey, since when did the other Alpha's start listening to you?” Jaxon asked, tilting his head. Novak stepped over to the table, grabbing another glass and filling it with wine. “Seems interesting that they would just go when you told them to.”

“This is my establishment. We have a system of respect in our culture. Something I am sure you know nothing about,” Novak replied bitterly, no longer forcing a smile. “You still haven't told me what you want.”

“Keep your strays closer to home,” Jaxon said before turning to walk out then stopped. “Oh, yea,” Jaxon said, tapping his head. "I almost forgot. He mentioned something about an army?" Jaxon shrugged his shoulders. "You wouldn't know anything about that would you?"

Novak tensed at the question and then relaxed, shaking his head. Jaxon nodded his head as if understanding.

"Well, it's just interesting that when I mentioned it to Tobias, he froze too. Granted, you recovered much faster than he did." Jaxon took a step closer. "Though, if you don't know anything about it. Why was he trying to warn you in your little conversation over there?" Novak's eyes narrowed.

"Yes, I can speak your language. At least well enough to understand that he was trying to warn you and you weren't willing to listen to anything he had to say." Jaxon's smile faded.

"Did you come here to threaten me?" Novak asked, stepping forward.

"I came here to see what the hell you thought you were doing." Jaxon answered, taking another step forward so that they were inches from each other. "You really think you could just create an army, and no one would notice?" Novak took another drink of his wine instead of answering "Ethan killed three families. Those deaths are on you, Novak."

"You have no idea what's going on," Novak snarled.

"Enlighten me."

"We're not building an army. At least not yet," Novak said with a huff. He bent down grabbing a small remote and pointed it out towards the wall. The metal walls lifted revealing the windows behind them. Jaxon could clearly see the humble skyline of Angoria.

"Three from my pack were killed by vampires," Novak said looking back at Jaxon. "I went to the other packs. Come to find out, the other Alphas were having similar issues."

"Do you know which clan?"

"Does it matter?" Novak snapped. "They'd deny it anyway."

'Then bring it to the Order."

"I tried," Novak argued. "They wouldn't even open the fucking gates!" He turned towards the windows. "The Covenant is dying, Jaxon. We will not allow ourselves to be attacked and eradicated by the clans."

"You would go to war?"

"Wouldn't you?" Novak asked, turning around. "We may be beasts to you and the rest of the world. But *they* are my family." He pointed towards the door where the other members had left through. "And I will protect my family."

"You start a war, you'll violate the covenant. The Order will be forced to side with the Clans."

"Of course, as you did before."

"You chose the wrong side in that war, Novak. Not us."

"It was always interesting to me that your precious order keeps everyone else in check. Yet, it was you and your order that slaughtered an entire village of *my* kind!" He was shouting now, and the shouts became a growl. His brown eyes flashed yellow before he closed them taking a deep breath, counting to ten quietly. When he reopened them, they had returned to their normal golden-brown.

"If you start this war. You will lose," Jaxon warned. "I will go to Balthazar and speak to him about the Clans."

"You do what you want," Novak muttered. "But we *will* defend ourselves and if necessary, we will go to war with the Clans." He turned his back and Jaxon made no attempt to continue the conversation, Novak was at his limit.

"Jaxon," he called out without looking at him. "If you ever come here and threaten me again… I'll kill you," he said as he took another drink of his wine.

"I'll remember that," Jaxon said as he entered the elevator. As the elevator descended Jaxon could hear Novak shouting in a fit of rage. Jaxon couldn't help but smirk.

Jaxon wasted no leaving the building and returning back to his vehicle. The engine roared to life as he started it, and the lights inside lit up. He pressed the center button of three that appeared on the dashboard and a screen lifted up. He pressed the microphone icon on the screen, and it began recording.

"Log Entry Number: No idea," he said. "Novak *is* forming an army or at least a loose coalition between the other Alphas. I will be going to see Balthazar. I'll report more as I find out." He pressed the 'end' icon and then sent the transmission. It would go to a database within the High Temple in Eri'Dor and would eventually make it to the council. He didn't care so much about that as he did about going to Balthazar.

Balthazar was not someone he wanted to see either. He had a better relationship with the 'Vampire King' than he did with Novak, but he still wasn't someone Jaxon wanted to be around. The last thing anyone needed was a war between the wolf packs and the vampire clans. It had nearly destroyed the Order the last time it happened, and they still hadn't fully recovered over the last 15 years since the civil war. He entered the coordinates on the screen and hovered upwards until he floored the accelerator disappearing into the darkness of night.

CHAPTER 8
Hidden

Arilynn waited impatiently as Clara methodically moved about the empty apartment. She watched Clara walk from corner to corner, touching everything and pausing for a moment before continuing. She knew what Clara was doing was important and there was a process. She also *didn't* understand what she was doing.

She wasn't a seeker and no matter how much she researched their ability or how many conversations she had had with others about the power Seekers possessed, she never truly understood it. No one did, and as far as Arilynn was concerned, no one ever could. So, instead she watched and did her best to stay quiet.

Clara stopped in the center of the room, looking up at Arilynn and shaking her head. Arilynn let out a disappointed sigh, nodding her head. She turned to open the door, but right before she could, it swung open. Markus entered with two men following him.

The first to enter was an older teenage boy. His shaggy dark brown hair almost covering his blue-gray eyes. He was taller than Arilynn with a lean build. His dark gray surcoat was neatly pressed and cleaned. Arilynn noticed that he had shined his gray Eri'Dorian armor which was reinforced with cybernetic fiber. His black leather belt wrapped tightly around his waist where his Umoya was clipped. The clanking of his shined boots disrupted Clara's concentration, making her frown.

"Briar," Arilynn said warmly. Approaching him, she placed her hand on the side of his face. He had just turned seventeen years old, though with a clean-shaven face he could pass for a very tall ten-year-old. She looked at him closely. "I trust your wound is healed." The thought of him being hit with a stray blast in heated peace talks raced through her mind.

"Yes, Lady Lynn," he said, lowering his head and his face flushing red. "I'm sorry it took me so long to get here."

"You're fine, Briar," she said quietly. "I'm just glad you're okay." It was clear he was embarrassed to have been injured. She couldn't help but think his embarrassment was misplaced. It wasn't his failure that led to his injury, it was hers.

"Me too," Briar said with a smile. "I'm glad to be back with you." He bowed his head before walking to the other side of the room looking around.

Arilynn paused when she saw the second man standing in the doorway. He fit the frame of the door with his broad shoulders and height. His short black hair was slicked back, black beard neatly trimmed. His brown eyes stared directly at her with a smile crawling across his face.

He wore white sculpted armor with blue accents between the sections under his blue surcoat. His coat was designed with a cape that draped over his shoulders and nearly touched the ground when he stood. His golden

Umoya, was prominently displayed instead of to the side like most knights carried theirs.

"Ari…Lynn," he said with a chuckle.

"Hello, Benjamin," she replied curtly. "I didn't know you were going to be here." She added, glancing at Markus who had moved next to Clara.

"Well, I wanted to make sure young Briar here made it to you safely."

"He's old enough to travel alone," Arilynn replied.

"Well, to be honest. I wanted to see if you needed help."

"Why would we need help?" Arilynn asked, looking around the room. She refocused her stare at him waiting for an answer.

He laughed nervously and looked to Markus who let out a snort and turned away, wiping his hands dramatically as if cleaning them off. "I didn't mean to offend you." Benjamin said, trying to validate her.

"You didn't," Arilynn commented. "Besides, I think we're at a dead end. Clara can't find a strong connection to the Oracle."

"Is it true that Isobella is back?" Benjamin asked, taking a small step inside the room.

"So, it would seem." She crossed her arms looking back over her shoulder to scan the apartment.

There wasn't much that they could use to locate her. Just normal things someone would find in an apartment or home. Except, there were no photos or anything that made it seem like the apartment was actually their home. More like a place to stay that they could leave at a moment's notice.

"Lady Lynn," Briar said, breaking her train of thought.

"Yes?" she answered, looking over at him.

"The police are here." He was pointing towards the doorway where three police officers were standing.

"What is it?" Arilynn asked in exasperation as she moved around Benjamin. The police were more of a nuisance than actual help.

"The man you talked to, Tylex. He's dead," the center man said quietly.

"What?" Arilynn asked, bewildered. "How?"

"Stabbed through the heart." He replied.

Arilynn looked back to Markus who looked at her with raised eyebrows and shrugged his shoulders as if to show that he wasn't surprised. "Take me to him," Arilynn commanded.

She looked back to Briar. "Stay here with them. I'll be back as soon as I can." Briar nodded in acknowledgement.

"I'll go with you," Benjamin said, following her out of the room.

Arilynn stood at the doorway of the small shop. Nothing seemed to be different, except for Tylex sitting on his chair, mouth agape and eyes open, but lifeless. The right side of his face looked bruised, his skin dark blue in the rough shape of a handprint. She walked in with Benjamin and the leader of the officers trailing behind her. The other two officers lingered back at the doorway.

"Do you have anything?" she asked when she reached Tylex. She touched his face and was startled by how unnaturally cold it was. There was a small hole through his chest where she could see droplets of blood and what appeared to be water on the floor beneath him. Benjamin came over and looked closely at the wound.

"Anything on surveillance?" Benjamin asked.

"No," the officer replied.

"Of course, not," Arilynn said, shaking her head.

She walked around the room and still couldn't see anything out of place. Just as she went to leave, she saw a faint red light blinking in the far corner. It was so subtle she wasn't sure she saw it until it happened again.

"He has his own surveillance," Arilynn spoke out loud. "Where is the feed?" she asked the officer who shook his head with a shrug.

"We don't have the authority to go through all of his belongings yet," the officer replied.

Arilynn ignored his statement walking into a small room near the back. She shut the door to muffle the outcry of the police officer.

The room itself was in complete disarray with files and receipts thrown all over the ground. She found a small holographic projector, pressing the center button it illuminated. The projector showed the entire store in a 3-D display. It even showed the officers standing outside. She could see Benjamin attempting to calm the angry officer standing next to Tylex's body.

She hit the rewind icon and the recording began to skip backwards at 20-minute intervals. It didn't take her long to find what she was looking for.

On the projector she could see Tylex was working at his bench like she had left him. He was so focused that he didn't notice as two people entered the store.

The male darted to the wall and walked along the side while the woman walked straight towards Tylex, who at this time realized he was no longer alone.

"Oh, sorry," he said from his workbench. "I'm closed." He let out a slight chuckle. "Should have…." His voice trailed when he recognized the woman.

Arilynn squinted her eyes to see who it was. The quality was poor, and it only showed a grainy shot of the side of her face.

"You're supposed to be dead."

"Well, surprise!" the woman said with an exaggerated bow. "Where is she, Tylex?"

"I... I won't tell you." Tylex argued. He looked over and saw the man approaching him from the side. "The Lioness has already been here," Tylex said. "I would leave if I were you." The woman made no reply as she walked towards Tylex slowly. "I'm not afraid of you, Nya."

Arilynn's heart stopped when she heard the name. She leaned closer and pressed every button she could find, trying desperately to see the woman's face.

"Tell me where she is, Tylex."

"Who?" Tylex said sitting back into his chair.

"You know damn well who!" Nya shouted. "I know Isobella is alive. Where is she? Where's the Oracle?"

"Bella?" Tylex repeated sounding confused.

"Enough!" Nya shouted. From the side of the room her companion rushed forward.

He grabbed Tylex by the throat, slamming him and the chair against the workbench and holding him down while Tylex struggled to break away.

"Tell us where she is, or we'll kill you," the man growled.

"I'm not afraid to die," Tylex said, his voice muffled. "Not anymore."

"Stop," Nya said, placing her hand on the man's shoulder. He hesitated before letting Tylex go, stepping aside.

Nya placed her hand on the right side of Tylex's face. After a moment he began to scream and writhe in pain, thrashing in the chair. The man quickly grabbed Tylex and held him down. The screaming stopped as Nya stepped away; Arilynn could hear Tylex cough while he gasped for air.

"Where is she?" Nya asked again.

"Far from here and far from you," he answered defiantly in between coughs.

"What did you tell, Lynn?" Nya asked, grabbing Tylex by the bottom of his face.

"It doesn't matter." Tylex coughed.

"You would betray your friend for the Lioness?"

"At least the Lioness is doing what she believes is right," Tylex argued with a strained voice.

"You don't know why I'm here," Nya argued.

"You're here for yourself and nothing more than that," Tylex muttered. "I'll never help you."

"I must admit, Tylex," Nya said, leaning over him, her hand on his chest. "You've impressed me." Tylex let out a gasp but made no reply. When Nya stepped away in her hand was a thin spike made of ice. She glanced up at the camera, not noticing the blinking light or not caring. Arilynn paused it on her face.

"This can't be happening," she muttered.

"What?" Benjamin asked standing at the doorway. She had been so preoccupied with what was happening she hadn't realized he was standing there.

"Nya's alive," Arilynn replied in disbelief. "It seems as if everyone is coming back from the dead," she added, irritated. She continued watching Nya and her partner discuss what they were going to do. Tylex lay dead but was in a different position now.

"What about him?" the man asked.

"Leave him, he's not important," Nya replied. "We should go before we run into Arilynn."

"Who's that?"

"Someone we don't want to meet," Nya replied flatly as they walked out. When the two left, Tylex gasped shouting for someone to help him. He attempted to stand but fell back on the chair as the coughing continued. He lifted his clenched fist before it fell, and he went still laying in the position he was at now.

She rushed out of the room and knelt next to Tylex. She closed his eyes and knelt in front of him. She couldn't help but feel some sense of responsibility for his death. Even though he was a defector, he was a defenseless old man, standing up she began pacing back and forth. There was a connection somewhere, but she wasn't seeing it, not yet. Nya and Isobella were both alive, but it appeared that Nya had no idea until just today.

"Tryxus Ilain," Arilynn said aloud as Benjamin approached her. "That's where Isobella is going."

"We have no idea where he is," Benjamin answered. "Also, how do you know that?"

"That's their connection." Arilynn replied. "If Isobella needed to flee and get away, she would go to Tryxus."

"Or Lio." Benjamin countered.

"No, at least not right away." Arilynn said as she began pacing back and forth. "They were all together, but Nya didn't know Bella was alive. Lio hasn't been seen in this realm since his defeat at Valemìr. We know Tryxus is active, *somewhere*, we just don't know where…"

"You're reaching," Benjamin replied, looking back out towards the street.

She was trying to stop herself from becoming annoyed. "It makes sense. Bella would go somewhere safe, Tryxus is safe."

"I guess," Benjamin muttered unconvinced.

"We need to find him," she announced looking at Benjamin with a stern look letting him know she was no longer entertaining the conversation.

He shrugged his shoulders with a nod, taking a step back to give Arilynn enough room to leave. He took one last scan of the back room and then followed.

When Arilynn entered the apartment where Clara waited, sitting on the ground cross legged. She jumped to her feet when they entered.

"Where is Markus?"

"Right here," he said walking in behind her. "We found out some more information." he announced to others in the room. "She is no longer on foot. She is traveling in an old *Volant*."

"What do you know about Tryxus Ilain?"

"Tryxus?" Markus repeated. "Big, strong, has a powerful swing, lacks stamina."

"I don't mean his prowess," Arilynn corrected. "I mean do you know where we can find him?"

"No," Markus admitted. "Jaxon mentioned he was on his trail, but that was a long time ago." Markus added. "Why?" raising an eyebrow. Arilynn explained her reasoning and what she saw on the surveillance feed.

"I think she's reaching." Benjamin commented with a shrug.

"It's the only lead we have." Arilynn retorted with flare of her nostrils.

"So, we are no longer just looking for the Oracle. We are racing to her," Markus said dreadfully as he stroked his beard. "The only thing I have ever heard consistently about Tryxus is he has a compound."

"But we have no idea where that is," Benjamin stated, still frustrated.

"Jaxon never found it?" Arilynn asked.

"If he did, he never told me or the council," Markus replied.

"That's not surprising," Benjamin scoffed. Arilynn shot him a glare to which he shrugged his shoulders in response.

"Do we know which way she was travelling?"

"West," Markus replied. "Nothing more than that. She could have changed directions or even started flying."

"She wouldn't fly," Arilynn replied.

"How can you be so sure?" Benjamin inquired.

"She hates flying," Arilynn replied dismissively, deep in thought. "I need a map," she said, searching the room.

"You think she has it written down?" Briar asked.

"No," Arilynn replied. "She would have memorized it. She's a Ranger and would always have a plan of escape wherever we went. She wouldn't want to be too far from any kind of safe haven." Arilynn explained as she shuffled through all the drawers.

When she found a folded map, she moved to the desk pushing everything onto the floor. Her violet eyes scanned the map quickly until she found what she was looking for. She then used her finger to trace the roads that lead westward from Olessa.

"She didn't pick Olessa by chance," she said as she continued tracing the map with her fingers. She could feel everyone was watching her. She often worked fast and expected everyone around her to just follow along and understand. It was something she struggled with. She found herself irritated having to explain what she was doing every step of the way.

"You said she was heading west, correct?"

"Yes," Markus replied leaning forward to get a better look at the map. His brow furrowed with concentration. "From what little footage we were able to see, she took this main highway." He traced the thick black line across the map.

"What do we know about Tryxus' compound?" she asked looking up at the others who were now standing in a circle around the small desk.

"It's hidden," Briar replied.

"It's only known by word of mouth and only those running or seeking asylum can know about it," Benjamin stated.

"Anything else?" Arilynn asked, looking to Markus.

"When Jaxon was searching for it. He mentioned it being in the side of a mountain."

"Cliff," Clara interjected. "He actually said the side of a cliff somewhere. Not a mountain." Arilynn scanned the map mouthing the information to herself.

"Here," she said finally. "The Argorian Canyon."

"That stretches for miles, Lynn." Benjamin scoffed. "That would take us days if not weeks to scour the entire canyon."

"She wouldn't want to go too far. This is an escape plan, quick and easy to get to."

"Well, we have nothing else to go on," Markus replied. "May as well check it out." They began to funnel out of the room, leaving Arilynn behind. She folded the map back into a small square being careful to make no new creases in the paper.

She walked around the apartment one last time. She wasn't searching for anything—she knew there wasn't anything else to find. She instead was looking to see how someone she once loved and respected, who had become an enemy. Disappeared and lived without anyone knowing for fifteen years.

CHAPTER 9

Revelation

Gwynne laid on her stiff thin padded bed, staring up at the metallic gray ceiling. The dim fluorescent light kept flashing in a pattern. Blink, blink, steady for three seconds, blink, blink, blink, steady for five seconds; repeat.

She didn't move, just kept watching the flashing light. She wasn't tired but didn't want to wake her mother who she could hear sleeping soundly on the bed across the small room.

They were supposed to have left by now. 'One night only', was what Tryxus had told them. He either forgot or changed his mind. Either way this was their fourth day here. Gwynne didn't mind. There was food and the people for the most part were friendly.

She also liked Tyron. He was nice and helpful—a little too helpful at times. Despite being overbearing, she was glad he was around. He made her feel normal which was something she never thought she would feel again.

He showed her around the compound. Which, to her surprise, was deceptively massive. It seemed to stretch on for miles, though Tyron insisted that it didn't. Most of the compound was made up of rooms for people hiding and traveling to other safe houses. The compound was a part of an intricate network run by many different leaders. She wasn't entirely sure of who they were all running from or if they knew each other, she just knew they were all wandering or lost like her.

Instead of paying money, Tryxus required those who stayed to work off their debt within the compound until they left. During their time there, Gwynne assisted Tyron to ensure all the security systems were in working order. She wasn't sure what her mother did; from what she could tell, her mother didn't do anything. Tryxus often stated she owed him nothing.

During their security checks, Tyron would ask questions about where she was from, what she did, food she ate. He seemed so fascinated by the smallest details of Olessa. Even when she tried to explain that Olessa was nothing compared to the main cities like Dorrenna or Ardonia. He didn't seem to care, he wanted to know as much as she was willing to tell him.

Tyron knew nothing but the compound. He couldn't remember a time when he didn't live there. He was only allowed outside when it was deemed necessary, and during those times, he would linger outside a little longer than *necessary.*

She knew that he would be by the room soon to start their daily routine. She didn't want to help. Not today. She just wanted to lay on her uncomfortable bed and stare at the ceiling, maybe even fall asleep for once.

Her mother suddenly sat up, kicking her feet over the edge and placed her head in her hands with her elbows resting on her thighs. She sat there for a moment, not moving.

"Are you okay?" Gwynne asked, breaking the droning hum of the light above them.

"Yes," her mother replied dismissively, standing up as she began getting dressed for the day. They washed their clothes over and over despite having other clothes in their bags. Her mother insisted they would have to leave at a moment's notice.

There was a soft knock at the door. *Right on time,* Gwynne thought. Tyron was a creature of habit. He was on the other side softly speaking Gwynne's name and asking if she was ready.

"She'll be ready soon," her mother answered before Gwynne could reply.

Tyron said 'okay' and the silence continued for a moment before Gwynne spoke again. "How long are we staying here?"

"However long we can or need to," her mother snapped. "I know this isn't exactly the greatest place to stay. But this is our home for the time being," she said in a much sweeter tone.

"I don't even know what is going on," Gwynne whined sitting up. "You won't tell me anything." There was a long pause as her mother stared at the wall where normally a window would be if they weren't underground. She let out a sigh and then plopped back down on the bed.

"You're right," she said after a moment. "I haven't told you anything and I should have…" Her voice trailed off. "Really should have" she added looking down at her hands, fingers interlocking. She then looked back up.

"You know what an Eri'Dorian knight is," she stated flatly. "I have seen you read so many books on the history of the Order, and I have seen your schoolwork reference them."

"Yes," Gwynne replied, not sure what else to say.

"I was an Eri'Dorian Knight," she said looking down at her hands again. "Before you were born. I was a Ranger within the Order." She paused. "A spy," she clarified.

"My job was to hide in plain sight—to watch and listen. To give information back to the Order or to whoever needed information for whatever ridiculous reason they made up." Her voice raised at the end, but she let out a sharp exhale.

"You have read about the Civil War that happened before you were born, right?"

"Yes," Gwynne answered nervously. "The… uh Covenant between the Clans and Wolfpacks. The Kingdoms treaty was put into place and the traitors…" She stopped talking and looked at her mother who stared back at her with a pained expression. "They were sentenced to…" She couldn't finish.

"Yes." Her mother's voice broke. "Well, most of that is true," she said more forcefully.

"Are you a traitor?" Gwynne asked standing up with a wave of anger. "Am I!?"

"Gwynne, listen," Isobella said, standing up and placing her hands on Gwynne's shoulders to hold her gently. "You are not a traitor."

"But you are," Gwynne flared, pulling away. "You are, aren't you?"

"Depends on who you ask."

"Okay, what does the *law* say about you?"

"Gwynne," Isobella said, stepping forward.

"I thought maybe someone was after us. Like a bad person. Not the people who are supposed to be protecting us!"

"Gwynne!" She shouted so loudly that it caught both of them off guard. "You need to calm down," she added in a calmer tone raising her right hand up while her left hand rummaged through one of her bags. "Take a breath and try to calm down."

Gwynne stared at her mother. It was the first time she had ever seen her actually look afraid before.

Gwynne glanced down at her hands and they were enveloped in fire that was slowly ascending to her elbows. Her eyes widened. "Mom!" she cried out. She couldn't feel the fire on her skin, but she could feel the heat it was emanating.

"Take this," her mother commanded, holding out a metal object that looked like the hilt of a sword.

Gwynne obeyed the command without hesitation and held onto it tightly.

"Focus." Her voice was calm and soft. Gwynne kept looking up to make sure her mother was standing directly in front of her. The expression of fear had been replaced with determination.

"Focus," she repeated.

"On what?!" Gwynne screamed.

"On what's in your hand," she replied. "All of your energy, your anger, sadness, everything you have. Focus it on what is in your hand. Picture a weapon, a sword."

"What?" Gwynne shouted. "I don't… I don't…!" Gwynne pleaded.

"Just do it," Isobella replied sharply. "Stop thinking about it."

Gwynne closed her eyes and focused on the metal in her hand. It was cool to the touch with slightly raised etching on the sides that helped her grip it. It was long enough that she needed both hands to hold it.

She could feel warmth from her chest slowly move to her hands. There was a crackling sound of electricity and when she opened her eyes, the object now had a sword made of pure lightning extending from it, with strands of energy straying outward. She looked down to her hands. The fire was gone, glancing up she saw her mother's face, a mixed expression that resembled both fear and awe.

Taking a deep breath, the blade of lightning disappeared back into the metal object in her hand. "What is this?" Gwynne asked frantically, dropping it on the ground. "What's going on?!"

"That is an Umoya," Isobella replied, picking it up. "The weapon of an Eri'Dorian Knight. It takes spiritual magic to activate and use."

Gwynne shuffled backwards until she felt the bed hit the back of her legs and sat down.

"I think you're the Oracle," Isobella said, still looking at the Umoya.

"The what?" Gwynne asked.

"The Oracle. There's so much I haven't told you," she added in a whisper. "I don't know if I have time to now."

They sat in silence. Isobella stared at the Umoya while Gwynne stared at her own hands. She kept moving her fingers as if she were to move them in a specific way something would happen. She couldn't help but feel eerie after seeing her hands and arms on fire more than once now.

She opened her mouth to speak as a soft knock on the door interrupted her. Neither one of them moved or answered, another knock.

"Um…is Gwynne ready?" Tyron asked from outside. Isobella looked at Gwynne who shrugged her shoulders and shook her head. She didn't know if she was ever going to be ready for anything ever again.

"Give me a moment!" Gwynne shouted as she stood up and quickly got dressed for the day. She looked back to her mother who was now sitting staring at the Umoya. "I'm gonna go."

"Okay," Isobella replied absently. "Be careful," she added looking over at Gwynne.

Gwynne nodded and rushed through the door nearly pushing into Tyron.

"We're late," Tyron stated. He was in his normal get up—a dark blue tunic over black leggings that tucked into black leather boots. A black leather belt wrapped around his waist with a ring of keys on one side and a wooden baton holstered on the other.

"Well, let's hurry up then," Gwynne replied as she rushed. She didn't care what they did, she just needed to be away from her mother. Away from the room and away from the Umoya.

"You okay?" Tyron asked as he hurried to catch up.

"Yes," she lied trying to rush ahead. Tyron had longer legs, and had no problems keeping pace with her.

"It's not that big of a deal if we're behind," he assured her. "I just like to do things a certain way."

"Then we should do them that way," Gwynne replied.

"Stop," Tyron said, abruptly grabbing her arm to force her to stop with him.

She could feel her cheeks turning red and tears welling up in her eyes as she looked at him. She pulled away, exhaling loudly as she tried to gather her composure. "Can we just get started, please?" she asked, turning her back to him.

He stared at her for a moment and then moved ahead, taking the lead.

The security checks were simple. There were multiple panels that were used to check the integrity of the wall or door. They regulated the temperature to ensure it didn't get too hot or too cold inside depending on the weather outside.

Each panel took roughly thirty to four seconds, according to Tyron who timed everything he did. He was a proponent of efficiency. He hated wasting time, and more than that, he hated being behind on his schedule.

Yesterday, Gwynne had been late and threw off his entire schedule. She didn't hear the end of it until it was time for her to go to bed. Even then, he commented on making sure she was ready in time.

Clearly, she wasn't ready, and they were even more behind today than yesterday. Today, Tyron made no comment. He just worked quicker than normal.

They walked mostly in silence. Except for when Tyron spoke out loud to himself as he checked panels. Gwynne wasn't entirely sure how any of them worked and didn't care to figure it out. She figured they would be gone too soon for it to matter.

When they reached the last door. He stopped and looked at her expectantly. She stared back at him with her arms crossed over her chest. "So, am I going to do everything today?" he asked.

"I don't know how to do… whatever it is, you're doing," she replied with a groan.

"Well, maybe you could learn."

"Why?"

"Because, you need to learn how to take care of things here while you stay."

"I don't think I'm staying for very long," she replied looking back down the hallway they came from. A group of people were walking down at the end, disappearing around the corner.

"Do you know who these people are?" she asked looking back to Tyron who had given up on trying to get her to work and was already checking the panel.

"Not all of them, why?" he asked, preoccupied.

"No, I mean do you know why they're all here?"

He stopped and looked over his shoulder. "What do you mean?"

"They're all criminals," she snapped. "Did you know that?"

"I wouldn't say they're criminals," he replied, turning back to the panel. He lifted his black tablet, pressing a button. His brows furrowed as the screen flashed blue. "Hmm, the temperature gauge is off," he noted. "Why do you care about these people?"

"My mom is a traitor," Gwynne replied bitterly. "Making me one too."

"What are you talking about?" Tyron said with a guffaw. "Your mom is a legend!" he said, shaking his head.

"What?"

"Yeah!" he said confidently. "Your mom is a badass. She led the revolt against the Eri'Dorian Order, saved my dad's life too."

She stared at Tyron confused as to how he could be so happy about what she had just said. "She's a traitor," she repeated.

"Depends on who you ask."

"The police, the Order, *people*?"

"Well, what about the people who supported her?"

"Like who?"

"The rest of the Eri'Dorian Knights who fought beside and followed her into battle," he argued. He powered the tablet down, setting it on the ground. "What do you know about the rebellion?"

"What is there to know?" she asked. "A group of traitors attacked the Valemìr Temple and attempted to take over. They lost and there was a war in which they also lost. Millions of people died. Seems pretty cut and dry."

"Your mom and my dad were two of the leaders in that rebellion. They didn't do it just to be in control. They did it because it was the right thing to do." As Tyron argued his point, his voice became stern. "My father built this place because when they lost. They were being hunted down and slaughtered like animals. The wolves and vampires got to go home and be safe. But everyone else who didn't fall under protection granted by the covenant? Well, they were left to fend for themselves. My father built this place so they could rest easy. Your mother isn't a traitor, she's a hero."

Gwynne didn't reply; she just looked down at her feet. She felt embarrassed and suddenly guilty. She had offended the only friend she had by calling his father a traitor. She looked back up and he was working on the panel again.

"I'm sorry," she squeaked. "I didn't mean to call your dad a traitor."

"I know," he replied without looking away from the panel. "It's not your fault you don't know anything about what happened."

"How do you?"

"My father told me everything. He wanted me to know everything that he did. The good and the bad, so that I wouldn't make the same mistakes he did."

Tyron let out a frustrated grunt hitting the wall next to the panel. "This panel isn't working. I'll have to have Dominic come down here and look at it," he announced. "You ready?" He looked back to Gwynne who was staring down at her feet.

"Sorry if I got a little defensive. It's just that I know my dad did the right thing and I can't help but get angry when people say he's a traitor. He's a good man and he protects everyone here."

Gwynne didn't know what to say, so she said nothing as she wrapped her arms around herself, feeling self-conscious.

"I want to show you something," Tyron said as he walked past her. He pulled at her arm to come along.

Tyron led them through a short hall that led them to a large room. It was mostly empty, except for racks of weapons at the front. There was one single light that illuminated the entire room.

"This is where my father taught me everything. From fighting to history and writing," Tyron said walking to the center. "You know how to fight?"

"That is one thing we have in common. My mom made me train every morning," Gwynne muttered walking around the room.

"They think you're the Oracle." Tyron said. The comment caught Gwynne off guard, and he noticed. "I heard our parents talking about it," he added with a shrug

"I don't even know what the Oracle is."

"From what my dad told me. The Oracle is supposed to be the most powerful being to ever live and they lead the world."

"Well, I don't feel that powerful," Gwynne groaned. "I feel trapped and stupid. I have no idea what's going on. My mom was a spy and I'm in an underground bunker with a training room and I have fire coming out of my hands." She paused. "Wait, can you use magic too?"

"No, not everyone can. Even *if* their parents can," he lamented. "Doesn't matter though, he taught me how to defend myself even without magic," he said smiling.

"I don't know what I'm doing," Gwynne whined as she sat down on the ground and then laid down looking up at the light. Tyron laid down beside her.

"You don't have to do anything. Not yet at least."

"I feel like I do," she replied looking over at him.

"Someday, you'll have to do *something*. But, today since my schedule is completely ruined anyway, we're not going to do anything."

Gwynne let out a chuckle. It felt foreign to laugh. This was the first time she felt anything outside of stress since leaving the city. She knew it wouldn't last, but she wanted to enjoy it.

~~~~

"What did she say?" Tryxus asked sitting across from Isobella at a wooden table.

A woman sat to Tryxus' right. She had long black braids with light brown highlighted ends. She had lighter skin than Tryxus and she was much smaller than he was. She had a slender build and her bright green dress wrapped around her tightly.

"Nothing really. She panicked and started to catch herself on fire. I taught her to use an Umoya that I stole from the Sentinel that attacked us," Isobella replied before putting her face into her hands "Tryxus, I've messed everything up."
~~~~

"You can't blame yourself," the woman said.

"I can, Moira," Isobella replied. "I should have told her years ago."

"You didn't know what she was," Tryxus countered. "You couldn't have."

"You still told Tyron."

"That's different," Moira replied. "We aren't living out there." She reached over the table, placing a comforting hand on Isobella's

"Did you hear anything about an unbinding potion?" Isobella asked looking up at Tryxus pulling away from Moira.

"No," He replied offhandedly.

"Where did you get the potion that bound you in the first place?" Moira asked.

Isobella glanced at Tryxus then at the table then finally looked up at Moira. "Jaxon," she replied.

"Jaxon?" Tryxus growled. "I can't believe you trusted that son of a bitch."

"He saved my life, Tryxus," Isobella argued.

"That man is a murderer!" Tryxus yelled. "I won't allow him to come here. He'll either kill everyone or bring the Order so they can."

"I'm not going to bring him here," Isobella scoffed. "Besides, I don't even know where he is," she added waving her hand. She was growing tired of the conversation.

"When's the last time you saw him?" Moira asked.

"The day before Gwynne was born."

"Is he her father?" Tryxus asked accusingly.

"Does it matter?" Isobella snapped back defensively. "I didn't come here for Jaxon or to get permission to find him. I came here because I didn't know what to do. If she wasn't…" Her voice trailed off. "I can't just go and hide," she grumbled. "Even if I did. The Seeker would eventually find her and even then, she needs to ascend or she'll…" She stopped herself from speaking the word.

"Have you reached out to Lionicles?" Tryxus asked.

"Are you kidding?" Isobella answered with a laugh. "That's the *last* person I need to deal with right now."

"I don't think bringing that man back into our lives is a good idea," Moira said, agreeing with Isobella's outburst. "He has a habit of making things worse."

"He would know where to take her," Tryxus argued. "You followed him before, why not now?"

"This isn't a war, Tryxus!" Isobella exclaimed. "This is my daughter we're talking about."

"You're the one who said we were still in one, not me," Tryxus snapped back.

"You don't even know where he is," Moira reminded him.

"I don't. But she might," Tryxus replied. looking at Isobella who let out a sigh of contempt shaking her head.

"I haven't seen him since the day we sacked the temple. I only know the rumors that he ran off to Vassah in Dereli."

"What's your plan then?" Moira asked, turning the subject away from Lio.

"I have to find Jaxon," Isobella said, shaking her head as if she couldn't believe the words coming out of her own mouth.

"What?!" Tryxus shouted. "Have you not heard a word I said? He'll kill you!"

"No. But, he's the only one I know who would actually hear me out before killing me."

"I have to agree with my husband, dear," Moira said, rubbing on his arm. "Going after Jaxon is not a good idea."

"At least someone listens to me," Tryxus grumbled, crossing his arms as he looked away.

"I don't know what else to do, you guys," Isobella admitted. "I can't just walk up to a temple and drop her off."

"Go to Eri'Dor," Tryxus said.

"Did you not hear what I just said?"

"Who's kidding now?" Moira asked, leaning back to look at him.

"We tell them who we have; they'll take her." Tryxus explained. "And…" He paused for a moment. "Maybe in exchange they'll pardon us."

"You want to use my daughter as a bargaining chip?" Isobella asked, insulted. Tryxus looked away again, letting out a heavy sigh. "How would we even get there?"

"You're not the only one who has an old vehicle," Tryxus answered.

"I don't think this is a good idea." Moira commented. "They can just kill you and take the girl anyway."

"Whatever we do. We need to hurry," Isobella urged. "We have been here too long as it is."

"Tryxus," Moira said looking up at him. "You need to speak to Vera." The mention of the woman's name made him shift uncomfortably.

"I don't think that's a good idea," he answered, shaking his head.

"I'm not saying I like it," Moira began, "But it beats going to Dereli or Eri'Dor. At least try her first."

"Who is Vera?" Isobella asked, looking at the two of them.

Their eyes met, before Tryxus answered. "An old…friend."

"You should at least try," Moira said, rubbing his hand before standing up to leave.

"Can she help with Gwynne?"

"I doubt it," Moira commented. Her demeanor changed to agitated. "But, she might be able to get your power back."

"Maybe," he admitted. "She works with potions, but that doesn't mean she would have what we're looking for."

"I don't care," Isobella replied. "If there's a chance, I'll take it. At least then I can protect her better." Tryxus shook his head but relented by shrugging his shoulders.

"Isobella, we will figure this out, don't worry," Moira said as she walked away, leaving them.

"I don't think this is a good idea," Tryxus muttered when Moira was far enough away not to hear.

"Yea, well, it beats going to find Jaxon or going to the High Temple." Tryxus shrugged his shoulders standing up.

"Well, we should head out as soon as we can."

It didn't take long for them to get ready. She'd decided it was better not to tell Gwynne she was leaving. She couldn't tell if that decision was to protect Gwynne or if she was doing it because she didn't want to face her. Either way, it seemed unnecessary to bring more stress to the poor girl.

Isobella waited at her *Volant,* and when Tryxus arrived, he rushed to get inside the vehicle. He was almost too big to fit, but managed to squeeze himself in. He was fully dressed, instead of being shirtless or a tank-top. He wore a brown studded suede jerkin under a long black leather jacket that barely zipped over his stomach.

"Where am I going?" Isobella asked looking over at him.

"Flatwood, small village not too far from here," he answered. "I'll tell you how to get there."

"How do I get out of here?"

"Same way you came in."

"I hate flying," Isobella muttered as she revved up the engine.

Despite the beginning of the short journey to Flatwood where she nearly crashed into the ground. It was rather uneventful,

Tryxus only spoke to give to directions and he seemed to be far away.

"I think it's amazing what you've done with the compound," she said, trying to break the awkward silence.

"It's taken a lot of work to get where we are now, but it's working," he said looking out the window.

"I should have been around more," Isobella said quietly. "I'm sorry I haven't been…"

"You have your own life to live, Bella. I don't blame you."

"Yeah, well, I don't show up for years and then come around when I have a problem doesn't exactly make me Friend of the Year."

"You've never been friend of the year," he said with a low chuckle. "But, you're here now, and that's what matters."

"Have you, uh, talked to any of the others?"

The question prompted Tryxus to look over at her. He regarded her for a moment before shaking his head. "Last I heard about Lio was what you said earlier. Nya died at the sacking of the Temple, and Daxus, I heard he's up north holding out for a comeback." Tryxus laughed again shaking his head. "We really thought we had a chance, huh?" he added with a snort.

"I forgot about Daxus."

"How?" Tryxus asked, confused. "The man is insufferable."

"That's probably why I forgot about him," she said with a shrug. "I never knew why Lio brought him in with us."

"He was an eager killer," Tryxus stated flatly.

"You see any Knights?"

"Nah, they don't come out here too often, and the few I've seen weren't any threat."

"That's good," Isobella replied awkwardly. She didn't know what to say or how to keep the conversation going.

"Here," he said pointing to the turn.

When they arrived, Isobella was surprised by how small the village was. There weren't any roads and barely any businesses. Mostly small homes with broken down, man-powered machines. It was clearly an agricultural town. Horses and cattle could be seen grazing lazily in the sun.

There were no clouds today, just bright skies with a cool breeze that carried the smell of manure into the village. Tryxus climbed out of the vehicle and took the lead, stomping ahead.

The conversation had officially died. Tryxus only spoke when someone waved hello. He would return their greeting with a smile and a polite 'hello', but would immediately revert to his scowl and continue walking.

Tryxus stopped short of a small cabin made of old moss-covered wood. It was well lit with puffs of smoke coming out of a stone chimney. He glanced back and took a deep breath before knocking on the door, slamming his fist so hard that the door shook.

"What the hell?!" a woman's voice shouted from inside. She swung the door open and the heat from inside that forced its way out of the door hit them like a wave and her expression of anger turned to annoyance.

"What the hell are you doing here?" she asked before looking at Isobella.

She was a petite woman with pale skin that was covered in splotches of red, dripping with sweat. . Her short brown hair stuck outwardly in random directions. She wore a faded maroon shirt that was far too large for her, stretching down to her knees. Isobella wasn't quite sure if she had pants on and didn't care to find out.

"I need your help," he said quietly.

"You need to get the hell off my property!" she scolded him with a glare. She turned her attention to Isobella and shook her head. "Honey, trust me, get away from this man. All he is, is trouble!"

"I'm the one who needs your help," Isobella blurted out.

Tryxus let out an aggravated snort throwing his hands up. He shook his head as he took a step away from the door.

"What the hell do you want?" she asked Tryxus, ignoring Isobella.

"He said you worked in potions," Isobella answered.

"Does Moira know you're here?" Vera asked, still ignoring Isobella.

"Yes, woman."

"Boy, you better watch your mouth with me!" Vera shouted, raising her hand as if she were going to slap him. "You need to get away from here and him," she said to Isobella before turning to walk back inside.

"Please!" Isobella yelped. "I need your help. I don't care about what happened between you two. I don't care if you like each other. I just need your help."

"What?" she asked impatiently. "I can't make him more loyal," she said glaring at Tryxus.

"What?" Isobella asked, confused.

"Oh, he didn't tell you?" Vera said with a scoff. "Of course, he didn't! He didn't tell me about his wife either!"

Isobella looked over at Tryxus who was looking down at the ground. He suddenly looked like a small child who was in trouble.

"Look, I don't care about any of that."

"What *do* you care about?"

"My daughter." The answer made Vera's expression change from annoyance to a brief glimpse of sadness.

"I can't bring people back," she said flatly. "No potion can."

"No, I- she's fine," Isobella replied walking towards Vera. "At least for now. I just… need your help to protect her."

"What can *I* do?" Vera asked confused.

"She needs an unbinding potion," Tryxus replied, interjecting.

"Was I talking to you, boy?" Vera said, suddenly enraged again. "No, so shut up and stay over there!" She turned back to Isobella and stared at her for a moment.

"What's your name, girl?" she asked.

"Isobella."

"Hartley?" she asked.

The question caught both of them off guard. "How did you know that?"

Vera looked around and motioned for them to come inside. Isobella hesitated but followed her with Tryxus trailing behind.

"Sit over there and be quiet," she said with a snap of her fingers, pointing at a small chair. Tryxus let out a frustrated grunt, but sat on the small chair that groaned under his weight.

Inside was uncomfortably warm with a blazing fire in the fireplace. Above the fireplace were stacks of vials filled with random assortments of dirt and liquids. Isobella scanned the area looking for something to stand out. The walls had all been repurposed into bookshelves where books and pieces of paper were stuffed to fit. Nothing was in order and the floor was covered in soot and ash.

"I can't help you," she said flatly.

"What, why?"

"I swore I wouldn't."

"Swore? To who?" Tryxus asked.

"What did I say?!" she screamed, prompting Tryxus to let out another heavy sigh before lowering his gaze to the ground. She then looked back to Isobella and smiled. "Jaxon Harwell."

Isobella stared at her for a moment, the only sound in the room was the crackling of the fire burning. She was already sweating from being inside, and now she found it harder to breathe.

"I…I don't understand," Isobella stammered. "How?"

"Well," she started, "he came here, broke down my door." She glared at Tryxus. "God, I thought he was going to kill me. Everyone knows Jaxon Harwell around here. Especially those of us involved in illegal potions. He stood in the doorway and said that I had two choices. He would destroy everything here and take me to Dorrenna to be tried and most likely executed for illegal potion use *or*, I could help him." She chuckled. "Doesn't take a genius to know which one I chose."

"That doesn't—" Tryxus started.

"Shut up," Isobella and Vera said in unison.

"Boy, never shuts the hell up," Vera said before sitting down on an old wooden rocking chair. She pointed to the chair next to her for Isobella to sit in.

"He said he needed a binding potion. Told me that I needed to make him one and that he would leave me alone."

"How long ago was this?"

"Oh, fifteen or so years ago," she answered. "I honestly thought he was coming after Tryxus. I wasn't going to tell him anything because I'm *LOYAL*!" she shouted, glaring at Tryxus. "Now, I wish I could have told him all about you. But he already knew where you were."

"Wait what?" Tryxus shouted angrily, standing up.

"Yes, he knows about your little compound," Vera said with a delightful laugh. "I guess that can make up for what you did to me."

"You never told me?!" he asked angrily.

"You never told me you were married!" she retorted.

"Stop it!" Isobella shouted. "I need that potion. Why can't you help me?"

"He told me there may come a day that you'll come find me, and that I am to tell you no. That if he found out otherwise, he would come down on me. I'm sorry to say dear, he's scarier than you are."

"I don't understand, how would he know I'd come here?" Isobella said, taking a deep breath.

"I don't know," Vera replied. "I'm assuming he knew you knew this bastard," she said pointing at Tryxus. "Either way, he comes by time to time. Doesn't say much, rarely asks for anything, but I always tell him that I haven't seen you."

"This is different. I think he would understand why I'm wanting my power back."

"I'm sorry. But I'm not breaking my promise to him. Not for any real reason other than self-preservation."

"So, I wasted my time coming here?" Isobella asked angrily.

"I'm afraid so," Vera replied with a shrug.

"You don't understand," Isobella said pleadingly.

"I understand just fine, honey. I'm not going to help you."

"You said you're not helping me for no other reason except self-preservation. What if I kill you if you don't tell me?"

"Bella!" Tryxus shouted standing up, he placed himself between her and Vera.

"Because I can see it in your eyes. You don't have it in you," Vera replied with a smug expression.

"You know nothing about me." Isobella countered. "If you did, you'd realize that for my daughter I'd do anything."

"That's enough," Tryxus said, placing his hand on her shoulder. She swatted it away and went to move around him. "Bella." He spoke sternly as he moved to intercept her.

"Get out of the way, Tryxus."

"Girl, just leave," Vera said, waving her hand. "I don't have time for this. I'm not going to help you, and you're not going to kill me."

"Let's just go," Tryxus said in a softer tone as he tried to usher her out the door.

Isobella let out a huff before nodding her head. She turned heading towards the door, with Tryxus' hand placed firmly on her shoulder.

As they approached the door, she stepped to the side. He moved to block her, only this time she twisted to the other side making him stumble as he tried to correct himself. She swung backwards, her elbow connecting with his chin. He let out a grunt as he staggered backwards.

Isobella knew that her window of opportunity was closing. Tryxus was clearly out of shape, but he was still strong and could easily overpower her with physical strength alone. Adding his magic, made him too formidable to take any chances.

As he reared back from the blow to his chin, she dropped down, pivoting off her knee so that she was now behind him. She slammed her forearm to the inside of his right knee, causing it to buckle. As she rose to her feet, she drew one of her daggers. A single blow to the back of his head would have been enough for a normal person. Tryxus shrugged it off, shouting in frustration as he went to stand up. She kicked the back of his knee again, and swung down.

Tryxus reached back, catching her wrist. He stood up lifting her with him. He yanked her forward so that she was in front of him. She kicked the side of his knee trying to knock him back down. She could see that Vera was on her feet now rushing to one of the bookshelves.

"Bella, stop!" Tryxus shouted.

"I can't!" she retorted, striking him in the throat, knocking him back. With another strike to his knee, he dropped to one knee, making it so she could strike him with the hilt of her dagger. The blow to his head drew blood as he staggered backwards.

He roared out in anger, lunging towards her. His massive hand wrapping around her throat, she reacted by cutting the inside of his forearm, forcing him to let go. As she moved to kick Tryxus back, she saw that Vera was grabbing a vial of vibrant orange liquid. Isobella threw her dagger, the blade piercing Vera's shoulder.

Vera let out a scream of pain dropping the vial. The glass shattered and the orange liquid ignited into a burst of fire. Isobella refocused on Tryxus who created a gust of wind that knocked Isobella into one of the shelves.

He stood up, shaking his leg as he stormed towards her. Isobella ducked under his wide swing, kicking the side of his knee again. She pivoted around him, grabbing the small wooden table, and smashed it across his back.

He was finally on the ground. Isobella didn't waste any time as she jumped on his back and stomped the back of his head. He let out a soft groan, but didn't move.

"Are you crazy!?" Vera shouted as she cowered away, holding the dagger in place as she tried to stop the bleeding.

"Tell me what I need to know, now!" Isobella shouted as she grabbed the dagger, ripping it out of her shoulder. Vera cried out as she stumbled using the wall to hold herself up. "I told you, I'll do whatever I have to, to protect my daughter." Isobella shoved her forearm into Vera's collar bone, and with her other hand held the dagger blade to her throat. "Give me what I need, and this all ends."

"Isn't he your friend?!" Vera cried.

"Yes, and I'll kill him if I need to." Isobella couldn't believe she heard herself speak the words, what made it worse was that she knew it was true. Tryxus was her friend, and that wouldn't stop her from killing him or anyone else. Gwynne was all that mattered to her.

"I don't have it!" Vera whimpered.

"Don't lie to me!"

"I'm not!" she shouted. "I can only give you the ingredients." Vera pointed to a shelf where a small box sat on the third shelf. "It's in there, it'll tell you everything you need to know."

"Why can't you make it?"

"It's not exactly easy to make a binding potion, let alone an *unbinding* potion!" Vera answered angrily. "Take it, and go!"

Isobella released her hold of Vera, rushing to grab the box. She could hear Tryxus was beginning to stir as she rummaged through the box. It was full of tattered pieces of paper, with random lists on each one.

"Which one is it?"

"Figure it out!" Vera shouted with a wave of her hand.

Isobella stopped and looked over at Vera whose eyes grew wide. "I'm sorry," she said, lowering her head.

"That one!" she said pointing to the one on the ground.

"If you're lying."

"You'll kill me," Vera said nodding her head. "I'm starting to think that's the best option."

"I'm sorry," Isobella said quietly. "I don't want to hurt anyone."

"Too late," Vera snapped. "Now get out of here!" she shouted. "You have what you want." When Isobella didn't move Vera shouted. "What are you doing?"

"Debating on if I should just kill you," she answered curtly. "You said it yourself, you would never lie to Jaxon. If I let you live, you'll tell him I was here."

"I won't!" Vera said, raising her right hand. "He hasn't been here in years, I doubt he'll come looking for you." Vera added with an unconvincing smile. "Besides, I'm sure you can handle him once you unlock your abilities."

"Don't patronize me!" Isobella snapped. She walked over to Tryxus as he began to move and kicked the side of his head knocking him back down. "If this is a lie, I *will* come back and kill you. When he wakes, tell him I'm sorry."

"Oh, I'm sure he'll understand," Vera said sarcastically, before lowering her head again cursing to herself.

"I'm not a bad person," Isobella said quietly.

"Who are you trying to convince?" Vera asked, sitting back down. "Just go."

Isobella took one last peek at the piece of paper before wedging it into her belt. She took another look at Vera and then Tryxus before rushing outside to her vehicle. She wasted no time as she started it, and took off towards the compound. She would have to work as fast as she could to get Gwynne out and leave before Tryxus would arrive. She had no desire to face him again, even if she'd won this fight with relative ease, it wouldn't be so easy a second time.

CHAPTER 10

Assault

Nya sat on her hover-bike, perched at the edge of a cliff. Looking through electronic binoculars that allowed her to see depth and distance, she scanned across the canyon. She placed them down in front of her on the handlebars. She looked over at Konan who was leaning forward on his handlebars staring down at his gauges.

"How long?" Nya asked, referring to the team of men that Konan had called when they first arrived. Nya knew the bunker well enough to get inside, and she also knew that under normal circumstances, Tryxus would more than likely let her in with open arms.

These weren't normal circumstances. Most people thought she was dead, which was something that she both enjoyed and hated. She hated it because she never saw her old friends. She was a ghost, lost in a very large world. On the other hand, no one would ever come looking for someone who was dead.

"Not much longer," Konan replied. "I don't know why we just don't go in there."

"We can't just walk in," Nya replied. "We don't even know if the code you got from that family will actually work." Nya commented. "Tryxus isn't a normal fighter, Konan. He's strong, physically and magically."

"I'm not worried about it," Konan replied dismissively. "I'm just tired of sitting here waiting in this damn heat."

"If the girl is actually the daughter of Isobella Hartley, this isn't going to be easy. She will be trained and will know how to run," Nya explained.

"I'm not worried about it," Konan repeated.

"Just stay here," Nya snapped, annoyed and defeated. "I'm going to go through the side entrance. It's away from the main entrance and most people don't go there."

"How do you know all of this?"

"I helped him build it," Nya replied. "Don't move until everyone is here and I have given you the signal." Konan rolled his eyes, as he nodded his head.

She glared at him for a moment before he nodded his head again raising his hands in mocked surrender. She pulled up a scarf that covered the bottom half of her face and pulled over a hood with goggles that covered the upper half. She then ignited the engine to her hover-bike and drove over the edge.

She flew down the side of the canyon and then revved the engine up so that she slingshot back up the other side being sure to avoid any security systems—at least the ones she had helped place.

From the looks of the area, nothing had been updated. Tryxus was lazy when it came to tedious work. She always warned him to keep up with it, and that it would come back to haunt him someday. Today was that day.

She flew up to a ledge shutting off the hover-bike. She pressed the back of her hand against what appeared to be stone, but the heat from the sun hitting the hidden metal nearly burned her.

She let out a frustrated sigh, holding her palm out in front of the metal. She focused on the metal itself and let out another frustrated grunt. The metal wasn't pure, and she would have to take her time trying to warp the metal by force—time she didn't have.

She opened her palm and ice began to form, spreading outward. She placed her hand back on the hidden door, and the ice continued to slowly spread.

~~~~

Tyron and Gwynne sat at their normal spot in the mess hall. Gwynne was in a better mood since they abandoned the schedule. They were eating, twenty-five minutes late according to Tyron. If it bothered him, he never said anything. He seemed to be okay with being out of sync, at least for the day.

The food was no different than most days. Bread, vegetables and water. She had somewhat gotten used to it. They told jokes and watched people around them in the mess hall, laughing at their clothes or mannerisms.

Tyron's tablet illuminated and began beeping loudly and repeatedly. He put down his cup of filtered water looking at the screen.
~~~~

He tilted his head in confusion and then shook his head.

"What is it?" Gwynne asked with her mouth half full of bread.

"That temperature gage on the far north door is going crazy," he said with a stifled laugh. "Says it's below freezing outside. Not this time of year."

"Didn't you send Dominic to go look at it?" Gwynne asked before taking a gulp of water.

"Yea, but he is probably taking his sweet time to get down there," Tyron replied with a huff. He began to tap his fingers rapidly on the table.

"Want to go back and check it out?" Gwynne asked, already knowing the answer. "We haven't really done anything today, and I can imagine you're dying to do *something*."

"No," he said defiantly. "It's someone else's job today."

"Tyron..." Gwynne replied skeptically. "Let's go. I know you want to."

Tyron exhaled with a loud chuckle nodding his head. "Okay," he said standing up hurriedly.

~~~~

Isobella let out a sigh as she entered the compound. Rushing to find Gwynne and leave as soon as they could. She first stopped at their room, and when she didn't find her, she quickly packed their bags. She closed the door behind her rushing to the mess hall.

She rounded the corner so fast that she nearly ran into Moira, who let out a squeal and a laugh patting Isobella on the shoulder. Isobella feigned a smile in return.

"I didn't know you two were back," she said looking around. "Where's Tryxus?"

"Uh…he's checking something on the vehicle. He'll be here soon," Isobella lied, the rush of guilt finally washing over her. "Uh, have you seen Gwynne?"

"Oh, she's been with Tyron all day," Moira said with a smile. "You know, those two have been inseparable the last few days."
~~~~

"Yeah," Isobella replied. "I need to talk to her about something."

"Oh, they were just in the mess hall." Moira barely finished her sentence before Isobella was already leaving.

~~~~

Nya knelt still, pressing her hand against the door. She watched the ice continue spreading. She ignored the sound of the metal groaning as the ice began to make the door fragile. Her communicator beeped, and she opened it to speak.

"You better hurry," Konan said over the frequency. "I think your friend Hartley arrived and I think your other friend Tryxus is approaching."

"Okay," Nya said, focusing her power.

"My men are here. We're going to make our assault."

"No, wait for me to get in!" Nya replied. "I'm almost ready."

~~~~

Gwynne and Tyron approached the malfunctioning door. Tyron was so busy looking at his tablet that he didn't notice that Gwynne had stopped.

"Tyron," she said in a hushed tone. He glanced back and then forward where the door was. He cocked his head trying to understand what he was looking at.

There was water pooling at the bottom while the door itself seemed to be covered in ice. He inched forward with his hand outstretched. He suddenly became aware that he was holding his breath and let out an audible sigh. When he touched the ice he jolted, pulling his arm back. It was so cold that it burned his hand.

"Tyron!" Gwynne ran over to him, pulling him away from the door. She grabbed his hand looking it over. His palm was reddened with his fingertips pruned.

"We should get your dad," she stated, looking up at him.

Before they could turn around, the metal in the door began to groan as it bent and twisted before it was thrown forward. Tyron shoved Gwynne to one side while he fell to the other side.

He sat up and saw a woman dressed in all black standing at the door. Her face was covered, and she had two daggers made of ice in her hands as she moved forward.

Tyron scrambled to his feet, grabbing the only weapon he had on him—his wooden baton—to charge the woman. She sidestepped the attack, throwing him to the ground. Tyron rolled through the throw, landing on his feet. Shouting, he charged her again.

Again, he was tossed to the side. This time she cut him with her blades, leaving a gash on his lower right abdomen. He winced at the pain as he tried to stand up.

Gwynne willed herself to stand as she saw Tyron on the ground with a woman standing over him.

"No!" she shouted. "Please don't!" Gwynne begged. She dropped to her knees raising her hands. The woman turned her back to Tyron and slowly approached Gwynne. "Please don't hurt us," Gwynne pleaded.

The woman didn't reply, but she stopped. The blade of her ice daggers disappeared, she holstered the hilts on her hips. She reached out with her hand open.

Before the woman could reach Gwynne, Tyron kicked the back of the woman's left knee causing her to buckle. She landed on one knee and swung back. Tyron grabbed her arm and slammed her into the ground. He stumbled backwards and hit one of the alarm systems on the panel near the door.

A loud siren began to sound, it was a piercing noise that echoed throughout the entire compound. It kept ringing so loudly that Gwynne covered her ears with her hands.

The woman seemed to be unaffected by the siren and kicked Tyron in his wound knocking him back. She raised her hand as the daggers of ice reformed.

Gwynne panicked and screamed. Throwing her hands forward, she felt a surge of energy release from her body. The woman turned just in time to raise her hands and a wall of ice appeared in front of her. The impact of the energy pushed the woman backwards, knocking her through the door.

Gwynne rushed to Tyron pulling him off the ground. She dragged him as she ran back towards the main compartment. Gwynne glanced back to see that the woman was already moving.

~~~~

"Attack the main entrance now." Nya winced as she struggled to stand up.

"What?" Konan said through her earpiece.

"I found the girl. Attack the damn entrance!" she shouted as she forced herself to stand up.

She hadn't taken a hit like that in all her life. The sheer power of the attack was enough to take her out of the fight. But she knew she couldn't stop.

She stumbled down the hall; her daggers were ready. She was not going to let her guard down again. That was a mistake she would be kicking herself over for a long time.

She ran around the corner where the two had disappeared, but was met with a small group of people. She scoffed at their appearance. They weren't true soldiers or
~~~~

guards. Just people Tryxus roped into protecting the compound. They were in a loose formation with wooden batons raised.

She lunged at them, forcing more than half to run. The rest who stood their ground didn't stand much longer. She cut through them with ease ducking and dodging their wild attacks. Even with being hurt by the Oracle, she managed to avoid any damage or attacks from the pitiful security force and continued after her target.

~~~~

Arilynn led the small team to the edge of the cliff. It was quite easy for them to realize where the compound was. A fleet of about 50 hover-bikes and other vehicles were attacking the hidden entrance they had heard about.

"Well, that was easy," Markus quipped with a smirk.

"Yes," Arilynn replied, not sharing his amusement. "What are the Red Scorpions doing here?" she asked, referring to the markings on the vehicles. The vehicles were using all their firepower. Their blasts pelted the side of the cliff, creating a cloud of dust.
~~~~

"What's the plan?" Briar asked from behind them.

"Take them down, eliminate all threats and capture the Oracle," Benjamin replied with a flat tone.

"You mean *find* the Oracle," Arilynn corrected. "We shouldn't be capturing anyone." Benjamin regarded her for a moment and then nodded.

"I will circle around and see if there are any other entrances. I can't imagine there is only one way in or out." Arilynn revved the engine to her hover-bike and shot off.

"Well, let's not keep them waiting," Markus said as he descended the cliffside. Briar and Clara followed directly after him. Benjamin hesitated, looking to where Arilynn went, but decided to follow after Markus instead.

Their hover-bikes were faster and more agile than the Junkers that the Red Scorpions used. They also had more firepower that they unleashed as they approached. The Red Scorpions suddenly dispersed as shouting became the loudest noise in the canyon.

Markus sent a wall of lightning that short circuited most of their vehicles, sending them crashing down to the stone canyon below.

The ones that remained began to fly in tight formations. The knights broke off and their battle began.

Markus dove down as a small formation of four riders chased after him. He shifted side to side and then shot upwards at such an incline that he nearly slipped off the seat. He sent a gust of wind behind him. The sudden gust of wind coupled with the intense speed and incline at which they were flying knocked three of the four off their bikes.

The fourth biker held on and began to close in on Markus who glanced around to see that the others were doing relatively well. The Three Tailed Scorpions weren't known for their fighting ability when it came to open combat. They were known for their assassinations and stealth or overwhelming numbers.

Markus pulled back and banked hard to the left heading straight for the damaged front door. He fired down with everything his hover-bike had on the one weak spot he could see.

As he approached, he reared his hand back and threw a fireball that blew the hole open wide enough that he could fit inside. The rider behind him followed through the attack, and one of his stray bolts hit the back of Markus' bike, hurling him forward uncontrollably.

Markus leapt off the speeder, and with another gust of wind, landed softly on the ground. He unclipped his Umoya and with a gust of wind, a thin rapier blade of air appeared. The man who followed him jumped off his bike, grabbing two daggers that were connected together at the hilt by a silver chain. He began to swing it back and forth as he made his approach.

~~~~

Tryxus shouted instructions to what remained of his security force as he marched through the main compound. His head ached and his face was bruised from Isobella. He didn't have time to think about her. He was too
~~~~

focused on making sure everyone was safe. He knew most of them weren't fighters, but they needed him to lead. As he continued down the hall he saw Gwynne hobbling forward with Tyron leaning on her shoulders. Giving out the last instructions before dismissing the security teams, he ran towards his son, Moira and Isobella running behind him.

"What happened?" he shouted as he lifted Tyron from Gwynne's shoulders.

"A woman, north door," Tyron winced. "I think she's after Gwynne." Tryxus shot a look at Isobella who was too busy checking with Gwynne to notice. "Get to the transport, both of you," Tryxus said looking at Moira. "Bella!" he shouted.

"Tryxus, we don't have time for this now!"

"Listen!" he shouted, waving his hand dismissively. "Take my son and wife to the transport. Get yourself and your daughter out of here."

"What about you?" she asked.

"I have to stay here and help my people fight."

"Tryxus," Isobella went to argue.

"This isn't about me. This is about *her,*" Tryxus said, pointing at Gwynne. "We'll discuss it later, but for now, just go," he said pushing her back.

"Son," he bent down so that Tyron could see him. "Take care of your mother until I find you."

"I'll do my best." Tyron winced. "Be safe."

"I love you, son," Tryxus answered, patting him on the shoulder. "Now go," he commanded.

Isobella and Moira helped Tyron walk ahead; Gwynne looked back at Tryxus. They locked eyes for a moment, before he nodded his head, instructing her to follow her mother.

He turned, running towards the hall that led to the north door and pushing past all the people who were trying to follow his instructions. He could hear people shouting that the main entrance had been compromised. He even heard the word 'Eri'Dorian'. The crowd was hysterical and trampling over each other as they tried to find a way to escape.

He ran to the small armory that was in complete disarray. He placed his hand on a black stone on the back wall. The stone illuminated with a surge of spiritual magic. He took a deep breath before taking out the weapon. His Umoya was a unique design where both ends of the weapon appeared to be where the blade would come from. As he held it out, the ends of the Umoya seemed to expand outward, transforming into a massive pike-ax with one of the ends creating a large handle and the other the blades.

When he ran back to the main hall, he focused on the shrouded figure moving towards him. He waded through the crowd with his pike-ax resting on his shoulder. The woman stopped when she saw him and rested all her weight on her right leg, popping her hip out to the side. He studied her for a moment before the realization of who it was came to him.

"Nya?" he said with uncertainty.

"After all of these years you still recognize me," she replied as she pulled back her hood and goggles to show her brown hair and eyes. "I don't want to hurt you or anyone else. Give me the girl, and this ends," she said firmly.

"You brought the Eri'Dorians?" he growled.

"What? No," she scoffed. "Why would I bring them? I'm here for the Oracle, Tryxus. I know she's here," she said showing him the burn marks on her sleeves.

"She's gone," Tryxus growled. "You hurt my boy, you know that?"

"I didn't mean to," she said, lifting her hands. "All right, I'm sorry. He attacked me and I reacted."

"Why do you want the girl?"

"It doesn't matter. Either way I will be getting her. I'd prefer it if you'd help me. "

"If you're not with the Eri'Dorians, who *are* you with?"

"Dammit, Tryxus!" Nya shouted. "We don't have time for this. Give me the damn girl, now!"

"I can't let you take her," he replied, lifting his pike-axe.

"Fine," Nya growled as she recovered her face.

He started his way towards her before stopping abruptly, looking beyond Nya which prompted her to look over her shoulder.

"Shit," Nya muttered when she saw the armored woman with the lioness helm walking towards them. She turned back to Tryxus who was glaring at Arilynn as she approached.

"We can work together and kill her, or she can kill us both!" she shouted as she ran towards him. Without hesitation Tryxus sent a bolt of lightning directly at her.

Nya threw herself to the ground, avoiding the attack. She looked back to see Arilynn simply raise her hand, catching the lighting in her palm. Tryxus continued the stream of lightning with both of his hands dropping his Umoya.

Arilynn seemed unbothered by the stream of lighting, simply holding it in her palm as she walked forward with little resistance.

"Good luck," Nya said as she ran past. He turned his head to watch her run off then turned his focus back to Arilynn. With a deep breath, he mustered everything he had and created another shockwave. This time it pushed Arilynn back a few steps. Tryxus relented, which allowed Arilynn to regain her footing.

He lifted his Umoya off the ground, raising it over his head transforming it into his pike-ax pointing the blade towards her.

~~~~

"Tryxus Ilian, Stand down!" Arilynn shouted. "No harm will come to you or your residents if you surrender now."

"And if I don't?!" Tryxus shouted defiantly.

"Then you'll die," she stated as a matter of fact.

"It won't be that easy to kill me!" Tryxus shouted, stepping forward.

"Stand down, Tryxus," she repeated, raising her Umoya.

He let out a grunt of frustration and charged towards Arilynn. Her Umoya erupted into a thin scimitar of silver metal, and she ran to meet him.
~~~~

He swung down with his pike-ax with all of his strength. Arilynn, at the last moment, sidestepped the attack, dropping to one knee and pivoted so that she was behind him. Her blade cut the back of his knee as she twirled to her feet. On his knee, she grabbed his forehead, pulling back exposing his neck and with one fluid motion cut his throat. He let out a choked gasp as she pushed his body to the ground and continued after Nya.

~~~~

Markus ducked back, avoiding another wild swing. He parried another attack, sidestepping the follow up and pushing the man forward.

"You remind me of an old pupil of mine," Markus said calmly. "All strength and attack, but you don't think of anything after that."

"Shut up!" Konan spat as he charged again. He swung the chain back and then shot it forward. Markus stepped to the side, avoiding the chain and dagger entirely. He stabbed forward so that his blade would become entangled.
~~~~

Konan smiled as he pulled back. To his dismay, the old knight was prepared for his attack. Markus braced himself and further wrapped his blade within the chain. He then grabbed the chain and sent electricity down the chain, shocking Konan and forcing him to drop the weapon.

Markus then simply allowed his blade to disappear. The chain fell to the ground and the thin metal blade returned.

"Now what?" Markus taunted.

"Why do you keep talking, old man?" Konan sneered, he could see the other knights were engaging the security forces of the compound.

"Because, you're attempting to kill me," Markus said with a smile. "I would at least appreciate some effort."

Konan grimaced, exhaling sharply through his nose. He grabbed a long dagger from behind his back, lifting it up and reversing his grip.

"I'll show you effort, old man."

~~~~
~~~~

Gwynne ran ahead of the group, consisting of her mother, Tyron and his mother. She could see the large vehicle that her mother had told them about—an old, rusted passenger-bus. The windows were tinted yellow from dust and sitting under ground. She wasn't even sure it would start when she jumped on, scrambling to the front seat.

She had learned the basics of driving with her mother, but this was above her understanding. It was an older model that had a manual transmission and steering system. She glanced back and saw that Tyron was hobbling on his own now, allowing her mother to rush to help. She pulled Gwynne back and started the transport with no difficulty.

"Sit and stay down!" Isobella commanded. Gwynne obeyed without question, sitting in the two seats directly behind her. She looked back to see that Tyron and his mother were sitting in the middle of the aisle.

The bus had two rows of seats; each seat was made for two people. A door at the back of the bus led to a small balcony for people to stand. The only protection the bus offered was a rusted metal canopy and a railing on the edges.

The bus began to lift off the ground as its thrusters strained, misfiring from non-use. Gwynne saw her mother's expressions change from focus to fear and back so quickly that she wasn't sure that it even happened. Gwynne had never seen her mother so stressed before.

Tyron's shouting prompted the two of them to look back. He was attempting to stand, pointing at the docking station they were trying to leave. The woman in black was approaching them. She was at a full sprint and then launched herself forward with a burst of wind.

Isobella veered the transport hard to the right. The sudden movement knocked Tyron back to the ground and Gwynne slid off her seat into the middle aisle. She clambered to her feet to see where the woman in black landed.

Tyron forced himself up rushing to the door, attempting to shut it. Before he could latch it, he was pushed back by the woman who followed up with a kick in the torso. He sprawled backwards onto his mother who pushed him back up to his feet. He swung, but the woman simply caught his arm. With a pivot, she flipped him over her shoulder, slamming him into the ground behind her.

Moira stood up to fight back and was hit in the face with a back elbow. She collapsed, unconscious, into one of the seats. Tyron let out a shout as he struggled to stand. Gwynne stood up raising her hands defensively and the woman mirrored her movements.

"Where's my dad?!" Tyron shouted as he forced himself up with the help of one of the seats. She ignored his question and when he charged her, she created a blast of ice that sent him backwards crashing into the far back door.

"Gwynne, behind me. Now!" Isobella shouted. The woman in black made no movement, she just stared at Isobella. Gwynne obeyed her mother's commands, hurrying to the front of the bus. She wedged herself into the front seat looking over the headrests.

There was a moment where none of them moved. Then suddenly the two women were interlocked in a fight. Gwynne had never seen her mom move so fast before. Her hands were almost a blur. She followed through every attack. Her kicks and punches aimed to hurt.

Gwynne began to think of all the times she trained and fought her mother. She had always considered herself on par with her. Their training sessions always ended with her mother winning, but she always thought she stood a chance if she ever decided to really try. She quickly realized how much her mother had been holding back.

~~~~

Isobella jabbed and swung with everything she had. Her opponent, who seemed familiar in her movements, was parrying each attack with such ease that it teetered on insult.

Isobella caught the woman's fist in her left hand and jabbed low with her right. The woman caught Isobella's hand and they began pushing against each other trying to gain the advantage. Isobella stumbled back, and it resulted in the woman using Isobella's own hand to punch herself in the face.
~~~~

Isobella stumbled back but recovered quick enough to duck under a swing and follow up with a jab that connected, repaying the blow. The woman took a step back and pulled her scarf and hood off showing her face. She stared at Isobella's surprised expression with an arrogant smile.

"Nya?" Isobella said in a hushed tone.

"I know, I'm supposed to be dead." Nya threw the scarf to the ground. "But, so are *you,*" she added before continuing her attack.

Isobella jumped back, startled from Nya's sudden aggression. She moved back and forth, parrying everything that she could and was quickly realizing how out of practice she was against a real opponent. Her arms were tired, and she was either slowing down or Nya was getting faster.

~~~~

Markus' blade change from metal to wind, swinging back, parrying Konan's long dagger. The wind blade created a gust each time he swung. Despite this; Konan was relentless, skilled enough to survive Markus' attacks, but not enough to outlast the fight.
~~~~

"You fight too hard," Markus commented as he parried another attack. "You're clearly outmatched."

"Shut up!" Konan screamed as he charged in an attempt to tackle the old knight. Markus sent a gust of wind, knocking him flailing backwards. Markus waved his hand to the side using a second gust of wind to further push Konan against the far wall. The impact left Konan dazed as he stumbled forward.

He swung so wildly with his dagger that Markus only had to move back or move his head slightly to avoid the blade. Konan was exhausted and was desperate now. Markus caught Konan's hand, twisting his arm. He expected Konan to stumble forward. To his amazement Konan was feigning his dazed state.

He pushed forward with such velocity that it knocked Markus off balance. The sudden burst of speed and strength left Markus vulnerable. He backpedaled to get as much distance as he could, but Konan was too quick and pressed the attack.

Markus ducked under another wide swing and threw a bolt of lightning. Konan managed to lift his dagger, the bolt bouncing off the blade. The force of the bolt knocked Konan back allowing Markus to follow up with a wide swing of his rapier creating a violent gust of wind that threw Konan back into the wall with enough speed that it knocked him unconscious.

Markus turned to see that Briar and Clara were finishing with the security team. They took special care to leave them all alive but incapacitated.

"Where's Benjamin?" Markus asked as he approached the two students.

"He ran off, sir," Clara replied. "What do we do now?"

"Now, I find Lady Lynn," Markus replied. "Stay here and guard the entrance. Contact me if anymore show up." With that he ran down the main corridor.

Clara stood tapping her foot impatiently. "I'm going," she announced running after her mentor.

"Hey!" Briar shouted. "What about me?"

"Stay here and guard the door!"

"Of course," Briar muttered. "It's always me."

~~~~

Nya pressed the attack, pushing Isobella back towards the main cabin. Isobella parried the second attack, dodged the third and absorbed the fourth. She was losing. and they both knew it. Nya was faster and ready for this fight.

Isobella ducked under a swing and charged. Her best chance was to get Nya on the ground and entangle her. Nya was prepared for the tackle and threw her legs back, dodging most of it. Isobella lifted her up, but a well-placed knee strike to the nose forced her to rear back. Isobella could feel the blood gush down her face.

Nya attempted a high kick, Isobella brought up her arm, blocking the kick, and with her other arm, trapped the leg to pull Nya forward and off balance. Isobella dropped her leg and tackled Nya onto the seat. She propped
~~~~

one of her knees on Nya's shoulder and crouched on top of her.

Isobella felt something snap inside of her. She was no longer tired, just angry and afraid. She held Nya down with one hand and with her other began to beat down on Nya's face and head. Her fist hitting wherever it landed. She was beginning to tire and gasp for air. Nya was still struggling to get free and exhaustion was beginning to set in for her as well.

Isobella paused at the sound of Tyron shouting. She couldn't understand what he was saying. She was too focused on Nya and her senses were blurred. She glanced up to see him rushing towards the cabin, pushing Gwynne out of the way; Gwynne was staring out the window when suddenly, she screamed.

Isobella looked back to see another woman standing in the doorway. Isobella stared at Arilynn in amazement. She didn't need to see her face to know that it was her.

Isobella's distraction gave Nya a chance to break free and push Isobella off. Isobella attempted to regain control with an elbow strike. Nya ducked to the side, grabbing Isobella and violently slamming her head into the side of the seat.

Nya stood over Isobella as she groaned, trying to get back up. Nya's face was battered and was beginning to bruise. Her lip had been busted open, and blood leaked from her nose. She grabbed her two daggers from their sheaths and turned to Arilynn boarding the bus.

"Well, Tryxus certainly didn't do his job," Nya growled as she connected the ends of her hilts together twisting so that they interlocked. Ice blades began to form on both ends.

~~~~

Arilynn replied in kind, lifting her Umoya. From the hilt a long whip made of water ending with two jagged ice prongs fell to the ground. Nya went on the offensive and moved towards Arilynn, leaving Isobella on the ground. Arilynn stepped forward, and with lightning speed, she cracked the whip. The end of the whip wrapped around Nya's
~~~~

weapon. Arilynn yanked it backwards pulling Nya with it. Arilynn lifted her knee to meet Nya's torso. As Nya stumbled backwards from the impact, Arilynn extended her leg, kicking Nya to the ground.

Isobella pushed herself up and swung at Arilynn. Arilynn swatted her hand away with her empty hand and then used the base of her Umoya to strike Isobella across the face, knocking her into one of the seats.

Arilynn took a step back, deactivating her Umoya. She clipped it back on her belt as the bus was too small for her to use it effectively. She turned back looking for what she had come for.

Gwynne backed up slowly, holding onto the seats as she stared down Arilynn who's helm only showed the roaring lioness.

"Hold on!" Tyron shouted as he lurched the bus forward. Gwynne fell backward from the sudden burst of speed. Arilynn took a step back bracing herself and keeping her balance. She turned in time to block another incoming attack from Nya. Nya punched and kicked with sloppy form. She was becoming tired.

Arilynn hardly had to move to block the attacks.

Her being a Soferian gave her an edge already. She was faster than most humans, saw things faster than they could, which was coupled with the heightened senses that most Eri'Dorian knights get with years of training. Her hands were already waiting for Nya's attack as she made them.

The surprise came when Isobella joined the attack. The two now working in tandem against Arilynn made it more difficult to stand against them. Arilynn persisted, ducking, dodging and parrying what she could, absorbing what she couldn't. Her armor helped in that aspect. When she managed to find any openings in their attacks, she used them. Her strikes hit harder than theirs, knocking them back and giving her a brief moment of reprieve.

She grabbed Nya's arm and flipped her over her shoulder. As she was slamming Nya into the ground, she kicked Isobella in the stomach, forcing her to stagger backwards. She knelt next to Nya, driving her elbow into Nya's torso to knock the wind from her lungs.

Arilynn stood up as Isobella prepared herself for another attack by shaking her hands. Arilynn raised her hands defensively. She caught Isobella looking behind her. Arilynn not wanting to waste any more energy sent a tornado of wind at Isobella, slamming her against the back door.

Arilynn pivoted off her back foot just in time to see Tyron lifting a large energy-rifle. His first shot hit Arilynn directly in the chest. The energy dissipated over her armor, but the impact knocked her back. His second shot was a grazing shot as the recoil was more than he anticipated.

He fired a third time, this time Arilynn met the blast with her hand using a fire blast to cancel out the bolt. She then followed up with another fire-blast. Tyron let out a shout as he dove to the ground to avoid the ball of fire.

Arilynn staggered backwards. The armor had done its job. There were no life-threatening injuries, but now she was hurt. She stood up straight doing her best to ignore the pain. She couldn't allow them to see her weakened.

She heard Isobella stirring behind her, and Nya was already on her feet. Arilynn was no longer interested in a physical contest. She threw a bolt of lightning at Nya who deflected it with a small shield of ice. Arilynn sent another gust of wind at Isobella, knocking her back down.

She moved towards Nya who returned a gust of wind that Arilynn waved away with her own, following up with a punch to the side of the throat that knocked Nya back down to the ground.

To her astonishment, Tyron was back up with his gun. She threw a bolt of lightning, hitting the gun. He dropped the rifle to the ground with a shout looking at his hands. She was impressed with his tenacity as he ran at her. He swung widely which allowed Arilynn to catch his wrist; she slammed the edge of her hand into the side of his throat. He coughed and fell limp as she pushed him to the seat on her right.

In front of her, she saw Gwynne attempting to keep the bus steady as it careened down the dark tunnel. Arilynn approached her carefully. She looked through the windshield to see lights approaching them and in the reflection, she saw Isobella attempting another attack. Arilynn turned abruptly, catching Isobella's wrist. Arilynn grabbed Isobella by the throat, noticing she had an old Eri'Dorian dagger, and with a sweep of her leg; she slammed Isobella into the ground. The bus came to an unexpected stop, nearly knocking Arilynn off her feet.

She then heard the distinctive crackle of lightning as an Umoya ignited behind her. She turned to see Gwynne standing with a sword of crackling electricity raised. Arilynn regarded her for a moment. She was clearly terrified—her stance was off-balance; her eyes wet and her face flushed red. Arilynn lifted the faceplate of her helm to reveal her face. She stared at Gwynne with her violet eyes. She did her best to soften her normally intense gaze.

"Stand down, child," Arilynn spoke calmly. "I do not wish to fight or harm you."

"Clearly," she said breathing heavily.

"It may seem that I'm here to hurt the ones you care about," Arilynn said, raising both of her hands up. "But I assure you. I'm not."

"You're trying to kill my mother."

"If I had wanted to kill her, I would have already," Arilynn replied. "She's out of shape and out of practice."

"Tryxus?" Gwynne whined. "Where is he?"

"Dead," Arilynn replied flatly.

"Did you kill him?" Gwynne demanded. Her eyes flashed white but immediately returned to their normal color.

"Let's just talk about this," Arilynn replied.

"Answer me!" Gwynne shouted, stepping forward. Arilynn could tell she was trying to act brave, and even though the girl had no control over her power, it was not something Arilynn wanted to face. She watched over Gwynne's shoulder as the pair of lights continued approaching them. They suddenly shut off, and there was nothing but darkness. She focused back on Gwynne as she attempted to inch closer.

Gwynne raised her sword higher; the blade crackled and wavered unevenly, when she saw what Arilynn was doing. Arilynn paused making sure to keep her hands raised. She could hear that either Nya or Isobella were moving. She didn't want to risk looking back to see who it was or what they were doing. She stayed focused on Gwynne who was focused on her.

It wasn't until she felt a hand on her shoulder that she reacted. She gave into the pull, pivoting off her back foot. She grabbed Nya's arm, torquing it so that she went forward. Arilynn unclipped her Umoya, igniting it to a single edged blade of metal, holding it to the back of her neck.

Isobella slowly pulled herself up once again. She grabbed Arilynn by the waist, trying to pull her back. Her muscles strained as she attempted to pull Arilynn. Arilynn dropped her elbow, hitting Isobella in the temple and knocking her back down. Isobella shook off the attack and charged Arilynn again. This time,

Arilynn let go of Nya and side-stepped Isobella. Nya and Isobella collided and then pushed off each other as they attempted to stand up right.

Nya grabbed for her connected daggers; Arilynn managed to get a hold of them first. She lifted the weapon into the air as ice blades began to form.

"Stand down," Arilynn commanded.

"You're outnumbered," Tyron groaned as he stood up.

"Yet, I am not the one who is outmatched," Arilynn replied confidently. "I'm not here to kill any of you. I'm here for the Oracle."

"She's not going anywhere," Isobella growled as she lifted her weary hands up for another fight.

"Yes, she is," Nya replied, hitting Isobella on the side of her face with a back elbow. Nya moved back to avoid Arilynn and jumped out the side door. She disappeared into the darkness of the tunnel, her footsteps receding.

"Well, that makes this easier," Arilynn commented, throwing Nya's weapon to the side. She once again allowed the blade to recede, replacing her Umoya back onto her belt. "Please, child. Come with me."

"No," Gwynne said defiantly.

"You do not understand the gravity of the situation," Arilynn persisted. "You are a danger to yourself and to everyone around you." Arilynn slowly moved forward. She could see that Gwynne was beginning to doubt her defiance.

She glanced down at Isobella who was still struggling to stand up. Tyron gasped as he pulled on the seats to keep himself standing.

"I don't want to hurt anyone," Gwynne whimpered.

"You've already killed," Arilynn commented. "The officer and the Sentinel."

"I….I didn't….I…"Gwynne stammered as she tried not to break down. She struggled to keep the Umoya up and steady.

"I know you didn't," Arilynn replied softly. "But you can't control your abilities, or power. Come with me and I will make sure you are taught correctly."

"What about my mom?"

"No harm will come to her," Arilynn replied. "I promise."

"Tyron and his mom?"

"Both are safe from me and the Order," Arilynn agreed. She was now within range to grab her but knew better. One wrong move and Gwynne would panic which would bring out the Oracle. Arilynn was doing everything she could to avoid that from happening.

"Please, put down the weapon and take my hand. I promise no harm will come to you." Gwynne stared at her with uncertainty and as she began to lower her hands. Arilynn's eyes grew wide.

"Benjamin, no!" she shouted, reaching out. Gwynne turned to see Benjamin crashing through the windshield with a fireball. Gwynne froze, and her eyes went white.

Arilynn grabbed her shoulder. "Don't!" she shouted. Gwynne simply swatted Arilynn's hand away in response. She sent a gust of wind so hard that it tossed Arilynn to the back of the bus, slamming through the metal door.

Benjamin grabbed Gwynne by the shoulders and tried to force her down. She ripped his hands away from her and grabbed him by the throat. Despite being much smaller than he was, she lifted him off the ground and held him there. Her eyes glowed as white energy pulsed through her hand into his neck.

He began screaming in pain as he struggled to pull away. She held him up in the air. She glanced over to Arilynn who was back on her feet. Arilynn made no hesitation, igniting her Umoya into a circular shield of gray stone. Gwynne reacted as she expected and sent a stream of energy at her. The impact of the power nearly knocked Arilynn off her feet again. She leaned into the power and pushed against it as hard as she could with no avail. Regardless of how hard she pushed her feet began to slide on the metal floor. She could feel that her Umoya was beginning to strain under the immense power. Arilynn dropped it, bringing up her hands creating a stream of fire.

She watched Markus leaping towards her from outside the bus. He was drenched in sweat from running and he created a stream of lightning against Gwynne. Gwynne reacted violently, throwing Benjamin through the front windshield. She turned towards them and was now using both of her hands.

Arilynn had never felt such power before, even with Markus, a Lord Knight of Eri'Dorian Order known for his power. They were losing, and they were losing quickly. Both of them were sliding on the floor as her power overwhelmed them. Arilynn could see that Gwynne was moving towards them effortlessly.

Arilynn saw Isobella stand up and try to stop her, but Gwynne simply stepped around her. Arilynn shouted as she struggled to stand against the young girl. She felt a hand touch her shoulder and looked over to see Clara standing there, she was now using wind to push back against Gwynne. This only seemed to slow Gwynne for a moment before she began to approach again.

"We can't hold her back!" Arilynn shouted. She drove her knee into the ground trying to push back harder. "We have to let go!" she shouted.

"We can't, she'll kill us!" Markus grunted. He was tired; running however far he ran, and his old age was catching up to him. He was beginning to falter as Clara reached out to steady him again.

"Let go!" Arilynn shouted. "NOW!" she commanded. Markus shouted, shaking his head defiantly. Clara obeyed, pulling Markus back.

Arilynn screamed at the sudden surge of power she felt pushing against her. She knew she couldn't defeat this. She also knew that she could withstand it long enough so that Markus and Clara and hopefully Benjamin could escape.

To her surprise, Gwynne relented. She looked up to see that Benjamin was now attacking her with a fire attack of his own. Gwynne was now simply absorbing their fire into her hands. It was beginning to build up, Arilynn stopped immediately once she understood what the girl was doing. She ran and jumped through the mangled back door.

She slammed onto the concrete of the tunnel rolling over to her back she saw the bright flash of light and then a shockwave that slammed into her so hard that it forced the air out of her lungs. She lay on the ground gasping for air, straining to sit up.

The entire tunnel was pitch black, she could hear Isobella shouting, but couldn't understand what she was saying. Everything had an echo and when the lights flickered back on, they were blurred. The engine of the bus roared to life and they quickly disappeared into the darkness.

CHAPTER 11

Ancient King

Jaxon parked and stepped out of his vehicle. He looked at the grand entrance of the old building. The late afternoon sun was being slowly blotted out by the wall of storm clouds approaching.

The building itself was made of old gray stone. Ancient gargoyles decorated the roof and the small towers at each corner. Their haunting eyes and faces looking down as he approached. The gate to the building was out of place. It was newly built with a shiny golden finish. There was no one at the gate or near them. It was eerily silent as it always was when Vampires were near. Animals had an ability to sense predators and Vampires considered themselves the greatest of all the predators.

Jaxon wasn't one to argue with their proclamation. They were faster than wolves and though not as strong, they still had great strength that outmatched other races. Sunlight only annoyed them despite the legends that they were 'allergic' or weakened by the sun. From what Jaxon could gather, the light bothered them like it did to someone who had a migraine. Ultimately, it was a bearable pain, but it was not something they often endured willingly.

Jaxon pushed through the gate which moved easily and made little noise as it swung open. He continued, cautiously looking and listening for anything that would warn him of danger. He allowed his face to be shown prominently. They would react to him differently than the wolves did. Though they were still dangerous, he had created a rapport with Balthazar—the leader of the largest clan and in more ways than not, a King of the Vampire race.

Jaxon stepped up to the old stone steps, which crumbled beneath his weight as he climbed them. The building was empty and mostly bare. The old architecture withstood the test of time with large stone pillars. Jaxon deduced that the tops and bottoms of each of the pillars had once been coated with some kind of precious metal that had long ago been stripped away.

He continued towards the center of the building until reaching his destination. It was a large stone circle that stood out much like the new gate. The gate was polished gold with an ancient symbol, two tear-drop shaped circles connected by a solid line. Separating them was a black line that created a small cross.

Jaxon knew the sign well enough to know its meaning. Each circle represented life and death; the line in the center separating the two represented the Vampire kin; they, like the line were in-between, and would never reach either side again.

Jaxon took a step back, lifting his hand to throw a small lightning bolt at the center of the symbol. The sound echoed throughout the building so loudly that the settled dust moved.

Jaxon waited in silence. The wind from the oncoming storm whistled through the old building. He crossed his arms becoming impatient.

He knew the building was a farce. Their true home was beneath him and this was the true entrance, not the golden gate outside.

After a few moments of no answer, he squatted down, placing his hand on the stone. He closed his eyes as he searched through the earth, one of his favorite magical abilities with Earth magic.

Below him was a cavern; he could sense the furniture and even a few *people* walking around. He knocked loudly and none of them seemed bothered. Jaxon let out a frustrated sigh, standing back up. He concentrated his energy into his fist and knelt back down, pressing his closed fist against the stone circle. With a strike coupled with his power of Earth magic, the stone shattered beneath him. He jumped through the new hole in the ground, landing beneath.

Despite being underground, the cavern was well lit. The ceiling had rows of lights that stretched as far as the walls. The beings he sensed before stopped abruptly staring at him. They bared their sharpened teeth as he walked through the cavern.

He made sure to keep his heartbeat and breathing steady. Vampires were keen to hearing such things. The faster the heartbeat, the more willing they were to attack him, but with a steady heartbeat, they were perplexed. His sudden and brash appearance into their dwelling surprised them, and they were all uneasy.

Jaxon entered through a small doorway that led into a room with a large wooden table that had a dark gray surface. Those surrounding the table all looked up at Jaxon, at first with annoyance, then surprise and finally anger. Three of them stood up hissing, baring their teeth with their arms stretched out to the side

"Where is Balthazar?" Jaxon asked, making sure his voice was low and loud enough for everyone to hear.

"Are you insane?" the woman sitting at the head of the table asked, standing up. She had dark black hair that was cut short just above her shoulders. Her cold black eyes glared at Jaxon. She wore a tight fitting sleeveless black gown that showed intricate, vampiric tattoos that decorated her body. They were solid black lines with a violet shine that intertwined, creating unique shapes and every so often, the Vampiric symbol.

"Where is he?" Jaxon asked, staring back at her. He was aware of the two men circling to flank him but kept his eyes fixed on her. She was the one in charge here and they wouldn't attack until she gave the order.

"I don't think we've had the pleasure," she said in a suddenly sweet voice. She smiled at him tilting her head slightly, her black eyes fluttering to blue irises. Jaxon recognized the sudden change and it put him on edge. Vampires were tricky and often used that to catch their prey despite their strength and speed. It was easier to catch prey that was already calm. Her pale skin brightened as if she were alive again. If he were to touch her, she would feel warm as if she were truly alive.

"My name is Jaxon Harwell," There were small murmurs that broke out within the room. "I'm here for Balthazar. Where is he?" he asked again, this time more forcibly.

"Well, Balthazar is not available, and *I'm* in charge here," she replied. "You shouldn't have come in here, Jaxon Harwell." She added. She sat back down and waved her hand, signaling the two men to attack.

Jaxon jumped onto the table, sending an arc of lightning hitting her in the chest that knocked her backwards in her chair. He then spun around with both of his hands outstretched, creating a ring of fire that forced all of them back hissing. He grabbed his Umoya, and with a burst of fire, it erupted into a flaming war-hammer that he threw upwards, crashing through the roof. The sunlight cut into the room illuminating it even brighter.

The Umoya fell back into Jaxon's hand, and he morphed it to a blade of lightning. He made sure to stay in the sunlight knowing it would make it easier for him to defend against their oncoming assault.

"Enough!" a loud, booming voice roared. Jaxon looked over to see Balthazar standing in the doorway.

Balthazar was once a Dru'Ny. His broad, heavily muscled frame filled the doorway. He was over 8 feet tall, towering over everyone in the room.

He was dressed in a heavy bear fur coat that draped over his shoulders. He wore a bright blue leather vest that stretched over his wide torso. Black leather pants tucked into black leather boots. He was bald headed, and his skin tone was pale brown. His black eyes stared at Jaxon and then at the woman on the ground. His arms were covered in tattoos similar to the woman's. His forearms had golden bracers with gems and precious stones embedded. Each finger had at least one ring, some as many as three ranging from gems and diamonds to bone and steel.

"Do you fools not recognize who this is?" his deep voice echoing in the room. They all bowed their heads not wanting to look directly at him. "Do you?!" he shouted.

"This is Jaxon Harwell of the Eri'Dorian Order," he scolded. "He is welcomed here, always," he growled. "Bow and show respect, for he is one of the greatest predators I have known in my lifetime." Jaxon regarded

Balthazar for a moment. That was not a statement Balthazar would say lightly.

Balthazar only looked around forty-five years of age, which even for Dru'Ny was a very young age. Despite his youthful look Jaxon knew Balthazar to be well over three-thousand years old. He was a god to many of the Vampires, and even his enemies gave him respect.

"Step down from there, you look like an idiot," Balthazar said to Jaxon as he walked over to the woman. He helped her up and checked to make sure she was okay. She was much more polite and soft in her replies in his presence.

"Now, everyone, leave," he commanded as Jaxon climbed down. He allowed the blade of his Umoya to fade, but it was still in his hand until they were alone in the room.

"What the hell are you doing here?" Balthazar snapped when everyone was gone. "And why are you breaking holes in my roof?"

"I needed to talk to you."

"Then ask," Balthazar scolded. He sat down on the small chair the woman had been, and motioned for Jaxon to sit next to him. Jaxon accepted the invitation.

It was rare for Jaxon to ever feel at ease with a vampire, especially one so large and as powerful as Balthazar. Their relationship had been going on for over twenty years which gave him a small sense of safety.

During that time, they could have killed each other and at times almost had. Despite their battles, they always maintained each-other's respect. Jaxon looked at Balthazar who stared back at him. All vampires had what many knights called "dead eyes.' There was no light in them, no pupil or iris. Just black unless they decided to mimic their old selves. This had once made Jaxon nervous, but now it was just another feature of the 'King' vampire.

"Why are you here, Jaxon?" Balthazar asked, relaxing from his rigid demeanor. "We have not broken any vows of the Covenant. Those who have in the past all have been severely punished." Jaxon found it odd that that was where Balthazar immediately took the conversation.

"We may have a problem," Jaxon said dusting some of the debris on the table away from him. "Novak is assembling an army." Balthazar chuckled but made no reply. "You already know, then?"

"No. Just doesn't surprise me," he added with another laugh.

"This isn't a laughing matter, Balthazar," Jaxon warned. "He has the packs and they're forming."

"Am I supposed to be afraid of them?" He leaned forward to place his large arms on the table. "If they attack us, *you* attack them, right? Let them come," he said with a grin.

"It's not that simple."

The grin faded from his face. "What the hell do you mean, it's not that simple?" he growled.

"Novak claims that wolves have been attacked and killed by members of the clans."

"You believe him?"

"Novak is impulsive," Jaxon commented. "Right now, he's being very reserved and thinking through his actions."

"Hmph, a dog that can think… imagine that."

"Have the clans been attacking the packs?" Jaxon asked firmly.

"No," Balthazar replied, matching his tone.

"Are you sure?"

"Are you calling me a liar, Jaxon?"

"No, I just have to be sure." Jaxon replied. "You've been expanding."

"And?" He asked. "That's not against our little agreement, is it?"

"No, it isn't," Jaxon answered. "But it brings into question how many of your people have violated the Covenant without you knowing."

"You think I'm losing control?" Balthazar asked, dejected.

"The woman, she had them attack me."

"I stopped it, didn't I?" Balthazar argued.

"And if you hadn't been here, and they killed me, would you have ever known?" Balthazar observed Jaxon with his typical, expressionless face.

"Let's be honest, you would have been fine," Balthazar said, leaning back with a smirk. "She shouldn't have attacked you."

"If Novak finds proof that it was one of the clan members, yours or not. They will bring it to the Order." There was a moment of silence between the two of them. Balthazar stared intently at Jaxon and then relented, glancing up at the hole in the ceiling.

"I will reach out to the other clans and see if they know anything." Balthazar shook his head. "Is that what you came here for? To accuse me of starting another war?"

"More or less," Jaxon replied with a smirk. "Who is the woman?"

"My new bride, Alamara."

"What happened to the old one?"

Balthazar shifted in his seat and for the first time since Jaxon had known him, he seemed uncomfortable.

"She left." He stood abruptly. "Walk with me," he said as more of a command than a request. Jaxon obliged and followed him into the main corridor.

They walked through the winding halls. They were dimly lit, they had no real use for light except for when they had visitors such as him. Jaxon could see in the dark better than most due to his own heritage. Despite this he was thankful for the lighting.

Balthazar rarely acknowledged any of the other vampires as he passed their bowing heads. Jaxon however noticed all of them. They glared at him with discontent, their dead eyes watching his every move. It was not common for a living person to be within their confines. Especially a Warden of the Eri'Dorian Order.

Jaxon followed Balthazar, his muscles tense and his hands ready to move at any time. He was sure if they decided to attack, he wouldn't stand much of a chance. There were too many of them, and he was just one person. Balthazar himself was more than capable of killing him.

They had fought many times before the Covenant had been reached, and he still had the scars to show. Regardless, most of the time that Jaxon managed a victory, it was due to something outside their conflict that allowed him to take the advantage.

"Here," Balthazar said quietly as he stopped in front of what looked like a dead end. Balthazar placed his hand on the back wall. It was nearly pitch black here, and Jaxon could only make out the outlines of the wall. After a moment, there was a soft beeping sound, and the wall began to move.

"We're upgrading," Balthazar said with a laugh and looked over his shoulder with a half-smile. "I'm sure you understand." He took a step back as the wall moved, and light began to pour in. "This is your exit, considering you put a damn hole in my roof," Balthazar said flatly. "Next time you'll pay for that."

"Luckily you're upgrading," Jaxon said with a smile. Balthazar chuckled softly, but his cold smile faded.

"We've known each other for a long time, Jaxon," he said grimly. "In that time I have fought beside and against you. I know you're a good man. An honorable man." He turned so that he was looking directly at him. "Which is the only reason I'm going to tell you this." He stepped into the light, his dead eyes squinting. His pale brown skin gleamed in the sunlight. "We know the Oracle has returned."

"Everyone does," Jaxon replied.

"Exactly." He turned looking directly at the sun. "You have never seen the world with an Oracle, but I have. Her power was incredible, and when she finally died, a vacuum of power was created. The world went to war as it always does. The Eri'Dorian Order assumed the mantle of power and has held it ever since."

"I feel like there's a point coming," Jaxon said, moving to his side.

"The world hasn't seen an Oracle in almost one thousand years. Now that the Oracle has returned, that vacuum will open up again."

"How so?" Jaxon asked. "The Order is still here, and the Order will raise and teach the Oracle as it always has."

"Do you really think the rest of the world is going to just let that happen?" Balthazar turned, facing him. "Other clans have already started their search. I wouldn't be surprised if the wolves haven't done the same. Who knows who else is out there doing whatever they can to get to the Oracle."

"What would you or anyone else do with an Oracle? You can't even help them to ascend."

"Imagine if she were to be turned into one of my kind?" Balthazar asked. Jaxon contemplated the thought, it was not one he enjoyed.

"You don't know if that would work," he countered.

"No, but her blood would be powerful."

"Her?" Jaxon asked; Balthazar smiled.

"We hide in the shadows, Jaxon," he said, leaning forward. "I may not see *everything,* but I see enough."

"What's your warning, Balthazar?" Jaxon asked, growing impatient.

"The Three Tailed Scorpions are not the only ones hunting the girl," Balthazar said flatly. "I only tell you because of who you are. If it comes between the Order and the Covenant or the Oracle. I'll choose the Oracle."

They stood in silence again. His statement was clear, which only made everything else worse. Jaxon's mind went to Novak and how he was already forming an army. He knew that when Novak found out that the Clans were hunting the Oracle, it was only a matter of time before they broke into conflict.

"Very well," Jaxon replied, breaking the silence "I hope it doesn't come to that."

"I have to do what is right for my people," Balthazar replied. "I'll check into the Wolf attacks. If any of them are guilty they will be dealt severe punishment."

"I'm sure they will be," Jaxon replied over his shoulder as he walked out. He could hear the door shutting behind him. Low fog floated across the lake ahead of him. It was so quiet he could hear the water lap against the bank from the growing breeze. He let out a long breath. Balthazar hadn't helped much. He gave him no new information, and openly threatened to take the Oracle if he had the chance. Now standing at the edge of the lake, he could see his vehicle waiting for him.

He knew that Balthazar was right. The Oracle returning would change everything. Even the council would lose most of its power when the girl came to age. They would only be there to council her while she made the decisions. Jaxon always considered it an idiotic practice to allow a child to lead the Order, but up until now he never thought it would happen again.

He made his way back to his vehicle. Sliding inside, he started the engine. It roared defiantly against the silence of the woods. He pressed open the computer in his center console and attempted to call Arilynn with no answer. He attempted it again and was about to give up when she answered.

He couldn't see her very well due to how dark it was. He could tell that she was lying on the ground and that her forehead was bleeding just above her right eye. She sat up, staring at the screen.

"What happened?"

"The Oracle," she replied bitterly.

"Are you okay?" Jaxon asked, concerned.

"No," she replied. "It seems your lie is becoming a bigger issue than we first thought." She stared directly at the screen and Jaxon slumped back into his seat letting out a loud sigh. "Isobella is the mother of the Oracle."

"What?"

"Yes," Arilynn replied. "Oh, and Nya is back."

"Nya?"

"Yes, just had…a meeting with both of them."

"They're working together?"

"From what I can tell, no." She replied. "You and I need to talk about this. But I don't have the time. The Oracle took off and The Red Scorpions are after her as well."

"Ari," Jaxon said softly. "You may have a bigger problem." She looked at him waiting for him to finish. "I just met with Balthazar. They know enough about the Oracle and I have a feeling they know more than what he was telling me. If the opportunity presents itself, they will take her."

"Great," she muttered. She shuffled around until she was standing up. He could see her straining while she walked.

"Where are you?"

"Tryxus Illian's compound."

"Tryxus?" Jaxon repeated. "You found it?"

"Yes. It was quite easy when we saw that they were being attacked by the Red Scorpions."

"Could have just asked me," Jaxon replied off-handedly.

"Of course, you knew where this was," she snapped. "Why didn't you tell anyone?"

"Because, he wasn't harming anyone," Jaxon replied. "Most of the people in there aren't even fugitives, just lost." Arilynn scoffed at the remark, she often attempted to keep him in line while he attempted to pull her out. It was why they worked so well. They both understood the importance of the Order. While she believed in the council, he did not

"So, you lied about one defector being dead and then you hid another one's presence."

"Ari…"

"No, Jaxon. This is not okay!"

"You're obviously upset."

"Oh, it's obvious that I am upset, thank you," she replied.

"We should talk about this in person and when you're not hurt."

"Do not try and sweep this under the rug, Jaxon."

"I'm not," Jaxon replied firmly. "But you're screaming at me in the dark. You clearly have more important things to worry about."

"Don't tell me what I need to worry about," she retorted. Jaxon let out an exasperated sigh. He knew this discussion wasn't going anywhere. Despite always being called the "stubborn one" she often outlasted him in their bouts. "Don't," she snapped. "What are you doing now?" She asked, softening her voice only slightly. He could see that she was walking and wasn't facing him anymore. He could only see glimpses of the side of her face.

"Going to the council," he replied. "I think this is becoming a bigger issue than I originally thought. Balthazar claims he has no knowledge of the attacks. So, either Novak is lying, or Balthazar is."

"Or he really doesn't know," Arilynn replied.

"Not likely. They don't call him the King for nothing."

"Kings rarely know everything going on," she commented. "But I agree you should go to the council, and if you're not too busy, you should come find us."

"Of course," Jaxon replied. "Ari, I'm—"

"I know," she replied, not allowing him to finish. "We will talk about it later." She stopped and lifted her arm so that she could look directly into frame. "I have to go. I just found Markus."

"All right, I love you."

"I love you, too."

CHAPTER 12

Beginning the Hunt

Arilynn shut off her communication with Jaxon and knelt next to Markus. He let out a grunt as he sat up. There was enough light from one of the Hover-bikes that she could see that he wasn't seriously injured.

"Well, that could have gone better," Markus said with a chuckle that ended in a cough.

"Where is Briar?" Arilynn asked Benjamin as he approached.

"Still at the front with everyone." Arilynn made no reply as she looked over to the hover-bike idling.

"I'm sorry," Benjamin said, breaking the silence. Arilynn glowered at him.

"What were you thinking?!" she snapped.

"I was trying to help you," he argued.

"I had it under control."

"Clearly," Benjamin scoffed. "You had a rifle pointed at you with the Oracle pointing her sword at you. Nya and Isobella near you; you were barely holding on."

"She was surrendering to me, peacefully," Arilynn countered. "Until, of course, you decided to interrupt and caused all of this."

"Both of you be quiet." Markus groaned as he stood up.

"You need to rest," Arilynn replied.

"And you need to pay attention." Markus nodded his head forward, pointing at someone approaching.

Arilynn reacted by grabbing her Umoya first. The flash of fire with the appearance of the sword illuminated the dark tunnel enough for Arilynn to see Isobella limping forward. She was holding her left arm as a trail of blood dripped down the side.

"Really, Lynn?" she said through labored breathing. "Do I look like I am here to fight you?" She plopped on the ground, crossing her legs. Arilynn watched her for a moment before she placed her Umoya back on her belt.

"Where are they going?" she approached her carefully, watching Isobella's every move. Even wounded Isobella was dangerous, and despite having the upper hand in the bus, Arilynn would never underestimate her.

"I had planned on going to Eri'Dor," she replied. "But, I doubt they'll do that now."

Arilynn shot a look at Benjamin who dropped his gaze to the ground. Markus moved around Arilynn and was standing over Isobella holding his hand out. She looked at him and then back at Arilynn and then back at him before she accepted his hand to stand up.

"I've missed you, Bella," he said embracing her. Arilynn rolled her eyes letting out a sigh.

"We need to find your daughter," Arilynn interjected. "So, who else was on that bus?"

"Moira, and Tyron, I'm sure you remember them." she replied; Arilynn tensed at the mention of their names, she hadn't recognized them, and felt foolish because of it.

"Where is Clara?" Markus asked as he began looking around. Arilynn glanced around and then back at Isobella who stood holding her arm.

"Where is she?"

"I think she's on the bus," Isobella replied.

"How?" Arilynn asked, annoyed. "I told her to get off."

"Yea, well, she was also told to stay with Briar," Markus replied. "She jumped back on to help you. She must have held on after the blast from the Oracle." Isobella winced at the word 'Oracle'.

"Great," Arilynn muttered. "We need to find them." She turned to Isobella and approached her, grabbing restraints from a small pouch on the back of her belt.

"Are you serious?"

"Yes," Arilynn replied flatly. "Turn around."

"This isn't necessary," Isobella replied. "We were on our way to Eri'Dor." Arilynn made sure to keep complete control of Isobella as she placed the restraints on her wrists tightening them. She grabbed the crook of Isobella's arm, pushing her forward.

"We need to get to Briar. Then we need to talk," Arilynn stated. "Benjamin, take Markus to the front. I will take her with me and walk through."

"All right," Benjamin said quietly. Markus was already making his way to the speeder and was waiting on Benjamin.

"Look at you, in charge of a whole new team," Isobella said with a sarcastic tone.

"This isn't a team," Arilynn replied, pushing Isobella forward again.

"Well, they listen to you like you're in charge."

"Markus respects me and wants me to lead. Benjamin is an idiot and couldn't lead himself out of a paper bag. The other two are apprentices. It's only natural that I'm in charge."

"Yea, that's how it was when we were kids," Isobella replied.

"We weren't children." Arilynn replied. "At least I wasn't." She heard Benjamin speed off with Markus to circle around the front.

"Must be hard, being so perfect," Isobella muttered.

"Maybe I can be a screw up like you and compare notes. Move," she said, pushing her forward again.

The walk to the main compound was a silent one, and while Isobella made no attempt to escape, Arilynn kept her grip on Isobella's arm tight. She did her best to stay calm but couldn't resist being tense the entire time.

The lights began to flicker as the emergency breaker attempted to turn on. The flashes of light made the walk disorienting and made Arilynn even more uneasy than she already was. Thoughts of what Jaxon told her about the clans made her picture vampires jumping out from the shadows.

As they approached the main compound, she could hear Markus speaking to someone about staying calm and that everything was going to be okay. There was a sudden roar of people talking over each other as Arilynn pushed Isobella into the entrance hall.

"Sit," Arilynn snapped, pushing Isobella down so she didn't have an option. "Don't try anything. I'm not in the mood," she added as she walked over to Markus and Briar who were busy speaking to a large group of people.

Most of them were women and children with only a few men standing near the back who she eyed carefully. Most of them were old men or too out of shape to be a real threat.

When she reached Markus, she glanced back to make sure Isobella was still sitting on the ground. Isobella caught her gaze and gave an exaggerated smile.

"We just want to go!" a woman shouted, prompting Arilynn to look away from Isobella. "You can't just come in here and kill all of us!" she screamed.

"Quiet," Arilynn snapped. "No one is going to kill you," she added more politely.

"Who are you?" the woman asked. She was a short, fat woman with short black hair dressed in dark gray coveralls.

"My name is Arilynn Harwell. I am a Warden with The Eri'Dorian Order. You are all being detained until further notice." There was a sudden roar of angry remarks and insults. "We don't care about any of you," Arilynn replied harshly. The blatant remark caught them off guard. "None of you are the reason we are here. We came here for her." She pointed at Isobella who was now on her knees. "And the girl that was with her. They left with a boy, the son of Tryxus Ilain."

"Where would they go?" Markus interjected in a much softer tone. "You give us a reason to go. We will. This compound isn't safe for any of you anymore, but we won't be taking anyone."

"Why should we help you?" the woman asked.

"Because, if you don't, every single one of you will be taken and transported to wherever you're running from." Arilynn replied. "So, what will it be? Save yourself or her?" She pointed back at Isobella.

"I know a place they would go," the woman replied. She stared at the ground and then looked up to Markus. "But you have to *promise* we can go."

"Of course," he replied with a polite smile. He lifted his arm placing it behind her ushering her away from the rest of the group.

"If any of you have any information step forward. If not stand by and out of the way." Arilynn stated as the crowd began to disperse to the back of the room. She turned to Briar who approached nervously.

"What should we do?" he asked quietly.

"About?"

"All of them?"

"Well, I think we're letting them go," Arilynn replied watching Isobella.

"Really?" Briar asked, surprised.

"Yes."

"I figured we'd turn them in."

"Most of them will be captured on their own. We have more important matters right now." She was still watching Isobella. Years of knowing Isobella, had taught her that she was dangerous, even in restraints.

"Is that her?" Briar asked.

"Yes, that is Isobella Hartley," Arilynn replied.

"She's pretty." Briar noted, his face flushed red when Arilynn looked over at him with a disdainful look.

"That pretty woman over there is one of the most dangerous Rangers the Order has ever had."

"I'll say," Briar commented. "She hid in broad daylight for almost fifteen years."

"You seem very intrigued by her," Arilynn said looking back at Isobella who was now staring at the ground.

"Should I not be?"

"Just be very careful around her and under no circumstances are you to talk to her."

"Why?"

"Because, I said so," Arilynn retorted walking towards her.

"So, what's the verdict?" Isobella asked without looking up.

"You're going to help us find your daughter and bring her back to Eri'Dor."

"Are you going to untie me?" Isobella asked, looking up with a polite smile.

"No. Get up," she demanded as she grabbed Isobella's arm lifting her to her feet.

"I don't know where they would go," Isobella said as she stumbled forward from the force of Arilynn's pull. "Neither does anyone here."

"One of the women over there is telling Markus everything we need to know"

Arilynn shoved Isobella past Briar who smiled and lowered his gaze when he saw Arilynn's disapproving stare. She guided Isobella to Markus and the woman who was becoming animated and clearly frustrated.

When Arilynn and Isobella arrived next to them, the woman quieted down and stared directly at the ground. Arilynn wasn't sure if it was her presence or Isobella's. Either way, the woman's loud posturing disappeared as told them of three other hideouts that Tryxus had mentioned in the past. They were safe houses in case something like today happened.

Arilynn had always considered Tryxus of lesser intelligence and made it known that she did not consider him an equal, but the network he had created surprised her. Despite her feeling of superiority, she had never thought of killing the man. Now that he was dead, she was surprised by the lack of guilt.

"Very good. Thank you," Markus said politely allowing the woman to hobble away. He noticed Isobella's restraints and looked back to Arilynn.

"No," Arilynn said without him having to ask. "What did she say?"

"Maybe we should—" Markus started.

"I'm going with you, may as well know where we're going. Who knows, I may even be able to help," Isobella said with another exaggerated smile.

"There are three other compounds, smaller in size and as far as she knows, no one uses them," Markus explained. "There are enough of us we can split up and go to each."

"No," Arilynn replied.

"I think we can handle it, Lynn," Benjamin interjected. She made no acknowledgement of him, still looking at Markus.

"I spoke to Jaxon earlier," she said, ignoring the scoff from Benjamin. "He warned me that the clans will be going after the girl."

"The clans?" Isobella repeated pushing herself into the conversation.

"And if the clans are getting involved it won't be long until the packs do as well," Markus said echoing Arilynn's thoughts.

"Where is Jaxon now?" Isobella asked.

"Going to the council," Arilynn replied sharply. "Don't speak."

"I *will* speak," Isobella argued. "She may be an Oracle to you. But she's my daughter and she is being hunted down."

"We will get to her first," Arilynn replied. "Maybe if you had just come to the council in the first place you wouldn't be in this situation."

"Yea, because you beat the Red Scorpions here," Isobella replied sarcastically.

"If we go together, we will need to go quickly. Which one first?" Markus asked.

"The closest and let's hope they are going there too," Arilynn answered.

CHAPTER 13

Pledge

Clara woke suddenly and sat up abruptly. Her body cried out in pain from the movement. She frantically looked around taking in her surroundings just as Markus had always taught her to do. She was on the cold metal floor in the bus. It took her a moment to realize her feet and hands were bound by old, frayed rope. She took in a deep breath trying to calm down and looked back to see that she was sitting at the end of the bus near the mangled door.

In front of her, she could see the Oracle and two people speaking too quietly for her to hear. They were parked in a field; the sun was getting low and the colors of the sky were beginning to change.

She looked at her hands and realized that the twine holding her limbs together wasn't magically bound. She could easily break from these restraints but decided against it, not wanting them to panic and see her as a threat. So instead she shouted for them.

The first one to notice was the male. He stood up with an energy rifle in his hand, pointing it at her. He cautiously moved towards her, each step was deliberate and thought out.

"I'm not going to hurt you," Clara said loudly. She kept trying to get a better view of the Oracle. She could sense her power but couldn't see her very well—just the side of her face and part of her blonde hair. The other woman standing in front of her blocked the rest of her view and seemed more concerned than afraid. She kept watching Clara fidgeting with her hands.

"We should just leave her here," the woman stated. "She's too dangerous."

"I'm not going to hurt you," Clara replied.

"How do we know that?" the male asked.

"Because, I'm here to serve the Oracle. That is my sole purpose."

"Tyron," the voice was almost like music to Clara. "Listen to her."

Clara leaned back and kipped-up to her feet. Tyron jumped back raising the rifle. Clara raised her bound hands over her head trying to show that she was not going to do anything. "Oracle, my name is Clara Amparo. I am the apprentice of Markus Troyan of the Eri'Dorian Order."

"Don't talk to her," Tyron commanded.

Clara glared at him for a moment before continuing. "Please, I'm not here to hurt any of you," she repeated.

"Your friend didn't seem to care if she hurt us," Tyron replied.

"Lady Harwell," Clara stated. "She…is… a little more forceful…than I am."

"Why should we trust you?" The Oracle asked, stepping into view. Clara stared at her almost forgetting what to say.

"Because," Clara said as she ignited her hands, burning the twine from her hands and then around her boots. "If I had wanted to. I could have attacked your friend here."

Tyron's eyes went wide, and he leaned into his firing stance. The Oracle stepped forward, placing her hand on him to lower the rifle to which he begrudgingly obliged. Clara dropped to one knee, and moved to grab her Umoya but realized it was gone. With a quick scan she could see that the old woman was holding it in her hands. Clara let out a sigh, shrugging her shoulders.

"Oracle, I am Clara Amparo, Seeker of the Order and I swear my weapon, my strength and my spirit….to you." Clara looked up and their eyes met. Clara couldn't help but look back down. She could hear Gwynne approaching slowly.

"Gwynne," Tyron whispered.

"I…I don't know what to do," she admitted.

"Accept my pledge. Or don't," she replied dreadfully. "Like I said, my sole purpose is to serve and protect you. Above all other things, your highness."

"And you will protect me no matter what?"

"Yes, your highness."

"Even against your friends?"

"Yes," Clara replied without hesitation. "I'm supposed to find, protect and guide you."

"Then I accept," Gwynne said nervously.

"What?!" Tyron snapped loudly.

"I don't know how to explain it," Gwynne answered. "I just feel... *safe* around her." Gwynne looked back at Tyron who was shaking his head. "I don't think she's going to hurt us."

"We don't know anything about her!" Tyron exclaimed with a slam of his fist on the seatback. "This could be a trick."

"It's not," Clara replied with a sharp tone standing up. Gwynne turned back to face her, and their eyes met. They were similar in build and height with Clara being slightly more muscular and an inch or so taller. They stared at each other for a moment before Gwynne spoke.

"Can you tell me what's going on?" Gwynne asked nervously. "Can you tell me what's happening to me?"

"I will do my best, your highness," Clara replied.

Clara tried her hardest to explain what a Seeker was in the easiest way possible. That she was to find and protect the Oracle when they were born. To serve them until their death. She also tried to explain the powers of the Oracle and what they did, but she was beginning to become frustrated.

"You're supposed to be a child," she said suddenly with a defeated sigh.

"What?" Gwynne asked with a nervous laugh. Clara looked over at her doing her best to ignore Tyron pacing behind them.

They had moved outside of the bus and were now in the middle of the field. The other woman, Moira, was kind, but cautious. She never took her eyes off Clara, and when Clara moved too quickly, both would react. Clara stepped away from them and raised her hand into the air.

"You are the Oracle, you will have to master all of the magical spectrums. There are three, Elemental, Mystical and Spiritual." She made sure to keep eye contact with Gwynne. "The strongest among these is spiritual." She motioned for Gwynne to come to her. With slight hesitation Gwynne obliged and stood in front of her.

Clara lifted her hands so that her palms were facing each other. She began to slowly move them side to side in unison, creating a wave like motion. After a brief moment, a small tornado formed between her hands.

She moved so that her left palm was under the small vortex, using her free hand to grab Gwynne's and place it under the swirling vortex. When their hands touched, the tornado grew and began turning faster.

"An Eri'Dorian knight uses elemental magic. There are 5 true elements that a knight will use. Air." The tornado flew into the air creating a gust of wind that blew Gwynne's hair back.

"Fire." Where the tornado once sat a burst of flame erupted and danced around her hand. Gwynne stumbled backwards from the sudden appearance. "Earth." She extinguished the flame by closing her hand into a fist and then knelt. She placed her hand on the ground and lifted. The ground shook before a pillar of stone grew from the ground.

"Water." Still kneeling, she placed her other hand on the ground just above the grass, and slowly, droplets of water began to form into a sphere that she lifted into the air. She was standing again and nodded her head for Gwynne to touch the water.

Gwynne's fingers ran through the water as it would if she were at a river. Though it felt the same as normal water, Gwynne could sense the power behind it.

"Finally, metal." She whipped her hand and the water that was once a globe in her hand turned into a whip-like shape and cut completely through the stone. She then faced her palm towards the stone and much like the water, small metallic flakes came to her hand. After another moment she closed her palm.

Her brow knitted as she concentrated. She opened her hand and in her palm was a small metallic flower.

"You're lucky the bus is mixed metal and that Lady Harwell was too busy dealing with your mother and Nya. Or she would have destroyed it." She handed the small flower to Gwynne who took it graciously staring at the simple design. It looked like a flower a child would draw with the large petals and the large circle in the center.

"You see, that's only a glimpse of what you can do," she saw Gwynne lift her arms up to wrap around herself, uneasily. "I'm not even that great, you should see the other knights, I'm just an apprentice." Clara added sheepishly. "You have control of this power as well as spiritual magic." She unclipped her Umoya that Moira had reluctantly given back at the behest of Gwynne. She held it up, and a blade of wind howled outwards, creating a consistent flow of wind that pushed against them.

Gwynne quickly grabbed the one behind her back and presented it to Clara. Clara's blade descended back, and she clipped it back on to her belt. She grabbed the one Gwynne presented, and then handed it back.

"Why did yours use wind but mine used lightning?" Gwynne asked, inspecting hers. "The other woman, Lady Harwell, used water."

"It depends on the person," Clara replied. "Lightning is the pure form of fire. Fire builds off your rage."

"Rage?" Gwynne said, feeling awkward to have brought it up in the first place.

"That will only work for a limited amount of time," she stated flatly. "You see, every knight has to create their own weapon. They can only create their Umoya when they have mastered all 5 or depending on who you ask, 6 elements, the last one being spirit and, well, blood."

"Blood?" Gwynne asked.

"It's the only time Eri'Dorians use Blood magic," Clara clarified. "The knight must give their own blood as the physical embodiment of their spirit. Besides this one ritual, it's forbidden."

"Why?"

"Because, blood magic doesn't always work the way people intend it to. Sometimes it affects both the target and the giver of blood." Clara replied.

"This one will fail?" Gwynne asked, raising the Umoya.

"Yes, it will work for a while with anyone. But it is connected to the spirit and blood of the knight who created it and, since he's dead, it will stop working sooner rather than later."

"He's dead," Gwynne echoed.

"Both Sentinels that you encountered are dead, Oracle," Clara replied. "They shouldn't have attacked you," she quickly added, lowering her gaze.

"I killed a man," Gwynne muttered. Her face turned red, and she suddenly looked fragile.

"I know," Clara replied. "Killing isn't something we enjoy. But sometimes it's necessary."

"I didn't have control."

"That's what I am here for," Clara replied. "As your seeker, one of my tasks is to help and train you until I pass on and a new seeker takes my place."

"How do you know I will outlive you?" Gwynne asked.

"I will only live to be about 120, if I'm lucky and stay healthy. Oracles live for thousands of years," Clara replied as if it were common knowledge. Gwynne's face paled.

"Why would I live that long?"

"All those who possess magic live longer than those without. Your magic is so powerful that you will live for a *very* long time."

"Oh," Gwynne said looking back down at the Umoya.

"I know it's a lot," Clara said quietly as she placed her hand on her shoulder. "But I'm here to help you." Clara looked up to see that Tyron had stopped pacing and was just watching them. "We need to keep moving," Clara said in the best commanding tone she could muster. "Nya will be searching for you as well as anyone else who wants the Oracle."

"Where do you think we should go?" Gwynne asked.

"Eri'Dor," Clara's reply was met with a scoff from Tyron who rushed towards them.

"Of course," he snapped, wedging himself between them.

"She will be safe there!" Clara snapped back.

"No," Tyron retorted. "The last two times an Eri'Dorian has come in contact with her. They tried to hurt her. I'm not going to allow you to do the same." Clara looked at Gwynne who was being pulled away by Moira.

Tyron had his rifle pointed downward, but when Clara took a step forward, he raised it. He glared at her with his jaw clenched.

"Tyron," Moira said calmly. "We need to go."

"No," Clara interjected. "I cannot allow you to leave without me."

"We're leaving," Tyron retorted. "We should have left you when we had the chance. You and your kind are killers and don't care about anything but your own power."

"I swore to protect her," Clara replied. "If you stand in the way of that. I will have to remove you."

"We've entertained this long enough." Tyron grunted. "We're leaving and you're not going to stop us."

"I can't let you leave without me," Clara repeated. She did her best to stay calm.

"I don't care what you want," Tyron replied. Clara glanced over his shoulder to see that Moira was holding Gwynne, preventing her from walking over.

"I don't want to hurt you, but I will," Clara said with as much confidence as she could muster. It didn't seem to work. Tyron made no move to stand down, stepping forward with the rifle still raised at her head.

She didn't wait for him to decide. She took a step back, raising her hands in surrender. She took one more step and as her back foot hit the ground, she sent a powerful gust of wind from the ground to the sky. Tyron fired but the gust of the wind pushed the muzzle up as she ducked down and charged him.

He repositioned, but she was already upon him. She grabbed the handguard of the rifle and ripped it from his hands. She threw it to the side throwing a ball of fire after it. The fire engulfed the rifle and the grass around it.

Tyron reacted angrily and swung at her. Clara ducked under the first attack and parried the second. He was stronger than she anticipated, and even when she blocked the strike, the strength of his swing knocked her off balance.

She moved backwards trying to give herself distance. Tyron kept closing the gap, and his attacks were unbelievably strong and faster than she expected.

She moved back and forth trying to avoid his strikes. He was relentless and she couldn't avoid all of them. Clara heard Moira and Gwynn shouting for the two of them to stop.

She absorbed another blow that knocked the wind out of her, causing her to stagger backwards. She tried to retreat but wasn't fast enough. He struck her again with a backhand to the face. She bit her tongue and fell to the ground, spitting out blood. He pressed the attack, attempting to knee her in the side. She rolled backwards, avoiding his attack.

She suddenly remembered what Markus had said about Tryxus "Big, strong, powerful swing, lacks stamina." Just as the thought entered her mind, she realized that Tyron was beginning to slow down. He would have short bursts of energy, most likely deriving from his anger.

Eventually her teacher's words rang true. Though this was the son of Tryxus, Tyron fought the same way—powerful, but lacking stamina. Clara focused on her speed and agility, allowing Tyron to tire himself out.

He wasn't tiring out as fast as she wanted, but he was slowing down, which gave her a chance to move out of the way. He would surprise her every so often with a burst of speed. Every blow he landed shot pain through her body.

She ducked under his wide swing and kicked the inside of his leg. He brushed it off and charged forward, pushing her back. She feinted a strike, and when he went to block, she kicked the inside of his leg again. He brushed it off, and the fight continued.

She made sure to avoid any contact. She couldn't allow him to get any real offense started or he would pummel her. She went to use a fire-blast, but decided against it. Beating him in a physical fight was the only way she could get him to respect her. If she used magic, he would just blame his loss on that. Also, not hurting Gwynne's friend was a benefit.

With another burst of energy, he charged. Clara sidestepped his attempt, causing him to stumble forward and crash into the ground. As he pushed himself up, she jumped onto his back, wrapping her arms around his neck. He stood up, lifting her with him.

She squeezed with everything she had while he began to repeatedly elbow her in the side. She was thankful that her armor absorbed most of the impact. He bent forward, throwing her off his back. She managed to flip in midair, landing on her feet. She kicked back, hitting him in the torso, knocking him away.

She followed up the attack, kicking the inside of his leg again. This time it buckled, and he fell to one knee. She slammed her elbow into the side of his face, causing him to stagger. She grabbed the back of his head and slammed his face into her knee. Tyron fell to the ground holding his nose, screaming out in pain.

"We are on the same side, Tyron," she said, breathing heavily. "But if you get in my way again. I will make sure you never get back up." Clara turned and walked towards Gwynne. Moira reluctantly let Gwynne go and then went to check on Tyron.

"We need to go. If you do not want to go to Eri'Dor, then where?" Clara asked, taking deep breaths.

"Dereli," Gwynne replied.

"Dereli?!" Clara repeated. "Why the hell would you want to go there?"

"That's not important, right now," Moira interrupted. "Right now, we need to get out of the open."

"You're right," Clara replied. "We shouldn't use the bus."

"What?" All three of them asked in unison. Tyron was still dusting himself off and wiping the blood from his face. He was glaring daggers into Clara. She did her best to ignore it.

"That massive boat of a vehicle will be easy to track. We need to avoid any roads, and flying isn't much safer. The Order has more than enough vehicles to fly through the air."

"There is a safe haven that Tryxus made in case something ever happened," Moira replied. "We aren't too far, and we could probably walk. It would just take us awhile."

"Well, we are in the middle of nowhere," Tyron groaned.

"Then grab your things, we should go."

"You're gonna help us hide from your own people?" Tyron asked with a scowl.

"Yes," Clara replied. "If her highness does not wish to be taken there, then so be it."

"Stop calling me that," Gwynne said in more of a request than a command.

"Why would you let her go wherever she wants if you keep saying we need to go to Eri'Dor?" Tyron asked Clara.

"Because her place is with the Eri'Dorian Order. But I cannot force her to choose that. She must choose it on her own,"

Clara replied, growing annoyed with Tyron. "Now get your things." She watched Gwynne who dropped her gaze to the ground. "Your...Gwynne, you never have to avert your gaze. When you realize your true power. Kings will kneel to *you*."

CHAPTER 14

Broken Covenant

Nya took another deep breath as she stared at a map, hoping that something would pop out at her as to where the oracle could have disappeared to. She could hear Konan pacing behind her, grunting and muttering under his breath.

Even if they weren't in a small tavern room, and he was a few steps away from her, she would have heard him stomping and breathing heavily.

"Can you stop that?" she asked without looking up.

"Can you find her?" he snapped back. He had stopped pacing but was still breathing heavily. "I don't understand how you lost her," He added as he began to pace again.

"Well, I wasn't exactly expecting Arilynn to show up," Nya replied inattentively, still looking at the map. "I don't know where they are."

"Then figure it out," he replied angrily. She turned to face him. He wasn't paying attention to her.

"It's not like I just sniff her out like a dog," Nya said sarcastically. He glared at her. She tensed up, realizing she had angered him. She immediately straightened her posture and lowered her gaze to the ground. He pushed up against her and then gently lifted her chin so that their eyes matched. He stared at her and then with a flash of anger he struck her with the back of his hand.

"Watch your tone when speaking to me," he said in a whisper.

The force of the slap knocked her off balance, but she managed to stay upright. He glared at her for a moment longer. He took a loud deep breath and turned away as he began to pace again.

The sting of the slap lingered on her face for a while. She clenched her fists, and realized she was holding her breath. She let out a long, controlled sigh, relaxing her hands. She could feel her magic in her hands waiting to attack.

She was sure she could catch him off-guard here. It would be so easy to kill him. But she knew she could never do it. He had saved her life—brought her into his world and given her a new reason to live. He had given her so much that she felt guilty every time she made him angry.

"I still don't know how to find her, Konan," she said trying to sound normal though her voice wavered.

"There are no other places they would go to hide?" he asked, walking back towards the map.

"None that I know of," Nya replied, tensing up as he approached her. "I only helped with the first one; back then, it was a bunker for the defectors. Everything he has done since then, I have not been a part of."

"Then we will need to find out and be quick about it," he replied, looking up at her. She could still see the anger in his eyes. His jaw was clenched as he took another deep breath.

"We could also just follow the knights," Nya interjected timidly. "As long as they don't find her, we're okay. They have more resources than we do, so it is likely they will find her first."

"I guess," he muttered, walking over to the map.

"I can go back to the compound and track them down. They won't be trying to hide like the Oracle," she stated, taking a step to the side to keep her distance. She did her best not act nervously around him. It would only make him angrier.

"And what will I do?" he growled. "Wait here like a lap dog?!" he yelled, forcing her to jump. She quickly controlled her impulse to move away further.

"No," she replied quickly. She forced a smile so that he wouldn't see that he had startled her. She reached out to him trying to ignore the stubborn sting on her face. "You can do what you're best at. Find those who know information and get it." She pressed herself against him and gently placed her hand on the side of his face. He kissed her and then lifted his head letting out a loud sigh.

"You're right, that could work," he said looking down, kissing her again. "I'll get more men, and you will follow the knights. If I'm as good as you think I am, we should meet at some point."

"Exactly," she said, pulling away. "I should go. They would have left the compound by now."

"Hey," he said, pulling her back. He caressed the side of her face that he had struck. He looked at her, and for a moment, she thought he was going to apologize.

"Be careful," he said, pulling away and turning back to the map. "Oh," he called out. "If something happens don't kill the old man."

"Markus?" she asked, confused.

"Yes, he's mine." he declared without looking up. Nya made no reply as she left the room.

She climbed down the rickety wooden stairs and out the main door, ignoring the innkeeper. She knew Konan was never going to pay for the room and would most likely just threaten him. She didn't want to see who it was. It was easier to ignore that way. Guilt was not something she could afford to feel.

She climbed back on to a hover-bike from one of Konan's fallen men. It wasn't hers, but it would get the job done. She ignited the engine, and without hesitation, raced back towards the compound as fast as the bike would allow her to go.

When she arrived at the compound, she was surprised to see it had been left untouched after their initial attack. She'd assumed the knights or the Clovi would be doing clean up as was custom for any damage caused during a conflict, but she could see that the doors were still mangled and debris left where it had fallen just days before.

She entered through the mangled doors and was even more surprised to see that there were still people inside. They all stopped what they were doing to look up at her. After they decided she wasn't an immediate threat, they continued doing whatever they were doing—most of them were packing and overloading their bags. Others were tending to the wounded or the dead, moving the bodies to one side of the large room.

Nya walked toward the largest group of people who dispersed as she approached, rushing to get away from her. She let out an aggravated sigh and turned to see a heavyset woman chuckling to herself as she sat on a large piece of broken wall.

"What?" Nya snapped.

"They don't like you," she replied.

"And I care, why?" Nya replied, turning to walk away.

"Cause' you're looking for the girl. Just like that Eri'Dorian bitch," the woman said with a wry smile.

"Do you know where they went?" Nya asked, softening her voice.

"Yes," she replied with a smirk.

"Are you going to tell me?"

"Perhaps," the woman said with a laugh. "What's in it for me?" Her smirk grew into a grin making her round cheeks turn red.

"I don't kill you," Nya replied sharply. The woman's smile faded but returned just as quickly.

"Nah, you won't kill me," she said confidently. "You won't know if I told you the truth, and if you kill me, you'll never know the truth."

"I could just take you with me." Nya replied, crossing her arms.

The woman tensed and then laughed shaking her head. "Nah, I am too heavy for your little bike over there."

"There are other people here that I can ask," Nya countered.

"They don't know," she replied. "I was the one who talked to them. No one else."

"What do you want, then?" Nya asked, becoming irritated.

"Well, I *am* pretty broke."

"I don't have money, and if you keep this up, I won't have any patience either."

"Well you gotta give me something." She cackled. Nya grew tired of the banter summoning a jagged piece of ice and threw it. The ice slammed into the wall next to the woman's head.

The woman screamed, falling backwards off the debris she was perched on. She let out a wail as she rolled around on the ground, trying to stand up. She began coughing uncontrollably as Nya approached.

"If you don't tell me what I need to know I will kill everyone here and *then* you."

"All right, all right!" the woman croaked as she managed to climb to her feet. "I was just trying to enjoy having the power for once," she said dusting herself off. "I told them about the three other compounds."

"Tell me," Nya demanded.

"Don't need to because I know which one they were going to." She smiled proudly. "Tryxus told me. It's not too far from here, and I told that Eri'Dorian bitch the wrong compound," she said with an expression of pride. "By the time she finds out, I will be long gone from here," she cackled with self-enjoyment.

"What about the other two?"

"The other two aren't even built. Tryxus got lazy and only left the one for an emergency."

"Why should I trust you?" Nya asked, creating another dagger of ice.

"Because," she began, ignoring the dagger. "I reckon you're after the same thing the knights are, and you're clearly not one of them. Besides, you and your friends are pretty terrifying," she said looking behind Nya.

"Friends?" Nya asked, looking behind her. She felt her heart jump and her stomach lurch downward. There were three men in black suits with black helmets covering their heads with black leather gloves over their hands. They stood in front of the hangar doors.

The one in the middle removed his helmet as he approached, revealing a pale skinned man with shaggy blonde hair and black, dead eyes. He winced at the sunlight that seeped through the wreckage of the doors.

"Hello," he said in a sultry voice as his black eyes turned to a shade of blue. Nya stared at him and she cursed to herself as she remembered she had lost her dagger hilts on the transport fighting the Oracle. She took a step back so that she was standing next to the heavyset woman.

"They aren't your friends, are they?" the woman asked meekly, backing up slowly. The other people there glanced between the three men and Nya.

"No," Nya replied in a hushed tone.

"We're here for the Oracle," the man announced, scanning the room and making sure to look everyone in the eye. "Now, there are two ways we can go about this. You can tell us what we want, and we leave. Or you don't. I'll let you figure out what happens if you don't." He smiled, which somehow made him more terrifying.

"You would violate the covenant?" Nya asked.

"The covenant isn't a concern for us anymore," His smile faded. Nya nodded her head and looked to the woman next to her.

"I'm sorry," she told the woman as she cut the woman's throat with a blade of ice. "I can't risk you telling them." The woman's eyes bulged as she grabbed at her throat, trying to breathe. Nya sent a blast of ice at the three men as the woman collapsed to the ground in a puddle of her own blood.

"Run!" she screamed to the room. She didn't care for them; she needed them to create a distraction, giving her a chance to get lost in the chaos. The three vampires roared out, pushing through the ice as Nya turned and ran down the corridor behind her. She knew she would never be able to outrun three vampires. She certainly wasn't going to be able to fight all three of them off. One would be challenging enough, even more so without her daggers.

She darted down the first corner and then the next and kept running. She could hear screaming and shouting behind her and quickened her pace doing, her best to get as much distance as she could. It didn't take long for the trio to start chasing her. She could hear their footsteps, and they were beginning to gain on her.

She was in a full sprint now. She did her best to keep her breath under control. She jumped over random debris scattered throughout the halls. Growls behind her made her run harder. She darted down another corner, but was pulled violently back.

She was thrown backwards into the metal wall, slumping to the ground. Before her attacker could reach down to grab her, she sent a bolt of lightning into his chest. He flew back down the hall she had just tried to run down. She glanced over to see the other two were rushing towards her. She slammed her hand into the ground and cried out as she pulled the metal from the walls, creating another wall in front of her. They slammed into the makeshift barrier, denting it, and began screaming while they clawed through.

Nya willed herself up, only to be slammed back into the wall by the first vampire to reach her. He was still in his helmet, but it was partly melted, showing the right side of his face. He grabbed her by the throat, lifting her off the ground with ease, pressing her against the wall.

She kicked and punched, hitting him in the torso and arms. It had little effect as he tightened his grip. She threw another lightning bolt at his head. He ducked out of the way. The bolt crashed into the ground.

She created a gust of wind that was strong enough to separate them. She fell to the ground and then used another ice blast that froze him in place. The other two were nearly through her makeshift wall, snarling angrily.

Nya turned the only way she could. She ran down the familiar corridor and stopped when she saw Tryxus' body on the ground. She took a deep breath, trying to bear the smell. She passed his body, but stopped again when she saw his Umoya sitting on the ground. She used a gust of wind to move the hilt to her hand, manipulating it so it appeared as a sword. The blade took a moment to form, showing that it was dying. She cursed loudly. It would have to be enough.

She continued running down the hall, doing her best not to look back. She could see the door that she had used the day of the attack. Outside she could see the front end of her hover-bike, left behind during the first assault. She'd convinced herself that the bike had been destroyed, yet there it was, waiting to save her once again.

She was beginning to tire, and her legs burned as she ran. Jumping into the air, she sent a gust of wind behind her that accelerated her forward. She finally dared to peek back and could see the trio were closing in on her. The leader of the trio swiped, catching her leg. Nya crashed onto the ground, rolling until she hit the hallway wall. She let out a groan as she pushed herself up, listening to the footsteps approach her. She pressed herself against the wall looking up at her attacker.

The leader grabbed her by the hair, torquing her head up and leaning forward so that their faces nearly touched. He let out a guttural growl as his mouth opened showing his now jagged teeth. She attempted to pull away, but he was too strong. He lifted her off the ground by her hair and wrapped his other hand around her throat. She struck him across the face with a palm full of ice. He shouted as the ice cut into his cheek. He leaned forward growling as his face began to heal itself.

"I'm going to enjoy this," he sneered. "Tell me what she told you," he said in a hateful whisper in her ear before licking the side of her face down to her neck.

He loosened his grip on her throat just enough for her to cough and breathe. She took in another deep breath and attempted to project another lightning bolt. He grabbed her wrist and broke her forearm with a violent twist.

Nya screamed, but her screams were drowned out by a horrific howling that echoed throughout the halls.

The trio froze, listening to the howling. Nya took the brief distraction and summoned another bolt of lightning with her uninjured arm. The blast hit the leader in the face, forcing him to let go of her as he was knocked backwards. She fell to the ground and created a gust of wind that propelled her forward. She slammed into her bike, powered it on and flung herself off the cliff.

She could hear the frustrated shouting from the trio as she plummeted towards the ground. She grabbed the handlebar and reared it up and accelerated with everything it had. She shot upwards and flew away without looking back.

~~~~

The leader of the trio growled as he watched his prey disappear into the sky. He took a step back inside, turning to see two
~~~~

large, brown wolves standing at the end of the hall. They were dressed in metallic armor that covered their shoulders, torso and forearms.

He sneered at the sight of them as he crouched down, his two companions growled baring their teeth. There was a moment of silence and stillness between the two races. As instinct took over, they lunged towards each other, reigniting their primordial war.

CHAPTER 15

Clovi King

It wasn't long before Jaxon began to question his reasoning of going to Eri'Dor. He hated it there. He wasn't fond of the high council either and considered most of them out of touch with what was actually happening in the real world. They were simply behind the times and refused to acknowledge their lack of understanding.

The members he did respect didn't have enough power to do much. He found it easier to just avoid the council all together as he often disagreed with their rulings and their reasoning behind them.

It was luck that he found a temple with a bar, and a Clovi he knew. Temples worked as both a place for food and rest as well as a portal home. He took one last drink of his whiskey, placing the glass on the bar. The bartender picked the glass up and went to refill but stopped when Jaxon motioned him not to. The man was dressed in a dingy tan tunic with a dark brown belt wrapped around his waist. He was in his early forties. He had a shined bald spot that was surrounded by the horseshoe of hair that covered the back and sides of his head.

"Thank you, Anderson," Jaxon said. He would have paid him, but Clovi had no need for money. They were given everything they needed. Everything outside of that was often condemned. They were held to the same standard as all knights, though they were treated far worse, and things a knight could get away with, a Clovi could not.

Instead, Jaxon gave him a golden Eri'Dorian coin. Which to many was considered worth more than money.

Eri'Dorian coins were a sign that a Clovi had helped or served a knight of the Order faithfully. The coin represented a favor of sorts. Anyone carrying a coin could approach a knight and ask for help. It was an ancient tradition that involved everyday citizens, though it had lost most of its meaning in the last few hundred years. Especially when people began to counterfeit the coins asking for ridiculous deeds to be done in the name of tradition. Among knights, the tradition continued.

Clovi were the men and women who attempted to become knights of the Eri'Dorian Order but failed to do so. Their powers were stripped with a binding spell, and they had a choice; to leave and possibly go home or to stay and serve the Order. Since most children given to the Order were abandoned or given up at such a young age, they know nothing of where they're from, and most chose to stay as a result. They were given food, shelter, clothes—the only thing they were rarely given was respect.

Anderson graciously accepted the coin, bowing his head. "Thank you, Jaxon, but I don't think giving you a drink is worth a coin such as this," he said, looking at the coin.

"I've known you a long time, Anderson," Jaxon replied. "You have always been good to me."

"It's my job, sir," he replied sheepishly.

"Jaxon," he corrected. It was uncommon for a Clovi to address a knight by their first name, especially a Lord Knight such as Jaxon, but Jaxon insisted that he just be called by his name. He never felt any better than those around him.

"Keep it," Jaxon replied, standing up. "You never know when you'll need a favor."

"Okay," Anderson replied with a chuckle. He tucked it into his pocket and began cleaning the bar. Jaxon glanced around to see other knights were there. Most he didn't recognize, and even if he had, he wouldn't have bothered to talk to any of them. He sauntered over to the shift-gate located at the back of the Temple. He hesitated before he approached the magical portal that would take him to Eri'Dor, scanning the room. Anderson had moved on from cleaning the bar to cleaning one of the many tables.

One of the knights scoffed at Anderson, shaking their head as he pushed passed him, most likely to go to their room. Anderson glanced up, meeting Jaxon's gaze, and shook his head, signaling for Jaxon not to get involved. Jaxon begrudgingly nodded his head and turned back to the shift-gate.

The shift-gate itself looked like any other room. The walls were made of dark brownstone and the floor had an engraved five-pointed star with a circle in the center that both separated and connected the points of the star. Each point had a different type of gem representing its element—a blazing amber for fire, polished obsidian for earth, moonstone for water, sapphire for air and finally shined steel for metal. The circle itself was made of carved diamond. The stones themselves held value, but it was what they did when combined with magic that made them reach their true potential.

On the wall directly next to the entrance was a bronze plate with a smaller formation of the stones. Jaxon pressed his hand against it and took a deep breath, closing his eyes. He could feel the power resonate in his hand and suddenly he was disoriented. It was a common side-effect that came with using the shift-gates. The burst of magical energy and sudden change of location would make anyone feel at least a little dizzy.

He stumbled forward keeping his hand on the bronze plate to hold himself up. He shook his head, looking up to see that he had reached the Great Valemìr Temple of Eri'Dor. He took another moment to gather himself. When he felt well enough, he stepped out entering the grand hall.

The lights above illuminated everything within sight, reflecting off the golden walls. The floor had another 5-pointed star. The gems at each point were as large as Jaxon's torso with the diamond in the center taking up most of the floor.

Jaxon looked around to see more than a hundred doors with golden arches. People moved in and out of the rooms. There were ten Sentinels posted strategically so that they could react to any part of the room in as little time as possible. Even though the shift-gates were usually only used by knights, they were still a gateway to the outside world.

Jaxon stepped forward and began walking across the massive star. He couldn't remember the last time he'd been to Eri'Dor. It didn't matter how many times he walked inside the Great Temple. He was always amazed by its beauty.

The detail in the architecture alone was enough to keep anyone enthralled for hours. The stone arches were carved and sculpted with incredible precision. Each wall was decorated with pieces of old art. The one that caught Jaxon's attention the most was the depiction of Ellyanna, the last Oracle.

He studied it for a moment. She was always depicted as young and beautiful. She stood in the center of a field with a river directly behind her that flowed away from her. On one side of the painting, the sky was pale blue with white birds flying towards the sun. On the opposite side of her, the sky was dark and gray with a looming storm approaching. Jaxon had never noticed how sad the young girl looked in the painting. Her painted green eyes staring directly at him, her hand raised, reaching out.

He looked away shaking his head, still trying to recapture his bearings. Using the shift-gate was disorienting and he couldn't remember the last time he used one.

He glanced back to see the poor Clovi who were designated to clean up the grand hall after those who couldn't handle the transport and vomited on the marble floors.

"Jaxon Harwell." Jaxon let out a sigh when he heard his name from a woman. He turned and smiled. Approaching, was a woman with dark brown hair and a pale complexion. She had black rimmed glasses and was dressed in a white dress with a deep blue sash that went over her slight bust, signifying that she was a Scholar within the Order.

"Ama," he said, embracing her. "It's been too long."

"I agree," she replied with a smile. "I'm surprised to see you without your better half," she said, looking around.

"She's not here," Jaxon said. "She's currently looking for the Oracle."

"Oh, yes, of course."

"Trust me, if I didn't have to be here. I wouldn't be," Jaxon said, eying one of the Sentinels who was making their way towards them.

"You know you *do* have friends here," Ama teased. "You don't always have to run off."

"Tell me, Ama," Jaxon said, ignoring her statement. "How is everyone reacting to the return of the Oracle?"

Her smile faded. She began nervously stammering as she went to respond. She cupped her hands in front of her and before she could answer the Sentinel interrupted.

"Your weapon, my lord," the Sentinel stated through his black helmet.

"I'm aware of the laws, Sentinel." Jaxon replied dismissively. He turned his attention back to Ama, but she was gone.

"My lord," the Sentinel persisted.

"What did I just say?" Jaxon grumbled. He had never understood the law that only Sentinels were allowed to be armed. Everyone else, even a Warden such as himself, couldn't keep his Umoya or any other type of weapon on him. Despite the fact that they could manipulate the elements, swords and guns, even magic, were strictly forbidden. The only exception was for scholarly reasons in designated training areas within the academy.

The Sentinel followed Jaxon as he approached a very large desk that sat at the center of the only entrance and exit of the grand hall and shift-gates.

At the desk was a heavyset man with dark russet brown skin similar to Jaxon's, his black hair shaved close to his head. He was facing away so that Jaxon could only see his back and the rolls of his neck.

"Place your weapon on the counter and fill out the form," he said offhanded without turning around.

"Really?" Jaxon asked. When the man heard his voice, he swiveled in his chair so fast that he almost spun around twice.

"Jaxon!" he bellowed. He scooted forward squinting his eyes. "Damn, I can't believe it's actually you!" He stood up from his chair and stepped down and around his large desk. He took Jaxon's hand and shook it vigorously. He regarded the Sentinel who stood by patiently. "They're really cracking down on the whole 'no weapon' thing," he whispered loudly.

Jaxon chuckled, shaking his head. "It's fine, Olnic." Jaxon replied, unclipping his Umoya. He handed the silver hilt to Olnic who grabbed it gingerly and waddled back to his desk.

"I'll need the dagger too," he said without looking up as he began filling out paperwork. Jaxon cocked his head and smirked.

"I know how you and your girl work. She has one, you have the other. Some kind of twisted love thing," he said, waving his hand for Jaxon to place the dagger on the desk.

Jaxon let out a chuckle, grabbing the smooth hilt of the dagger from behind his back underneath the cape of his surcoat. The blade had a slight curve and was single edged. The hilt was pale blue in color and had the same slight curve in the opposite direction. The pommel had silver markings in the Soferian language.

"You know 'The 'twisted love thing' that you're referring to has nothing to do with love. It's actually an Eri'Dorian tradition," Jaxon stated. "Knights give or trade their weapons for a period of time. It's supposed to show deep trust and faith. It's called Credina."

"Thanks for the history lesson, professor," Olnic said with a laugh. "I know what Credina is. I still need the dagger."

"I'll be sure to let Ari know you made me give it up."

"She gives hers up all the time," Olnic replied with another laugh. "You know how she is with the rules."

"Trust me, I do," Jaxon replied, shaking his head. "She's always making me follow them," he added sizing up the Sentinel who made it a point to look away.

Jaxon regarded the dagger for the moment it took Olnic to grab it. He and Arilynn had performed Credina, but with twin daggers. They were made in opposite fashion—one represented tranquility and compassion while the other represented power and rage.

Jaxon carried tranquility and compassion as he was known for his temper and his power while Arilynn carried rage and power because she was known for her control. She had chosen the dagger in hopes to learn to let go of that constant need of control.

It was a private agreement between the two of them and a gift from the High Queen of *Elivenii*—Sedella Ellenstar, Arilynn's mother. Once it was discovered, everyone was sure to make a comment whenever it came up.

Jaxon watched as Olnic placed both of his weapons into an old wooden chest with the same 5-pointed star engraved into a golden clasp. He slammed the top down, closing the chest, and after a moment, there was a small flash. When he opened it back up, it was empty.

The chest was enchanted to send whatever was inside of it to another chest. In this case, it was sent to the armory that would place his weapons in a specific spot designated by his name and the form he had filled out.

The council assured everyone that this was secure, though Jaxon and many others were not convinced. They did not have much of a choice in the decision, but it was the standard procedure for all weapons.

"Thank you, my lord," the Sentinel said before he stepped away. Jaxon nodded his head and looked back to Olnic who smiled, stretching out his hand for another handshake.

Jaxon obliged, and they spoke briefly about the Temple and how everything was being run. Olnic had his normal list of complaints about the knights bullying him and the other Clovi. Olnic also told him that everyone had been acting very differently since the return of the Oracle. He said there was a tension in the air, as if everyone was waiting for something to happen. This made Jaxon think about Ama and her reaction when he asked her about it. He took a quick look around hoping that somehow he would see her again but had no such luck.

After a few minutes of catching up, Jaxon took his leave and allowed Olnic to get back to his duties. Jaxon exited the grand hall, and even with its beauty, it was nothing compared to the actual temple.

The ceilings towered overhead, all of them decorated with various pieces of art. The first ceiling showed the image of Philos, the ancient King of the Gods. His long wispy white hair draped down his shoulders and blended into his white beard that stretched down to his waist. Behind him, a massive owl sat perched on a large oak tree.

Unlike the Oracle's painting, Philos was surrounded by pale blue clear skies. His eyes were painted gold, and his expression was stern as it stared down at the passing knights who paid no attention to the piece of art.

Each room had a beautiful archway as the entrance. The massive pillars were made of white granite with golden rings wrapping themselves around the base of the pillar all the way to the top. The floor was made with shined marble that reflected the light from overhead.

The temple served more than just as a meeting place. It was the hub of the city, some considered the City of Valemìr all of Eri'Dor, and in many ways, they would be right as there was very little outside of the Grand Temple.

The temple was the center of the city. Outside the temple you would see what most people would think looked like a normal city. Any knight or person who lived here knew better.

Schools and training grounds made up most of Valemìr. Beyond that were the barracks where many would stay. Especially those who never left.

Knights were not permitted to buy or inherit land. Every so often, the council would allow certain knights to take a plot of land to build their own home on. This was typically reserved for the highest-ranking members of the order and was often given when the knight was nearing the age of passing. Jaxon considered the gesture a sham and only done to give the false pretense that the council cared.

Jaxon continued his walk down the main hallway. He peered through the colorful stained-glass windows on the bridge he was crossing. He could see the white rooftops of the buildings and could even hear the shouting of cadences and instructions being screamed at the combat recruits.

His mind began to race through all the memories he had of this place. Very few of them were pleasant, making him want to leave sooner rather than later. He continued, doing his best to ignore the shouting and force the memories from his thoughts. He eventually made it to where he wanted to be. He found the traveling rooms that the temple would provide for those who did not have a barracks room. Jaxon was sure he had a room somewhere, but he didn't care to find it, this would do. He couldn't remember the last time he had taken a warm shower. When chasing after a wild wolf pup, finding warm places and hot showers was a rarity.

After his shower, he shaved his beard just as his wife always preferred it. He brushed his long black hair to the sides and stared at his in front of the mirror. Even though he was forty-five years old, being clean shaven made him feel like he was a little boy again. His Dru'Ny heritage and magical connection would allow him to live to well over four-hundred years of age if he died of natural causes. Though he had accepted a long time ago that he would never reach old age.

He looked down at his wide chest, the left side was scarred with a burn mark that stretched across to his side. On his abdomen he had 4 distinct claw marks that stretched from the middle of his stomach just above his belly button to his right oblique. On the other side, he had a scar from when he had been betrayed by a friend and stabbed between the ribs. The rest of his scars were faded, or he couldn't remember where they came from.

His left arm was completely covered in a ritualistic tattoo of his Dru'Ny heritage. It was in the image of a *Dra'thyron, m*assive, bear-like creatures that roam the Dru'Ny realm, *Manu.* Due to their appearance, they were often called *K'waado bears,* which loosely translates to 'angry bear'.

The tattoo resembled the animal well enough. It had a large mane around its thick neck. White stripes spread all over its body. A thick bushy tail with rings starting from the tip of the tail until reaching its hindquarters. It stood on its hind legs, its mouth open in a roar, and its pointed ears perked forward. The large arms and paws stretched out in an attacking motion.

Many years ago, he went searching for his father and found that he was a drunkard and banished chieftain. But, the tribe itself had accepted him with open arms and he had been celebrated and given the title *Tso Weda,* which to them was Great Bear or Strength. Jaxon wasn't sure on the exact translation, but he didn't think it mattered as the Dra'thyron was renowned for its strength in their culture.

It was the brand on his right forearm that always caught his attention. Every time he saw it, he could remember the pain that came with it. That brand itself was smaller than the size of his palm.

He could remember the day he had been branded. He and other hopeful students were considered too difficult to train. They seared his arm with the sigil of the Clovi, the black ant.

Now that he was so much bigger than when he was nine, the brand was distorted and barely resembled anything close to an ant. He knew what it was and anyone who saw it did as well. His stare lingered for a moment longer reminding him on why he never felt truly at home here.

He was a Clovi, and despite breaking through his binding spell and becoming a great knight in his own right, he always felt a kinship to the other Clovi. Other knights, especially the elders, still considered him an outsider.

He got dressed but decided against his usual armor. Instead he wore a dark blue sleeveless tunic with a black leather belt wrapped around his waist over black leather pants. He tied his hair back into a loose ponytail, letting it drape between his shoulder blades.

He made sure to grab his bracers to cover up his forearms, ensuring the brand on his right arm wouldn't be seen.

Jaxon made his way down the main hall; every cross section seemed to spiral off into multiple directions. Despite the halls being crowded, he never stopped moving. Everyone from the students to other knights would all simply step out of his way.

He was used to the stares and the quiet whispers as he passed them. He never cared to hear what they said; he knew it was either false or hateful. He would walk, and they would move. It was something he had grown accustomed to, and whenever it was disrupted, he was always taken aback. Fortunately for him, today everyone moved, and it allowed him to get to the main elevator to the council chamber that much faster.

The elevator had gold doors that contrasted with the silver walls that surrounded them. The doors were flanked by two Sentinels.

There were six towers within the Great Temple of Valemìr, each connected to the council chamber suspended in the center. They were all interconnected by strong, magically strengthened suspension bridges and arches and were enclosed in fortified glass windows that allowed the person walking to see out and see the landscape of the *Eri'Dor*.

The sun was in the middle of its descent as he made his way down the main bridge. The city lights were beginning to turn on. The landscape of the outer area was hilly with fields of flowers interrupting their pattern.

Jaxon sauntered down the bridge until he reached the doors to the chamber. They were closed which was uncommon and most likely meant they were in the middle of a meeting or hearing they wanted no one to be a part of.

The two Sentinel guards stepped forward to intercept him. The smaller of the two stopped and took a step back nodding his head to the other, who begrudgingly agreed. "Welcome back, Jaxon," he said, nodding his head hello.

"Thanks," Jaxon said offhandedly as he passed. He wasn't sure who it was, and it didn't really matter much to him.

The doors opened to a spiral staircase that he climbed up until he was at a second door made of solid dark redwood. In front of this door was one last Sentinel that stepped forward.

"No visitors at this time," the Sentinel said automatically. "Wait, Jaxon?" he said, quickly removing his helm showing a round headed bald man with a full beard and brown eyes. He towered over Jaxon with broad shoulders and a wide base.

"Hello, Rayland," Jaxon said with a smile. "Guarding the council now?"

"Better than guarding that damn academy," he said with a loud laugh that he quickly moved to silence by covering his mouth. "But really. They said no visitors," Rayland said, trying not to smile.

"It's important, friend."

"Isn't it always?" he asked, crossing his arms over his chest. "You're gonna get me yelled at," he commented as he stepped aside, shaking his head.

"I'll be sure to let them know you put up a fight," Jaxon said as he walked in.

There were seven seats in total with the center chair placed on a thick slab of granite that raised it just slightly above the rest. The room had a domed ceiling and the walls were made of the same glass that protected the bridges, which allowed the light to come in from the descending sunlight. There were electric lights that hung around the circular room with old torches that remained unlit. The floor was polished black marble with the Symbol of Valemìr in the center of the room.

The conversation stopped abruptly as the council members looked over at Jaxon who stood in the doorway. He acknowledged each of the six members. Half of the members stared at him with either blank or annoyed expressions and the other half seemed joyed that he was there.

When he was in the center of the room, he clasped his hands behind his back and bowed his head to the man sitting in the center chair.

"We need to talk," Jaxon said, his voice echoing in the chamber.

Jaxon spent the next few minutes explaining everything that he had learned from Novak and how he had managed to make himself the Alpha over all the packs.

He made sure to look at each member as he spoke. Each member sat in their own chair, which were more like thrones with specific decorations chosen by the owner of the seat. Jaxon glanced at the only empty seat, which belonged to Markus Troyan, before his attention went back to the center chair.

Lorrennius Zuul sat rigidly with his arms laying flat on his thighs. He was dressed in a large black robe that was adorned with small sigils embroidered down the sides representing each of the classes within the Order.

Lorrennius was the Commandant of the Order. He was also considered the face of the Order. He was the one who spoke to the other leaders around the world and other realms as their elected leader. Ultimately, if a decision needed to be made, it would always fall upon him to make it.

"How do you know that Novak is the Alpha of the other Alphas?" Andaar Maxwell asked, leaning forward stroking his long graying goatee.

Andaar was the High Lord of the Rangers. He had a slim build and wore a dark green cloak that draped over his shoulders.

Jaxon could still see the Ranger sigil on the right side of his cloak—hawk eyes with the bow and arrow placed above them. His long, gray hair was pulled back behind his ears with a single braid. He glared at Jaxon with his unblinking, dark blue eyes. Andaar was known for his sour attitude and sharp tongue. He and Jaxon had never seen eye to eye.

"When he spoke, the other Alphas in attendance listened, and when he gave them commands, they followed."

"So, you don't know," Andaar replied. "You're speculating."

"What I *do* know," Jaxon countered, turning away from Andaar, "is that he told me himself that he is amassing the packs. There were members from other packs, and they weren't fighting each other. This is dangerous and is reminiscent from before the Covenant.

"You spoke to Balthazar as well, did you not?" Robert Quin asked. Jaxon turned to Robert and nodded. Jaxon admired Robert. He was the High Lord of the Scholar class.

Robert had light brown skin and a round face. He wore thin rimmed glasses that perched at the bottom of his bulbous nose. He was a stocky man with a broad back. His head was mostly bald except for the horseshoe of black hair that was neatly combed. He wore a silver robe with a sigil of the owl for his class.

"I did," Jaxon replied. "He denies any involvement, but Novak is convinced the attacks were carried out by a vampire."

"This isn't good," Robert commented.

"No, and with the added allure of the Oracle, we are in a very dangerous place," Jaxon stated looking back to Lorrennius.

"What about the Oracle?" Lorrennius asked.

"Balthazar in a very roundabout way told me they wouldn't hesitate to take the Oracle if the opportunity presented itself."

"That would be against the Covenant," High Lady Zora Ezell stated flatly. Zora represented the Healers of the order. Despite her small stature and slight build, she was known for her tough demeanor. Her jet-black hair was pulled back so tightly it pulled the skin of her face back. She wore a white robe with a golden dove brooch clasped just below her collar.

"He doesn't care," Jaxon replied. "They're willing to risk punishment if they can get their hands on the power of the Oracle. And if they do, could we really stop them?" The question lingered in the air for a moment. It was something that no one really wanted to think about.

Lady Ethyia Jalice broke the silence by clearing her throat. Ethyia was a Dru'Ny and the largest in the chamber. She stood out among the others with her immense size and because she was wearing her Sentinel armor. The armor was similar to all of the other Sentinels except that hers had red accents in the abdomen and shoulders. Her breastplate had a decorative bullhead that was the sigil of the Sentinel class. The horns stretched to her shoulders where a deep red cape was clasped on.

She was the High Lord of the Sentinels and the youngest member of the council. She was appointed at twenty-one years of age, holding the position and title for the last fifteen years with no dispute.

"This is concerning," she said in a soft voice that seemed peculiar coming from her large form. Her pale blue eyes contrasted against her umber colored skin. She was bald with a shined dome. "We cannot afford to go to war with either one of them right now. Let alone both."

"We won't," Lorrennius said, taking over the conversation as he stood. "The priority right now is Novak and his followers. Arilynn and her team are closing in on the Oracle as we speak. It won't take them long to bring her back here." He turned to Jaxon and approached him.

"You will go after Novak and bring him here. He will need to be punished for his violation of the Covenant."

"I don't think he's going to just take my hand and follow me back here," Jaxon replied.

"No, I don't think he will," Lorrennius agreed. "That is why I have decided that Lady Jalice will go with you as well as Lord Kalix

Torin." Jaxon couldn't help but let out a sigh of disdain when he heard the name.

"What about Balthazar and the alleged attacks?"

"Balthazar and his…people…haven't been seen since your little conversation," Andaar replied accusingly. "The Rangers out there have no trace of him."

"Perhaps he is the one we should be going after then?" Jaxon asked. "We know where Novak is, he won't be hard to find."

"Why don't you let the council decide these matters and you just do what you're told," Andaar retorted. There was a moment of tension until Ethyia broke it again by standing up and announcing she would leave with Jaxon.

Ethyia ushered Jaxon out of the chamber with a gentle hand. She towered over him standing nearly ten feet tall. Her heavy footsteps echoed in the bridge and each Sentinel they passed gave her a salute.

"Damn, Jaxon," she said as they entered the elevator after walking the bridge in silence. "He really doesn't like you."

"The feeling is mutual," Jaxon replied with a deep breath.

"I've missed you!" she said with a loud laugh, embracing him in a tight hug. She nearly lifted him off the ground. He laughed and returned the embrace. "You need to come around more often," she said as the elevator doors opened.

"I hate it here," Jaxon replied flatly as he stepped out of the elevator.

"I know," she replied solemnly. "But there are some of us who would consider you a friend, and we do miss having you around."

The statement sent a wave of guilt over Jaxon and reminded him of Ama. He nodded, placing his hand on her shoulder. "I've missed you too," he said quietly.

"Don't get all soft on me," she said with a laugh, shrugging his hand off. "Go get your armor, and I will meet you down here. I need to get a few things myself." With that she turned walking off.

He looked ahead and saw all the people walking by. Most would acknowledge and greet her, while the rest would awkwardly look at him before scurrying off.

He made sure to hurry to get his belongings and climb back into his armor. He wasn't sure why he even bothered changing out of it. He inspected the scratches and marks before placing his surcoat over it. When he was ready, he rushed to find Ethyia. When he couldn't locate her, he waited. He never felt comfortable here. He had been brought here when he was just nine years old. His time within the temple was short lived, and most of that time he was treated poorly due to his designation as a Clovi.

Thoughts of the other students who ridiculed and excluded him entered his mind. All but his brother Lionicles and Arilynn. It would be another two years before he was reinstated by the council and given to Markus Troyan as an apprentice. Despite how long ago that had been and how apologetic those who had wronged him were, he never forgot those feelings. He never forgot the loneliness created by those who now call him brother.

"You *really* need to come back more." Ethyia said breaking his train of thought."

"I'll try," he replied dryly.

"I'm sure many people would enjoy that," she said in reply. "Not just the Clovi either."

"They're not bad people."

"I never said they were," she replied sounding offended.

"Your words didn't, but your tone did," Jaxon said looking back at her.

"Well, not everyone can be the 'Clovi King'," she added with a smirk

Before he could speak, a low voice shouted for them. Jaxon's calm demeanor was replaced with annoyance. He turned to see Kalix Torin approaching them.

Kalix was a handsome man. In fact, he was often called the 'Handsome Knight' by those who fawned over him. He had olive colored skin with bright blue-gray eyes. He had a lean muscular build and a strong jawline. He smiled his perfectly white toothed smile and stuck his hand out for Jaxon to take. Jaxon with slight hesitation accepted.

Kalix was also known for his lavish armor and accessories. He was a Warden, like Jaxon, and his armor was even similar to his. It differed in its pearl white color with golden accents, from the white surcoat with gold etching down the sides and seams to his traditional knight helm and armor.

"I hear we're hunting wolves," he said with a joyous smile. "Beric!" he shouted over his shoulder behind him. A young man rushed over. Compared to Kalix, Beric looked overweight and his armor in poor condition despite being polished.

"This is Beric Dane, my apprentice," Beric bowed his head and both Jaxon and Ethyia nodded their heads hello. "Beric, go get our vehicle ready." Beric nodded his head and hurried off. Kalix turned back to the two of them. "I assume we're traveling separate?"

"Yes," Jaxon replied before Ethyia could. She rolled her eyes nodding her head with a slight shrug.

"Well, then I'll meet you at Novak's last known location." He handed both of them small info-chips. "I was already briefed before you came down here. See you there." He flashed another smile before leaving.

Jaxon made no reply as he placed the info-chip into his right bracer. It flashed and the small screen provided the coordinates of where they were meeting. He recognized that it was the same place in Angoria. Jaxon shook his head at the slim chance that Novak would still be there.

He wasn't sure why he was so surprised that the council was giving them outdated information. It was quite common for them to do so, despite having rangers who were supposed to be the best at locating targets.

He glanced up to see that Ethyia was staring at him with her head tilted.

"What?" Jaxon asked, looking around.

"You could be a little nicer," she replied with a laugh. "I know you two don't exactly get along, but need I remind you, you won." She placed the info-chip into her own bracer.

"It's not that."

"It's not?" she asked, not convinced. "Because, I know you didn't like him, what 10 years ago? The man has worked hard and is now a Lord. If anything, you could be a little more respectful."

Jaxon sighed in response.

Ethyia continued her lecture about him and Kalix. That their rivalry was over and that Jaxon needed to 'grow up'. Jaxon nodded in response, allowing her to finish.

Jaxon would never admit it, but he had been threatened by Kalix. Kalix was an accomplished swordsman and was well liked by the other knights. Something Jaxon never received which made his disdain for him that much stronger.

"Still can't believe you managed to get Arilynn to marry you," Ethyia said, breaking Jaxon's train of thought. "That woman is *way* too beautiful for you."

"Thanks," Jaxon replied sarcastically.

"All I'm saying is, if those two had ended up together. Damn they would have been gorgeous."

"You sound disappointed," Jaxon commented bitterly.

"Not at all," she replied with a flash of her smile. "I just love seeing you squirm."

"You're not a very good person," Jaxon replied with a smirk. She laughed as they made their way inside the hall with the shift-gates. Olnic looked up and he sat up straight at the sight of Ethyia.

"Lady Jalice," he said with his voice cracking. "Uh, how can I help you?"

"I don't need anything. But my friend here needs his weapon back."

"Uh, of course!" Olnic said as he rushed around. He opened the small chest and placed the form that Jaxon had signed and closed it. After a moment and two bright flashes he re-opened the chest and grabbed the items. He handed Jaxon his Umoya first and then the dagger.

"Does someone just sit there all day and wait for that?" Jaxon asked, taking the weapons.

"Yeah," Olnic replied as if the answer was obvious. "Just like I sit here all day. Not everyone can be great like you," Olnic teased.

"Thank you, Olnic," Jaxon said. Ethyia gave him a quizzical look when he said the Clovi's name.

"Of course, Jaxon!" Olnic said with a bright smile that faded when Ethyia looked at him. "Sir" he said quickly, correcting himself before looking back down. Jaxon clipped his Umoya on his belt and then sheathed the dagger as he walked away.

"They really love you, don't they?" she said as she caught up to him. Jaxon made no reply. "Perhaps if you focused on making friends with other knights the way you do with the Clovi, you'd have more friends."

"I have all the friends I need," Jaxon replied as he stepped into his shift-gate. "I'll meet you at the designated area." With that he walked into the shift-gate placing his hand back on the wall.

"Whatever you say, Clovi King," Ethyia said as Jaxon vanished.

CHAPTER 16

Deal

"She lied," Arilynn growled, showing Markus around the unfinished compound. Her brow furrowed with concentration and annoyance. He could see that Briar and Benjamin were standing with Isobella who kept letting out long sighs to show her contempt.

"I'm not sure what to do," Arilynn admitted. "Anything happen for you?" She looked back down at her wrist to the image of Markus sitting in what looked like a wooded area.

"Oh, yes," Markus replied with a slight smile. "Nya returned just as you thought she would." Markus showed his surroundings, a thick forest of redwood trees. "But she was quickly followed and chased out by vampires. It seems Jaxon's warning came to fruition."

"I was hoping it wouldn't," Arilynn replied from the hologram. "Do you know where she went?"

"I'm trailing her now, though I fear I may have lost her," he muttered. "I'll let you know once I figure that out." Markus clicked off the hologram and continued forward.

The forest was dense and dry. The leaves that littered the ground crunched loudly under his boots. He made sure to make as much noise as he could while walking, digging his heels into the ground and kicking up dust with every step. He was never meant to be a quiet walker or someone who snuck around.

He preferred to be in the fight and was always in the open. He took another step, his ears listening intently for anything out of the ordinary. He could hear the branches brushing against each other as a breeze came through. The birds sang their songs while the buzzing of bugs seemingly tried to drown them out.

He stopped in a small clearing where the ground was mostly flat, so he knelt on one knee removing his gauntlet and pressed his bare hand on the ground. He closed his eyes and searched through the ground.

With his mastery of all the elements, seeing through the earth was a simple task at this point. He could see worms, bugs and dead carcasses that had been reclaimed by nature. He could see the roots of trees and the trunks they belonged to. He could sense the small vibrations of rodents scurrying around. The snake hiding, patiently waiting for its time to strike.

He expanded his senses, trying to see more. Every sound seemed to illuminate his vision of the earth. He ignored everything that was "normal" for a forest until he finally saw what he was looking for.

A small heap laid against the base of a wide tree trunk. They were letting out slow and controlled breaths. He could almost sense their heartbeat. All he could see was their shape, but he knew who it was. He took a deep breath standing up, opening his eyes.

He continued forward making sure to avoid the heap that was hiding just a few meters ahead of him. He made sure to approach at an angle so that his back was towards her. He let out a mocked frustrated sigh and began to press buttons on his wrist.

"I lost her," he said to nothing. "I'm going to circle back and will meet you as soon as I can." He clicked another button that made a small beeping sound.

He then turned to walk from the way he came. He could hear her shuffling behind the base of the tree.

He knew she was injured simply because he *could* hear her. He knew Nya very well as he had known her since she was a child. She was too good to be caught without being hurt, and he knew she would most likely just hide and wait for him to leave.

He moved to the center of the clearing and stood for a moment. He let out a long-exaggerated sigh as he continued forward making sure to walk past her and doing his best to not tense up as he did so. He was tired and was far from ready for a fight. Even injured, Nya was a formidable opponent who could simply outlast him. He had no business running around with young knights and facing an adversary like Nya and her friend.

When he passed and she didn't attack, he let out a chuckle. He turned around so that he was facing the large tree. It was so tall he couldn't see the top and so wide he could barely see around it.

"You must be very tired or very hurt, Nya," he said loudly, unclipping his Umoya. "If you would be so gracious and step out."

He waited for her to decide, whistling while he did so. He inched closer towards her slowly. When he finally rounded the tree, she was gone. He let out a defeated sigh, turning to go back the way he'd come.

Before he could finish his breath, she sprang from her hiding place. He sidestepped her attack, forcing her to stumble forward. She swung backwards wildly. He caught her hand pulling her towards him. She resisted, so he let go, and she flung herself to the ground.

She scrambled to her feet and turned around just as he sent a concentrated gust of wind, slamming her into the ground.

"Nya, stop," he said calmly as he walked towards her, placing his Umoya back onto his belt.

"Why, so you can just kill me?" she spat back.

"If I had wanted to kill you, I would have when I first noticed you hiding behind that tree," he replied with a confident smirk. He raised his hands to show that he was not a threat to her. "I'm not after you. At least for the moment."

Nya hesitated before she relented, slumping on the ground, cradling her right arm. Her breathing was uneven and labored. She stared up at him as she always had. With a soft expression with anger lurking in the background of her eyes.

"You know where she is," Markus said as he approached, dropping his hands to his side.

"What makes you so sure?"

"You threatened that woman," Markus replied. Nya looked up at him surprised by the statement. "I was watching from quite a distance, so I have an idea of what she said."

"Well, it doesn't matter what she told me."

"On the contrary, it does," he argued, kneeling in front of her.

"Well, don't you know everything?" Nya taunted. "It still doesn't matter." To her astonishment, he laughed and sat down on the ground directly in front of her.

"I have missed your snarky attitude, Nya." He smiled at her while she glowered back at him. "I have to know, why are you searching for her?"

"What?" Nya asked, caught off guard by the question. She pulled her arm inward, shifting so that her side was facing him.

"I understand why The Order is after her. I even understand why the clans and the packs are after her. I could understand Kings and Queens and other world leaders searching for the Oracle. What I don't understand is why are *you*?"

"I'm not," she replied, looking up at the canopy above them. "The Three Tailed Scorpions are. Specifically, the Red Scorpions."

"Yes, but even that doesn't make much sense," he replied. "None of them can unlock her power."

"But world leaders can?"

"They have more resources and money to throw at a problem," he replied "Perhaps they would hire someone to unlock her power. Perhaps they would hire you?"

Nya rolled her eyes, looking back down at her arm. She let out a wince as she shuffled further away from Markus.

"Why are you here, Nya?" Markus asked in a more serious tone.

"What do you want me to say?" she asked quietly.

"The world thought you were dead. You could have stayed hidden and enjoyed your life."

"The Order isn't the world," she retorted. "People knew I was alive, and those people *own* me. This is my way out." She looked up, glaring at him before looking back down at her arm. Markus looked at her for a moment. Her face was red and bruised, her hair ruffled and matted to the side of her head.

"Ah, freedom is what you seek," Markus stated as he stroked his beard. "Perhaps we can come to an agreement then?"

"You have nothing to offer me."

"Freedom."

"I'm already free of the Order," she replied without looking at him.

"Are you?" Markus replied grimly. "I could kill you right now for treason. Any other knight that comes across you will have the same authority, and most are going to take the chance to kill the fearsome Nya Dulay." Nya's gaze shot up when she heard her last name.

"I can handle any knight that comes looking for me."

"Except an old man like me," Markus replied with a laugh.

"I could kill you, Markus."

"Hmm, probably," he admitted. "You're a great fighter and much younger than I am." He stroked his beard looking up at the canopy above. "We can test that if you'd like."

She stared at him; he could see her tense up as she debated on what to do. She glanced down at his Umoya and then his hands then back to his face. She took a deep breath before looking back down at the ground in front of her.

"If you help me find the Oracle. I will ensure that you are pardoned by the Order."

Nya looked back up at him, stunned by his statement. She opened her mouth to reply. She stammered and then tried again.

"You can guarantee that?" she asked, trying not to sound too excited.

"Yes," Markus replied. "They will have no choice to accept it if you're the reason we're able to find her."

"That doesn't help me with Red Scorpions," she muttered.

"They'll be too busy dealing with the full force of the Eri'Dorian Order to worry about you. Besides, a great Ranger like you can hide anywhere she wants." She regarded him for a moment. Then looked back down at her arm.

"You can have the life you wanted," he spoke softly resisting the urge to reach out.

"You don't know what I want," she argued.

"I know that you weren't happy with the Order. You clearly aren't happy now. Quite frankly, do *you* even know what you want?"

Nya shot him another dark look.

"Tell me what the woman told you. Help me find her, Nya," Markus implored.

"I'll need a map," she replied quietly.

"You got it," Markus replied.

"You're also going to have to heal my arm," she said, lifting it up gently. Markus slowly reached over. He looked up at her; she nodded giving him permission.

He gently placed the palm of his hand on her broken forearm. He hesitated again looking at her. "This will hurt," he warned.

"Just do it," she grumbled.

Markus nodded his head and gripped her arm tightly. He could feel her tense from the pain despite her not making a sound. He closed his eyes to concentrate on the wound. With his other hand he pulled the moisture from the ground. There wasn't much for him to find, but there was enough that he clasped his second hand over his hand holding her forearm.

He held it as tightly as he could. The water seeped through his fingers onto her arm. The water became warm as it enveloped the broken bone. Water was the great healer of all the elements. He was no true healer, but he could heal a simple fracture.

She began to wince in pain until there was an audible snapping sound, and she screamed, violently pulling away. He let go knowing that the fracture had been fixed.

"That was almost as bad as when it was broken," she growled as she tried to catch her breath. She moved her hand and fingers to make sure everything worked.

Markus stood up taking a few steps back. He watched her carefully. He wasn't entirely sure if she was going to hold her end of the bargain and he had to be ready.

"I'm not going to attack you," she said as if reading his thoughts.

"Good," he said with a smile. "I'm getting too old for this."

"Even if I did get the jump on you and managed to kill you, Arilynn or Jaxon would come after me, and I don't need that."

"Well, I'm glad my life is that important to some," he said with a smile.

"We're not friends, Markus," Nya scowled.

"Of course not. We're sworn enemies destined to hate each other," he replied mockingly. "We used to be friends, remember?"

"I was a child," she grumbled.

"Ah, yes, I remember," Markus said, looking off into the distance as if he could see back in time. "You were always the one who tried her hardest every day." He glanced back at her. "You've always impressed me."

"I don't care," Nya said, annoyed. "I'm not that person anymore."

"I suppose you're right," Markus replied with a mournful tone. "I remember the day you left with Lio and Isobella and the day you three came back at the head of an army." He was looking down at the ground. "Interesting how both of you are alive and Lio is nowhere to be found."

"Lio isn't my concern anymore," Nya said flatly. "Let's just get to the damn girl so you can get me my pardon, and I can move on with my life. Finally."

"Very well," Markus said as he stepped to the side with an exaggerated bow and a wave of his hand, showing the way to go. Nya rolled her eyes as she stood up. She hesitated before walking ahead.

~~~~

Nya did her best to hide her elation. Being free of the Red Scorpions was one thing. Being free from the Order was something else entirely. She could finally find some peace in her life. If the Order went after Seticus and Konan, she wouldn't have to worry about them. The Red Scorpions or even the entire organization couldn't handle an enemy like the entire Eri'Dorian Order.

She stopped when they reached the end of the forest where his speeder was waiting for them. She went to take another step when her belt began to beep loudly. She looked down to see that it was Konan attempting to contact her. She quickly grabbed it and opened it so that he was facing away from Markus.
~~~~

"Where are you?" Konan asked. His eyes narrowed, and his brow creased with frustration.

"I got a little sidetracked."

"With?"

"Surviving," she replied trying to control her tone. "I was attacked by vampires and then wolves showed up. It was a party," she said with as much sarcasm she could muster. She could tell by Konan's expression he did not enjoy her attempt at humor.

"Where are you?"

"On my way to a possible location, you?"

"Following that knight, like we planned."

"Anything?"

"No, the dumb bitch hasn't found anything."

"We didn't expect them to."

"The old man is missing."

"He is?" She asked, trying to sound surprised. "He may have gone back to Eri'Dor."

"They have the girl's mother."

"They do?" she asked looking through the hologram at Markus.

"Yes, looks like she's a prisoner of theirs."

"Well, keep your distance. I'll look at this other location and see if there is anything there."

"Where are you going? I can meet you."

"No," she said curtly and then rushed to explain herself. "I mean, no point in wasting both of our time. Just stay there. I don't even know if I can trust this woman's intel. She claimed she lied to Arilynn; she may have lied to me."

"Where is she?"

"Dead," Nya replied.

"Well, just let me know if you find anything."

"Of course," she said with a smile. Konan stared at her with his normal blank expression, and the transmission cut out. She placed the small disk back onto her belt and turned to Markus.

"Do you trust me yet?" she asked defiantly.

"In time, we'll see how far your trust actually goes," Markus replied.

CHAPTER 17

Failure

Clara sat in the center of a small room with Gwynne sitting across her. She could hear Gwynne breathe in and out, doing her best to stay in a steady rhythm.

"Just focus," she whispered to Gwynne who nodded her head slightly. Clara tried to speak as slowly and clearly as possible.

She kept thinking of her own training with Markus, and how he had taught her to focus on each element. She was nowhere near a master of the elements, but she knew enough to get Gwynne started.

"Open your hands," Clara commanded. Gwynne obeyed. "Remember what I showed you." Gwynne began moving her hands in unison slowly. Her hands swayed back and forth, palms facing each other.

She began to pick up speed until finally a small tornado formed between her hands. It twisted and bent, threatening to disappear before it became steady and held its place centered between her hands.

Clara looked up to see that Gwynne was smiling. She stared in amazement, watching her hands move back and forth. The small tornado dissipated for a moment before it came back. She continued the motion moving faster and faster. Every few seconds she would look up at Clara seeking validation.

"This is amazing!" she exclaimed.

"This is nothing compared to what you're capable of, Oracle," Clara replied.

Gwynne's nose wrinkled at the word of 'Oracle', but she managed to keep her concentration on the small vortex of wind in her hands. "I want to learn more!" Gwynne said eagerly, letting the tornado dissipate.

"It'll take time, usually you learn one element, and then move on to the next. Air, earth, water, metal, and then finally fire. Air is the easiest to conjure, but it is quite powerful."

"How do I learn all of them?"

"A Master will teach you," Clara said calmly. "Once you get a Master, you'll be amazing!"

"I don't want to go to Eri'Dor," Gwynne muttered. "All of them except you have tried to hurt me or capture me."

"That's because they're afraid of you, but at the Temple, they have the greatest minds and masters who will teach you everything they know."

Gwynne leaned back so that she was resting on her elbows and looked around the metallic room. It was empty with no windows. All the rooms they searched were the same. It hadn't taken them long to find the compound. It wasn't nearly as hidden as the first one. It wasn't submerged into the ground just hidden in the depths of a small forest.

Clara could hear Moira and Tyron speaking outside the door. She couldn't understand them, but she had an idea about what the conversation was about by their tones. They didn't trust her, and the feeling was mutual.

Clara knew that they would never do anything to intentionally hurt Gwynne. She also knew that they didn't care about going to Eri'Dor. They didn't care about her or the

Order, and they would do anything to make sure that Gwynne never made it to them.

~~~~

Gwynne laid all the way down on the cold ground, looking up at the dim lights. Her thoughts kept reverting to wondering where her mother was. She wavered between guilt, anxiety and anger, and sometimes she would experience all three simultaneously.

She was angry because she never asked for any of this. She was even more angry at her mother for not telling her anything about what she did before she was born. This fueled her guilt for being angry at her mother.

But the anxiety was the worst. It would hit her unexpectedly. She would be fine and then suddenly feel as if the entire weight of the world was on her chest and she couldn't breathe. She would start sweating and become disoriented to the point that she would have to sit down. How long it lasted varied, making it even worse.

Clara had been there the last time it happened. When they first arrived at the compound, Gwynne suddenly became
~~~~

overwhelmed looking at the empty room. Her mind began thinking about those who were chasing her, and if her mother would ever be able to find her.

Clara just knelt next to her, placing a hand on her upper back. She didn't say anything or rub her back. She just kept her hand there. Knowing that someone was with her made the experience slightly less awful.

Gwynne closed her eyes just trying to relax. She knew Clara was still there, but she wasn't saying anything. The silence in the room allowed Gwynne to hear the muffled argument going on outside. She rolled to her side, turning her back to the voices.

"Are you all right?" Clara asked.

"No," Gwynne said flatly. She was concerned with how honest she was with Clara. She barely knew the girl but felt she could tell her anything and that Clara would never judge or condemn her. "I want to go home," Gwynne whispered.

"I know," Clara replied softly as if she shared the sentiment. "Sometimes things are asked of us that we don't like, and we can't go home."

The statement didn't make Gwynne feel better. It actually made her feel worse. The thought of her never being able to go home was overwhelming. She surprised herself with a laugh that echoed in the room. Sitting up, she saw that the laugh had caught Clara off guard as well.

"I hated my home," she said with another laugh shaking her head. "Yet, here I am wishing I could go back." She started laughing harder. Clara stared at her, unsure of what to do. Which only made Gwynne laugh harder. Even she didn't understand why she was laughing. She suddenly couldn't stop, and the laughing abruptly became sobbing.

She felt the familiar hand of Clara clasp hers. She tried her best to control her sobbing, but the harder she seemed to try, the harder she cried.

"You didn't ask for this," Clara said quietly. "But you will get through this." The confidence in her voice was strangely comforting. She looked up at Clara, and even though they were nearly the same age, Clara seemed so much older.

Gwynne opened her mouth to speak before Tyron pushed through the door. He looked at Gwynne and then shot a dark glare at Clara. He rushed to Gwynne kneeling next to her. He placed his hand on Gwynne's pushing Clara's away.

"Are you okay?" he asked, his voice full of concern.

"I think so," she answered, feeling embarrassed. "I'm just tired."

"Me, too," Clara and Tyron replied in unison. They traded stern looks before refocusing on Gwynne.

"We shouldn't stay here too long," Clara announced, breaking the silence.

"I agree," Tyron said bitterly. "My mother is resting in the other room, but we should move sooner rather than later."

"How far is Dereli?" Gwynne asked, looking at both Tyron and Clara.

"We can't go there," Clara replied.

"Why not?" Tyron asked.

"Because, Dereli is dangerous and not somewhere we should take the Oracle," Clara argued. "Why do you even want to go there?" she asked, looking to Gwynne.

"My father said there was someone there that could help us," Tyron answered before Gwynne could speak.

"Who?" Clara asked, narrowing her eyes. Then an expression of recognition replaced her skepticism. "You're looking for Lionicles Harwell." She shook her head letting out a laugh.

"What's so funny?" Tyron asked angrily.

"No one has seen him since his defeat in Valemìr. He's most likely dead; you're chasing a ghost," she added with another laugh.

"Our parents both agreed that it was a good idea!" Tyron growled.

"I don't doubt it," Clara retorted. "Your father had a bad habit of following Lionicles around."

"Don't speak about him like that," Tyron growled.

"Stop, both of you," Gwynne interjected. "Do you really think Lionicles is dead?"

"No one really knows," Clara admitted.

"We should at least try." Tyron said, looking to Gwynne. "Your mother will find us."

"If she's not already with Markus and Arilynn," Clara countered. "If you go to Dereli, they'll just follow you. Gwynne, please come to Eri'Dor. No harm will come to you or your...*friends*."

"I'm not going to Eri'Dor," Tyron snapped. "And if I see Arilynn I'll kill her myself." To his disdain Clara laughed loudly. "What?!" He shouted.

"You couldn't even beat me, and you really think you have a chance against *the* Lioness of Valemìr?" She laughed again shaking her head. "You could train for a thousand years, and she'd still kill you."

"We'll see," Tyron snarled.

"Why do they call her that?" Gwynne asked. The question caught Clara off guard.

Gwynne glanced up at Tyron who looked expectantly at Clara.

"She kills everything without remorse," Tyron said when Clara didn't answer.

"That's not entirely untrue," Clara replied. "She *is* known for her tenacity and ruthlessness."

"Oh, so that's why?" Gwynne asked, looking at the two of them.

"No, she was named that after the battle of Utende."

"Yea, she murdered a great hero," Tyron sneered.

"She killed a traitor," Clara growled angrily. "She and the Prince of Ardonia; Kylos Lefaye and their soldiers were ambushed by Dru'Ny named Tiber the Unbreakable." Clara shifted. "The story changes depending on who tells it. But what stays the same is that Tiber and his forces attacked the Utende tribe and the valley the Order was using to replenish supplies against the *traitors*." She glared at Tyron before continuing. "Arilynn and her forces were massacred, she and Prince Kylos were the only ones left and he was too injured to fight. Tiber wanted to kill Arilynn himself and descended on the valley. She fought him as best as she could, before he broke her armor and her Umoya." She looked over at Gwynne who was enthralled by the story.

"Arilynn managed to break through the armor protecting his neck. He held her down and depending on who you asked, some say he intended to rape her, others say he was just going to strangle her. Either way, she clawed at the opening in his armor, and when he was close enough, she bit down and ripped his throat out." Gwynne's eyes grew wide.

"The people of the Utende tribe said she looked like a Lioness who had just finished a kill. She's been called the Lioness ever since."

"So that's who's after me?" Gwynne asked nervously.

"Yes," Clara replied. "But she isn't after you to kill you."

"That's comforting," Gwynne muttered. "Do they all have names like that?"

"No," Clara replied. "Most don't actually."

"What about the other woman?" Tyron asked.

"Nya? No, she was a ranger… and a Seeker like myself."

"So, she can sense me too?"

"Yes."

"Great," Gwynne groaned, laying back. "I have a woman who bites people's throats out and someone who can find me no matter where I go chasing me."

"Except Eri'Dor," Clara commented. Tyron glowered at her, but she did her best to ignore it.

There was shuffling outside the door. Tyron was the first to move. When he opened it, Moira stepped in. They whispered for a moment before he turned around.

"Someone's here," he said in a hushed tone. Clara was on her feet before Gwynne could understand what Tyron was saying. "We need to get you out of here."

"Take her and go," Clara stated firmly. "I will handle whatever threat there is." This time Gwynne caught the flash of doubt across Clara's face.

"I don't understand how they found us," Moira said holding the door open as they exited.

"Maybe someone led them here," Tyron said accusingly, looking at Clara.

"I told you, I'm here to protect her," Clara scorned. "Just get her to the old vehicle we found in the bay. I'll see who it is," Clara commanded.

~~~~

To Clara's amazement, the three of them moved without argument. She wasn't sure if it was because they didn't care what happened to her or if they really trusted her to handle it. She decided she would figure it out later. Clara waited for the three of them to disappear down the dark corridor of the compound before turning towards the only entrance that wasn't in the bay. She grasped her Umoya tightly, anticipating an attack.

She could hear footsteps approaching. They were heavy footed, but they weren't alone. She could hear a second pair of footsteps that were lighter and quicker. They were approaching her quickly which made her begin
~~~~

to panic. She did her best to listen to her own words that she spoke to Gwynne and tried to calm down.

Despite how small the compound was. It was quite the maze to navigate. There were more turns and tighter hallways. Most of the lights didn't work, and the ones that did barely illuminated the space they were in.

She pressed herself against the metal wall at the corner and waited. She could feel her heart beginning to race. She was so nervous, she nearly forgot to breathe. She cursed at herself for being so afraid. She was supposed to protect the Oracle. This was her one job.

When she heard the steps approach, she tightened her grip on her Umoya and prepared to launch an attack. When the two people stepped around the corner. She threw herself forward, her Umoya whooshed into an air blade. She stabbed at the first person she saw.

Clara's heart sank when she saw that she was attacking Nya. She tried to push her fear back and attempted to follow through the attack, but was stopped by Markus' hand who swatted the blade away, with a gust of wind. He stepped in between the two of them.

"Sir?" she asked confused and then looked back at Nya. "What's going on?"

"Put your weapon away," he commanded softly. "Where is the Oracle?"

"Why are you with her?" Clara asked, pulling away from him.

"We have an arrangement," Markus replied. "Where is she?"

"No," Clara said defiantly.

"No?" Markus repeated.

"I can't let this woman near her, and you shouldn't either," Clara replied, trying and failing to stop her voice from shaking.

"Clara, listen to me," Markus said in a soothing voice. "We need to get to the Oracle. The situation is far different than when we last saw each other."

"Yea, kid. I'm not here to hurt her," Nya said with a mocking smile. "Hurry up," she added in a harsher tone.

"How did you find us?" Clara asked, looking to Markus.

"I asked around," Nya said sarcastically. "You're wasting my time." She went to push through Clara. Clara pushed her back; pointing the blade at Nya.

"Child if you do not move out of my way…" She didn't finish her sentence as Markus stepped in between them again.

"I know it doesn't seem like it, but it's okay."

"How can you trust her?" Clara exclaimed.

"I don't," Markus said flatly. "But she is outnumbered and outclassed." The last part of the comment caused Nya to glare at Markus, but she returned her gaze to Clara. "She wants to go home, and her giving me the Oracle is the way she does that."

"I can't," Clara argued. "Not with her here."

"Would you feel better if I were in handcuffs?" Nya asked with a smirk.

"I would feel better if you were dead," Clara replied, prompting Nya's smile to disappear.

"Enough," Markus shouted. It was the closest to yelling Clara had ever heard him. "Stand down, now." His voice was firm.

"No," Clara said more confidently.

"Clara!" Markus growled. "I am your master, and you will do as I say."

"I am sworn to the Oracle now," Clara replied proudly. She stood up as tall as she could.

"Good god," Nya said with a sudden lightning bolt that caught Clara in the chest sending her sprawling backwards. She hit the back wall so hard that it knocked her unconscious.

"Nya!" Markus shouted. He grabbed at Nya who pulled away.

"She was never going to move, Markus," Nya replied. "She's fine."

Nya made her way down the winding corridors as Markus checked on Clara. When he made sure she was fine, he rushed to catch up.

Clara struggled to sit up. Her chest aching, and the remnants of the electricity pulsed through her body. It took her a moment before she remembered what happened and jumped to her feet. She sprinted down the hallway to where Gwynne and the others were.

She could hear shouting as she rounded the corner. She was blinded by the sudden appearance of light just as she reached the end of the corridor. She entered the transportation bay, raising her wind bladed Umoya once again. She could see Markus and Nya were standing over Gwynne who was bound by the hands. Tyron was on the ground with Moira tending to him. She looked up to see that the doors to the bus were blown open.

"What did you do?" Clara shouted.

"She's fine," Nya sighed. "She's just bound until she learns to calm down." Clara charged Nya but was cut off again by Markus.

"Clara!" he shouted. "That's enough!" Clara fell forward at the side of Gwynne who wasn't moving.

"She is bound, you got your Oracle," Nya said to Markus. "We had a deal, right?"

"We did. But you need to help us get her back."

"That wasn't part of the deal, Markus," Nya argued. "I lead you to her. You get me pardoned, and you deal with the Three Tailed Scorpions."

"I need your help, Nya," Markus replied. "The quicker you help me with this, the quicker you move on with your life."

"Haven't heard that one before." Nya sighed.

Markus carried Gwynne back into the bus while Moira helped Tyron on the other side. The bus was similar to the one at the last compound only much smaller. Clara glowered at Nya who smiled as she walked past.

Markus jumped down from the transport and went to the back of the bay. As he passed Clara, he whispered to her. "Be ready." Clara knitted her brow trying to make sure that was what he said. She glanced back to Nya who was looking down at a small disk. Clara wasn't quite sure, but it looked like one of the older communicators that the older knights used.

Clara looked back to Markus who was now standing next to the bus helping Moira strap Tyron in. Whatever had happened before Clara arrived had hurt Tyron enough that he was barely moving. He was still talking and shouting so she knew he would be all right.

"Be ready for what?" she asked through gritted teeth. "Are you afraid the traitor you brought the Oracle is going to do something awful?" she asked, crossing her arms.

"You should always be ready," he replied, not looking at her.

"I can't believe you brought her here," Clara said, looking directly at Markus who was stroking his beard watching Nya.

"Sometimes you have to do what is necessary," Markus replied.

"Leading that woman to the Oracle was necessary?"

"She led *me,*" he replied. "And yes." He turned towards her. "There will be many times in this world where you can't do something by yourself. You will need the aid of those you do not trust. Sometimes you will have to do what is *necessary* to achieve your goal."

"She's evil," Clara declared. "You brought an evil woman to the Oracle."

"Oh, dear girl," Markus said with a laugh. "Nya is not evil."

"You don't think she's evil?" Clara asked, surprised by his defense of her.

"Selfish, rude, misguided, yes. But evil? No." He looked back over to where Nya was standing. "You have never seen true evil, my apprentice, and I hope that you never do."

He patted her on the shoulder and walked towards the bus, leaving Clara alone. She took a deep breath doing her best to calm down. She wanted to trust Markus; he had never lied to her. But now she wasn't loyal to him. She was loyal to the Oracle, and he brought a very dangerous threat right to her.

"We need to go," Markus announced, breaking her concentration. Clara hesitated before she walked up to the transport while Nya lingered looking at the small disk for a moment longer before sure placed it back in her belt.

It was the first time Clara had really seen Nya up close. Her hair was pulled back in a messy ponytail that showed more of the pale complexion of her face. All her clothes were dirty. Clara glanced down at her own armor. The once clean and unscarred surcoat and armor was now torn to shreds with scorch marks.

"Nya," Markus said, trying to get her attention. Nya looked over at him but didn't move right away. Clara's eyes darted back and forth between the two of them.

Nya finally moved towards the bus nearing the entrance. Clara followed behind her trying to keep her distance. She couldn't help but start to shake again, only this time from anger instead of fear. She did her best to control her breathing and act as if nothing was wrong.

"You can fly this, right?" Markus asked. Nya nodded her head, continuing forward. As she passed Clara and Moira, Clara peeked back at Markus who was watching Nya intently.

As Nya climbed into the transport, there was a loud boom that echoed in the room. The entire bus rocked back and forth. It caught everyone off guard, prompting everyone to look around to find the source. Nya started the bus while Clara ran towards the door.

Markus turned towards the loud sound and the drumming of footsteps approaching them. He activated his Umoya, the metal blade pointing down at his side. He turned back towards Moira, motioning for her to run to the bus. When the door swung open, he sent an arc of lightning hitting the first three men to enter the room. After they fell to the ground, another group charged inside after them, Konan among them.

~~~~

"Dammit," Nya said as she slammed the accelerator to the ground. When nothing happened, she cursed and stood up.

"Nya!" Konan shouted to get her attention. Nya glanced down at Konan and then Markus. She couldn't breathe. It felt as if her heart had climbed up her throat and was pounding.

She knew the right decision was to honor her agreement with Markus, but it was her fear that won out. She wasn't as afraid of Markus as she was Konan. She sent an ice blast at Markus who raised his hand, swatting it away.
~~~~

She lifted her hand to attack again. Before she could summon more magic, Markus threw a bolt of lightning at her; she brought up her hand blocking the arc. The force of the impact knocked her backwards, nearly hitting Clara as she fell.

"We have to go, now!" Markus shouted. Clara managed to push Nya off, both of them scrambling to their feet.

"Open the bay!" she heard him yell as more of Konan's men began to funnel in.

Markus sent a wall of fire that pushed the men back down the hallway. It was clear he had no patience to use non-lethal attacks. Not anymore. He raised his weapon and cut down the first three he intercepted with relative ease and continued to engage the oncoming threat.

Nya jumped off the bus and ran towards Markus. Markus pivoted around and returned with a blast of fire. Nya rolled away, conjuring another ice blast that he deflected to the ground with his blade and sent one back in return. She brought up her hands and with them a wall of stone ripping through the metallic ground. The ice shattered upon impact sending shards of ice everywhere.

"You lied to me!" Markus shouted.

"No, I didn't!" Nya replied, lowering her hands. She grabbed Tryxus' Umoya from her back and attempted to use it. It took a moment before it activated but the curved blade of jagged ice finally appeared. "I had no idea he was coming," she said, lifting her weapon up.

"Then why?" he asked, lifting his blade, the metal turning into fire.

"I have to survive. That's all I know how to do, Markus."

~~~~

Markus hurled a bolt of lightning that she avoided by simply ducking out of the way, charging at him.

Markus backpedaled, parrying her attacks. She was angry and was using as much strength as she could behind every attack. He glanced back to see what Clara was doing.
~~~~

Then refocused on Nya when he felt a cold gust of wind as her blade swung near his chest.

He parried her attacks again, swatting them away with ease. Each time their blade met, there was a sizzling sound, and steam would appear. While he was far superior in sword combat, she had youth and anger on her side. He had to make sure the fight was as short as possible.

He led their fight towards the bus and when he was close enough, he sidestepped her, kicking the back of her leg. He knocked her down and then backhanded the side of her face with his hilt, hammering her to the ground.

He returned his focus to the men rushing in. They were now too far in that he couldn't push them back down the hall. He noticed Konan shouting directions but was staying behind, allowing his men to fight without him. Markus sent a blast of fire behind him to launch himself forward. He landed between a small group, throwing lightning at their feet. He morphed his blade back into metal, and cut them down as they convulsed.

The second group were armed with energy rifles that they raised and fired. He parried the first blast with his metal blade, before taking a step and morphing it into a wind blade. They fired again, this time he avoided the first blasts, before parrying a second, he followed through with his swing and created a gust of wind that blew them off balance. With his free hand he conjured another blast of fire behind him. He summoned another gust of wind beneath him that launched him forward and into the air, allowing him to land behind them. Markus created a barrier of fire that engulfed the group. He cut down the ones closest to him and allowed the others to burn, turning to face the others.

~~~~

Nya pushed herself off the ground. She turned to the sound of the bay doors opening and saw that Clara was at the control center. She began regretting her decision at the sight of Markus making easy work of Konan's men. She shook her head, letting out a frustrated grunt. She couldn't think about it anymore. She
~~~~

had chosen her side, again. Upon standing up, she threw an icicle at Clara.

Clara easily avoided the projectile, but it was enough of a distraction for Nya to close the distance. She ran towards Clara but was thrown forward from a searing hot jolt in the right shoulder blade. Nya slammed into the ground, shouting out in pain. She couldn't stand the pain of being hit with a lightning bolt. She rolled to her back and sat up. She let out a frustrated scream, looking at Markus.

Markus had turned his attention back to fighting Konan's men. She stood back up looking to see Clara was now in the driver's seat and the bus began to rise with its thrusters screeching. Nya wasted no time as she sprinted, launching herself towards the bus with a burst of wind. She landed on the roof of the transport. She forced Tryxus' Umoya to work one last time, with a blade of fire, as she stabbed down through the roof. She ripped the blade away and created a stream of fire which began melting the hole, causing it to split open.

When it was opened wide enough, she dropped down. When she landed, she was immediately hit with another bolt of lightning. She crumpled backwards and looked up to see Clara running towards her. Her blade was raised, and she didn't wait for Nya to get up before launching her own attack.

~~~~

Markus deflected another blast and cut through two more of Konan's soldiers. They were beginning to panic, and their ranks had broken rather easily. Markus pressed the attack, moving as fast as his body would allow him to.

Markus lifted his blade up and cut down. His swing was forced to a stop when a chain wrapped around his wrist and pulled against him. He yanked it forward, but whoever was on the other end was too strong and pulled back, knocking Markus off balance, causing him to fall to the ground.

Markus scrambled back to his feet and turned to see Konan running towards him with his chained daggers. Markus sidestepped the first attack and then parried the next two.

Markus was already tired before this and was now beginning to slow. Konan was
~~~~

fresh and ready for a fight. Markus parried only the attacks that mattered, no longer able to create gusts of wind to aid his movements. If the attack wasn't going to hit, he let Konan waste his own energy. He fell into a defensive stance and knew that Konan would gladly be the aggressor. Markus backpedaled again, trying to get to where the bus was. It was now hovering with Clara fighting Nya inside.

~~~~

Nya relentlessly attacked Clara, shouting with every swing. Clara was young and inexperienced, but her youth and not being injured was her advantage. Nya pressed the attack as hard and as fast as she could, trying to exploit her inexperience. Clara did her best to keep up but was quickly falling behind as Nya's attacks became more complicated.

Finally, Nya broke through Clara's basic defense, pushing her to the back of the bus. Clara continued to parry every attack she could until she slammed into the back of the bus. Nya spun and kicked Clara in the lower abdomen so hard that Clara began coughing
~~~~

up blood. Clara desperately swung her metal blade with every ounce of strength she had. Her blade cut nothing but air as Nya sidestepped her, slamming the back of her elbow into Clara's mouth.

Nya grabbed Clara by the side of the face, slamming her head into the wall repeatedly. Nya only stopped when she heard movement behind her. She turned and was met with Tyron tackling her into the wall next to Clara slumped on the floor.

She screamed out in frustration as she began to beat down on his lower back, causing his knees to buckle. She pulled him back by his hair and kneed him in the face forcing him to stagger. She then kicked him in the groin, causing him to double back over. She grabbed him by the back of his neck and slammed the top of his head into the wall. She staggered backwards, looking around. Most of the bus seats had been ripped out leaving a wide space for cargo.

Nya went back and pushed Tyron over, walking towards Gwynne laying on one of the seats at the front of the bus. When she went to grab her, someone pulled her by the hair, torquing her neck backwards. Nya screamed in a flash of rage as she turned around to see her new attacker was Moira. The bus suddenly crashed into the ground causing the two of them to tumble to the floor.

Nya pushed herself up and ripped her hair from Moira's grasp. Moira staggered Nya by charging her and swinging wildly, trying to strike her. Nya covered up as Moira punched and clawed at anything she could. Nya caught Moira's hand and cranked it back until she could hear the bone snap. Moira let out a piercing scream as she crumpled to the floor, holding her arm. Nya followed up the attack and kicked Moira in the head, knocking her unconscious. In her anger, Nya shouted, throwing a blade of ice that hit next to Moira's head.

Nya looked around trying to see why the bus had crashed. She could see fire burning at one of the thrusters. A stray bolt had hit it, seizing the engine. She turned her attention back to Gwynne who was beginning to stir. She rushed over and hit Gwynne across the face, making sure she stayed unconscious. Despite having binding ropes wrapped around her hands, Nya knew they wouldn't work for very long and was not prepared to fight the Oracle.

She grabbed Gwynne, lifting her up over her shoulder. The task proved harder than she anticipated due to her exhaustion. Once she had Gwynne off the ground, she began to fumble around on her belt. She let out an agitated grunt as she searched for what she needed.

Clara cursed as she forced herself up, storming across the length of the bus and stabbed at Nya. Nya moved back, dropping Gwynne to the ground, kicking Clara in the torso. She created two icicles and prepared for another attack.

~~~~

Sweat poured down Markus' face as he parried another attack from Konan. By now Konan had shouted for the others to stay out of the fight. His pride was taking over, and this gave Markus the advantage however slight it may have been.
~~~~

Konan charged again, this time Markus was too slow to react. Konan slammed his shoulder into Markus' sternum. The impact caused Markus to drop his Umoya and stumble backwards. Konan followed up the attack and began cutting and slashing and eventually he started to move so fast that he was no longer holding the daggers, just swinging the chains.

Markus did his best to avoid the chain and the deadly blades attached. He was too tired to summon any kind of magic, offense or defense. He relied on his armor to absorb the blows from the chains. Despite how strong his armor was, the impact of each hit was taking its toll.

Eventually, Konan was beating Markus to the ground and was relentless. Konan began screaming as he continued swinging the chain. He stopped as he gasped for air and grabbed the hilt of his daggers. He drove down both daggers but was surprised to see that Markus was still fighting back by grabbing his wrists.

Konan bore down on him with all his weight and strength. He could see the tip of the blades inching closer with every passing second.

"Is that all you got boy?" Markus shouted. Konan paused for a moment confused by the statement and then grew angrier.

~~~~

Nya slammed Clara into the wall, forcing her to fall to the ground. Nya was too fast and better trained. Despite her lack of speed and ability, Clara kept willing herself to stand up, only to be kicked back down. Finally, Nya grew tired of the fight and kicked Clara in the side of the head, sandwiching it against the wall. She crumpled to the ground. Nya turned back to grab Gwynne and began dragging her away.

Moira groaned as she reached out, grabbing Gwynne's leg. Nya turned around and viciously kicked the side of Moira's face, forcing her to let go. Nya then pressed the heel of her boot onto the side of Moira's face, pressing down until Moira begged for her to stop.

Nya finally relented, turning her attention back to Gwynne. She dragged her to
~~~~

the side exit of the bus. She thumbed her belt and grabbed the Amulet of Indiza, which allowed her to use a shift-gate wherever she was and take her wherever she could think of.

She knelt, grabbing Gwynne and held the amulet up, taking a deep breath preparing to use the magic. She glanced up and saw Clara was crawling towards her. Blood ran down the side of her face from the deep cut on the side of her head from Nya's boot.

"You fought well kid," Nya said.

"You're supposed to protect her!" Clara cried as she crawled forward.

"You're young," Nya replied. "Someday you'll learn that when you spend your life serving everyone. They'll just throw you away when they don't need you anymore."

"I'm going to kill you!" Clara shouted angrily, lunging forward.

Nya shook her head, slightly impressed by the young apprentice. She regained her focus and with a flash Gwynne and Nya were gone.

~~~~

"No!" Clara screamed out reaching for Gwynne. When her hand hit nothing but air, she collapsed to the ground. She could hear more shouting and the familiar hum of the hover-bikes landing. She sat up, leaning against the seats, and could see fire and lightning arcing through the windows but could not see who was fighting.

After a moment she didn't need to, she could sense Arilynn had arrived. The feeling of comfort didn't last. She had lost a hard fight, and she had lost badly.

She looked around the transport. Moira was weeping on the ground. She looked to where Gwynne had just been before disappearing into thin air.

She could feel a pit forming in the bottom of her stomach. It still felt as if her heart was lodged in her throat. Getting kicked in the face and torso coupled with the taste of blood filling her mouth made it even harder to breathe.
~~~~

She had failed her only duty—her sole purpose in life. Just as she went to lay her head against one of the seats, she glanced to where Tyron had been. When she didn't see him, she looked around frantically. She let out a frustrated sigh. She had lost Tyron, but more importantly she had lost the Oracle.

CHAPTER 18

Abandoned

Jaxon stared out the window looking down at Angoria. It looked far different during the day. The streets were busy with people rushing around following their normal routines instead of drunkenly stumbling around.

He couldn't help but wonder what they thought of the world. How their days went and if they ever thought of all the things happening around them. If they ever noticed the danger that seemingly lurked around every corner.

He was expecting to see Ethyia and the others any moment. They insisted on scouring the area for any kind of clues as to where Novak and the pack had disappeared to.

Jaxon wasn't hopeful. He knew how the packs worked and that Novak was incredibly thorough when he left any den. Still, Ethyia and Kalix insisted on looking, and he didn't care to spend the energy arguing with them.

He didn't consider Novak the threat. Despite the two of them being less than friends. He believed Novak. It was Balthazar that made Jaxon nervous. The open threat should have been enough for Jaxon to go after him and bring him in or cut him down. Yet another decision the council made that he disagreed with.

The elevator doors opened, breaking his train of thought. He turned to see Ethyia in the lead with Beric. Behind them was another man that Jaxon recognized.

"Oh, dammit!" Tobias screeched. "Damn, man!" he said, shaking his head. He looked worn down. His suit was dirty and had a few tear marks across the torso and back.

"Tobias," Jaxon said, walking forward with his hands behind his back. "I'm surprised to see you here."

"I didn't want to be here," Tobias muttered.

"Then why are you?" Kalix asked, pushing him forward. Tobias stumbled, giving Kalix a dirty look before turning his attention back to Jaxon.

"Novak wanted me to come back and make sure everything was cleared out," Tobias replied.

"Ironic," Jaxon said with a smirk. "If you hadn't come back, we wouldn't have any way of finding Novak."

"What makes you think I'll tell you?" Tobias said, standing up straight to show his size. Ethyia stepped forward, dwarfing him. He glanced over at her and slumped his shoulders, shaking his head.

"Look, I'm not trying to get killed, all right?" he said glancing up at her.

"Then tell us where he is," Jaxon replied.

"I don't know," Tobias said. "I swear! He was pretty pissed at me for letting you in that night," he added, pointing to the tears in his suit.

"He attacked you?" Kalix asked.

"Uh, yeah," Tobias said as if it were obvious. "He couldn't attack you, so he had to attack someone. I'm just glad we heal fast," he said with a scoff.

"Where were you supposed to go after you were finished here."

"Nowhere," he replied.

"What?" Ethyia asked, confused.

"I was being left here until they decided to let me back in," he said.

"So, Novak just left you with nothing?" Jaxon asked.

"Yes."

"He left you here to be discovered by us."

"Well…" Tobias said scrunching his face while he thought about the question.

"In hopes that we or someone else would find you, torture or even kill you to find him," Jaxon said. "He left you to die."

"No…" Tobias' voice trailed off as his eyes darted back and forth. He shook his head and then looked at Jaxon.

"Where is he?" Jaxon asked firmly. "We'll let you go."

"No," he said shakily. "He wouldn't." His tone was firmer this time. "NO!"

"Calm yourself," Kalix warned. Tobias glared at him, his eyes flashing yellow.

"Quiet," Jaxon admonished. "Look at me, Tobias."

"I have always been faithful to him," Tobias growled.

"I know," Jaxon answered. "I need you to be loyal one more time."

"What!?" His voice dropped low. He kept taking deep heavy breaths. "How would telling you make me loyal?"

"He may be in danger," Jaxon replied.

"Well, he left me to die," he said, still not believing it.

"Then to the pack," Jaxon countered. "We need to find him."

"I don't know. I think they were meeting up at one of our hideouts. Something about the clans."

"What about them?" Ethyia pressed.

"He wants to stop Balthazar from doing something. That's all I heard before…before he sent me here."

"Where were you?"

"On the road," Tobias replied dismissively. He dropped to the ground on his knees rubbing his temples. "I can't believe he would abandon me."

"Where is the hideout?" Jaxon asked, squatting down. "I need to speak to him. I think he's going to do something very foolish." Tobias looked up at him and nodded his head.

"For the pack," he said with a gulp. "For the pack."

It didn't take long for Tobias to spill everything. He was distressed and would waver between anger and sadness. Most of the information that he provided was useless.

The only part that stuck out was that Novak was moving against Balthazar in an attempt to stop him from getting to the Oracle. Jaxon mused at the irony that he and Novak were now on the same side.

Once Tobias gave all the information, Beric and Kalix escorted him out, leaving Ethyia and Jaxon upstairs. Jaxon stared down at the people, his thoughts returning from earlier. How quickly the world was changing around them, and none of them seemed to notice.

"What's our next move?"

"We find Novak," Jaxon replied. "We should attempt to reach out to Arilynn and the others."

"I agree," Ethyia said, walking over to stand next to him. "How do you think this is going to go?"

"Not well," he replied grimly. "Novak will never accept that we are there to help him."

"We're not," Ethyia replied.

"Say again?" Jaxon asked looking over at her.

"We are there to apprehend him, Jaxon," she replied looking down at him. "That is our mandate."

"The mandate has changed," Jaxon replied, turning away from the window.

"The mandate does not change until the council changes it," she replied firmly.

"It changes when it changes," he replied with a scoff. "The council isn't here."

"It is here."

"You're the council now?" Jaxon asked with a laugh. "I had no idea."

"Don't give me your attitude Jaxon." she snapped. "The mandate is to find and apprehend Novak for violation of the covenant."

"What about Balthazar?"

"He hasn't done anything but speak idle threats. That's all he ever does," she replied, stepping away from the window. "We're not going to go after him for simply speaking. That would set the clans off and we cannot afford that."

"It was a threat."

"A veiled one," she replied. "Even you said it wasn't an outright statement."

"You can't be serious?" Jaxon asked incredulously. He stared at her for a moment, trying to understand how she could think this was a good idea. He took a deep breath and spoke. "The girl is in danger. We need to find her and protect her."

"That is under Markus' mandate."

"I never knew you to be so concerned with all of the mandates," Jaxon said as he entered the elevator.

"The council makes the decisions. Not you."

"The mandate is to do what is right, Ethyia," Jaxon replied as the doors closed.

~~~~

Ethyia watched as the numbers above the door counted down. She turned back to the window and began a transmission that was immediately answered by Lorrennius.

"What is it?" he asked, sounding annoyed by the interruption.

"We are in the process of locating Novak."

"And?"

"Jaxon is being difficult," she replied grimly. "He wants to allow Novak to attack Balthazar. One of Novak's followers claims that he is only trying to stop Balthazar from getting to the Oracle. Jaxon wants to aid him in attacking Balthazar if he follows through with his threats."

"We cannot allow that to happen," Lorrennius replied curtly. "You know what is at stake.
~~~~

"I do," Ethyia admitted. "I tried telling Jaxon that setting off the vampires would only cause problems."

"Jaxon will never understand what we do," Lorrennius replied snidely. "Ensure he doesn't do anything to jeopardize Markus' mandate."

"I will," she replied, ending the transmission.

CHAPTER 19

Deal Kept

Markus struggled to stand up with piercing pains spreading throughout his body. He winced when Arilynn grabbed his arm helping him move to a place to rest. Briar and Benjamin chased after Konan and his men, leaving Arilynn and Markus alone with Isobella who rushed to the bus checking on Moira.

"Where is the Oracle?" Arilynn asked aloud, looking around. She ignored the bodies that littered the floor and then located Clara limping towards them. Half of her face was covered in blood, her black hair matted and the other side of her face already beginning to bruise.

"She's gone," she whimpered as she did her best not to cry. "So is Tyron," she admitted as she fell to the ground.

"Dammit!" Arilynn shouted in frustration. "I should have been here sooner," she added, turning her anger inwards.

"Well, where did she go?" Markus asked with a grimace.

"I don't know," Clara replied. "She used some kind of amulet. She was here one second and gone the next."

"She has the Amulet of Indiza," Markus stated with another wince of pain. "We have been wondering where that relic went," he said with a chuckle that made him grimace.

Benjamin and Briar returned shaking their heads, signaling that they did not catch anyone. Benjamin instructed Briar to look around to see if there were any survivors before walking over.

"We lost, didn't we?" Briar asked.

"Not yet," Arilynn replied defiantly. "That Amulet can go anywhere she can think of. We just need to think of where she would go." Even as she said it, her optimistic resolve lessened.

"No, I have an idea of where she may have gone," Markus stated with a pained sigh. "Clearly, she is working with the Red Scorpions. But she is only working for them so she can break free of them."

"Where?" Arilynn asked.

~~~~

Nya slammed Tyron back into the ground as he struggled to stand. He pushed himself to his hands and knees. She replied by kicking him in the stomach, rolling him over. Nya summoned a blade of ice.

"Stop!" Gwynne shouted as she fought to break free of the rope that bound her hands. She took a deep breath trying to focus like Clara had taught her, but nothing happened.

"Those ropes are for more than binding your hands. They're enchanted. You won't be breaking free of those anytime soon," Nya explained as she plunged the blade into Tyron's stomach. He let out a gasp of air and began shouting, trying to grab at Nya's hand as she ripped the blade away.

"Please, please! I won't fight you or do anything. Just let him go!" Gwynne pleaded. Nya regarded her for a moment and shrugged. She let the ice turn to water and splash on Tyron. She stood up, looking around her room.

Everything was the same as she had left it. The bed was made and the bookcases full.
~~~~

She couldn't help but smile and enjoy the feeling of being at home. Her smile faded once she remembered that she would be leaving again, this time permanently. Her eyes fell on Gwynne who was huddled against the corner.

"What are you going to do to me?"

"I'm not doing anything to you," Nya replied. "You're a means to an end for me. That's all." Nya opened the door and shouted for someone to come to her. She returned to Tyron, looking down at his wound, he was staring up at her, but stayed still.

"I never wanted this life," Nya said suddenly without looking over at Gwynne. "I never wanted to be an assassin, to be a knight, to be a *seeker*. I just wanted to live a normal life, know my parents, my brothers and sisters, to get married, maybe have a family…" Nya looked over at Gwynne and laughed, shaking her head. "I don't know why I'm telling you all of this." Gwynne opened her mouth to reply, but was interrupted by the arrival of four men, standing up she approached the first.

"Tell Seticus that I have the Oracle," Nya said and then opened the door wider.

"Also, I need this one taken out of here," Nya added pointing to Tyron. The servant nodded her head and rushed away. Nya watched Tyron roll to his stomach, dragging himself towards Gwynne, still whimpering in the corner.

The three men began trying to grab and lift Tyron off the ground. When he struggled, they would drop him. Just as he would crash into the floor, they would immediately begin to kick and punch him until he stopped fighting. This continued multiple times until Tyron finally gave up and stayed limp. They grabbed him by the arms, hoisting him up. His head hung back as they carried him out. He stared at Gwynne and moved his mouth to speak but nothing came out.

Nya couldn't help but feel a hint of remorse for them. She could remember a time where she crawled towards someone knowing that it was a futile attempt. She shook her head, removing the memory from her mind. That didn't matter anymore.

"You promised you wouldn't do anything."

"I'm not," Nya replied. "He'll live." she shrugged. "Most likely." she grabbed Gwynne, yanking her to her feet, pulling her along as they left the room.

~~~~

They entered the hall and Nya's fingertips dug into Gwynne's upper arm causing her to wince. Gwynne took a brief look around the hall. It was well lit with dark orange and red painted walls. The floors were bright white and looked freshly cleaned.

Nya shoved her into another room, causing her to fall onto a soft couch. Gwynne pushed herself up as best she could with her hands being bound. She glanced around the room. It was wide with large windows that were covered with heavy curtains. She wasn't entirely sure where she was anymore.

What caught her attention the most was the fireplace on the other side of the room. The fire looked normal, but she couldn't help but think something was off about it. When she started to focus on it, the door opened. She turned to see an older gentleman enter the room. He was followed by a large woman who
~~~~

trailed behind him, closing the door. Nya rushed from the mirror she was using to fix her hair.

"Here she is," Nya said eagerly. "We got a deal, right?" The man looked down at Gwynne. His green eyes lingered for a moment before looking back at Nya. He hobbled over with his red cane and sat down across from Gwynne.

"Is it really you?" he asked in a quiet raspy voice.

"My name is Gwynne Hartley."

"But are you really the Oracle?" he asked in a sterner tone.

"That's what everyone keeps telling me," she muttered. To her surprise he laughed, showing his yellow-white teeth.

"A deal is a deal," he said standing up, looking to Nya. "Where is Konan?" he asked looking around the room.

"I don't know," she replied. "It's not my problem anymore." When she turned to leave, the large woman stepped in front of her. "We made a deal, Seticus," Nya said angrily.

"We did," he agreed. "But you can't walk out with that marking on your arm," he said looking down at Gwynne with a half-smile.

Gwynne was too busy looking around the room to notice his lingering stare. It was large and open with beautiful art and expensive furniture. A skinny man entered the room and began removing the curtains, showing the windows. It was dark outside, and it was the first time Gwynne had seen outside in a few days and was the first indication she'd had of what time it was.

She was mesmerized by all the city lights that lit up the skyline. She had never seen such a city before. Even now as terrified as she was, she couldn't help but marvel at the beauty. She looked over to Nya who was removing the armor from her left arm. She had a panicked look on her face but held her hand out. The large woman took a dagger and very meticulously cut the Scorpion marking from the inside of her forearm. A puddle of blood formed underneath her arm ruining the freshly cleaned floor.

Gwynne was amazed Nya didn't scream. She gritted her teeth, closed her eyes, tears formed in the corner of her eyes, but she never made a sound. When the woman was done, she threw the skin to the ground, sheathed the large knife back on her belt and nodded her head for Nya to leave.

"Good luck, Nya!" Seticus said, waving his hand. "I'll be sure to send Konan all your love." He was still focused on Gwynne who was now matching his gaze.

"What are you going to do with her?" Nya asked, looking at Gwynne. Their eyes met for a moment before Gwynne switched her focus back to Seticus.

"That is none of your concern now, goodbye," Seticus said dismissively. Nya's gaze lingered for a moment before turning and leaving the room.

"I'm not going to harm you, child," Seticus stated. "But you are going to help me achieve something that no man has ever achieved." He turned to the woman. "Leave."

"Are you sure?" she asked looking at Gwynne.

"She's bound. I'll be fine. Go," Seticus replied in a harsh tone. She bowed her head and left the room with the frail man who opened the windows following her. Gwynne couldn't understand it. She knew the woman most likely wouldn't have helped her, but with her gone, Gwynne was suddenly even more afraid.

~~~~

Balthazar stood at the edge of a building, his black eyes scanning each person at ground level. Ten of his followers stood behind him. He couldn't see who was all there, and he didn't care. The only ones that stood out to him were three male siblings. All blonde with lean builds, wearing matching black and orange armor.

Balthazar gripped the hilt of his falchion. A wide single edged sword with a curved point. The hilt was made of very old blackwood and had been worn down to fit his hand perfectly. The gold pommel was shined and gleamed in the bright city lights.

"I know some of you are afraid of what we're about to do here," he said, looking back
~~~~

up at his followers. "What we are going to achieve tonight will set the course for the next few hundred years. The power we are about to obtain will replace us in our rightful position at the top of the mountain!" he growled.

"No longer will we have to share our stature with the filthy dogs. No longer will we have to endure the mind numbing and painstaking idiocy of the order!" The group began to shout and cheer as he continued to speak.

"We are here to set things right," he said calmly. "Some of you may die today. In fact, I'm certain some of you will." The group looked around nervously.

"Your death will not be forgotten," he said solemnly. "You will be forever remembered by those who come after you as part of this group. *This* group that started a new era where *we rule.*"

Balthazar looked at each of the followers. They all wore similar armor meant to protect against Eri'Dorians and wolves. It stretched from their neck down to their wrists, encasing their torso and legs within the ancient vampiric armor. It was light and pliable allowing them to move freely without losing any of their speed. Their faces were covered with horned helmets. The armor blocked out all ultraviolet light allowing them to fight at any time.

"Grab your weapons and prepare yourselves." He turned back towards the city. "I will go after the Oracle alone."

"Are sure that's wise?" Alamara asked. stepping from the side. "Perhaps, a *lesser* of our kind can do the honors."

"No," Balthazar replied. "It has to be me. I'm the only one here strong enough to resist her magic, at least long enough to turn her."

"I don't think—"

"No, you don't," Balthazar interjected. "You're not supposed to think. You're supposed to *obey*." He glared at her. "Get them ready and wait for when I need you."

"When will that be?" Alamara asked, looking down at the ground submissively.

"You'll know."

~~~~
~~~~

"Get up," Seticus commanded. His sweet demeanor softened, and he was now pushing her with his cane. Gwynne tried to focus and summon *any* kind of magic, and again nothing happened. She let out a frustrated grunt when he pushed her again.

Gwynne began to panic. She could hear Clara's voice telling her to focus and to stay calm. She took a deep breath and when she knew he was going to push her again she moved out of the way, causing him to stumble forward. She slammed her shoulder into his side, knocking him to the ground.

He let out a shout as he crashed to the floor. Gwynne ran across the room, but the large woman had already rushed in.

Gwynne scanned the area trying to find any route of escape. She took a deep breath and tried to focus again. She felt something this time and she focused harder, but before anything could happen, the sound of glass shattering and gust of cold wind caught her off guard. Gwynne opened her eyes to see that the far window was gone. The woman was on the ground convulsing, and a very large man stood over her.

He was larger than she was, and his pale brown skin seemed to absorb the light from the surrounding buildings. He wore peculiar armor she had never seen before. It was black with gold highlighting the edges and joints of the armor that covered his entire body. The breastplate had a gold symbol etched in the center of his chest. There was a black leather belt that wrapped around his waist. Strapped to the belt on his right side was a large sword with a gold pommel.

He turned and looked at Gwynne with dead black eyes. He didn't move with his eyes locked onto her. She suddenly felt very small and weak. Her skin felt like it was crawling, and suddenly, she became very aware of her breathing. She couldn't help but stare at him, frozen, despite a voice in her head screaming for her to move.

Gwynne was woken from her trance when Seticus fired a small pistol. The bullets seemed to do nothing, but bounce off him. The large man moved so fast and with such velocity, that when he passed, she barely saw him and was nearly knocked over.

She looked over to see him holding Seticus by the shoulder and ripping out his throat with his free hand. Seticus gurgled on his own blood as he tried to cry out, his hands pointing at the fireplace. The man threw Seticus through the other window, looking back at Gwynne.

"You will forgive me, Oracle," he said, his voice was low. "My name is Balthazar Zaan and I am here to ensure the survival of my race." He moved toward her with such blinding speed that she barely had time to blink.

He grabbed her by the shoulders. She could feel his strength in his grip. He towered over her and effortlessly lifted her off the ground. "This will burn," he said flatly.

He opened his mouth, showing his jagged teeth. Gwynne screamed out kicking and thrashing around as much as she could; it was no use. He was too strong, and her effort was wasted.

There was a loud crash that knocked into Balthazar. They both glanced down and saw Tyron holding a broken piece of metal from the windowsill.

Balthazar let out a growl, he kept Gwynne lifted in the air and with his other hand he grabbed Tyron, throwing him backwards. Balthazar turned his attention back to Gwynne, who was still trying to summon any kind of magic. There was a loud pop that made everyone pause for a moment. Tyron stood shaking holding Seticus' pistol. The bullet bounced off Balthazar's face and hit Gwynne on the shoulder burning into her skin. Gwynne let out a shout of surprise and pain. Balthazar calmly looked over at Tyron, a smile spreading across his face. Tyron was bloodied and as he stumbled forward as a team of Red Scorpions funneled into the room. Balthazar dropped Gwynne to the ground and stepped forward to meet them.

CHAPTER 20

Grasp for Power

Jaxon knelt behind a cement barricade, Kalix and Beric knelt to his right while Ethyia was to his left. Tobias' information had paid off better than he had expected. They were hidden in the shadows created by the high-rise lights, watching a small group of wolves near a construction development. The ambient light of the city just beyond them created a purple and pink sky against a dark backdrop. Jaxon had made sure they were downwind in their approach.

"What's with wolves always looking for abandoned or unfinished buildings?" Kalix whispered.

"Quiet," Jaxon snapped. He was focused on the group. He could see a few members he recognized from the last time. Then he saw Novak's distinctive long black hair. Novak was in the center of the pack, and it was then that Jaxon realized that it was only part of his pack there.

Novak commanded one of the largest packs in the region and if he had control of all the other packs, it was quite peculiar for him to be here with such a small number.

Novak was speaking in *Luguia* as he paced back and forth. He was beginning to shout, and Jaxon did his best to understand him. The members of his pack shouted back in agreement.

"We should make our move," Ethyia suggested.

"No, not yet," Jaxon whispered.

"What are you thinking?" she asked.

"I'm thinking they're about to go on a hunt." Jaxon replied. "Their numbers are too small for just a meeting, but large enough they can hunt something down."

"You'd think they use a larger number to go after Balthazar," Kalix commented.

"We don't know what they're doing," Ethyia noted. "We need to move while there are only a few of them. More could be coming."

"You're still going to go after him?" Jaxon asked, looking over at her.

"It's our mandate," Jaxon said with her, shaking his head.

"It's a foolish mandate," Jaxon replied. His wrist began to flash to which he quickly covered. He glanced down and saw that the hologram projector switched on, and Arilynn's face appeared.

"Are you serious?" Ethyia grumbled in a whisper.

"You try ignoring her," Jaxon lamented. He looked at the screen. "Now's not a good time."

"Listen," Arilynn said, ignoring his statement. "We lost the Oracle.'

"What?" Ethyia asked leaning over. Kalix shook his head, keeping an eye on the pack.

"Nya used the Amulet of Indiza." Arilynn explained. "We think she went to the stronghold held by Seticus. I'm sending the location, I need your help in trying to find her."

"All right," Jaxon said, clicking off the projector. "He's not too far from where we are."

"All right?" Ethyia repeated. "We are in the middle of our own mission."

Jaxon gave her a quizzical look. "I would argue this is more important than Novak," Jaxon said, pointing to the screen. "She's not far, and I'm willing to bet that Balthazar is near."

"That is not for you to decide," Ethyia argued. "We are to capture Novak first, and then we will go after the Oracle." She spoke with a tone of voice that reminded him of their conversation in Angoria. They maintained eye contact for a moment before Jaxon started standing up.

"Jaxon," she hissed, pulling him back down. "I am the ranking knight on this mission. You will do as commanded!" Her voice was coarse and began to shake.

Jaxon let out a laugh shaking his head standing up. "You're a fool if you think I'm going to just let that girl die because of some *mandate*." Jaxon looked over to where the pack was sitting, and Novak was no longer there. "Too late anyway," Jaxon muttered. "We will get him later."

"Jaxon!" she scorned. "I understand that you like to do things your own way, but when I give you a command you will obey it!" She was now standing over him, her torso bumping into him to push him back.

"The girl is not far from here," Jaxon repeated as calmly as he could. "Novak is either after Balthazar or the girl. Either way, we will get him, but our priority is to protect the Oracle."

"You really think we can handle both of them?" Kalix asked, looking back at the pack that was now leaving.

"He isn't going to allow Balthazar and the clans to get to her first," Jaxon explained. "The girl isn't far which, unless you believe in luck and coincidences, this makes sense as to why Novak is here. He's hunting Balthazar." He looked back up at Ethyia. "Do you want to keep being in charge or do you want to do your job and protect the damn girl?" He walked off before allowing her to answer, heading towards his vehicle.

Ethyia let out a growl of frustration. She glowered at Kalix and Beric who hesitated before rushing over to their own vehicle. Ethyia tapped onto her wrist and Markus appeared. She was startled to see him so beaten and bruised.

"What is your status on your mandate?"

"It's taken a little longer than I expected," Markus replied with a sarcastic smile pointing at his face.

"Jaxon is on his way to intercept the girl. You need to get to her first," Ethyia said, cutting off the transmission.

~~~~

Gwynne pushed herself backwards as fast as she could, trying to reach the fireplace. Still being bound and now shot in the shoulder made movement difficult. She persisted, doing her best to ignore the pain. When that stopped working, she rolled over to her stomach and pulled herself forward, using her legs to push.

She wanted to help Tyron who had been thrown against the wall. Somehow, he was the lucky one. The others Balthazar attacked either ended up torn to shreds or thrown out of the windows falling to their deaths. Lucky for both of them, there were enough people attacking
~~~~

Balthazar to keep him busy as he continued to dominate them.

Gwynne finally reached the fire and threw herself forward putting her wrapped hands into the fire. The flames of the fire flashed and turned to white. She squinted her eyes; she thought she saw someone reaching out to her. Before she could see what it was, she was pulled from the fireplace.

She looked back expecting to see Balthazar but saw a thin man with shaggy blonde hair with the same dead eyes. He smiled at her as he lifted her off the ground by her foot. She kicked him with her free foot, but it didn't seem to faze him. He tossed her back onto the couch; the impact flipped the couch onto its back. Gwynne rolled off and began crawling as fast as she could, trying to get away.

The slim man stood over her and grabbed her again, this time under her arm, hoisting her off the ground.

"Let's go," he said. He looked over the edge of a broken window and then back at her and smiled. His smile disappeared just as a blast of ice hit him in the neck, forcing him to stumble. He was still holding Gwynne off the ground as he stumbled and fell over the edge.

He and Gwynne began to fall, but she suddenly stopped while he continued his descent. Gwynne floated in the air frantically looking around. She looked up and saw Nya straining with her hands out. Gwynne suddenly realized that she was on *air* and began to panic even more.

Nya gritted her teeth, straining as she lifted Gwynne up with another gust of wind. Gwynne crashed into Nya, knocking her onto the ground. Nya growled, shoving Gwynne off her. She scrambled to her feet as Balthazar leapt towards her.

~~~~

Nya ducked, barely missing one of his swipes, and she was not fast enough to avoid the second. The back of his granite-like hand smashed into her side, knocking her down. Pain shot through her torso when she took a breath. She tried standing, but her strength failed, and she fell back to the ground.
~~~~

Balthazar grabbed her by the back of the neck, lifting her off the ground. He violently turned her so that she was facing him.

"I owe you a great deal of gratitude," he said in a smooth and polite tone. "I never would have found her if it hadn't been for you."

Nya kicked and swung at him, but they ricocheted off him as he dangled her in the air and slowly began to tighten his grip. "It took me a moment to realize when the three I sent to the compound began telling me about you, but when Reuno described you, I knew exactly who he was talking about." He glared down at Gwynne who was crawling towards Tyron.

"The assassin of the Three Tailed Scorpions, more specifically the *Red* Scorpions was after the Oracle and it was only a matter of time before Seticus' little errand girl came back with his prize." His grip tightened until Nya fell limp. He brought her down to his face and chuckled before throwing her through the wall by the main door.

~~~~
~~~~

Balthazar grabbed Gwynne just as she reached Tyron. He effortlessly lifted her off the ground and launched himself out the window. His speed coupled with his enormous strength propelled him to another building across the street. He lifted her up and bit down where her neck and shoulder met.

The bite woke something inside of Gwynne. She screamed out in agony thrashing around, trying to get away. The bite burned and seemed to trickle down her shoulder and arms and up to her chin. The burning became more and more intense until it stopped suddenly.

The burning dissipated, and she could feel what she had been trying to focus on all day. Balthazar felt it too, letting go of his grip. Instead of falling she stayed in the air and began to levitate in place. The rope around her hands began to glow as the power within her pushed its way out until it finally exploded. The circle of energy that she expelled hit Balthazar, knocking him back and down to one knee.

It was the first time that Gwynne had control. She could move freely, and the power was at her disposal. She instinctively pointed her hands at Balthazar who raised his hands up defensively. Suddenly rage overcame her. and she began to lose what little control she had. She felt as if someone else was fighting to keep her hands raised as she tried to lower them.

Movement to her right caught her attention. As she turned, a blur tackled her to the ground. Piercing pain stabbed into her lower abdomen. She looked down to see blood pooling in her shirt. Standing over her was a creature she had never seen before. Its black fur glinted in the city lights, menacing yellow eyes stared down at her as it snarled. Its hand was covered in the black fur with long curved claws that dripped with her blood. It let out another snarl and then a howl before turning its attention to Balthazar.

"Novak," Balthazar said. When he turned, Gwynne was able to see him fully. He had matte black armor that protected his entire torso, his shoulders and neck.

Novak charged Balthazar. When they slammed into each other they began to claw and bite one another, each aimed to kill. They thrashed about with muffled snarls in between each attack.

Gwynne took the opportunity she had to try to crawl away. The pain in her side was so unbearable she nearly passed out every time she moved, causing her to become dizzy and nauseated. She kept trying to summon her power but every time she did, the pain of her wounds pulsed, forcing her to stop.

She scooted to a temperature gauge unit for the building, a large metal box that hummed and was warm to the touch, and rested against it. She did her best not to look back at the sounds of the two monsters fighting each other. She took a moment to try to catch her breath. Her shirt was soaked through now. As the blood poured out, it caused the shirt to stick to her torso. She felt numb, and the heat of the metal she was leaning against was soothing.

She could feel herself falling asleep, but a sudden touch jolted her awake. She opened her eyes to a man kneeling in front of her. His vibrant blue eyes stared at her with concern. He had long thick black hair and wore the surcoat of an Eri'Dorian. She kept looking into his blue eyes that stood out against his dark russet colored skin.

"I need you to stay awake," he spoke calmly, his voice sounding far away. He turned and said something to another person: much larger than he was. Gwynne could tell she was a Sentinel from dealing with the last one back at Olessa.

"We need to get her out of here, now," he said in a commanding tone.

"How do you even know it's her?" the woman asked through her helm.

"Look at her, she looks just like Bella," the man replied as if it were obvious. He glanced over to where Novak and Balthazar were tearing at each other.

This time Balthazar got the upper hand, throwing Novak onto his side and with a swipe to the side of the head Novak yelped falling to the ground. The large Sentinel knelt next to Gwynne before lifting her off the ground. Gwynne tried to resist but she had no more strength left. She warily watched as the man turned towards Balthazar.

"Go, I'll handle this," he said confidently without looking back.

~~~~

Jaxon unclipped his Umoya but did not summon a weapon. He made sure to keep eye contact with Balthazar as he sauntered over towards him. Despite his battle with Novak, he seemed perfectly fine, except for the gash on his right cheek and two puncture wounds on his shoulder. His black blood trickled down his torso, smearing across the vampire symbol.

"Jaxon Harwell," he said as if he were singing. "You always seem to show up where you're not wanted."

"You broke the covenant," Jaxon stated firmly. Novak had reverted to his human form. "You attacked the wolves, why?"

"I had nothing to do with that," Balthazar replied. "I already told you that."

"So, the girl then?"

"You act as if I didn't warn you." His smile was gone. He was leaning against one of
~~~~

the main vents with his arms crossed. "I don't care about the covenant. That girl changes everything."

"How?"

"You've never seen the world with an Oracle," Balthazar replied. "I have and let me tell you how the world works when *she* is alive," he said, pointing at Gwynne who was dangling in Ethyia's arms. "Half of the world won't accept her presence and the other side will expect everyone to do so. It doesn't matter. With her power, no one stands a chance against her. What's to stop you or Novak from deciding my kind is no longer allowed to be tolerated? What then?" Balthazar roared. "The covenant was never going to last!"

"So, you break the covenant and attempt to make the Oracle your own personal pet?" Jaxon asked incredulously. "Stand down while you still can."

"I'm not going to surrender to you or your order," Balthazar growled in response.

"Then I have no choice," Jaxon replied as he peeled off his surcoat, throwing it to the side. He lifted his Umoya, knowing that the moment he summoned the blade, he would be in the fight of his life.

CHAPTER 21

New Alliances

Nya coughed as she tried to sit up. She gave up and decided it was better to just lay in the rubble of the broken wall. She could hear footsteps and shouting all around her. She closed her eyes, listening to Tyron cursing everyone around him as he was being recaptured.

She let out a sigh, allowing him to be taken. He wasn't important to her, and she was no longer a member of the Red Scorpions. Once they saw that, they would try to kill her, just because they could. She was too weak to fight them off even with the boy's help. It just wasn't worth it to her.

She rolled to her side forcing herself to sit up. Her hair was sticking to the drying blood on her forehead. When everything went quiet, she looked up and saw Konan standing at the wall she had been thrown through. His dark eyes stared at her. His jaw clenched as he grinded his teeth, his temples pulsating.

"Where is she?" he asked in a whisper.

"Dead, I think," Nya replied with a hard swallow.

"Get up," he said calmly. Nya struggled but managed to get to her feet. She stumbled forward, catching herself by placing her hand on what was left of the wall. She went to step over what remained of the wall, but Konan grabbed her wrist, torquing her arm so he could see her forearm.

She looked down and saw that it was still bleeding where the marking once was. She had healed most of the wound herself. She had planned to finish her healing after she decided to help the Oracle. It was a choice she had been regretting every moment since she made it.

She looked up at Konan whose expression went from confused to cold and emotionless. They stood in silence while he figured out what had happened. He shook his head, and then he looked back at her as if he had decided what he was going to do.

He yanked her forward, throwing her to the ground and began to kick her in the stomach and torso. As she tried to crawl away, he grabbed her by the hair, lifting her up and slamming her back down into the ground.

"I can't believe you would do this!" he shouted. He then dragged her by the hair towards the fire. Nya fought as hard as she could to break away from his grip.

He stopped, slamming her back into the ground. He held her there pressing her face into the ground and the glass that covered it. He started raking her face back and forth, the shards cutting into her skin. After what seemed like an eternity to Nya. He grabbed her, throwing her forward nearer to the fireplace. He kicked her in the side before kneeling and grabbing her hand.

"Since you hate fire so much!" he shouted as he held her right hand into the flames. His shouting and cursing were drowned out by her screaming. She tried to pull away, but he was too strong.

He finally pulled her hand out. He held her arm by the wrist and started kicking the side of her chest and ribs. Eventually, he stopped aiming and began kicking furiously not caring where he struck.

Nya tried to cover up, but it was no use with him holding her hand out. She tried to cry out for him to stop, but his kicks kept knocking the wind out of her lungs not allowing her to. She became resigned to her fate as she began to lose consciousness.

"That's enough!" Markus roared, throwing a lightning bolt that hit Konan's shoulder as he tried to avoid the attack. Konan stumbled backwards. Using the wall, he pushed himself forward. He had been too busy tormenting Nya that he hadn't realized that his men had been overtaken.

Nya curled up, holding her burned hand against her chest. She could hear Markus giving instructions before engaging Konan. She didn't care anymore. She was done fighting; she just laid there. She could feel herself slipping out of consciousness again. As her eyes began to close, she saw a hand reach out of the fire. The flames turned black and before she closed them, she was pulled into the fire.

Nya fell onto hard black stone. The room was hot with a massive fire pit. The flames climbed towards the vaulted ceiling.

She wasn't entirely sure, but she felt that she had just come out of those flames.

The pit was centered in the middle of the room. She sat up groggily glancing around the room. One thing she noticed immediately was that she had suddenly begun to feel better with every passing moment.

She looked to her hand and her eyes widened as the burned skin slowly began to heal. She wasn't sure if it was actually happening or if she was hallucinating. She touched her hand gently waiting for the pain to shoot down her arm. When nothing happened, she pressed against her hand harder. To her surprise, it was completely healed. She could breathe easier and felt *rested*. Something she hadn't felt since the day the Oracle returned.

She jumped to her feet, suddenly aware that she wasn't alone. She turned, raising her hands up defensively. She attempted to summon ice, but nothing happened. She looked down at her hands with concern and then raised them again when a man suddenly appeared in front of her.

He had long black hair that rested on his shoulders. He wore a bright red robe that was embroidered with gold markings she had never seen before except for the Emblem for the Eri'Dorian Order on the right side of his chest. His fingers were covered in gold and silver rings. The one that stood out was a golden ring with a dark green emerald embedded into the band proudly resting on his left ring finger.

He stood rigid, his clean-shaven face showing youth. His dark brown eyes were cold and off-putting. He smiled. It was not a polite smile which made her feel even more uncomfortable.

"Your power won't work here, I am afraid," he said in a soothing voice. "Despite how powerful you may think you are, you are not nearly powerful enough to summon any kind of magic, here." He lifted his hands gesturing to the room.

"Who are you?" Nya asked, refusing to lower her hands. "Where is here?"

"My name is Daaro Sahir," he replied calmly. "And if you want to survive this encounter you will help me."

~~~~

Markus parried Konan's frenzied attack, sidestepping him, and with a push, he sent him falling to the ground. Konan cursed as he scrambled to his feet. Markus took in a deep haggard breath as he prepared for another attack. He was too tired to fight this man for much longer. He had sent the others to find the Oracle. Moira had outright refused, staying behind to tend to her son who was sitting on a pile of debris pressing against his stomach wound.

Markus' only goal was to keep Konan away from them and from Nya who had disappeared sometime during his fight. Konan ran at Markus. Markus sent a bolt of lightning. The bolt was not as strong as he was used to, but the impact still stopped Konan in his tracks, staggering him backwards. Markus kicked Konan in the torso, sending him through an already broken wall.
~~~~

"We need to go," Markus said with labored breathing. Moira nodded her head pulling Tyron to his feet. Markus turned back to see where Nya was, but couldn't find her. He heard Konan shuffling behind the broken wall and decided it wasn't worth looking for her any longer.

He rounded the corner and with a loud *POP!* Markus hit the ground with agonizing pain shooting down his arm. He looked over and saw that his armor had been pierced and bright red blood began to ooze out. Markus rolled to his side to see more of Konan's men had arrived. They now had Tyron and Moira and were pushing them into the main hall.

Konan stumbled out of the broken wall with a projectile-pistol raised. He smiled with blood covering his teeth. He stumbled forward, trying to keep his balance as he approached.

Markus lay on the ground, trying to push himself to stand but couldn't find the strength. Konan moved so that he was standing over him pointing the pistol at his chest. To Konan's surprise Markus laid there quietly and smiled.

"You think you've won," Markus coughed.

"I did, old man," Konan snapped back.

"He's going to kill you when he finds you," Markus said faintly as he closed his eyes. He felt himself fading, the world around him was no longer loud. It was quiet and almost peaceful.

Konan fired the pistol repeatedly until there was nothing left. He tossed the pistol to the side and let out a triumphant yell, stomping on the body. When he was done, he looked over his shoulder and saw more of his men entering. They scattered around the room with their weapons raised.

"We need to go," Konan said shakily, taking a deep breath. "This place is lost, and this is no longer our fight." Stepping over Markus' body, he stopped suddenly and grabbed the old man's Umoya before walking towards the exit.

He looked back once, scanning the room for Nya. When he was satisfied that she wasn't there, he went to leave. He stopped when one of his men stepped into his path pointing to

Tyron and Moira sitting against the wall. He regarded them while his man asked what he wanted done with them.

"Take them. I'm sure they are worth something to the White Scorpions."

"What about Seticus?" a man asked.

"He's dead," Konan replied without looking back. "I'm in charge."

~~~~

Nya was suddenly on the building's roof. She felt amazing and could feel her magic return to her. She made her way to the side of the building, peering over the edge. There was an all-out fight spilling out in the middle of the streets.

She could see a group of werewolves fighting Vampires. The vampires were being led by the one she pushed out of the window. There were other knights arriving, joining the fight.

Nya scanned the chaos erupting everywhere, and located Gwynne. She was being held by a Sentinel that Nya recognized as Ethyia right away by the bull-horned
~~~~

helmet. She saw the 'Handsome Knight' and a young apprentice following him.

They rounded the corner, trying to stay away from the actual fighting that was taking place down at the street level. Nya could see Arilynn had arrived and was too busy fighting a rather large werewolf to be bothered with Nya's presence.

Nya crouched down and watched as Kalix and his young apprentice ran to Benjamin and Clara who were struggling to keep away from two vampires. She watched as another apprentice ran to help Arilynn.

She searched and finally found Isobella running back and forth, trying to get people who weren't involved out of the battle zone. Nya wasn't surprised with Isobella's role. She was an accomplished fighter, but without her magic, she was next to useless against these beasts.

She took the opportunity and leapt from the roof. She held out her hand as the earth came hurtling towards her. When she was close enough, she sent out a gust of wind that slowed her fall, and she rolled through to her feet.

Nya watched Ethyia run, still trying to avoid anyone. Nya watched her intently and when they came close enough, she wasted no time sending a stream of ice into her back, causing her to fall forward. When Ethyia over corrected to stop herself from falling, she dropped Gwynne. Nya ran, pulling her backwards, kicking the back of her legs. Ethyia and Gwynne crashed into the ground while Nya stepped out of the way.

She ripped Gwynne from Ethyia's grasp and tried to hoist her over her shoulder. Ethyia was surprisingly fast to her feet, pulling Gwynne back with such force, she nearly pulled Nya to the ground.

Gwynne groaned as they dropped her. Nya ripped her shoulder away from Ethyia's grasp and conjured another stream of ice that Ethyia blocked with a blast of fire.

Nya danced backwards, avoiding the fire, and charged again. She made special care to stay out of Ethyia's grasp. Daaro had given her new weapons similar to the ones she had lost, but they were lighter, and their grip seemed made specifically for her. She created her ice blades and charged again.

Ethyia retrieved her Umoya and created a flail with a spike as the pommel. She swung the flail with a destructive grace that Nya was not prepared for.

Nya wanted to get close so that she could neutralize the flail, but had to be careful of the large spike on the pommel. That and Ethyia's large hands were deadly up close.

Her only advantage was that she was quicker and rested. She continued moving back and forth, trying to tire the Sentinel. As soon as she realized this Ethyia only moved when she needed to. Nya used another stream of ice that Ethyia blocked with her hand.

Nya was growing impatient. She couldn't see her face, but she was certain that Ethyia was smiling underneath her black and red bull shaped helm. Ethyia always enjoyed a good fight.

Nya jumped too soon and was hit with a backhand to her abdomen. Fortunately, for her it was Ethyia's hand and not her flail. Despite it being a glancing blow, it still knocked the air out of Nya's lungs and sent a sharp pain through her ribs.

Nya scrambled to regain her balance as Ethyia retreated to stand over Gwynne. Nya let out a frustrated huff. A werewolf howling caught her attention. It tore angrily at Kalix. Nya threw a small bolt of lightning hitting the werewolf on the side of its face. It wasn't meant to hurt but to get its attention.

To Nya's delight it worked as he backhanded Kalix to the ground. The werewolf snarled and ran towards her. Nya could tell by its relative small size, and erratic movements, that it was a young wolf. Too young to use reason or be capable of controlling its urges. It would attack with strength and pure aggression and not think of the consequences.

Nya ran, giving it something to chase which fueled its base instincts. She ran towards Ethyia who took a step back, raising her flail. As Nya approached, she jumped into the air using another gust of air to propel her up and over. Ethyia tried to follow Nya, but now had to deal with the wild werewolf that was now charging her.

Nya landed safely behind Ethyia, pulling Gwynne as the wolf slammed into Ethyia who shouted out in anger, pushing back against the wild beast. Nya quickly lifted Gwynne up to her feet, placing her arm over her neck holding her up.

"I know where to keep you safe, come on," Nya said as she half dragged Gwynne away while Ethyia fought desperately to go after her. The werewolf clawed the back of her armor, latching onto her shoulder. She shouted as she was thrown backwards.

Nya carried Gwynne as she tried to pull her away from the battle. She looked over to see that Clara and Isobella had spotted them. Isobella was shouting for Clara to stop her.

"Come on," Nya said to herself as she lifted Gwynne onto her shoulder. Gwynne shouted incoherently, trying to pull away. Nya turned in time to see Clara charging at her. Nya dropped Gwynne to the ground, sidestepping Clara.

Clara stopped abruptly and swung backwards with her sword. Nya dodged the first attack, bringing up her daggers to parry the next. Nya moved with every attack that Clara threw at her. She was impressed with the girl's sudden aggression.

"You're outmatched, girl," Nya said as she trapped Clara's blade with her daggers. Clara yanked the blade back, shouldering Nya and knocking her off balance. Clara then pushed forward again and with a backhand knocked Nya to the ground.

Nya rolled to her feet in a crouching position. She took a moment to wipe the blood from her lip and smirked. The smirk disappeared when she saw a young man grabbing Gwynne. Nya sent a shockwave through the ground. The earth lifted up and shot towards Clara who jumped over the spike of stone. When she landed, she charged Nya.

Nya was no longer in the mood to entertain the fight. She lunged into the attack and began cutting and slashing so fast that Clara couldn't keep up. Nya knew that her daggers wouldn't pierce the Eri'Dorian armor, but it would still hit and still hurt.

When Clara stumbled backwards, Nya spun around kicking her in the lower abdomen. As Clara doubled over, Nya grabbed her by the hair and threw her to the side.

"Briar! Get her out of here!" Clara screamed as she pushed herself up. Nya sent a gust of wind that lifted Clara off the ground, sending her into the side of one of the buildings.

She turned her attention to Briar who was now carrying Gwynne away. She raised her hand to summon the Earth beneath him. Just as she felt the Earth within her grip, Isobella tackled her to the ground.

"You bitch!" Isobella shouted as the two of them rolled over each other. Nya kicked Isobella off. She climbed to her feet but was kicked in the side of the face for her efforts.

Nya sat back up, ducking under Isobella's swing. She threw a shock of lightning that knocked Isobella to the ground.

"I don't have time for this!" Nya grumbled as she stood up. She scanned the area looking for Briar.

The wolves were outnumbered but were holding their own against the vampires. Kalix and his apprentice were enthralled in a fight with a female vampire wielding a spear with deadly purpose.

She finally found Briar who was hobbling away with Gwynne on his shoulder. He glanced back, meeting her gaze. His eyes grew wide and he lifted Gwynne off the ground, trying to move faster.

CHAPTER 22

Old Battles

Balthazar sprang forward, cutting down with his falchion. Jaxon sidestepped, not bothering to parry the attack. Balthazar swung back and charged again. His blinding speed coupled with multiple lifetimes of experience made Balthazar one of the deadliest duelists in the world.

Jaxon moved as quickly as he could, parrying every attack he could and avoiding the others. He focused on his spiritual magic, which allowed him to move faster, giving him a chance against the ancient king. The sound of their blades crashing crackled, as Jaxon's blade of lightning splintered small bolts around them. Balthazar would move in sudden bursts. Changing his tactics from speed to absolute strength and power. Jaxon did his best to keep the same pace, but even with his spiritual magic, he wasn't capable of keeping up for long.

Balthazar broke through Jaxon's defense, slamming his blade into his torso. Jaxon collided into the cement guardrail at the top of the building. His Umoya slipped from his grip as he groggily fought to stand up. He ducked warily under Balthazar's swipe and blocked the backhand that followed.

Despite his own strength given to him by his Dru'Ny heritage, Jaxon wasn't as strong as Balthazar. He could contend against him for moments at a time, but eventually Balthazar always won out. Jaxon ducked under another swipe. He countered with a strong punch that staggered Balthazar. Balthazar recovered quickly and was back on the attack. Jaxon rolled backwards grabbing his Umoya, summoning it into a Warhammer of fire.

He swung the hammer up, catching Balthazar off guard as he cut down. The head of the hammer struck Balthazar's sternum, cracking and scorching his breastplate. Balthazar retaliated by swinging down and clawing at Jaxon's chest.

Jaxon's armor absorbed most of the blow and scratch. The armor was already strong by Eri'Dorian standards, but it had also been blessed by his father's tribe. He had never really believed their blessing would do anything, but today he was starting to.

Balthazar grabbed Jaxon by the shoulder and lifted him up over his head then slammed him into the ground. Jaxon coughed as he scrambled back to his feet, raising his hammer defensively.

"You have always impressed me," Balthazar sneered. "I could just slam you into the ground and bite your neck and be done with it." Jaxon backed himself up trying to create distance between the two of them. "But because of my respect for you. I won't. I will simply kill you in a *traditional* way."

"Thanks," Jaxon said sarcastically, waving his hand for Balthazar to attack again. The vampire lord grimaced as he let out a guttural growl. Jaxon fell to the side as Balthazar rushed forward, avoiding contact, and rolled to his feet. He knew that Balthazar would eventually kill him if he kept trying to stand against him physically.

They had fought before, more times than Jaxon cared to count. This time it was different. This time there wasn't the normal banter or Elena, Balthazar's wife, to stop the fight. Jaxon knew that if Balthazar had the chance to kill him, he would take it.

Jaxon ducked back avoiding a deadly swing of the falchion. He pivoted off his back foot and sent an arc of lightning that stabbed into Balthazar's side. Jaxon followed the attack with a wall of fire that Balthazar walked through and was met with another arc of lightning that hit him in the center of the torso. Balthazar leapt forward, swinging the massive sword hitting nothing but air.

Jaxon jumped back and with a gust of wind, flipped over Balthazar. He landed behind the vampire lord and sent another bolt of lightning into his back. Balthazar roared out in frustration. He swung back, forcing Jaxon to tumble backwards to avoid contact.

Jaxon ran into one of the vents. Laying his arm flat against the metal, he concentrated as he moved and warped the metal around his clenched fist creating a rigid metal glove in the shape of a clubhead. He changed his hammer into a short blade of fire.

When Balthazar ran up against him, Jaxon swung with everything he had. The force of the punch would have killed most people. Balthazar only staggered backwards, dropping to one knee, holding his chin that had cracks crawling up the side of his face. He let out a snort shaking his head.

Jaxon followed up the attack, not wanting to let Balthazar resume control of the fight. He punched down with his metal wrapped fist. Balthazar grabbed Jaxon's hand just before it connected. Balthazar was so focused on Jaxon's metal club that he didn't see Jaxon stabbing with his other hand. Jaxon plunged the blade into Balthazar's underarm just above where the breastplate ended.

Balthazar's black eyes widened. He roared as he shot to his feet, lifting Jaxon into the air and slamming him into the ground. He stumbled backwards, placing his hand underneath his armor. When he pulled his hand out, it was covered in the thick, black blood. His face contorted between anger and fear. He looked over at Jaxon who stood with his fire blade slowly turning back to lightning; the point of the sword facing him. Balthazar shuffled forward, letting out a growl as he approached.

"Stand down, Balthazar." Jaxon winced.

"You know I can't," he replied as if he contemplated it. "Not now." He took another step forward, baring his teeth. Crouching down, he leapt towards Jaxon but was stopped abruptly by a large black wolf-hand. He cried out, backhanding Novak who jumped out of reach and then launched himself forward, tackling Balthazar down to the ground.

Jaxon let out a groan of frustration as he let down his guard. He jumped when he felt a hand touch his and spun around lifting his blade.

"It's me," Arilynn said breathlessly. Her armor was badly damaged, and her face was covered with dirt and grime. Her normally vibrant red hair was dingy and matted down with sweat.

"Are you all right?" he asked, glancing over to see that Novak had Balthazar pinned to the ground and was tearing into his chest and neck. "We need to get you out of here"

"I'm fine," she said. "I got here as fast as I could."

"What took you so long?" he asked with a smirk.

"Do you have any idea what is going on down there?" she asked, not amused.

"No, been too busy fighting a vampire king," Jaxon replied, the metal clanging at his feet as he relinquished his hold of the metal wrapped around his fist. He turned when the commotion of Balthazar and Novak came close. Balthazar had gotten the upper hand despite his wounds and was now on top of Novak.

"We should let them kill each other," Arilynn commented.

"Normally, I would agree," Jaxon began with a heavy sigh, "But I think Novak is actually trying to help us." Jaxon raised his Umoya. Arilynn did the same, and together they created streams of lighting that intertwined and hit Balthazar in the side of the face. Their combined power was enough for

Balthazar to fall to the ground, writhing in the pain as a lightning pattern burned on the side of his face.

Jaxon jumped first and stabbed down, missing his strike. Balthazar leapt to his feet and threw himself over the edge of the building. Jaxon dove over the edge, catching Balthazar on the way to the ground. Jaxon fought to hold on as they plummeted downward. Balthazar flipped himself over, throwing Jaxon forward. Jaxon created a pocket of wind that slowed his descent. Balthazar reared backwards, pushing his feet downward.

Jaxon slowed his fall enough that he landed lightly. Balthazar crashed into the ground, the concrete crumbling as he did. He stood unfazed and sprung forward from the newly formed crater. He moved too fast for Jaxon to react, shouldering him into the ground. He ripped at Jaxon's armor and tore the breastplate off, showing his sweat soaked blue tunic. Balthazar growled unevenly as he stabbed at Jaxon with his claws.

Jaxon yelled in pain as Balthazar's claws dug into the right side of his abdomen and then again at his torso. Jaxon summoned everything he had and a bolt of lightning from the sky slammed into the both of them. Balthazar flew backwards from the impact, slamming into the building's wall. Jaxon laid on the ground gasping for air, trying to bear the pain.

Balthazar staggered forward, crawling on his hands and feet. He bared his teeth as he inched closer. He stopped abruptly when he saw Gwynne pushing away from Nya with Briar on the ground. He stepped over Jaxon and ran towards them. He moved so quickly that neither Gwynne nor Nya saw him. He hit Nya, knocking her to the ground, and grabbed Gwynne who tried to pull away.

"If I can't turn you," he growled. "Then no one may have you." He gripped her throat, slamming her into the ground and began to strangle her.

Jaxon rolled to his stomach. His tunic was already soaked from all his sweat; he couldn't tell where the blood was without looking down. He tried pushing himself up, but his strength failed. He heard Arilynn land next to him, but she paid no attention to him as she ran towards Balthazar.

Jaxon glanced up to see Novak was looking down at them in his human form. He let out a howl, changing back into his wolf form, and his pack began to circle Balthazar. Jaxon looked around as the other knights closed in on Balthazar, the wolves flanking them.

The local law enforcement had finally arrived and were aiming their weapons at Balthazar as well. Jaxon saw three men standing behind Alamara watching from a distance. When Balthazar turned and saw her, he shouted for her and the others to join him.

"Together we can turn her!" he shouted, ignoring everyone closing in on him. "Help me, Alamara!"

Just as she started moving forward, a large carrier ship descended. It hovered in place as the doors slid open. Jumping out were at least 20 Eri'Dorian Sentinels who landed with their shields raised and their Umoyas became spears of stone and metal.

The three men hesitated and then turned, running away. Alamara shouted for them to stay, but they were already gone, leaving her alone. She turned back, glowering at Jaxon and then looking mournfully at Balthazar who kept shouting for her to help him. With one last glance at Jaxon, she ran after the other three.

Jaxon rolled to his side, still trying to stand. He could see that the Sentinels were moving to surround Balthazar and the girl, who he was afraid was already dead.

CHAPTER 23

Ascension

Arilynn ran towards Balthazar while Isobella continuously shot Balthazar with an energy rifle. Clara and Beric sent gusts of wind, trying to keep Balthazar away from Gwynne. He had lifted her off the ground and was now holding her by the throat with one hand.

He was shouting for his followers to aid him, but none were left. When the ship came with the Sentinels, he began trying to bargain with everyone. When this failed, he decided to attack again, absorbing the punishment. He threw Gwynne onto the ground, standing over her.

Every time he attempted to escape, he was stopped by one of the Sentinels forcing him back into the middle. He let out a frustrated cry, slamming into Clara, knocking her down on the ground. He turned, grabbing Isobella off the ground, throwing her to the other side of the street. He grabbed Beric by the breastplate of his armor. Kalix rushed behind, stabbing Balthazar in the back, causing him to roar in pain.

He backhanded Kalix, knocking him to the ground. Beric attempted to stab Balthazar but was stopped when he grabbed the blade and ripped the weapon from Beric's grip. Balthazar then bit down on Beric's throat, ripping it out, and then threw his body to the side.

The police opened fire and Balthazar was on the move again. Even injured, he was dangerous. He began to tear through the police force until he was interrupted by Arilynn's water whip wrapping around his arm, pulling back. He fought back, yanking her forward. She resisted as much as she could before he closed the distance himself. He slammed his palm in her torso, denting her armor, causing her to collapse to the ground.

A fire blast hit the side of his head and could see Benjamin throwing another ball of fire. Clara reacted quickly, summoning vines that broke through the concrete, wrapping around Balthazar's legs.

The Sentinels held their defense, and began creating a wall of stone. Arilynn cursed for them to do something other than simple containment. Balthazar roared in frustration, struggling to break free of Clara's vines. Arilynn threw a bolt of lightning, hitting him in the chest knocking him to one knee allowing more vines to entangle him.

With one last shout he broke free of the vines slamming into Clara again. Still using his speed, he clawed Benjamin across the chest and then lunged at Arilynn, knocking her back to the ground. He lifted his hand up to swing down, but movement caught his eye.

He turned his attention back to Gwynne who was standing. He used his speed and grabbed her by the throat again. She coughed as he reared his hand back. Arilynn used her whip to grab his arm. It was a futile attempt as he pulled back with much more strength, dragging her forward.

That was when she saw the light forming in Gwynne's eyes, and eventually the light engulfed her body. Balthazar screamed out, letting Gwynne go as she began to lift off the ground. She sent a wave of energy outwards, knocking her back down to the ground. She rolled to her side to see that the Sentinels had braced themselves with their shields.

Arilynn coughed for air from the force of the energy wave. She scrambled to her feet and saw that another wave was coming at her. This time, she brought up her hands and prepared for the wave. She summoned her own spiritual magic to try and push against it. The wave hit, but then came another and another until eventually, it was no longer a wave but just a steady dome pulsating outwards.

Arilynn looked around to see that the others had decided to do the same. The Sentinels lifted their shields and began to push against the dome, trying to force it back to no avail. Inside the dome, Balthazar knelt on the ground, holding his hand shouting. He stood up, lunging towards Gwynne in a desperate attempt to catch her off guard. He was stopped abruptly, shouting out in surprise.

He attempted to move and when he couldn't, he began thrashing around as if something was holding him in place. Gwynne stretched out her hand with her palm facing him. She slowly turned it so that it looked like she was lifting something. As she moved her hand upward, Balthazar rose with it.

"W-what are you doing?" he shouted as he flailed around in the air, trying to break free. She closed her hand into a fist. He cried out and strained to speak. "P…please, don't," he pleaded.

Gwynne stared at him with a blank, unapologetic stare, and with a twist of her hand, he turned to ash that fluttered into the air where he once existed.

Gwynne hovered in the center of the dome for a moment before descending to the ground. She spun around slowly looking at everyone as they strained against her pulsing dome that continued to push outward. She lifted her hands up, facing them outward and the dome receded and for a moment Arilynn felt relief until it came back twice as forceful.

Gwynne's face was no longer a blank expression, but an angry one.

"Gwynne!" Clara shouted as she pushed against the energy. "Stop! It's okay now!" she shouted, but her voice was drowned out by the energy itself and the strained cursing and shouting from the other knights.

Arilynn dug her heels into the ground and pushed as hard as she could but felt her feet sliding. She pressed both of her hands against the energy and cried out in surprise when she saw her fingers and hands were beginning to disappear into the energy.

She took a chance and looked behind her to see that the Sentinels were sliding backwards with her. One of them let go and went to charge Gwynne. She turned her attention towards him and sent a concentrated stream of energy that shot through his shield and armor, killing him instantly.

Arilynn let out a shout, watching the Sentinel crumple to the ground. She turned to see that Jaxon was finally on his feet and was limping towards her. She tried to yell for him to stop, but her words were drowned out.

He stepped next to her, placing his hands on the energy, and pushed back with her. Arilynn felt relief and her hands began to reappear. She looked at Jaxon who was so focused on Gwynne that he paid no attention to Arilynn's warnings.

Arilynn watched in amazement as Jaxon managed to take a step forward into the energy. She had always known he was strong, but this was different. He was moving through the energy, pushing it back. As he moved, she could follow behind him and tried to help him.

It didn't take long for Gwynne to notice Jaxon approaching. She turned her focus towards him, lifting her hands. Arilynn nearly fell over as the dome disappeared. Jaxon was beginning to strain, grunting as he moved forward. Arilynn could only see the bright white light of the energy. She watched as his black hair slowly began to streak silver.

"Jaxon!" she cried out, wanting to stop him. She tried moving towards him but was stopped by Clara who watched with her.

Arilynn looked around to see that none of the other knights were doing anything. She pushed Clara off her and ran forward but was immediately stopped with piercing electrical shock that dropped her to her knees. Gwynne had created a barrier between them.

She struggled to stand as Clara came to help her. It was then that she noticed the sun had broken above the horizon. She would have never known that the sunlight was there. Except for the small rays of light that broke through the massive cloud that circled above them and was expanding outward. Flashes of lightning illuminated pockets of the cloud and the low rumble of thunder growled overhead.

~~~~

Jaxon pushed with everything he had. He couldn't remember the last time he felt so much pure power bearing down on him. He was growing tired with every step, but he managed to keep pushing forward. He wasn't sure how he was doing it, and he didn't care. His only focus was to get to the child.

He took another step forward until he was close enough to grab her hands. When he did, they burned the gauntlets off his hands,
~~~~

searing his skin. He shouted in anguish, clasping his hands over hers.

Gwynne's eyes looked up at Jaxon, and her expression went from angry to one of recognition. She tilted her head slightly and opened her mouth to speak.

She spoke a word in a language he had never heard before. It was almost melodic, and the energy stopped at the sound. She swayed back and forth until he knelt and grabbed her by the shoulders to keep her steady. She looked at him with her normal pale blue eyes.

"You're okay," he said as blood splattered onto his face. He sat there for a moment before wiping his face, confused by what had just happened. He heard a horrific scream from behind her.

He looked up to see her coughing and choking. An arrow was sticking through her neck. A second one pierced her torso, the arrowhead inches from his face. Gwynne choked as she fell backwards. Jaxon immediately summoned a wall of stone surrounding the two of them trying to protect her from more harm.

He pulled her towards him, slowing her fall and laid her gently on the ground. He did his best to stop the bleeding but there was nothing he could do as Gwynne choked on her own blood. She kept reaching outward. Jaxon kept the wall until he could hear Isobella screaming from outside.

When he lowered the walls, Isobella was there, holding her hand. Isobella wailed as Gwynne convulsed and her blood in her mouth began to discolor into a dark greenish-blue. Isobella tried to hold her before Jaxon pushed her back.

He lifted his Umoya, a blade of metal forming, and with a quick thrust stabbed the girl. She let out a gasp of air, before dying. Isobella screamed out, throwing herself at him. Jaxon pushed her off, grabbing her arms, holding them tightly. Clara knelt next to them, staring down at Gwynne.

Jaxon felt as if the whole world had stopped. Everything seemed to slow down; he took long deep breaths, holding Isobella who had given up fighting him. He held her while he looked down at the girl he had never met.

He knew that Isobella was sobbing, but she seemed so far away.

The sunlight was breaking through the dark cloud as it dissipated above them, and the giant rock wall that he had created around them slowly descended back into the earth. He finally moved and could see Arilynn who stood staring down at the ground. He looked around, trying to find anyone or anything that could make this better. All he saw were knights and others looking down at the ground, none of them daring to look at her.

He heard a howl from Novak, prompting the other wolves to run off. Above, Jaxon could see that Novak was changing back to his human form. He lingered for a moment, surveying the area before walking out of sight.

Gwynne's skin was beginning to discolor into a light purple. He couldn't take his eyes off her. She was so young and unprepared to live the life that had been chosen for her. He finally stood up looking to see where the arrow had come from, but he saw nowhere that was close enough for it to make sense.

He felt Arilynn place her hand on his shoulder. It was comforting, but the heavy feeling on his shoulders never went away. He feared it never would.

"Tell the council," he said quietly. "That the Oracle is dead."

CHAPTER 24

A Changed World

Jaxon stayed next to Gwynne while Arilynn took Clara away. Isobella went between sobbing and cursing at Jaxon. She sat up, staring directly at him as he slowly raised his head to meet her gaze.

"You killed her," Isobella said in a flat tone. Her cheeks and eyes red. Her pale blue eyes looked darker as she glared at him.

"I spared her," Jaxon replied

"Really?" Isobella snapped.

As she went to speak, pillars of light and sirens began to go off, signaling the death of the Oracle, which only made Isobella's face turn redder.

"You have no idea what could have happened—"

"She was dying, Bella," Jaxon replied. "Those shots alone were fatal, add the poison. She would have died a slow and painful death. This was a mercy."

"Mercy?!" Isobella went to lunge forward. She stopped when she saw Arilynn shift, grabbing her Umoya. Jaxon waved his hand for Arilynn to stand down.

"I'm sorry, Bella," Jaxon said quietly. He lowered his gaze towards Gwynne. "I really am." He stood up leaving her to grieve alone.

"Where is Markus?" he asked Arilynn as he approached. He glanced around to see that most of the Sentinels had moved to the side in a tight formation.

~~~~

Lorrennius knelt next to Markus, glancing around the room, surveying the damage and bodies that littered the floor.

"He failed his mandate," Ethyia said from behind.

"It doesn't matter," he said without looking up. He placed his hand on Markus' breastplate.

"What do we do now?"

"We go back to normal," he replied standing up. "We continue to protect the realms by protecting the Order."
~~~~

"Jaxon isn't going to take this very well."

"I'm not worried about how Jaxon handles anything," Lorrennius replied dismissively. "You did well, Ethyia."

"Not well enough," she replied glumly.

"You did fine," Lorrennius assured her.

"The girl will need a new mentor."

"Yes, I'm aware," Lorrennius replied, walking towards the broken windows, stepping over the dead bodies. "I am already thinking of a replacement," he said, looking down at everyone surrounding Gwynne. His eyes fixated on Jaxon. He looked over as Ethyia walked over to him.

"Jaxon?" she asked, confident she already knew the answer.

"It will help keep him in line."

"Or pull her out of it," she countered.

"Either way, we can keep better tabs on him," he replied.

"What about Markus' replacement on the council?"

"One thing at a time," Lorrennius replied. "Can you carry his body?" he asked, looking back to Markus. Ethyia nodded, walking over to his body. She lifted him off the ground and cradled him in her arms.

As she passed Lorrennius to leave, he stopped her. He placed his hand back on Markus' chest. Then leaned over to kiss the top of his forehead.

"Goodbye, old friend," he whispered before nodding for her to continue. He looked around the room one last time. The fire in the fireplace caught his attention. It was flickering in an odd way that made him watch for a moment. It flickered again and suddenly went out, leaving the room eerily dark. He hesitated, never taking his eyes off the fireplace. After a few moments of nothing happening, he left.

~~~~

Jaxon shifted when he heard loud footsteps stomping towards them. He let out a sigh when he saw Andaar approaching with his scowl.

"Arrest this woman!" Andaar shouted as he marched towards him.

"She just lost her daughter, Andaar," Arilynn snapped. "Give her a damn moment."
~~~~

"We have our orders," Benjamin argued.

"Anyone touches her, and they'll deal with me," Jaxon said, looking at each of them before returning his attention to Arilynn.

She moved closer, resting her head on his chest. It was unusual for her to show affection in front of anyone. She took a step back, inspecting the cuts from Balthazar. Jaxon attempted to wave her hands away, but she persisted. She let out a gasp when she saw the wounds. She then grabbed his wrists so that she could see his hands, inspecting his injuries.

"Are you all right?" She asked, looking up at him.

"I will be," he replied, looking down at his hands. The palms were mostly fine, it was the back of his hands and forearms that had burn marks. The wounds on his chest looked far worse than they really were.

"Your silver hair is back," she said brushing her fingers through it.

"The name will definitely stick now," he replied with a smirk.

"I should have been here sooner," Arilynn whispered, returning her head on his shoulder.

"It's not your fault," Jaxon replied. "Someone killed her, and we need to find out who."

Clara shouted, startling everyone around her. Jaxon looked over as Ethyia came by, carrying Markus in her arms.

Jaxon felt a sudden drop in his stomach as if he were falling. His body tensed, and he couldn't find his breath. A rush of emotions overcame him so quickly, he couldn't decipher what he was feeling.

Thunder grumbled overhead, prompting Arilynn to glance up. She then looked at Jaxon giving him a quizzical look.

"What?" he asked, looking over at her.

"Nothing, I'm just sorry…" she said lowering her head. "I'm so sorry, sweetheart," she repeated, wrapping her arms around him.

Clara rushed over to Ethyia, trying to hold his head up. She did her best to stop crying as she walked with Ethyia.

"Grab her!" Andaar growled, looking around. Everyone looked over to see Nya kneeling over Gwynne. She stood up, raised one hand up with an arrowhead, while her other hand was placed behind her back. She stared at Jaxon and then Arilynn before disappearing in a flash of light.

"Where is Isobella?!" he shouted. His eyes scanned the area before falling on Jaxon.

"You'll be punished for this!" he snapped.

"How could you possibly blame me for this?" Jaxon asked, shaking his head, trying to control his anger.

"You disobeyed a direct order."

"I do that all the time," Jaxon replied dismissively. "She's gone and isn't a threat to us anyway."

"Where do you think Nya went?" Arilynn asked quietly.

"She's long gone by now," Benjamin replied. "We'll catch her later."

"Yea, because both of them weren't hiding for the last fifteen years," Briar said as Ethyia and Clara passed him.

"Get his body to Eri'Dor. We need to get her body and leave this place," Lorrennius commanded. Ethyia nodded her head, walking towards the ship with Clara and Briar following.

Jaxon and Arilynn knelt next to her body and noticed that both arrowheads were missing. Which meant that Isobella had the other. Only the shaft and fletching of the arrows remained. Jaxon thumbed the synthetic gray and white feathers. He let out a sigh of disappointment when he looked at Gwynne again.

"I'm sorry," he whispered.

As he spoke, the ship began to descend until it was on the ground.

"Jaxon…" Lorrennius started.

"Not now," Jaxon snapped.

"I just wanted to say I'm sorry for your loss," he said quietly. "Markus was a good man."

"He was a great man," Jaxon replied.

"The girl," Lorrennius stated, changing the subject. "She's going to need a teacher." He nodded his head towards Clara as she approached the ship.

"You think you're up for it?" Andaar interjected. Jaxon stared at Clara who was fixated on Gwynne while still holding Markus' head up. She glanced over and their eyes met for a moment before she refocused on Gwynne.

Jaxon looked up at the sky, letting out a sigh. He wasn't sure if he was capable of being a teacher like Markus. He knew that he had no other choice. Markus had trained him, and Clara would need someone to show her the rest of the way. He took a deep breath and nodded his head without looking at either of them.

He took a step back as a group of Sentinels came for Gwynne's body. He watched them gently lift her onto a platform and carry her back to the ship. Only Arilynn was left standing next to him.

"You sure you want that?" Arilynn asked, glancing at the ship.

"I don't think I have much of a choice," Jaxon replied. "The girl needs a teacher, and well, I can be that. If not for her then for

Markus." Arilynn made no comment which either meant she was satisfied with the answer or she didn't want to argue the point.

"I'm sorry," Jaxon said, breaking the silence, looking back down at the ground where Gwynne had been.

"For?"

"For lying," he replied looking up. "I should have told you about Bella. I just…I figured it was easier this way." She again made no verbal reply as she walked over. She placed her hand on the side of his face and kissed him intensely.

"I'll forgive you later," she replied. "I'm too tired to even think about it right now."

"Lucky me," Jaxon replied with a smile.

"I really thought the world was going to change. I guess we'll just go back to normal."

"I think the world has changed. We just don't know how yet." Arilynn shrugged, nodding her head. She stepped away, walking towards the ship.

Jaxon knew the world had changed with the arrival of the Oracle and would change again with her death. He wasn't worried about the change itself. He was worried about *how* it was going to change.

CHAPTER 25

Search

Jaxon stood rigidly at the back of the council chamber with Clara standing next to him, watching Novak speak to Lorrennius. He felt anxious being so close to Novak with no weapons to defend himself with. He glanced around to the team of Sentinels that lined the walls of the chamber and even *that* failed to comfort him.

"We will uphold our commitment to the covenant," Novak said calmly. He brushed his black hair back, glancing at Jaxon.

"On behalf of the high council of Valemìr," Lorrennius started as he stood up, "We are happy to no longer see you as adversaries, but as allies." There was a slight applause from the council members and the others in the room.

Jaxon looked over to Arilynn and Briar who both were watching Lorrennius speak. Jaxon scanned the wall. Kalix stood with his arms crossed over his chest with his armor and surcoat completely cleaned and repaired. Benjamin stood to his right, his eyes fixated on Arilynn until he noticed Jaxon looking at him.

"What of the clans?" Novak asked, looking to the other council members.

"Yes, we are aware that the clans and the loose treaties between them are incredibly fragile with the death of Balthazar."

"What is going to be done about them?" Novak asked firmly. "If they attack us, what should we expect from the Order?"

"You should expect a swift response," Andaar replied.

"Yes," Lorrennius agreed. "I would implore you to not interfere with our response."

"If they attack us, we will retaliate," Novak said flatly. Lorrennius narrowed his eyes and then nodded as he sat back down.

"It will not come to that," Lorrennius said with a smile. He waved his hands signaling the Sentinels. They all took a step forward in unison. "The Temple Guard will escort you to the shift-gate and take you home."

Novak went to speak again before he decided against it. He nodded his head and turned to leave the chamber with the team of Sentinels following him out. He maintained eye contact with Jaxon until he was out of the chamber.

When the door shut behind them, Jaxon stepped into the center with Clara walking beside him. They both bowed their heads, and Lorrennius waved his hand for them to speak.

"I'm here to inquire what is being done about the murder of Markus Troyan?" Jaxon asked, looking to the empty seat where he once sat. There was a twinge of pain in his chest when he saw the empty chair. He refocused on Lorrennius who let out a sigh. He too was looking at the seat.

"What do you think should happen?" he asked.

"I would ask permission of the council to go after the man who murdered him."

"Do we even know who it was?" Ethyia asked. She spoke with more confidence than Jaxon was used to. She shifted in her seat;

Jaxon assumed it was because she was not used to her robes instead of her armor.

"From what I could gather his name was Konan. No last name," Jaxon replied.

"What is your plan?" Lorrennius asked.

"To find him and bring him to justice."

"How do you plan to do that?"

"We know where most of the hideouts for the Three Tailed Scorpions are. The Red Scorpions are only a fraction of the entire organization. If we put pressure on them, they will likely turn him over to avoid any issue with the Order." Jaxon glanced around the chamber, and the members all nodded their head in agreement.

"Go," Lorrennius said as if he was going to regret the decision. Jaxon nodded, and with a bow he turned to leave. Clara stayed, stepping forward. "Yes?" Lorrennius asked.

"What is being done to find the Oracle's killer?" she asked, looking up shyly.

"Lady Lynn has been chosen to lead that investigation," Lorrennius replied.

"I would like to help," Clara announced.

"Your place is with your new teacher," Andaar stated. "You will remain with him."

"Yes, sir," Clara replied quietly. She bowed her head before turning to leave. She glanced over at Arilynn who rushed over to her.

"I will find whoever did this," Arilynn promised. "When you and Jaxon find Konan, you should find me. You can help me then." She looked to Lorrennius who scoffed before nodding his head.

"This council is adjourned," he announced standing up.

"Let's go, Clara," Jaxon said, standing at the door. Clara bowed her head and quickly left the chamber. Jaxon turned to Arilynn, grabbing her hands and kissing them.

"You sure you're ready for this?" she asked looking at Clara.

"No," he replied with a chuckle. "But she's a smart kid."

"You'll probably learn something from her."

"I hope so," he replied. "The woman you're looking for, her name is Kalisso."

Arilynn furrowed her brow looking back at him. "The arrows, they were almost identical to hers."

"Almost?"

"There were some differences, not enough anyone who doesn't know what they're looking would notice."

"But *you* do?" she asked, crossing her arms. "I'd almost forgotten about her."

"Yea, well, it seems you'll get a chance to reacquaint yourself."

"Ah," she replied, shaking her head. "Another one of your old flames."

"Ari, she's dangerous, but she wouldn't do this."

"Why didn't you say anything to the council?" She lifted her hand before he could answer. "I don't even know why I asked. You're always protecting people who don't deserve it."

"The council is always condemning those who don't deserve it," he countered.

"Where will I find her?"

"I don't know," he replied. "But she likes to drink and gamble in Dereli."

"Great," Arilynn replied, shaking her head. "Dereli here we come." She leaned in, kissing him on the cheek. When she went to walk away, he grabbed her hand, pulling her back. She laughed, shaking her head, and kissed him. "I can't wait to see her," she said, pulling away.

"Be careful, Ari."

"Goodbye, Jaxon," she said, pivoting off her back heel to walk away. Jaxon watched her leave for a few moments before turning back to look at Markus' old seat. He stared at the seat, focusing on his anger. He took a deep breath before leaving the chamber.

~~~~

The two of them sat in his vehicle in awkward silence. Clara shifted uncomfortably, doing her best not to touch anything. He often acted as if she wasn't there.

"Do you think we'll find him?" Clara asked, watching him prepare the vehicle.

"Yes," he replied confidently.

"How are you so sure?"

"We are going to destroy and burn down every stronghold they have."
~~~~

"Wait, what?" Clara asked, confused.

"Two things will happen. He will either come out on his own to stop us. Or they will turn against him and spit him out. Either way, we'll get him."

"What about the council?"

"What about them?" he asked, looking over at her.

"Won't they be upset?"

"Probably," he said with a shrug. "I'm not worried about the council."

"You *are* different from Markus," Clara said, leaning back into her seat to get comfortable. To her surprise, he laughed. It was an odd thing to hear him laugh. The last few days, he had barely spoken to her and barely showed any facial expressions. His silver hair was what she fixated on when she looked at him.

"Markus was worse than I ever was when it came to this kind of stuff," Jaxon replied. "He just started acting better when he joined them."

They reverted to their normal silence while Jaxon began thumbing through a database on the screen, centered in the dashboard.

"Clara."

"What?" she replied, looking over at Jaxon who looked up at her with a confused look.

"I didn't say anything," he said, turning back to the screen. She stared at him for a moment. He leaned back into his chair and started the vehicle. The engine roared to life.

"Clara, it's me," Clara eagerly scanned the area around her. She could hear the voice, and it clearly wasn't Jaxon. "Find me, Clara," The voice came in clear this time.

"Gwynne?" Clara whispered.

"What?" Jaxon said looking over.

"Uh…nothing," Clara said hesitantly. She shook her head, taking a deep breath. It was impossible. The Oracle was dead, Gwynne was dead. In the droning of the engine and between her breath, Gwynne spoke again.

"Find me."

EPILOGUE.

Nya stumbled in front of the fireplace. She took a deep breath, looking back to make sure no one had seen her. The entire building and the surrounding area was still under Valemìr control with Sentinels and local law enforcement patrolling the area.

She felt Daaro's hand grab her, and suddenly she was in the hidden room again. She stumbled from the dizziness this time. The same warm feeling overcame her. It took her a moment to feel normal.

"Where is she?" Daaro asked, looking around frantically. "What took you so long?"

"The place is crawling with knights," Nya replied.

"Where is the Oracle?" Daaro asked, ignoring her answer. His expressionless demeanor made her feel uneasy.

"Dead," Nya replied, looking down at the ground not wanting to meet his gaze. She felt so much more vulnerable without her magic. She glanced up and saw that his expression hadn't changed much. He looked down at her hands, so she promptly held them up. It was an arrowhead with the Oracle's blood still on it.

"This is all that I could bring, I'm sorry." Nya lowered her gaze again. She didn't want to admit it, but he terrified her.

He stepped forward, grabbing it gently from her. He lifted it up to the light above and then closer to his face as he inspected it. He made no indication on if he was happy with this or not.

"This will have to do for now," he said, waving his hand dismissively. "Now go."

"I'm free to go?" she asked, hopeful.

"Free?" he asked, turning around. He let out a soft chuckle. "Freedom is such a relative term. What may be free to someone may be prison to someone else."

"So, I'm not free then?" she asked.

"Go and enjoy your *freedom*. If I ever need use of you again. I will find you."

"How will you find me?"

"I have always known where you were, Nya," he said quietly. "How do you think Konan found you in the first place?"

The question sent a chill down her spine. She had never told him her name nor Konan's. She had never told him anything. She only agreed to help him because she felt she had no other choice. Even without her magic, she could still sense his power. He had more power than anyone she had ever encountered except that of the Oracle herself.

"Go," he said, turning away.

"They will be looking for me," Nya commented.

"Then I suggest you find a really good hiding spot," he answered. Without turning around, he waved his hand, and she was gone with a burst of light.

He quickly moved to the other side of the room, pushing the door. It opened to a grand hall that was covered in shadow. He rushed down the red carpeted walkway where it ended at a throne.

The throne towered over Daaro as he approached. The front of the arm rests were adorned with large humanoid and animal skulls while the back was fortified with spinal cords wrapped in old leathered skin.

At the bottom of the steps, in front of the throne, was an immense casket. The casket itself was made of forged black iron with black gemstones embedded in the sides. It had intricate markings at the head of the casket, matching the ones embroidered on his robes.

With a wave of his hand, Daaro moved the top of the casket off, creating a cloud of dust that spread out through the air. He dropped the stone cover onto the floor with a loud thud that echoed throughout the hall.

He approached the casket, climbing up a small stool so that he could see down inside. Inside was a large pale white man. He was heavily muscled and was dressed in ancient black armor with a gaping hole in his chest that looked fresh. What would normally be red blood was colored silver.

Daaro climbed into the casket, doing his best to stand over the hulking body. He delicately began removing the blood from the arrowhead, with the tip of his finger. Once removed he threw the arrowhead to the side, clanging in the distance. He dangled his finger over the wound of the man, letting the droplets of blood fall inside.

Daaro began chanting and held his hand over the wound, pressing down. He stayed as still as he could, and when the wound began to close, he jumped from the casket, stumbling to the ground as he did. He turned and immediately knelt to the ground, lowering his head.

There was a soft groaning that began to crescendo into loud wailing. The grand hall began to shake, unsettling old dust from the corners. A loud gasp came from the casket followed by a sudden shout.

The man inside the casket had sat up. He scanned the room, his wide eyes started off white then faded into black and back to white. The large man stood up climbing out of the casket. His pale skin began to darken, and his thick silver hair seemed to glow in the absence of light.

The man stopped once he realized he was not alone. He stepped forward. looking down at Daaro who lifted his head to match his gaze. He stared in amazement as a smile slowly stretched across his face.

"Welcome to the new world, Lord Demieses."

Made in the USA
Coppell, TX
14 December 2020